ALSO BY SUSAN HOWATCH

THE DARK SHORE *1965*
THE WAITING SANDS *1966*
CALL IN THE NIGHT *1967*
THE SHROUDED WALLS *1968*
APRIL'S GRAVE *1969*
THE DEVIL ON LAMMAS NIGHT *1970*
PENMARRIC *1971*
CASHELMARA *1974*
THE RICH ARE DIFFERENT *1977*
SINS OF THE FATHERS *1980*
THE WHEEL OF FORTUNE *1984*
GLITTERING IMAGES *1987*
GLAMOROUS POWERS *1988*

ULTIMATE PRIZES

ULTIMATE PRIZES

Susan Howatch

ALFRED A. KNOPF

NEW YORK 1989

THIS IS A BORZOI BOOK
PUBLISHED BY ALFRED A. KNOPF, INC.

 Published in the United States by Alfred A. Knopf, Inc., New York, and simultaneously in Canada by Random House of Canada Limited, Toronto. Distributed by Random House, Inc., New York. Published in Great Britain by William Collins PLC, London.

ISBN: 0-394-58064-8
LC number: 89-45303

Manufactured in the United States of America

Contents

PART ONE

CRISIS

"It is in the failure to achieve integration . . . that personalities too often make shipwreck, either breaking down (physically or mentally) under the strain of conflict or abandoning any real desire for an effective synthesis."

CHARLES E. RAVEN
Regius Professor of Divinity, Cambridge, 1932–1950
THE CREATOR SPIRIT

I

"Many of us have a hard fight to control our passions . . ."

CHARLES E. RAVEN
THE CREATOR SPIRIT

I

THE most appalling feature of the morning after I nearly committed adultery was my lack of surprise. I was scared out of my wits, racked by regret and almost prostrated by shame, but a virtuous amazement was notably absent. For some time my life had resembled a ball of wool kidnapped by a kitten, and now, after the preliminary unravelling, I was apparently experiencing the start of the inevitable tangled mess.

As we all know, adultery is far from uncommon, particularly in spring-time and particularly among people in the prime of life, but it happens to be an activity which disqualifies me from my job; if a clergyman commits adultery he becomes spiritually disabled, unfit for further service. Even in that spring of 1945, when the entire population of England was no doubt gripped with the desire to celebrate the war's end by wallowing in corybantic copulation, clergymen were still expected to keep their minds on God and their eyes on their wives. And why not? In my opinion such exemplary behaviour is the least that the Church of England should expect of its men. Everyone knows that all the best clergymen live in domestic bliss and never have an adulterous thought in their lives.

I was one of the best clergymen. I was forty-three years old and had already risen to a rank usually occupied by men in their fifties and sixties. "What is an archdeacon?" my Germans had asked in their prison-camp on Starbury Plain, and when I had begun to explain how the diocese of Starbridge was divided into two archdeaconries, one of the Grade C men, the unrepentant Nazis, had exclaimed impressed: "Ah, so you're the Bishop's Gauleiter!" I was sure I was no such thing, but the implication that I was a man of power and authority was true enough. As my Uncle Willoughby would have said, I had "Got On" and "Travelled Far" in my chosen profession, with the result that any possibility of moral failure was now quite unthinkable.

I thought about it. "Let him that thinketh he standeth take heed lest he fall," St. Paul had written to the Corinthians, and on the morning after I almost committed adultery I found these words had assumed a new and sinister immediacy.

I knew what I had to do: I had to repent (which I did, with every fibre of my being), pray for forgiveness (which would be granted because of my genuine repentance) and go on being the first-class Archdeacon which I undoubtedly was. Yet when I sank to my knees I found the formula was failing to work. My repentance, though genuine, was ill-defined and ultimately ineffectual. I did not understand why I had wound up in such a mess, and without understanding, how could I promise that my appalling behaviour would never be repeated?

I remained kneeling, not chatting garrulously to God like some woolly-minded mystic but trying to concentrate on the spiritual force of Christ as I struggled for enlightenment, and gradually I felt strong enough to face a very unpalatable truth. The main reason I was now in such a spiritual mess was because three years ago, in the May of 1942, I had met Miss Diana Dorothea Tallent.

With a shudder I began to recall that seductive first meeting with Dido.

2

THE fatal dinner-party was given by my Bishop, Dr. Ernest Ottershaw, at his episcopal palace in Starbridge. This statement evokes a grandeur which unfortunately, by that stage of the war, was little more than a memory. Gone were the lavish sophisticated dinner-parties of Dr. Alex Jardine's pre-war episcopate. Dr. Ottershaw, who had succeeded Alex in 1937, offered a hospitality which war-time economies and the increasing dearth of servants had systematically drained of glamour.

Both wings of the palace were now closed. In the main section of the house the Ottershaws were cosseted only by the butler, Shipton, a famous ancient monument, and by a couple of elderly maids, who were obviously retained more for charitable than for utilitarian reasons. It was rumoured that Mrs. Ottershaw had learnt how to boil an egg to present to her husband at supper on Sunday nights when the servants were resting their varicose veins, and it was even said she was keen to acquire more advanced culinary skills, but Shipton refused to countenance such ambition. He was still recovering from the Bishop's attempt to learn to drive after the chauffeur had gone into the Army—we were all still recovering from that well-meaning episcopal whim which had destroyed one of the palace gate-posts—and Shipton, an arch-conservative, was firmly of the opinion that bishops and their ladies should never develop ideas below their station.

Heaven alone knows who had produced the food on the evening when I met Dido, but it was well in accord with the recent Government edict which proclaimed that no restaurant could charge more than five shillings for a meal or serve more than three courses. Rationing had become increasingly severe; in the dark mysterious stew which emerged from the episcopal kitchen, lonely chunks of meat could occasionally be glimpsed swimming alongside the potatoes and carrots. Pudding consisted of bottled plums covered by a sauce which Mrs. Ottershaw tried to pass off as custard. She even said it contained a real egg, a disclosure which made me wonder if the Bishop had nobly volunteered to forego his Sunday supper that week. Fortunately the meal was redeemed by a claret provided by one of the guests, the Earl of Starmouth, who had a reputation for being benevolent to the clergy.

Lord and Lady Starmouth were the most aristocratic guests present but they were not the guests of honour. The dinner was being given for Dr. Ottershaw's predecessor, my mentor Alex Jardine, who had been living near Oxford since his premature retirement in 1937 and who was now visiting Starbridge to consult the official records of his episcopate; he was working on his autobiography. Alex was keen on claret and lukewarm towards Dr. Ottershaw, two facts which led me to suspect that the Earl of Starmouth had provided the legendary St. Estèphe not merely out of Christian charity but in a desire to ensure that the dinner-party fell well short of disaster.

The other guests consisted of the Dean and his wife, who were almost as old as the Ottershaws but not nearly so endearing, their neighbour in the Cathedral Close General Calthrop-Ponsonby, who could talk of nothing but the Boer War, the Ottershaws' unmarried daughter Charlotte, now a Wren at the Naval base in Starmouth, and Charlotte's new friend, the former debutante of the year and the darling of the society gossip columnists, Miss Dido Tallent. Marooned improbably among so many nineteenth-century relics, she exuded such vitality that I was at once reminded of a diamond, glittering wickedly among a prim collection of pearls.

Like Charlotte Miss Tallent was serving in the Navy, and as soon as I saw her I thought how appropriate it was that she should be able to call herself a Wren. She was slight, bright-eyed, quick, sharp and volatile. Her dark hair was immaculately waved, her sleek uniform swooped in and out of a dramatically small waist and her scarlet lipstick emphasised the whiteness of her teeth. She had a small bosom, but that was of no consequence to me. I'm not one of those men who are obsessed by the symbols of motherhood. I like legs. Naturally I was unable to see Miss Tallent's legs from top to bottom, but one glimpse of her ankles inspired me to imagine firm gleaming thighs. In fact so absorbed was I by this potent fantasy that I barely heard Charlotte Ottershaw's introduction and had to ask for the name to be repeated.

"Haven't you heard of me?" exclaimed Miss Tallent amazed. "What a sheltered life you must lead!"

"Archdeacons never lead sheltered lives!" retorted Charlotte. "This one's constantly roaming the north and west of the diocese in order to pounce on any clergyman who misbehaves!"

"What happens in the south and east?"

"Not much. The other Archdeacon prefers to play croquet."

"What's wrong with croquet? I adore all games with balls," said Miss Tallent in a formidably innocent voice, and gave me a very straight look with her impudent bright eyes.

I cleared my throat, wondered dizzily if the ambiguity had been intentional and asked myself why I was so suddenly unable to think of anything but sex. Who exactly was this fantastic creature? I had heard of her but my knowledge was sketchy because I never read gossip columns unless the sexton accidentally left his *Daily Express* behind on the churchyard bench; like all good clergymen I confined my excursions into the world of secular journalism to *The Times.* However with the aid of the sexton's *Express* and the glossy magazines which nervous tension drove me to read in the dentist's waiting-room, I had learnt that Miss Tallent moved in the best society despite the fact that her father was a self-made Scottish millionaire. I had of course long since dismissed her as a frivolous creature I would never meet, and yet here she was, in a bishop's drawing-room—in *my* Bishop's drawing-room—giving me impudent looks and talking about balls. I could hardly have felt more confused if I had been confronted by one of Orson Welles's invaders from Mars.

"Dido, how can you possibly say you enjoy all games with balls?" Charlotte was protesting, sublimely unaware, just as a bishop's daughter should be, of the sensational double-entendre. "Only the other day you remarked that cricket—"

"Oh, don't let's start discussing English perversions! What did you say this distinguished clerical gentleman's name was?"

"Neville Aysgarth."

"Neville! How dreadful—I *am* sorry! Mr. Chamberlain's ruined that name for all time. I think you should be called Stephen, Archdeacon, after the Christian martyr. It has such noble, serious, earnest associations, and I can tell you're noble, serious and earnest too, blushing at the mere mention of such a frivolous sport as croquet . . . oh, there's the exciting Bishop Jardine—introduce me, Char, quick, quick, quick! I'm simply passionate about controversial clerics . . ."

She skimmed away. After a while I became aware that Shipton was offering me a glass of sherry and I had to make an effort not to down the drink in a single gulp. Images of gleaming thighs and croquet balls chased each other chaotically across my mind until the Dean, buttonholing me purposefully, began to hold forth on his current nightmare: Starbridge Cathedral's possible destruction. The Germans had recently announced plans to bomb every illustrious British city which had been awarded three stars in the Baedeker guide, and although Baedeker in fact never awarded more than two stars no one believed that this little inaccuracy meant the Nazis were joking. Three heavy raids on Exeter had damaged though not destroyed the Cathedral; Starbridge, not so many miles east of Exeter, was now in the front line.

"Read any good books lately?" I said when he paused for breath. The prospect of a blitzed Cathedral was so appalling that I preferred not to talk about it. The Dean might choose to relieve his anxiety by speaking the unspeakable, but I preferred to tell myself that once all precautions had been taken to minimise the damage there was no sense in agonising over something which might never happen.

"Books? Ah, it's interesting you should ask me that . . ." Diverted at last from his Cathedral, the Dean began to talk about the fashionable Crisis Theology, which was now sweeping through the English ecclesiastical ranks in a tidal wave of gloom and doom, but I soon ceased to listen. I was aware that Miss Tallent was trying to vamp my mentor, while Alex appeared to be greatly enjoying the experience. His wife, Carrie, had not accompanied him to Starbridge, and Alex, a youthful sixty-three, was a past master at cultivating the *amitié amoureuse,* that peculiar pre-1914 relationship between the sexes in which close friendship was celebrated while sex remained taboo. I found this concept delectably erotic and only regretted that the changed moral climate currently made any attempt to achieve such a liaison far too liable to misinterpretation. Nowadays the only men who could safely take such a risk were men like Alex—a retired bishop well over sixty who could not conceivably be suspected of wrong-doing. On that evening in 1942 I had only just turned forty and any flirtation, even of the most innocent kind, was out of the question.

"Neville dear," said my hostess Mrs. Ottershaw, massive in moss-coloured velvet, "will you take Miss Tallent in to dinner before Dr. Jardine bears her off and upsets Lady Starmouth?"

This was a shrewd request. Lady Starmouth, who looked about forty-five but was probably pushing sixty, was Alex's closest platonic friend. She was watching Miss Tallent's antics with an indulgent smile which was rapidly becoming glazed, but possibly she was merely trying to keep awake as General Calthrop-Ponsonby expounded on the siege of Mafeking.

"Why did Bishop Jardine retire so early?" Miss Tallent asked me as we advanced together to the dining-room, and after I had explained that a mild heart complaint obliged Alex to lead a quiet life, she commented: "How boring for him! I suppose his wife has to toil ceaselessly to keep him entertained—or is she too antiquated to be amusing?"

"Mrs. Jardine's not as young as she used to be, certainly, but—"

"Poor thing! It must be awful to be old!" said Miss Tallent with feeling, and as she spoke I perceived the source of her charm. She was curiously artless. She said exactly what she thought. Her sincerity, as she spoke compassionately about Carrie Jardine, was genuine. In the artificial world of high society this honesty, coupled with her vitality, would make her so striking that few people would notice how far she was from being pretty. In addition to her irregular features she had a white scar on the side of her forehead and a nose which looked as if it had been broken more than once in the past; by the end of the first course I was telling myself firmly that I had never seen such a plain girl before in all my life.

"I expect you're wondering how I got my broken nose and my fascinating scar," she said, tearing herself away from her other neighbour, the Earl of Starmouth, in a burst of boredom halfway through the stew. "I fell off a horse. I've fallen off lots of horses. I like to live dangerously."

"So do I," said the prim Archdeacon, chastely encased in his archidiaconal uniform. "That's why I went into the Church. Charles Raven once wrote: 'Religion involves adventure and discovery and a joy in living dangerously.' "

She was captivated. "Who's Charles Raven?"

"One of the greatest men in the Church of England."

"Singing my praises again, Neville?" called Alex, teasing me from his position on the far side of the table.

"Don't be so naughty!" said Lady Starmouth. "You heard the name Raven just as clearly as I did!"

"The greatest man in the Church today must surely be William

Temple," said Dr. Ottershaw, naming the new Archbishop of Canterbury, who had indeed dominated the life of the Church for decades.

"Temple's a very remarkable man," said Alex, "but I distrust his politics, I distrust his philosophy and I distrust his judgement."

"So much for the Archbishop!" said Lady Starmouth as Dr. Ottershaw looked appalled. "Now let's hear you demolish Professor Raven!"

Alex instantly rose to the challenge. "How can one take seriously a churchman who favours the ordination of women?"

"My dear Alex!" I protested. "You can't write off Raven on the strength of one minor eccentricity!"

"Very well, I'll write him off on the strength of his major eccentricity! How can one take seriously a churchman who in this year of grace 1942 is still a pacifist?"

"But his pacifism proves he has great moral courage," said the Dean, unable to resist gliding into the debate, "and great moral courage should always be taken seriously. For example, none of us here may agree with Bishop Bell's criticisms of the Government, but his moral courage is surely—"

"Oh, we all know George Bell's been soft on Germans for years," said Alex, "but I'd call that pig-headed foolishness, not moral courage."

"I must say, I rather agree," said Lord Starmouth, "although nevertheless one can't doubt Bell's sincerity. What do you think, Archdeacon?"

I said in my most neutral voice, the voice of an ecclesiastical diplomatist who was determined never to put a foot wrong in influential company: "Dr. Bell's a controversial figure and it's hardly surprising that his views are hotly debated."

"Speaking for myself, I adore the Bishop of Chichester!" said Dido, as if anxious to inform everyone that despite her ignorance of Professor Raven she knew exactly who Bell was. "He's got such beautiful blue eyes!"

"You've heard him preach?" I said at once, hoping to discover an interest in church-going.

"No, I heard him speak in the House of Lords ages ago about the internment camp on the Isle of Man—no wonder they say Bishop Bell makes Mr. Churchill foam at the mouth! It's all terribly Henry-the-Second-and-Becket, isn't it?"

"Let's hope Dr. Bell doesn't wind up a corpse on the floor of his Cathedral."

The mention of the internment camp stimulated a discussion of the proposed camp for prisoners of war on Starbury Plain, and it was not until some minutes later that I had the chance to resume my private conversation with Miss Tallent.

"Are you a member of the Church of England?" I said, mindful that the Scottish father might have been a Presbyterian.

"But of course! My father—being a self-made man—was most anxious that his children should have all the social advantages he never had!"

"How amusing for you—and does the Church rank above or below Henley, Ascot and Wimbledon as a place where a successful society girl should take care to be seen?"

She laughed. "I've shocked you, haven't I?"

"No, fortunately for you I have a sense of humour. Do you ever actually go to church at all?"

"How dare you imply I'm a heathen! Of course I go to church—I'm *devoted* to the Church—why, I go every Christmas, and I never miss any of the vital weddings and christenings in between!"

I at once spotted the omission. "What about the funerals?"

The vivacity was extinguished. Her plain, impertinent little face was shadowed and still. After a pause she said flatly: "The last funeral I attended was the funeral of my favourite sister. She died in 1939. After that I vowed I'd never go to another funeral again."

I saw her wait for me to make some banal religious response, but when I remained silent she added unevenly: "She died after childbirth. The baby died too. Afterwards I felt as if someone had chopped me to pieces. I'm still trying to stitch myself together again."

"Easier said than done."

"Yes, sometimes I think I'll never get over it. At first I thought that the war would be a ghastly sort of blessing as it would give my life a purpose—I saw myself as a noble heroine, sacrificing my comfortable life in order to join the Navy and fight Hitler—but of course I was just being stupid. I'm not required to be noble. I'm just a *chauffeuse* at the Naval base. I have a wonderful social life, heaps of friends—and every day I despair because life seems so pointless and unheroic."

"Heroism comes in many shapes and forms. Your heroism may lie in the fact that you're struggling on, day after day, even though you're bored and miserable. I think you're being very brave—and I also think that if you keep struggling you'll eventually break through into a more rewarding life."

She stared at me. Her bright eyes were now opaque, suggesting endless layers of mystery beneath the artless candour of her conversation. All she said in the end was: "I wish I'd met you after Laura died."

Recognising the oblique appeal I said at once: "You must tell me about Laura," but at that moment we were interrupted by Alex, who was keen to lure Miss Tallent back into the general conversation, and her opportunity to confide in me was lost.

At last the stewed plums and the extraordinary custard were either consumed or abandoned, the ladies withdrew, and the gentlemen, with the exception of General Calthrop-Ponsonby, who had been mercifully reduced to silence by the legendary St. Estèphe, began to talk in a desultory manner about current affairs. I was afraid the Dean would start talking about the Baedeker raids again, but instead he showed signs of wanting to resume our earlier theological discussion. I wondered if I ought to warn the Bishop that the Dean was drifting dangerously towards neo-orthodoxy. In my experience, conversions to Crisis Theology—or indeed even to the more moderate forms of neo-orthodox thought—inevitably meant fire-and-brimstone threats from the pulpit and much embarrassing talk about sin, not at all the sort of clerical behaviour which would be welcomed by the visitors who attended services in the Cathedral.

". . . of course Niebuhr's modifying Barth's theology in important ways . . . If Hoskyns were alive today . . ."

I broke my rule about allowing myself only one glass of port and reached for the decanter to drown my irritation.

By the time the Bishop led his flock to the drawing-room I was sagging beneath the impact of the Dean's enthusiasm, but as I crossed the threshold my spirits revived. Miss Tallent pounced on me. My pulse-rate rocketed. I was aware of a reckless urge to take risks.

"Will you think me terribly fast," said this dangerous creature whom I knew very well I had a duty to avoid, "if I invite you to walk with me to the bottom of the garden and gaze at the river? I feel I need a calm beautiful memory to soothe me during the next air-raid on Starmouth."

"What a splendid idea!" I said. "Take me away at once before the Dean begins a new attempt to convert me to Crisis Theology!"

Could any response have been more inappropriate for a dedicated archdeacon?

"What's Crisis Theology?" demanded Miss Tallent as we drifted discreetly outside onto the terrace. "It sounds thrilling!"

"Do I look thrilled?"

"No, you look wonderfully serene and austere—in fact I was thinking just now in the drawing-room how simply miraculous it is to stumble across a man who's not utterly beastly. Speaking confidentially, Archdeacon dear, I'll confess to you that the main reason why I'm not married is because men are in general so utterly beastly to women . . ."

By this time we had left the terrace and were wandering across the unkempt lawn towards the river which glittered beyond the willows. The moonlight was very bright. I thought of the Baedeker raids, and for a split second I prayed for Starbridge, perhaps under sentence of death for the crime of being beautiful, for the sin of earning two stars in a famous travel guide.

". . . and in fact I wouldn't mind not marrying at all, but of course a woman has to be married if she wants to be a success in life, and I *burn* to be a success. So what am I to do? I'm twenty-seven years old. I've got to take action soon or I'll wind up a spinster, and one can't be a successful spinster, it's a contradiction in terms. I did think of being a successful nun, but they keep such peculiar hours, and I'm sure I'd hate being deprived of my silk underwear—"

"I agree it does sound as if you're not called to celibacy in the cloister"—I somehow managed not to dwell on the image of Miss Tallent in her silk underwear—"but plenty of women are called to celibacy in the world and manage to live happy, successful, productive lives. The big question here is not, as you seem to think: how will society judge me if I don't marry? but: what kind of life does God require me to lead?"

"As far as I can make out, God just wants me to loaf around Starmouth fending off passes from drunken sailors."

"Fine. Keep loafing and fending and I'm sure the way ahead will eventually become clear."

"But *dearest* Archdeacon—"

"Despite the drunken sailors I can't quite understand why you're so convinced most men are beastly to women."

"Well, it's all that pawing and pouncing, isn't it? Heavens, why I haven't been pounded into dust years ago I really can't imagine, and it's entirely because most men can think of nothing but sex—sex, sex, sex, sex, *sex*—and it ruins everything, simply ruins it, and sometimes it all seems so sad I want to cry. But I'll tell you this, Archdeacon dear: if I ever do marry it'll be to someone high-minded who won't just look at me and think: What a nice pair of legs! I can't possibly settle for a man who isn't high-minded, not possibly, anyone low-minded is quite unthinkable."

"If a man loves you he'll see far beyond your legs. I mean—good heavens, what am I saying—"

"But how do I know if a man loves me, Stephen? You don't mind if I call you Stephen, do you, it's such a good pure noble high-minded name—"

"Miss Tallent, I hate to say this, but I think you'd be bored to death by someone high-minded. Think of that prig Arabin in *Barchester Towers*! Everyone agrees he's quite the most tedious hero in Victorian literature."

"But if it's a question of choosing between someone high-minded and someone who's sex-mad—"

"Why choose? Why not have someone high-minded *and* sex-mad?"

"Heavens, what an amazing suggestion! But does such a man exist?"

"The human race is infinitely diverse." I glanced back over my shoulder at the house. "Well, now that we've seen the garden by moonlight, perhaps we should—"

"But I want to go down to the river! I want to sit on that wooden seat underneath the willows and have an enthralling discussion with you on the heroes of Victorian literature!"

I looked at the wild garden shimmering in the pale light. I looked at the willow trees, swaying against the night sky. I looked at the glittering water of the distant river. I looked into the land of countless fairy-tales where the hero is changed from a frog to a prince by the casual wave of a magic wand, and I said: "Well, all right. But only for five minutes."

As I had already confessed to her, I liked to live dangerously.

3

THE river curled around Starbridge in a loop to divide the city from the suburbs, but at the point where the water glided past the Cathedral Close there were no buildings on the opposite bank, only water-meadows, woods and farmland. The inter-war building developments had taken place on the other side of the city where there was no river and no need to build expensive bridges. The water-meadows and fields, owned by the Dean and Chapter, were leased to the nearest farmer and bore silent witness to the fact that Starbridge, though a county town, was not an industrial centre driven to expand in all directions. The countryside remained unspoilt beyond the river, and the line of willows at the bottom of the Bishop's garden completed the illusion that we stood many miles from a city.

"This was a great garden in Bishop Jardine's day," I said as we sat down on the ancient bench by the river-bank. "But when the gardeners went into the Army Dr. Ottershaw had no alternative but to sanction a wilderness."

"*Much* more exciting! I think the garden in Tennyson's *Maud* could have been a wilderness, all tangled and steamy and exotic—"

"I wouldn't have thought a modern young woman like you would be interested in Victorian literature."

"It was the only thing our stupid governess knew about."

"You never went to school?"

"No, and if I had I'm sure I'd have run away and begun my outrageous society life much earlier—with the result that I'd now be worn out. In fact if I'd been the heroine of a Victorian novel—"

"Oh, you'd have died of consumption by now, no doubt about that," I said, making her laugh, and we began to talk of all the literary heroines who had paid the price demanded by society for the flouting of convention.

The conversation glided on, just like the river, glinting, glittering, gleaming, a hypnotic pattern coalescing into a unity beneath the white bright slice of the moon. Time glided on too, the time which should have been spent in the drawing-room, and every few minutes I told myself we should return to the house. Yet I never moved. The fairy-tale in which I was travelling had become more clearly defined; I now realised I was enacting the role of a male Cinderella and that when the clock began to strike twelve I would be compelled to flee from my princess, but meanwhile I preferred not to think of those inevitable midnight chimes. I thought instead how amazing it was that I, entombed in my sedate cathedral city, should be enjoying a scintillating dialogue with a society girl, and beyond my amazement lurked the absurd satisfaction that I, Norman Neville Aysgarth, the son of a Yorkshire draper, should be conversing in a palace garden with a millionaire's daughter who had danced with the former Prince of Wales. I always tried hard not to slide into the repellent snobbery of the social climber, and of course I knew a good clergyman should be quite above such embarrassingly worldly thoughts, but the night was very beautiful and Miss Tallent was very amusing and I was, after all, only human.

The metaphorical midnight arrived so suddenly that I jumped. Far away by the house Charlotte Ottershaw called: "Dido! What have you done with Neville?" and I saw my fairy-tale draw to a close.

"I've ravished him!" yelled Miss Tallent, and added crossly to me: "What a bore! Now we'll have to return to the drawing-room."

"And I must be getting home." In my imagination I heard Cinderella's clock relentlessly chiming the hour.

"Must you? Already? But why?"

The moment had come. I had reached the point in the fairy-tale when Cinderella had been reclothed in her rags after her unforgettable night at the ball. "Miss Tallent," I said, "I'm sorry, I should have told you earlier, but I'm hardly at liberty nowadays to keep late hours with charming young ladies. I have a wife waiting for me at my vicarage. We've been married sixteen years and have five children."

For one brief moment she stared at me in silence. Then heaving a sigh of relief she exclaimed: "Thank God! Now I shall never have to worry about you pouncing on me, shall I? After all, what could possibly be safer than a married clergyman with five children?"

"What indeed?" I said, smiling at her, and that was the moment when

I realised what a prize she was, so clever, so stimulating, so attractive, so rich, so celebrated and—most alluring of all—so utterly beyond my reach. The familiar powerful excitement gripped me; I was always deeply stirred by the sight of a great prize waiting to be won. Then I pulled myself together. This prize at least could never find its way into my collection. There was no other rational conclusion to be drawn. In my politest voice I said: "It's been a great pleasure to meet you, Miss Tallent. I doubt if our paths will cross again, but I shall certainly pray that you find the happiness you deserve."

"Don't be silly!" She was aghast. "Isn't it patently obvious that our paths are already divinely interwoven? As soon as you told me at the dinner-table that I was heroic I knew God had sent you to my rescue! Now look here. I want to begin a meaningful new life: I want to be good, I want to be wise, I want to be *Christian.* You can't just say blithely: 'I doubt if our paths will cross again,' and sail away into the night! Of course I know how busy you must be and naturally I wouldn't want to take up too much of your time, but if you could just write me a little spiritual note occasionally—"

"But my dear Miss Tallent—"

"You see, I feel I've reached the time of life when I simply must have a spiritual adviser. You can write and explain God to me—oh, and you must tell me all about Professor Raven and Bishop Bell and Archbishop Temple and all the really *vital* people whom I ought to know about—and that reminds me, talking of vital people, I'd simply adore to meet your wife. May I call at the vicarage tomorrow?"

I cleared my throat. "How kind of you to offer, but unfortunately my wife's unwell at present. That's why she didn't accompany me this evening."

"What a pity! But perhaps next time I'm in Starbridge—"

"I'm sure she'd be delighted to meet you," I said, diplomacy personified, but I already knew that Grace wouldn't care for Miss Dido Tallent at all.

4

NO doubt I have now succeeded in conveying the impression that I'm a sex-obsessed, claret-mad, world-fixated ecclesiastic who deserves to be defrocked without delay. One always runs the risk of creating a false impression when one sets out for the purest of motives—honesty and humility—to portray oneself "warts and all"; the warts have a habit of commandeering the artist's canvas. Let me now try to redress the balance.

First, I doubt if I'm more obsessed by sex than the average man. I admit this mythical "man on the Clapham omnibus," as the lawyers call him, probably spends too much time thinking about sex, but the point I'm trying to make is that I doubt if I'm in any way abnormal when I meet an attractive woman and find myself picturing gleaming thighs. Nor need these harmless fantasies signify a tendency to immoral behaviour. A childhood spent among ardent chapel-goers ensured that I learnt early in life about the wages of sin, and out of an acute desire to avoid these terrible deserts I later acquired immense self-control in sexual matters. As a young man I was earnest, idealistic and chaste (more or less; one really can't expect adolescent boys not to masturbate). Grace had been my first and indeed my only woman—apart from a disastrous lapse before my marriage when I had been an undergraduate up at Oxford. Embarrassment prevents me from disclosing much about this incident, so I shall only say that it followed my introduction to champagne and that the female was a shop assistant at Woolworth's. From that day to this I can never cross the threshold of any branch of Woolworth's without experiencing a small secret shiver of shame.

The truth is that on moral issues I hold views which are currently held to be old-fashioned. I believe fornication is degrading to women, who should be treated with the utmost reverence as befits their unique contribution to humanity as wives and mothers. Adultery I look upon not merely as a moral error but as a crime, breaking sacred promises, destroying trust, poisoning love, wrecking the lives not only of the guilty but of the innocent. Sex is like dynamite. If it is used in the right place and at the right time the results can be beneficial, but unless the proper regulations are observed there can only be a disastrous explosion. Those people who indulge in sexual activity as casually as they would down a couple of cocktails are always the sort of people who would find it amusing to play with matches in a bomb-factory. As a clergyman I would be guilty of a most un-Christian lack of charity if I bounded around yelling "Stupid!" at all these fools, but I do find it an effort sometimes to treat the perpetrators of such mindless incidents—as a Modernist I won't use that Victorian word "sinners"—with compassion.

My strict attitude to sexual license extends to the human race's other pastime which causes so much trouble: drink. The Primitive Methodists of my childhood used to thunder away on that subject with as much verve as they devoted to sexual immorality, so it was hardly surprising that I became a most abstemious young man. In fact my catastrophic initiation into the pleasures of champagne up at Oxford shocked me so much that not another drop of alcohol passed my lips until the day I told Uncle Willoughby that I was going into the Church, but contrary to what the preachers had always proclaimed, this benign brush with whisky failed to consign me to perdition. I was much too poor to afford whisky regularly, and moreover as soon as I became a clergyman I knew I had to be careful in my drinking habits. Successful clergymen never drank spirits. Even as time passed and my tastes became more sophisticated I always made it a rule to drink moderately, and although I concede that on the evening of my meeting with Dido I bent this rule by tossing off an extra glass of port, this was an exceptional, not a commonplace, lapse.

I never drink twice a day. I do smoke, I admit, but never in public and only in my bedroom, usually after sexual intercourse. I like eating, but only wholesome food such as roast beef and Yorkshire pudding. I was brought up to believe that frivolous snacks, such as chocolate, stimulated the sin of gluttony and constituted an unforgivable extravagance. It was only when I was a young man courting Grace that I finally dredged up the nerve—and the money—to rebel against this austerity. I took Grace to the cinema and bought a box of chocolates. I can still remember the fearful guilty thrill of watching Clara Bow oozing "It" as I sank my teeth into a sumptuous peppermint cream.

Now, no doubt, I've created the impression that I'm not a rake worthy of defrocking but a prig worthy of a kick on the bottom. How hard it is to get the balance of a self-portrait right! Let me stress that I try very hard not to be priggish. Christ came into this world to be at one with us, not to stand apart and look down his nose at our antics, and as a Liberal Protestant who believes strongly in the centrality of Christ I can hardly ignore the example he set. Certainly, despite my strict views on morality, I never feel morally superior. How can I, when every time I pass a branch of Woolworth's I remember that I'm as prone to error as anyone else? Moreover, although I have strict moral standards I don't consider myself strait-laced, and I suggest that anyone who does consider me a trifle on the sober side has no idea what being strait-laced is all about.

Being strait-laced, as anyone brought up among strict Non-Conformists knows, means not only spurning extra-marital sex, chocolates and the demon drink but avoiding the theatre, the cinema, the wireless, playing-cards and novels. I have insufficient time and money to go often to the cinema or the theatre nowadays, but I enjoy playing cards with the children and I never miss the broadcast of *I.T.M.A.,* that most perfect of comedy programmes. I also read modern novels for relaxation. I may not read about sex in the *News of the World;* that would be dabbling with prurient trash. But I do read about sex in the work of D. H. Lawrence; that, I submit with all due respect, is keeping abreast of modern literature.

Grace enjoyed reading in the old days, but by 1942 her life as an archdeacon's wife and the mother of five children barely allowed her enough time to open a book. At this point I must state unequivocally that Grace was the most wonderful woman in the world and the best possible wife for a clergyman and I adored her. I do want to make that absolutely clear. For sixteen years we had enjoyed the most perfect married life without a single cloud marring the marital sky. At least, if I'm to be entirely accurate, I have to admit little wisps of cloud did occasionally appear but they seldom lasted long. Even the most perfect marriages have to suffer little wisps occasionally. One is, after all, obliged to exist in real life and not between the pages of a romantic novel.

Garnishing my perfect marriage, like gilt lavishly bestowed upon the gingerbread, were my perfect children. I know that as their parent I may be judged hopelessly prejudiced, but people outside the family did constantly comment on my offspring's good looks, good manners, high intelligence and remarkable charm, so I venture to suggest I can't be entirely deluding myself. Needless to say, it was a matter of the very greatest satisfaction to me that I had succeeded in winning two of the ultimate prizes of life: a perfect marriage and a perfect family.

Now I suppose I sound smug, worthy of another kick on the bottom, so let me add honestly that family life did have its ups and downs. However the problems never seemed insuperable and the children never seemed intolerable. My favourite was Primrose, whom I thought quite beautiful, although I know men always view their daughters through rose-tinted spectacles, particularly when they have only one daughter to view. Grace and I had called her Primrose in memory of the first flower I had given Grace many years before at St. Leonards-on-Sea, the genteel resort on the Sussex coast where my mother had spent her widowhood in the company of my sister, Emily. My brother, Willy, and I had never lived at St. Leonards; we had been boarded out in London in order to receive our education, but three times a year, at Christmas, Easter and in the summer, Uncle Willoughby had given us the money for the train journey to Sussex, and it was on one of these seaside holidays that I had met Grace, who was visiting cousins. I was seventeen; she was two years younger. When I gave her the primrose she kept it, pressed it, framed it and finally gave it to me on our wedding night seven years later. Even now the memento still hung over our bed. In view of this flagrant—but not, I suggest to any revolted cynic, unusual—sentimentality, it was hardly surprising that we should have decided to call our first daughter Primrose, and finally, after the advent of Christian, Norman and James, Primrose made her grand entrance into the world. Our perfect family was now complete. All that remained for me to do was to work out how I was going to pay for the public school education of three sons.

It was at this point that one of those little wisps of cloud appeared in the sunlit marital sky, and unlike all the other little wisps in the past, this one failed to fade away. Grace and I discovered to our shock that Primrose had not after all completed our perfect family, and in 1941 Alexander (named after my mentor Bishop Jardine) arrived at the vicarage.

When I had finished accepting the will of God, just as a good clergyman should, I decided I would have to adopt a much more rigorous approach to contraception. This subject, I need hardly add, is one of the most awkward matters with which a clergyman can ever become involved. As far as I can gather, everyone in the Church practises contraception, even bishops, but no one in a clerical collar will ever admit to such behaviour because the Church can never surmount its ancient conviction that interfering with procreation is a bad thing. The last Lambeth Conference had barely softened this negative attitude, and a vast amount of hypocrisy had attended the debates on married life. It was noticeable that those bishops who thundered most eloquently on the evils of contraception were always the celibates. The married bishops with their neat little families of two or three children tended to sink into a deafening silence.

Having been brought up to believe God helps those who help themselves, I had never agonised over the rightness of contraception; it had always seemed plain enough to me that it was my responsibility, not God's, to protect my wife's health, and so the question which bothered me most about contraception was not whether I should practise it but how it could be achieved. "French letters" may have been widely available since the end of the First War, but a clergyman can hardly be seen to purchase them. Nor can he seek help from his doctor, who might be scandalised by such a questionable resolution of the Church's murky official attitude.

I knew from the start of our marriage that the responsibility for regulating the arrival of children must be mine; it was inconceivable that Grace should be soiled by knowledge which should belong only to fallen women, and after Christian's birth I made the sensible decision to ignore the ancient religious disapproval of *coitus interruptus.* This form of contraception has a dubious reputation, but if one regards it as a discipline which is capable of developing one's control and thus enhancing one's performance, the obvious disadvantages soon cease to be intolerable.

I confess I didn't practise this discipline all the time. That would have been too demanding, even for a man who enjoyed a challenge, but Grace's monthly health was so regular that it was easy to work out when special care was required. After Christian's birth in 1927, Norman arrived in 1930, James in 1933 and Primrose in 1937. No exercise in family planning could have been more successful, and that was why we were so shocked by Alexander's conception. None of the other children had begun life as an accident.

After he was born I pulled myself together, made the necessary unpalatable deductions and began my travels in "mufti" to the port of Starmouth to forage anonymously for French letters. I disliked these sordid expeditions very much. I felt they constituted conduct quite unbecoming to an archdeacon, but I refused to regard my behaviour as morally wrong and I had no doubt that Christ, who had held marriage in such high regard, would forgive these unsalubrious machinations to protect my wife's health, maintain my emotional equilibrium and preserve my happy family life.

By this time that happy family life had become more than a little frayed at the edges, and although my new approach to contraception prevented further unravelling, I became conscious, as time passed, that the frayed edges were failing to repair themselves as swiftly as I had hoped. In fact by the May of 1942, when I met Dido, I had begun to be seriously worried about Grace as she struggled to survive the stresses and strains of life at the vicarage.

It's not easy being a clergyman's wife. Parishioners make constant demands. Social obligations multiply. Her husband requires her support in a multitude of ways both obvious and subtle. Even in a peaceful country parish these responsibilities can be oppressive, but we were no longer living in the country. The Archdeaconry of Starbridge was attached to the benefice of St. Martin's-in-Cripplegate, a famous ancient church in the heart of the city, and I was also an honorary canon—a prebendary, as they were called in Starbridge—of the Cathedral. I knew everyone who was anyone in that city, and as my wife, Grace was obliged to know them too. Grace was a cut above me socially; her father had been a solicitor in Manchester, but people from the north can be intimidated by people from the South, and Starbridge, wealthy, southern Starbridge, was not a city where Grace could easily feel at home.

Alex had appointed me to the archdeaconry in 1937, shortly before Primrose had been born. Christian had been away at prep school, but Norman and James had still been at home. Struggling with two active small boys, a newborn baby, a large old-fashioned vicarage, unfamiliar surroundings, a host of unknown parishioners and an increasingly elaborate social life, Grace had slowly sunk into an exhausted melancholy. Alexander's arrival had been the last straw.

In vain I suggested remedies. I proposed extra domestic help, but Grace found it tiring enough to cope with the charwoman who came every morning of the working week. I offered to engage a live-in nursemaid instead of the girl who appeared in the afternoons to take the children for a walk, but Grace, who was the most devoted mother, could not bear to think of another woman usurping her in the nursery. I told her not to get upset if the house became a little dusty or untidy, but Grace, who was a perfectionist, could not endure living in a home which was other than immaculate. Thus the melancholy exhaustion had persisted, aggravated when she was unable to live up to her impossibly high standards, and on the evening of the Bishop's dinner-party she had been too depressed to attend.

"I've nothing to wear," she said. "Nothing." I refrained from pointing out that this was inevitable so long as she persisted in spending all her clothing coupons on the children, but when I assured her that she would always look charming in her well-worn black evening frock, all she said was: "I can't face Lady Starmouth." This was an old problem. Lady Starmouth, effortlessly aristocratic, faultlessly dressed and matchlessly sophisticated, had long been a source of terror to Grace. I saw then that any further attempt at argument would be futile; I could only plan a suitable apology to offer the Ottershaws.

When I arrived home from the palace that night I was alone. Alex was staying with us, but he had lingered at the party, as befitted the guest of honour, and we had agreed earlier that we would return to the vicarage separately. As my wife was supposed to be suffering from a migraine it would have looked odd if I had failed to leave the palace early.

My key turned in the lock, and as soon as the front door opened I heard the baby howling. Seconds later Grace appeared at the top of the staircase. She was white with weariness and looked as if she had been crying. "I thought you were never coming home! I'm so worried, I can't think properly—Sandy can't keep his food down, won't go to sleep, won't stop crying, and I can't bear it, can't cope, can't—"

"My dearest love . . ." As she staggered down the stairs into my outstretched arms and collapsed sobbing against my chest, I thought of all the letters which I had written to her during our long courtship. After we had become secretly engaged I had always addressed her in my romantic correspondence by those same words. "My dearest love, today I finally put my schooldays behind me . . ." "My dearest love, today I arrived in Oxford for the start of my great adventure . . ." "My dearest love, today I finally gave up all thought of a career in the law, so I'm afraid I shall never make my fortune as a barrister . . ." "My dearest love, I know young men aren't supposed to marry on a curate's salary, but if one takes into account the little income you inherited from your grandmother, I see no reason why we shouldn't be together at last . . ." How I had chased my prize of the perfect wife and what a delectable chase it had been! In fact the chase had been so delectable that I had even feared marriage might be an anticlimax, but fortunately I had soon realised there would be new prizes to chase on the far side of the altar: the perfect home, the perfect marital happiness, the perfect family life . . .

The baby, bawling above us in the nursery, terminated this irrelevant exercise in nostalgia. "My dearest love," I said firmly, "you really mustn't let the little monster upset you like this! Go to bed at once and leave him to me."

"But he vomited his food—I think he might be ill—"

I finally succeeded in packing her off to bed. As she stumbled away I noticed that the hem of her nightdress had unravelled and for a second I knew I was on the brink of recalling Dido Tallent, smart as paint in her Naval uniform, but I blocked that memory from my mind by invading the nursery.

Alexander was standing up in his cot and looking cross that he had been obliged to scream so hard for attention. He fell silent as soon as I entered the room.

"I'm afraid this behaviour is quite impermissible," I said. I never talk down to my children. "Night-time is when we sleep. Noise is not allowed."

He gazed at me in uncomprehending rapture. Here indeed was entertainment for a fourteen-month-old infant bored with his mother. I patted his springy brown hair, which reminded me of my brother Willy, stared straight into the blue eyes which were so like mine and picked him up in order to put him in a horizontal position on the sheet. He opened his mouth to howl but thought better of it. Instead he said: "Prayers!" and looked so intelligent that I laughed. "That's it!" I said. "Prayers come before sleep." I felt his forehead casually but it was obvious he had no fever, and I suspected he had only vomited out of a desire to discover how much fuss he could create. As he watched fascinated I recited the Lord's Prayer for him, said firmly: "Good night, Sandy," and retired to examine the picture of Peter Rabbit which hung on the far wall. After a while I glanced back over my shoulder and when I saw he was watching me I exclaimed: "How quiet you are! Well done!" At that point he smiled and allowed his eyes to close. I was still taking another long look at Peter Rabbit when I heard the welcome sound of even breathing and knew I could safely creep away.

"The Kraken sleeps," I said to Grace as I joined her in our bedroom. By this time she was dry-eyed but very pale.

"How on earth did you do it?"

"I let him know who was the boss. Sometimes I think you're too soft with him."

"I'm not soft with him! I'm just a normal loving mother, and if you'd ever had a normal loving mother yourself—"

"My mother adored me."

"Well, I suppose she did in her own peculiar way, but—"

"Grace, is this really the moment to start talking about my mother?"

"It's never the moment to start talking about your mother!"

"Then why drag her into the conversation?"

"Oh, I'm sorry, I'm sorry, I'm sorry—" Once more Grace dissolved into tears.

Guilt smote me. "My dearest love . . . forgive me . . ." Sinking down on the bed I kissed her in despair but when the tears continued I announced: "I'm going to say my prayers," and escaped to the dressing-room. For ten seconds I concentrated on breathing deeply. Then having steadied my nerves I stripped off my clothes, stood naked in the middle of the floor and stretched myself until my muscles ached. This manoeuvre also proved soothing. When I shed my clerical uniform I felt younger, more flexible, possibly more light-hearted, certainly more adventurous. Perhaps women undergo a similar psychological liberation whenever they shed their corsets.

Having donned my pyjamas, I said my prayers at a brisk pace, gave the Bible a thoughtful tap, stared into space for two minutes and came to the conclusion that my next duty was to embark on a ministry of reconciliation. Accordingly I extracted the necessary item from the locked box at the back of the wardrobe and returned to the bedroom.

Grace had dried her eyes. That boded well. She had also brushed her hair. That boded well too. Grace had long straight dark hair which during the day she wore twisted into a coil on the top of her head. That was how she had worn her hair when her mother had first allowed her to abandon her pigtails, and I had never allowed her to wear it in any other way. During the 1920s she had wanted to cut her hair short but I had said: "Why destroy perfection?" and the crisis had passed. Later, in the 1930s, she had wanted to curl her hair, but that idea too I had refused to countenance; I had always felt that Grace's delicate Edwardian look was the last word in beauty and elegance. She was five feet four inches tall, a height which was perfect because even when she was wearing high-heeled shoes there was no risk of her being taller than I was. Even after bearing five children she was still remarkably slender and graceful—not quite as slender as she used to be, certainly, but then one really can't expect one's wife to look like a young bride after sixteen years of married life.

As soon as I returned to the bedroom she said in her calmest, most sensible voice: "Darling, I'm very, very sorry. How boring for you to come home to such a tiresome scene! How was the dinner-party?"

I was conscious of a relief of gargantuan proportions. My wife was being perfect again. All was well. "Oh, dreadfully dull," I said, sliding into bed and giving her a kiss. "I envied you missing the meal. There was a most extraordinary custard which was supposed to have had an egg in it."

"What sort of an egg?"

"Mrs. Ottershaw wasn't saying." I switched off the light.

"Was Charlotte there?"

"Yes. With a friend."

"A man? How exciting! I do hope Charlotte gets married!"

"Unfortunately it was just another Wren. And General Calthrop-Ponsonby was there, still breathing fire against the Boers, and Mrs. Dean was holding forth about the Girl Guides as usual, while her husband tried to convert me to Crisis Theology or neo-orthodoxy or whatever one wants to call the latest variation on the theological rubbish fathered by Karl Barth—"

"How glad you must have been to get home!"

"I'm always glad to get home," I said, unbuttoning the fly of my pyjamas.

"Darling, I really am sorry I was so awful earlier—"

"No need to say another word about it. We'll ring down the curtain on the scene, pretend it never happened and celebrate your splendid recovery. At least . . . you have recovered, haven't you, darling?"

"Oh yes!" she said at once. "I'm fine now. Everything's absolutely fine, just as it always is."

A vast relief overwhelmed me again as I prepared to bring my ministry of reconciliation to a triumphant conclusion.

It never even occurred to me that I might be grossly deluding myself.

II

"First loves do not always keep their glamour."

CHARLES E. RAVEN
A WANDERER'S WAY

I

I HAD just stubbed out my post-coital cigarette when I heard the front door close in the distance and realised that Alex had returned from the palace. Beside me Grace had already fallen asleep. Leaving the bed, I pulled on my discarded pyjamas, grabbed my dressing-gown and padded downstairs to attend to my guest.

Alex had paused to read the headlines of the *Starbridge Weekly News* which had been delivered that morning and abandoned on the hall chest. He was a man of medium height, just as I was, but we had different builds. I'm stocky. He was thin as a whippet and as restless as a cat on hot tiles. His thinning grey hair was straight, sleek and neatly parted. His ugly yellowish-brown eyes radiated an impatient vitality which was defiantly at odds with the heavy, sombre lines about his mouth. As always he was immaculately dressed.

"Would you like some tea before you turn in, Alex?"

"A corpse-reviver would be more appropriate! Why on earth did Ottershaw invite that old bore Calthrop-Ponsonby?"

"I think he feels sorry for him."

"How typical! Ottershaw would even feel sorry for a man-eating tiger who wanted to eat him for breakfast . . . How's Grace?"

"Sleeping."

"Hm." He dropped the newspaper abruptly on the hall chest. "Can we go into your study for a moment, Neville? I'll decline your kind offer of tea but there's something I'd like to say to you."

Obediently I led the way across the hall. I was anxious to return to bed as I was now very tired, but Alex was not only my present friend but my past benefactor and I always made every effort to oblige him.

I had first met him in 1932 when he had become the Bishop of Starbridge. Having long since decided that it was best to live in the South if one wanted to Get On and Travel Far, I had pulled all the Oxonian strings at my disposal and sought ordination from Alex's predecessor, Dr. Hargreaves, who had been scholarly, moderate in his Protestantism, tolerant of Modernist thought—and in fact exactly the type of leader I had had in mind when I had been called to enter the Church. Eventually I had become a curate in a village only two miles from Starbridge, and every morning I had been able to look out of my bedroom window at the distant Cathedral spire as it soared triumphantly upwards, symbolising my high hopes for the future.

After my curacy I had been appointed Rector of Willowmead, a picturesque market-town in the north of the diocese, and it was here, after Dr. Hargreaves's death in 1932, that Alex had entered my life.

I disliked him at first. He was abrupt to the point of rudeness, but I discovered later that he had had many problems on his arrival in the diocese and the strain of solving them had temporarily taken a toll on his charm. The next year, on his second visit to my parish, he was at his best. He enquired courteously about my life-history and when he discovered we had much in common—the early loss of a parent, the grinding experience of genteel poverty and the increasing determination to triumph over the inequities of the British class system—I was at once adopted as a protégé. Possibly I would have been promoted without his special interest, but that was by no means certain. In a national institution such as the Church of England, which was hidebound by tradition and dominated by men of the upper classes, a self-made man could only rely on help from another self-made man who knew what it was to struggle against prejudice and discrimination. Alex was a Fellow of All Souls, but he had never been to public school. United by our modest backgrounds we had long since entered into the conspiracy which had enabled me to squeeze under the closed door of the established order into the privileged room beyond, and it was this tacit comradeship, acquired on the battlefield of the class system, which gave our mutual respect a strong emotional edge. Of course we never displayed emotion to each other; we were, after all, Englishmen. But although we belonged to different generations I considered him my closest friend.

In the summer of 1937 he began to have trouble with the Archdeacon of Starbridge, an elderly man who had developed the habit of flying into senile panics, and after this millstone had been manipulated into retirement Alex offered me the archdeaconry. I myself was not sorry to leave Willowmead. I had organised the parish into a model of Christian efficiency and had been secretly longing for some time for new worlds to conquer. My translation to Starbridge came at the most appropriate moment, but unfortunately no sooner had I been installed at St. Martin's in the September of 1937 than Alex was obliged to retire from the bishopric.

At first I was much upset, not only because I was fond enough of Alex to be concerned about his health but because I was acutely aware that I could ill afford to lose such an influential patron. I awaited Dr. Ottershaw's arrival with trepidation, but to my great relief my fears proved groundless.

In general there are two types of bishops: holy bishops and what I call chairman-of-the-board bishops. The latter are by nature businessmen with gregarious personalities and a flair for organisation; their inevitable worldliness is mitigated by the spirit of Christ, and their success as bishops depends on the degree of mitigation. Holy bishops, on the other hand, usually have no talent for administration and need much time to themselves in order to maintain their spiritual gifts; their success as bishops depends less on the grace of God than on their willingness to delegate their administrative duties continually to talented assistants.

Alex was a chairman-of-the-board bishop. Dr. Ottershaw was a holy bishop. I was the talented assistant who thrived on delegated administrative duties—and within a month of his arrival I had realised that Dr. Ottershaw and I were made for each other. I even realised that had Alex remained in office we would almost certainly have quarrelled. Alex had a notoriously combative manner; I had an equally undesirable weakness for wielding a verbal sledgehammer. That premature retirement might have been unfortunate in many ways, but at least it had enabled us to preserve the friendship which now in 1942, ten years after our first meeting at Willowmead, we both valued so highly.

As we entered my study that night he said almost before I had closed the door: "Will you think me intolerably impertinent if I offer you some paternal advice?" and at once I said lightly: "You know very well I enjoy your impertinence—go ahead!" But I was alarmed. I have an aversion to people in authority who dole out paternal advice. Such behaviour always reminds me of my Uncle Willoughby.

"It's about young Miss Tallent."

"Oh yes?" I said, somehow contriving to remain cool as the temperature in the room appeared to soar to a tropical heat.

"Yes." Alex, whose hatred of hypocrisy and endless crusades for truth had won him plenty of enemies during his episcopate, was hardly a man to be deterred by coolness. "Neville, next time you meet an alluring young woman at a dinner-party, don't disappear into the moonlight with her for more than five minutes. And next time you meet Miss Tallent—if there is a next time—don't disappear with her at all. I'm a great believer in the pleasures of an *amitié amoureuse,* but such friendships are best conducted with happily married women escorted by their happily married husbands. Dabbling with a fast little miss isn't conducting an *amitié amoureuse.* It's playing with fire and asking for trouble."

"Quite." To my fury I realised I was blushing; this unfortunate adolescent handicap is one which I have never quite managed to outgrow. Deeply embarrassed I turned aside to realign the photographs of my children on the mantelshelf.

After a pause Alex said tersely: "I'm sorry if I've upset you, but I always speak my mind, as you know, and on this occasion I'm speaking purely out of a concern for your welfare. You mean a great deal to me, Neville. I'm very fond of you—and I'd hate to see your career take a wrong turn."

I was outraged. To spell out his affection—to indulge in sentimental utterances—to violate our delightful friendship by acting like some mawkish heavy-handed father: it was intolerable. Speech was quite beyond me. I could only grab the photograph of Grace and start polishing the silver frame furiously with my sleeve.

"Don't misunderstand," said Alex at last. "I'm sure the little escapade tonight was innocent. But where an attractive woman's concerned, any man—even a clergyman—perhaps especially a clergyman—has an almost limitless capacity for self-deception."

I finished polishing the frame and set it back on the mantelshelf. Then I said in my politest voice: "I take your point. Thank you for your advice. Is there anything else you wish to say?"

"Well, as a matter of fact there is." I should have remembered that when Alex was exercising his compulsive candour he was virtually unstoppable. "Can you tell me if there's a financial reason why you don't have a nursemaid living in to attend to my delightful godson in his more exuberant moods? Because if there is indeed a financial reason I hope you won't be too proud to accept my offer of help. I've money to spare and I'd be happy to do anything which might ease the situation."

Once more I was appalled. In my stiffest voice I said: "What situation?"

"My dear Neville, I've been staying here for three days and I'm neither blind nor deaf! It's patently obvious to me that Grace is at the end of her tether!"

"Nonsense. I concede she's a little tired at the moment because she's still recovering from the Easter holidays, but now that the three older boys are back at school she'll soon recover. Very good of you to offer help but it's not necessary. No problems financially. No problems of any kind, thank you."

"Neville, I know you're a proud man, but wouldn't you find it helpful—just for once—to admit that everything in the garden isn't quite as lovely as it ought to be? If Grace is so exhausted that she can barely cope with her domestic duties, how can she possibly deal satisfactorily with her responsibilities as an archdeacon's wife? She deliberately evaded the dinner-party tonight, didn't she? Well, as it happens that wasn't a disastrous evasion, but what are you going to do when a really crucial engagement turns up, an engagement vital for the well-being of your career? Or in other words, how is Grace going to summon the extra energy she'll need to keep up with you in the future? If you were to engage a nursemaid—"

"That's not what Grace wants. She couldn't bear another woman constantly in the nursery."

"Then engage a full-time cook-general!"

"That's not what Grace wants either. She couldn't bear another woman constantly in the kitchen."

"I'm getting rather tired of hearing what Grace wants! What do *you* want? It seems to me, judging from your behaviour tonight, that you're beginning to feel short-changed!"

Somehow I managed to control my temper. I heard myself say in my most colourless voice: "You couldn't be more mistaken, Alex. You've utterly misread the situation, but on the other hand, why should I expect you to read it correctly? The truth is no outsider can really know what goes on in any marriage."

"Well, that's true enough," said Alex dryly, deciding to wipe the tension from the conversation by exercising his caustic wit. "No one knows the half of what's gone on in mine." He turned aside, but as he opened the door he was unable to resist the urge to proffer still more unwanted advice. "Deposit Primrose and Sandy with a kind neighbour," he said, "and take Grace away for a second honeymoon before you get tangled up with another fast little miss."

"There won't be another fast little miss. Perhaps you can't be blamed for drawing quite the wrong conclusions from my idiotic behaviour with Miss Tallent, but let me assure you now, once and for all, that Grace is a perfect wife and I adore her."

"Splendid! Very well, I'll now stop overstepping the mark in my usual outrageous fashion and take myself off to bed before you try to hit me with those clenched fists of yours. Good night, Neville. God bless you. And do try to remember that I've spoken only with your welfare in mind . . ."

2

I WAS so angry with this cavalier attempt to meddle in my marriage that although I was tired I lay awake fuming for over an hour in the dark. I hated Alex thinking that Grace was temporarily less than perfect. I hated him telling me facts I already knew. And I hated him suggesting facile solutions when I knew very well that the problem was more complex than he in his ignorance supposed. I could not simply impose a cook-general or a nursemaid on Grace against her will. After all, it was she, not I, who would have to deal with the woman, and if Grace felt unable to cope with a stranger in either the kitchen or the nursery, any effort on my part to employ someone suitable would only be a waste of time. Also I knew from past experience that Grace interpreted my suggestions about employing additional help as implied criticisms of her ability to be the perfect wife and mother. Then no matter how hard I tried to reassure her that no criticism was intended, she became more depressed than ever. Eventually, I was sure, the problem would be alleviated when Sandy ceased to need constant maternal supervision and embarked on his career as a schoolboy, but until that golden moment when he skipped off to begin his first day at kindergarten, it seemed my best course of action was to help Grace by being loyal, loving and endlessly sympathetic. I had to make up my mind never to complain about her melancholy, never to reproach her for shying away from the social life she should be sharing with me and never, never, never to lose my temper. I was always mindful of the fact that Sandy could hardly have been conceived without my assistance, and if he was now complicating our lives I had a moral duty to ameliorate the situation by being a perfect husband.

Remembering my loss of temper earlier I winced, but at least I was able to console myself by recalling my subsequent ministry of reconciliation. How wrong Alex had been to assume that I was being short-changed in the bedroom! Even after sixteen years of marriage I was never deprived in that area—except on those occasions when Grace was in an advanced state of pregnancy or suffering from migraine or too exhausted to do anything but pass out. However, those exceptions were of no consequence, since one could hardly expect married life to be one long sex-romp. Even D. H. Lawrence had never tried to describe Mellors and Lady Chatterley with five children. My brother Willy had smuggled a copy of *Lady Chatterley's Lover* into England after a holiday in Paris and I had read the book with interest, but personally I thought it was greatly inferior to Lawrence's other work.

Remembering that Lawrence's own marriage had been childless, I began to think of Alex again. His childless marriage was certainly far from successful, and it occurred to me to wonder how far his own marital discomfort had influenced his interpretation of my dilemma.

Alex had said lightly that no one knew much about his marriage, but I suspected I knew all too well what had gone on. Having married his intellectual opposite after a whirlwind courtship, it seemed clear that he had long since regretted his folly. Even with no children to distract her, his wife Carrie had been unable to master her increasing responsibilities as Alex had travelled rapidly up the Church's ladder of preferment. In 1927, when he had been appointed Dean of Radbury, he had even been obliged to engage someone to keep her life in order, and it had been this companion, an icy virgin with a deceptively steamy appearance and a brain like an adding machine, who had run first the deanery at Radbury and later the palace at Starbridge. The companion had eventually left to get married, much to the Jardines' fury, and since 1937 a variety of women had been hired and fired in the unending struggle to keep Carrie organised. Even now, when Alex was living quietly in a small village, Carrie was incapable of running her life without help. What a burden for any husband! Alex used to joke bravely about his *ménage à trois,* but I thought his marriage must be the height of dreariness.

The one redeeming feature was that Carrie in her elderly way was still pretty. It had seemed logical to assume the Jardines enjoyed something which resembled a sex-life—how else could Alex have made his marriage tolerable?—but now I found myself wondering if the heart condition which had terminated his career had also terminated the intimate side of his marriage. Curiously enough he always seemed very fit, bursting with energy, but if he had been so quick to detect a nonexistent sexual frustration in my marriage it seemed logical to deduce he was no stranger to sexual frustration in his own.

I sighed, feeling sorry for him, and with my anger finally conquered I succeeded in falling asleep.

The next morning I was confused to discover that I still felt angry with him but for a different reason. I could accept that he had spoken out of the best of motives; I could even accept that he had been justified in feeling concern about Grace; but what I found hard to accept was the way he had conducted the interview. Displaying the delicacy of an elephant and the sensitivity of a rhinoceros, he had charged around trying to impose his conclusions upon me without regard for my willingness to accept them, and although such behaviour might possibly be forgivable when displayed by some well-meaning Victorian father, I thought it was quite unforgivable when displayed by a clergyman. I myself had no great pastoral gifts. My talent was for administration, but I knew enough about pastoral work to realise that when counselling someone in trouble one's prime duty was to listen, not to make speeches, to nurture trust, not to destroy it. In some fundamental way my trust in Alex had been impaired by that bruising interview. I still admired him as a man; I still respected him as a friend. But I did not want to discuss my private life with him ever again.

This was a disturbing conclusion, but fortunately in the early mornings I was always too busy to dwell on unpleasant thoughts. My first task was to make the tea. I always performed this chore because I felt that the least Grace deserved was a husband who delivered the early morning tea to her in bed. Having accomplished this ritual I withdrew to my dressing-room, read the office and meditated conscientiously on the appointed verses from the Bible. Being Low Church in inclination if not in practice—my services were carefully aimed at the middle-of-the-road moderate majority in the Church of England in order to avoid unfortunate controversy—I preferred to focus my spiritual exercises on the Bible before applying myself to my prayers.

After this interval I shaved and dressed. Usually I wore my archidiaconal uniform, but if my engagements were informal—or if the weather was so hot that the wearing of gaiters became intolerable—I had enough courage to resort to a plain clerical suit. I'm not the kind of man who enjoys tripping around in an antiquated fancy-dress.

When I eventually left my dressing-room I headed for the nursery, where Sandy would be waking up, and put some toys in his cot to keep him quiet. By seven o'clock I had reached my study, where I aimed to put in an hour's work before breakfast. On that particular morning I caught up with my sympathy letters—after three years of war one had to take great care that the sentiments expressed sounded genuine—paid a couple of bills and studied two archidiaconal files, one relating to new gutters for a church with a persistent damp wall and the other concerning a parish quarrel over a new font. I decided it would be prudent to ask the diocesan surveyor to look at the old gutters and even more prudent to ask the diocesan lawyers to advise on whether the font was, legally speaking, a font. The outraged churchwarden was insisting that it reminded him of a lavatory.

I yawned. The archdeaconry was quiet. No fallen steeples, no dispute about plastic flowers on graves, no rural dean suffering from delusions of grandeur, no curate going berserk with choirboys, no vicar letting off Anglo-Catholic liturgical fireworks, no verger blowing his brains out.

Finding myself with five minutes to spare before breakfast, I drew up a plan for my Sunday sermon and plucked a few pertinent quotations from my trusty memory. My brother Willy always said I had a mind like a vacuum cleaner; I can effortlessly absorb any information, from the sublime to the ridiculous, and regurgitate it, sometimes years later, with an efficiency bordering on the robotic.

At breakfast I admired the new bow in Primrose's hair, glanced at the headlines of *The Times,* read the latest letter from Christian at Winchester, answered the telephone, picked Sandy's rusk off the floor twice and asked Alex if he intended to spend all day in the Cathedral library, where he was studying the records of his episcopate.

"No, I'm having a rest from my autobiography today," he said, surprising me. "I've decided to take a train to Starvale St. James and call on Lyle."

Lyle, now Mrs. Charles Ashworth, was the icy companion who had run the Jardines' household so efficiently before her unwelcome defection to the state of matrimony in 1937.

"She probably won't want to see me," Alex was saying as he idly applied marmalade to his toast, "but I thought it would be too ridiculous if I left the diocese without calling on her. I intend to arrive on her doorstep waving the olive branch of peace."

"Better late than never, but why not phone her first? Your olive branch will be wasted if you arrive on her doorstep and find she's gone out for the day!"

"I'll take the risk. If I ring she might simply slam down the receiver—I can't tell you what a tangle we all got into back in 1937—"

"I always thought it sounded the most grotesque storm in a tea-cup and I can't believe Lyle won't welcome the chance to end the estrangement. Do you want a lift to the station?"

He accepted the lift. I noted with compassion that he had bought expensive presents for Lyle's two sons. Evidently he was anxious that his olive branch should be substantial.

"Remember me to Lyle, won't you?" I said. "As it happens I'll be coming her way soon. An incensed churchwarden at Starvale St. James is complaining that the new font looks like a urinal."

"Oh yes?" said Alex vaguely, and when he failed to smile I knew his thoughts were far away.

Leaving him at the station I called at the diocesan office on Eternity Street to collect my special allowance of extra petrol coupons, suffered myself to be cornered by various officials who saw me as a channel to the Bishop, escaped into the High Street to buy cigarettes and finally parked my car in the old vicarage stables behind Butchers' Alley just as the clock of St. Martin's chimed the half hour. I was fractionally late for the morning conference with my curates, but to my relief I saw no bicycles parked outside the vicarage gate. I disliked my curates arriving ahead of me and looking insufferably virtuous as I walked into the room. Much better that they should arrive panting and apologetic while I was sitting coolly behind my desk.

I opened the front door. I withdrew my key from the lock. And I paused, paralysed with shock, as my hand remained on the latch. I had heard a laugh in the morning-room where we received the parishioners who called on us, but this laugh belonged to no one who lived within the parish of St. Martin's-in-Cripplegate. Automatically, without stopping to think, I blundered forward into the hall.

Grace was saying: "That'll be Neville. If you'll excuse me, I'll just tell him you're here."

I plunged across the morning-room threshold. Grace, who had almost reached the door, hastily recoiled. As our visitor sprang to her feet, I saw us all as three puppets jerking on the ends of some exceedingly erratic strings.

"Hullo, Stephen!" said Dido, whose memory I had, of course, been conscientiously suppressing all morning, and gave me a bold, bright, impudent smile.

"Good morning, Miss Tallent," I said, rigid with rage behind my clerical collar. I was acutely aware that Grace was wearing her oldest dress, the one she wore only around the house, and that she looked faded, fatigued and unfashionable. In contrast, Dido, seemingly poured into her sleek Naval uniform, looked saucy, sexy and scintillating. I could have slapped her.

Suddenly I became aware of Sandy's presence. In the profound silence which followed the formal exchange of greetings he staggered across the floor and offered me one of his toy bricks.

"Thank you, Sandy." I took the brick and gripped it so hard that my fingers ached. Then in a passable attempt to achieve a smooth social manner I said to Dido: "How kind of you to call, but I'm afraid you must excuse me. I have an urgent meeting now with my curates."

"Oh, I wouldn't dream of troubling you when you're so busy!" exclaimed Dido with that wide-eyed candour which I found so fatally compelling. "I just called to leave my card and enquire if your wife was better." Giving Grace her warmest smile, she added confidentially: "You didn't miss much at the Bish's dinner-party—your husband was the only redeeming feature."

The doorbell rang.

"I'll go!" said Grace, scooping up Sandy.

"No, I'll answer it—"

"No, it's all right, Neville—"

We collided in the doorway before Grace succeeded in escaping into the hall.

"I'm obviously causing chaos as usual," said Dido. "I'll leave at once."

I realised I was still holding Sandy's brick. It was bright red, the colour of violence, volcanic fire and Technicolor blood. It also matched Dido's lipstick. Setting the brick down on the table with meticulous care, I somehow managed to say to Dido in my politest voice: "If you feel you must go, then I shan't try to detain you, but I apologise if you've been made to feel unwelcome."

"Oh no, your wife was charming! We got on terribly well!"

"Miss Tallent—"

"Oh, I do wish you'd stop calling me that! Why don't you call me Dido, just as everyone else does?"

"I'm most flattered that you should wish to be on such friendly terms with me, but I'm afraid a clergyman has a duty to be formal towards a young lady he's known less than twenty-four hours."

"But I'm sure Jesus would have called me Dido without a second thought! He *never* bothered to be formal with the good-time girls!"

I opened my mouth to say coldly: "I fear I can only consider that remark to be in excessive bad taste," but the words were never spoken. To my horror I realised I was smiling. "You're outrageous!" I exclaimed in despair. "What on earth am I going to do with you?"

"But don't you remember? You're going to be my spiritual guide and write me uplifting letters!"

"But my dear Miss Tallent—"

"You didn't think I was serious, did you? You didn't think I meant what I said, but I swear to you I'm deeply in earnest and absolutely desperate. I know you think I'm stupid and frivolous and not worth bothering about, but—"

"Everyone's worth bothering about. But don't you think your local clergyman would be better placed than I am to give you the guidance you need?"

"That celibate fish? He's only fit to be lightly grilled on both sides and served to the congregation with parsley sauce!"

I made a quick decision, the kind of quick decision capable administrators make, a cool practical decision untainted by emotional involvement. There was no doubt this girl was genuinely distressed and adrift. It seemed reasonable to suppose she was suffering from that particularly debilitating confusion which so often follows a severe bereavement: an appalled recognition of her own mortality and a consequent questioning of her way of life. With the right help this self-examination could lead to a vital spiritual growth. Who was I to regard her with such un-Christian cynicism because she had spent too many years as a mindless society girl? In a very real sense Dido's tasteless comment about Jesus had hit the mark of truth. He would never have walked past her with his nose in the air, and since I was one of his followers neither should I.

Abruptly I altered course. "Very well," I said, adopting a crisp authoritative tone. "If you honestly believe I can help you I'll answer your letters—but on one condition. You must address me as 'Archdeacon,' I must address you as 'Miss Tallent' and our correspondence must be a model of propriety."

"That's three conditions, not one! But never mind, I accept them all with rapturous gratitude." She smiled radiantly at me. "Goodbye, Archdeacon dear. I'm off to the post office to buy a large supply of stamps." And leaving me wondering how on earth I could have been quite such a fool, she sailed triumphantly from the room.

3

"WHY didn't you tell me?"

"I didn't think it was important."

"But she's famous! She almost married that millionaire—and then there was the film star—and everyone knows she flirted with the Prince of Wales!"

"I don't find that sort of thing very interesting."

"Well, she obviously found you very interesting indeed! Why in heaven's name did she call you Stephen?"

"The name Neville reminded her of Mr. Chamberlain."

"But what was she doing calling you by your Christian name when you'd only just met her?"

"Oh, society people have very peculiar manners these days. Like people in show business."

"Well, it all sounds very fast to me! Why, she even said she talked to you on your own for half an hour in the garden!"

"Only about Victorian literature."

"But what did everyone think when you disappeared for half an hour with a society flirt?"

I cleared my throat. "I think that designation's a little uncharitable, Grace. Not even a society girl's beyond redemption."

"Don't tell me she wants you to redeem her!"

I cleared my throat again. "Well, as a matter of fact she did show signs of wanting a complete change of direction. I've promised to write her a line or two in response to any queries she may have about spiritual matters."

"Honestly, Neville! I wouldn't have thought you could be quite so naive!"

"And I wouldn't have thought you could be quite so catty and cynical!"

Grace suddenly drooped as if all the strength had drained out of her. Immediately I hated myself. "My dearest love"—I took her in my arms—"I know it all seems highly irregular, but what's a clergyman to do when he's asked for spiritual advice? He can't refuse to give it simply because the person in search of help is someone with whom he'd never normally associate!" I kissed her before adding: "Of course I'll show you every letter."

"Don't be silly. You know that's not necessary." She clung to me briefly before turning away with the abrupt comment: "The curates have arrived."

"Bother the curates." I grabbed her back into my arms and said in my firmest voice: "I love you very much—as I trust I proved to you last night—and for me you'll always be the only woman in the world. Why on earth should I even look twice at a saucy little piece of nonsense like Dido Tallent?"

That indeed was the question.

4

ALEX returned at noon after bearing his olive branch to the village of Starvale St. James, where Lyle had rented accommodation a year before. She normally lived in Cambridge, where before the war her husband had been a canon of the Cathedral and a theologian at the University, but after Ashworth had been sent overseas with his regiment Lyle had preferred to retreat temporarily to the country so that her young children would be in a safe place. Ashworth had an elderly friend in Starvale St. James—none other than the irate churchwarden who was now persecuting me about the font—and Lyle, already familiar with the diocese after her years with the Jardines, had decided she ran less risk of being lonely there than elsewhere in the English countryside.

When Alex returned I had just finished speaking on the telephone to the Bishop, who was in a flap about the proposed prisoner-of-war camp on Starbury Plain. It was by no means certain that we would be allowed any contact with the prisoners but the Bishop felt we should at least plan as if some form of pastoral work, no matter how limited, would be permitted. Unfortunately the camp, if built, would stand in the other archdeaconry, and the other Archdeacon, Hubert Babbington-French, was now openly proclaiming that the only good German was a dead German. No wonder the Bishop was in a flap; it wasn't every day he had to deal with an eminent cleric bent on bawling out un-Christian slogans. Obviously the idiotic Babbington-French would have to be steered away from the wretched Huns, but I had a nasty feeling that the Bishop in his despair was planning to steer me towards them. I was willing to do my duty and attempt to behave in a Christian manner towards even the most repulsive Nazi, but the prospect was far from enthralling, particularly when we were all waiting to see if Hitler opened his Baedeker guide at the wrong page. I was now privately very worried indeed about the prospect of an attack on Starbridge, for my vicarage was in the centre of the city, but Grace, following the example of the Queen, had said that the children stayed with her and that she intended to stay with me—and I, of course, had to stay at St. Martin's. I could only thank God we had a good air-raid shelter and pray that Hitler, diverted by the fighting on the Eastern Front, would lose interest in reading travel guides.

I was just wondering if I should hold daily services at lunch-time for all the city workers who would be experiencing a strong compulsion to pray for deliverance, when the door of my study opened and Alex strode in. There was a spring in his walk, a smile on his face and a carnation in the buttonhole of his smart lounge suit.

"Do I deduce that the hatchet was safely buried?" I said amused after we had exchanged greetings.

"I think it would be more accurate to say that we managed to ease the hatchet into a coffin to await a full burial later—but at least that's a step in the right direction! We sat in the garden and drank tea for twenty minutes."

"Only twenty minutes?"

"She had to attend a committee meeting of the Women's Institute. But she sent her love to Carrie, so it would seem the ice is definitely broken."

"Splendid! And what did you think of her boys? That little Charley says he wants to be a clergyman."

"So he told me." Alex, who had been pacing around the room in his usual restless fashion, now stopped jingling the coins in his pockets and started eyeing the telephone. "I'd so much like to tell Carrie about the meeting," he said. "Would you mind if I put through a call on your extension upstairs?"

"Not at all—go ahead," I said, and embarked on a letter to the Red Cross about the parish food parcel for British prisoners of war.

I was halfway through this task when I was interrupted by the arrival of my diocesan *bête noire,* a clergyman named Darrow about whom I shall say more later. I mention him now only because it was at this time that he began his career at the Theological College in the Cathedral Close, a fact which became of considerable importance to me in 1945 after I had almost committed adultery.

On that morning in 1942 when Darrow arrived without warning on my doorstep and breezed arrogantly into my study, the Theological College was in the midst of a crisis because of the war-time shortage of staff, and on the previous evening at the palace Alex had been able to provide Dr. Ottershaw with the vital information that Darrow had had experience in the training of clergymen. Darrow had had experience in many other clerical fields too—driving archdeacons well-nigh round the bend was only one of his more esoteric activities—but now is not the moment to expand on his buccaneering career in the Church. His purpose in calling at the vicarage that morning was to thank Alex for recommending him to the Bishop, but he wound up by delivering an insufferably priggish lecture on the theme that the ultimate prize for any priest—as a bigoted Anglo-Catholic he always called clergymen "priests"—could only be union with God.

"How did I manage to keep a civil tongue in my head?" demanded Alex as soon as Darrow had stalked out. "I must be getting saintly in my old age! And to think that according to Lyle her husband remains one of Darrow's most devoted admirers!"

"Ashworth's busy being an Army chaplain in North Africa. If he was trying to run an archdeaconry where Darrow was on the rampage, he'd soon modify his admiration, I promise you! What on earth will life be like at the Theological College once that pirate prances through the front door?"

"I prophesy charismatic wonders, incense in the College Chapel and a collective nervous breakdown for the remaining staff. And talking of nervous exhaustion . . . Am I forgiven for speaking my mind to you about Grace last night?"

"Of course."

"I really am sorry if I upset you, Neville."

"My dear Alex, let's ring down the curtain on the scene and forget all about it!"

"Very well, but before the curtain finally reaches the ground, may I just ask if you're taking my advice about bearing Grace off on a second honeymoon?"

"Drop the subject, Alex, there's a good fellow—just drop it," I said, brandishing a voice of steel alongside my friendliest smile, and he hastily began to talk of other matters.

But that night in the bedroom I found myself saying to Grace: "How would you like a week's rest before the school holidays begin? We could leave Primrose and Sandy in Manchester with Winifred and go to a hotel in the Lake District."

Grace, who had been brushing her hair, paused to stare at me in the triple mirror. "But is it still possible to take holidays there?"

"I'm sure it is. Holiday-makers are only banned from the south and east coasts."

"But I couldn't possibly leave Sandy with Winifred! He'd wear her out."

"Maybe she wouldn't mind being worn out in order to give you a rest! After all, you're always saying what a wonderful sister she is."

"Yes, but she's not as patient as I am, and—"

"No one's as patient as you are with that little monster! Personally I think a touch of impatience now and then would do him no harm at all!"

"But Neville—"

"Why are you beating around the bush like this? The issue's really very simple: Do you or don't you want a second honeymoon?"

"I suppose I'll have to say I do, won't I?"

"For heaven's sake!" I exclaimed, no longer making an effort to conceal my exasperation. "What sort of answer's that?"

"The sort of answer which I'm sure you require of a perfect wife."

"Grace, if you weren't so constantly obsessed with perfection you wouldn't make such ridiculous statements!"

"*I* obsessed by perfection? But Neville, *you're* the one who's obsessed! You—chasing the prizes of life, never able to rest, never being satisfied—"

"What rubbish—of course I'm satisfied! I've got the perfect wife, the perfect home, the perfect family—I've won all the ultimate prizes of life! Well, nearly all of them—"

"Darling, listen to me." Rising to her feet, she turned her back on the triple mirror and we faced each other. "I'm not a prize. I'm a person. I can't just be kept in a glass case on a mantelshelf. I have to move in the real world, and in the real world I can't be this perfect wife of your dreams. I do try to be—I keep trying and trying—I try so hard because I don't want to disappoint you, but—"

"You could never disappoint me."

"No? Supposing I tell you that I don't want to go away to the Lake

District unless we take Sandy and Primrose with us? Darling, we simply can't dump them on poor Winifred for a week! It's just not fair to her, and besides I wouldn't enjoy myself—I'd spend my whole time worrying in case they were unhappy. I admit I do want a rest, but I'd much rather wait until our family holiday in July."

"Very well." I turned away.

"Neville—"

"No need to say another word. You've spoken your mind and I still think you're perfect. Happy ending. Now let's ring down the curtain on the scene and forget I ever mentioned the idea," I said in the most equable voice at my command, and withdrew at once to my dressing-room.

5

I FOUND myself unable to concentrate on the evening office, and an attempt to pray proved futile. However when I eventually returned to the bedroom in my pyjamas, Grace said at once: "Darling, could we compromise? If we changed our plans and spent our family holiday in the Lake District instead of Devon, we could leave all five children with Winifred for the first forty-eight hours and have that little holiday alone together after all. I don't think Sandy could destroy Winifred in two days, and since Christian and Norman are old enough to be helpful with the younger ones, I wouldn't spend all my time worrying about how they were getting on."

"Splendid! I'll cancel Devon immediately."

"We've left it rather late in the day to change our plans—and of course it would involve a longer journey just when the government's telling us we shouldn't travel unless we have to—"

"We do have to—and I'm sure we can easily find a cottage to rent. I'll look at the holiday advertisements in today's *Church Gazette.*"

She kissed me. "You're not cross with me any more?"

"My dearest love!" I said. "When have I ever been cross with you?" And before either of us could answer that question I took her in my arms.

6

THE letters began to arrive. Dido wrote as she talked: fluently, with eccentric punctuation. She used a pencil, which always began sharp and ended blunt, probably as the result of her copious underlinings.

Dear Archdeacon,

Before I *bare my soul* to you I must tell you *all* about my background so that you can see my troubles in some sort of *illuminating perspective* . . .

I learnt that her father had made a fortune by profiteering during the First War and had consolidated his wealth by adventurous skulduggery in the City. He was currently chairman of an enterprise called the Pan-Grampian Trust and played golf regularly with various luminaries of the Bank of England in an effort to consolidate his hard-won respectability. In addition to his house in Edinburgh and his nine-bedroom flat overlooking Grosvenor Square he had not only the usual millionaire's castle in the Highlands but a country mansion in Leicestershire, where his daughters had pursued their passion for hunting. His wife, however, never left Edinburgh.

. . . poor Mother is a good person but *very shy.* How glad I am that I haven't inherited this *devastating* handicap! Fortunately Father's mistresses have all possessed gregarious dispositions in addition to superb connections in Society, so my sisters and I have been able to surmount the difficulties which were inevitably created by Mother's beautiful retiring nature.

Merry (that's my sister Muriel, now Lady Wyvenhoe) and darling Laura (who became the Honourable Mrs. Anthony Fox-Drummond) and I (who's so far become no one at all) were always invited *everywhere,* and since Father spent money like *water* on our coming-out, I can't say I ever found it a handicap to be a jumped-up Scot—indeed quite the reverse, we were all regarded as exciting novelties and given a license to be entertaining. So no matter how outrageous we were, people just said: "Poor little things, they don't know any better, but what a gorgeous breath of fresh air they are, blowing away all the boring cobwebs from London Society, let's invite them to *masses* more balls and tea-dances and cocktail parties so that we can all continue to be *madly* amused!" So that was what happened and we were a simply enormous success, even when for a laugh we put on our Scottish accents, although of course our governess was told to make sure we knew how to talk like English ladies and in consequence we grew up bilingual.

Anyway, Archdeacon dear, you may disapprove of me talking faultless English and so pretending to be what I'm not, but let me assure you that in every other respect I'm *entirely honest.* I always say to a new friend right from the start: "My father's a self-made man (though one of Nature's Gentlemen, of course) and my mother doesn't go out and about in Society because she's afraid she'll be thought common (a fear naturally enhanced by her beautiful retiring nature)"—and once all that's been said everyone relaxes because they know exactly where they stand and no one feels in the least deceived . . .

In another letter she told me about her three brothers, all employed in her father's financial empire, but I realised that since they were many years her senior they had played little part in her growing up.

. . . but I've always been *very close to my sisters*—well, we had to stick together, you see, because since Father was so busy making money and my brothers were so busy at public school learning how to be English gentlemen and Mother was so busy being retiring, no one had much time for us except Blackboard our Governess (Miss Black) and even she was always wishing she was somewhere else, so Merry and Laura and I formed what we called *The Triple Alliance* in order to conquer the world and make everyone take notice of us. I was *devastated,* simply *devastated,* when Merry married that sporty bore Wyvenhoe, all polo and fishing and shooting thousands of poor little birds in August (I think he only married Merry to gain permanent access to Father's grouse-moor). Her marriage destroyed our Triple Alliance and I knew things would never be the same again and I was right, they never were. She lives up in Leicestershire now, although of course she has a house in London, and I seldom see her. But I recovered from losing Merry. It was losing Laura that nearly killed me.

Darling Laura was the *light of my life,* we were *closer than most twins,* only twelve months apart, we did everything together, everything, Merry was always the odd one out as she was two years older than Laura, three years older than me. Laura and I were presented at Court together and shared our first Season, and later the Prince of Wales (I'm sorry, I know he's the Duke of Windsor now, but for me he'll always be our gorgeous Prince of Wales)—he said he would have danced with both of us simultaneously if he had had two pairs of arms (my dear, Mrs. Simpson was simply *seething!*) and life was thrilling, *such fun,* how we laughed, and then Laura, darling Laura, fell in love with Anthony, and at first I minded dreadfully but after a while I told myself it was wicked of me to begrudge her such happiness, so I made up my mind not to be jealous of him, and once I'd done that I realised he was *such* a nice man, so sweet-natured, the son of a peer but really quite normal, and they got married in 1938 and they were so happy, living in London—which meant I could still see Laura every day—and then she started a baby and she was so thrilled—we were all so thrilled, even me, although I did have a little shudder at first at the thought of having to share her with yet another person—ugh! how contemptible of me, I despised myself for being so selfish!—and then . . .

Disaster, tragedy, DEATH. Why do such things have to happen, why, why, why, I cried for days, I felt as if half of myself had been amputated and all the world seemed such a dark place without Laura's special light—and when I looked back at all the parties, all the champagne and the caviar, I could only think: Death always wins in the end. Oh, what a dreadful moment that was, so black, so brutal, so absolutely terrifying—and suddenly all my party memories seemed so sinister, I seemed to see a death's-head grinning at every feast, and that was the moment when I knew parties would never be the same again because I would always be thinking: EAT, DRINK AND BE MERRY FOR TOMORROW WE DIE, and the word DIE would always remind me of horrors past and horrors still to come.

Well, when I realised there was no escape from that terrible truth, no escape on the dance-floor, no escape in the saddle at a hunt, no escape among the cocktails at Grosvenor Square, I saw that the only thing to do was not to run away but to stand my ground and try to look Death straight in the face—and once I'd done that I knew I had to *live,* and when I say *live* I mean not frittering away time but using time profitably—I knew I had to find some way of life which was *real,* as real as Death, the toughest reality of all.

At that moment the war arrived, and as I told you, I thought the answer was to join the Wrens, but that hasn't worked out as I'd hoped. What I now find—and this is really *most* peculiar, in fact highly unnerving—is that the person I appear to be in public, the person everyone thinks I am, has *nothing to do with my new true self.* Everyone thinks—including you, I suspect, Archdeacon dear—that I'm still just a frivolous little piece of nonsense, but that old false self's smashed to bits now, all the fragments are gone with the wind, and my current great task is to find the right life for my new true self and so make myself into a real person at last—because only when I become a real person, living in harmony with my new true self, will I be able to face that other real person, Death, on equal terms and not be afraid of him any more.

Well, I know that all sounds rather turgid, so I'll spare you further soul-searching by announcing that I believe I see the first step I have to take: I must get married. (I mentioned this when we met, but now I can explain the decision in its proper context.) The plain fact of the matter is (as I more or less implied earlier) that despite emancipation and women voting and being doctors and bus conductresses and so on, our society considers any woman who's not married is a failure, and I think that if I'm to have a meaningful life and be truly *me,* I've got to be a success. I mean, I wouldn't be happy otherwise, and how could I live meaningfully if I was miserable?

Now, Archdeacon dear, I know you were terribly original and said it could be fulfilling to be celibate (by which I assume you meant not only unmarried but chaste although I believe, strictly speaking, to be celibate merely means to be unmarried) but to be brutally frank I don't think celibacy would suit me at all. I wouldn't mind doing without sex, which has always seemed to me as if it must be quite dull in comparison with hunting—although darling Laura said it was all rather heavenly—sex, I mean, not hunting—after all, hunting's *really* heavenly, no "rather" about it—and . . . oh bother, I've lost my way in this sentence, I'll have to start again. I wouldn't mind doing without sex (as I was saying) but I simply couldn't bear the social stigma of being unmarried. But *please* don't think I'm just enslaved by a *rampant pride.* You see, the one thing I'm good at is being social, so I feel sure that God's calling me to be a social success, but of course now I realise it can't just be the kind of facile self-centred success I used to enjoy when I was my old false self. It must be a *meaningful* social success—the social success of a wife who strives to help her husband (who of course must be a really *worthwhile* man) in his dynamic and outstanding career. Then I could feel useful and fulfilled knowing that he was feeling useful and fulfilled and I'm sure we'd both live happily ever after.

It's a glorious vision, isn't it? Or so I think now, but when it first unfurled itself I confess I did have grave doubts because I knew very well I felt so lukewarm towards men that I couldn't quite conceive of ever summoning the desire to marry one of them. I did tell you at the dinner-party, didn't I, about my lukewarm state, but I wasn't quite honest with you about my reasons for being anti-man. I said I couldn't bear the way men regarded me as just a pair of legs, but there's rather more to my antipathy than that. You see, I'm still recovering from being in love with the wrong man for six years. His name's Roland Carlton-Blake. (If I tell you he likes to be known as Rollo you'll guess at once what kind of a man he is, so I shall merely confirm your suspicions by telling you that before the war he called himself a gentleman of leisure and other people called him a playboy.) Now he's a soldier in Cairo and as he's got some sort of desk-job I doubt if he sees any fighting, but I can imagine him passing his leisure hours by riding around the pyramids and pretending to be Rudolph Valentino in *The Sheik.*

Why did I fall for this ghastly creature, you ask? Well, primarily for all the usual reasons, he was so handsome, so glamorous, he rode to hounds so beautifully, and life always seemed to be so gay and amusing when he was around, but the real reason why I liked him was that he never tried to jump on me and I appreciated this so much that I began to believe he really did love me for myself and not just for my legs. So I wound up thinking: That's the one man I could bear to marry—I shouldn't even mind if he was disgusting when he was having sex—because quite frankly, I don't see how men can avoid being disgusting when they have sex, so the great thing is not to mind when they do.

Anyway, earlier this year before he was posted to Egypt I decided to propose to him. After all, it was obvious after six years that *he* wasn't going to do it, so I proposed and then he told me he was in the midst of an affair with an actress.

As a matter of fact I knew her, she was rather nice, but when I found out I felt absolutely *crushed,* and I said to Rollo: "Why did you never ask *me* to be your mistress if you're the kind of man who does that sort of thing?" He just laughed. He said: "You'd have said no and slapped my face!"—which was actually true, as I can never see the point of coming second (being a mistress) when one can come first (being a wife). I've always thought fornication was a dead-end career for a woman, almost as futile as lesbianism.

Very indignantly I said to Rollo: "All right, I admit I wouldn't have been your mistress, but I could have been your wife and then you wouldn't have had to skulk around fornicating in such an undignified manner." Oh, how cross he was when I said that! "I'm always *very* dignified when I fornicate!" he cried indignantly. "All my mistresses consider me a *paragon* of discretion!" "*All* your mistresses?" I shouted. "You mean you've had others?"

Oh Mr. Aysgarth, you'll think me very naive, especially as I'm a Society Girl who's supposed to be the last word in sophistication, but you see, I loved him and love is blind and I wanted so much to believe he was pure and noble behind his dashing facade, quite different from all the other men in the world, who appear to see me as a cross between a cream-cake and an ice-cream cornet. Even Father, who's so well-behaved with his mistresses, only having one at a time and never in the same city as Mother—even Father and my brothers seem to see me as no more than a box of chocolates whenever they take time off from their full varied interesting lives to remind themselves of my existence.

How I wish I'd been born a man! Gender's such a prison sometimes, especially when one wants one's new true self to be recognised and respected.

Anyway, to return to Rollo, I said: "How would you feel if I were to tell you that I'd been sleeping with everyone in sight for six years despite the fact that I'd regularly been saying that I loved no one but you?" And Rollo said as if I was being very stupid: "Oh, that wouldn't have been playing the game at all! A man with mistresses is just living a normal life. A woman with lovers is just being a slut. That's the way of the world, isn't it?" At which point I drew myself up to my full height and looked him straight in the eyes and declared: "Your world, perhaps. *But not mine.*"

I told him I never wanted to see him again, but the awful part was I did want to, I missed him *terribly,* and it was just as well he was sent to Egypt or I might have weakened. I still loved him even though I could see he was just a selfish lout with the brains of a flea. I thought: That's the last straw—I've lost first Laura and now Rollo, why don't I just fling myself in the Thames? But I couldn't bear the thought of being a failure and anyway I'm not the suicidal type, so I staggered on day after day until finally I had a big stroke of luck: I met Charlotte Ottershaw when I was transferred to the Starmouth Naval Base, and as soon as she started talking about her father the Bishop I saw my salvation. It was the Church of England. I thought: *There's* where I can find a man who's good and noble and pure, who won't see me just as a box of chocolates and who'll never betray me with someone else! Clergymen have to be virtuous because it's all part of the job, and so adultery and fornication would be absolutely OUT.

Well, Archdeacon dear, I knew at once that I'd had a *revelation* and I was fearfully excited because I thought I could see the way ahead at last, but then I started feeling depressed again because I realised I knew *nothing,* beyond a few random facts, about the C. of E. and *absolutely* nothing about theology and philosophy and all the earnest things good pure noble men talk about. So I told myself that I'd got to find someone who'd teach me what I needed to know because my good pure noble man would at least expect his wife to be able to talk church-language intelligently, it would be a sort of minimum requirement for the job. I think I'm actually quite clever, though it's a wonder I ever learnt anything from Blackboard. Father thought education for women was a waste of time and Mother thought it was positively harmful so I suppose I'm a victim of a bizarre form of child-neglect, but although I expect I often appear quite scatterbrained I'm not really stupid at all.

So now that you've agreed to be my Guide, Philosopher and Friend I must urge you *not* to assume I'm a fool and water down your erudition accordingly. I want to know *everything,* even the difficult bits. Can we start with the Church itself? I'd be so grateful if you could give me some information about the most important people, the sort of information which isn't in *Who's Who*—although I had such a fascinating time with *Who's Who* the other day, I looked up the Archbishop of Canterbury and I think it's so extraordinary that *his* father was Archbishop of Canterbury too—I wonder what the odds are against such a thing happening? It makes the Temples into a sort of dynasty, doesn't it, and fancy Frederick being over sixty when William was born, maybe more men should take up religion so that they can keep bounding around when rakes like Rollo are chairbound with gout and hardened arteries.

I think William Temple will be a tremendous Archbish, he's so substantial, isn't he, and I don't just mean in weight. He's so human and sympathetic, not like that pompous old prig Archbishop Lang who was so *beastly* to the Prince of Wales. Now, what I want you to tell me is this: What does William Temple *think?* Someone said he was a Christian Socialist and someone else said his thought is a blend of Hegelian Dialectic and Platonic Idealism. I've heard of Plato (just) but who or what is Hegelian? It sounds like a kind of cloth—or possibly a very grand butler—and the syllables have such a thrillingly sumptuous ring. Write *soon,* I implore you, and expound on these esoteric mysteries to your most grateful disciple,

DIANA DOROTHEA TALLENT.

Much amused I immediately picked up my pen and seized the chance to divert myself from the problems I was unable to face.

7

I THOUGHT she would soon lose interest in the intellectual aspects of the Church, but her desire to learn persisted until I could only conclude her interest was genuine. I kept my explanations simple, in the belief that clarity is more important to beginners than complex detail, and I did make an effort not to talk down to her. Again Dido responded with gratitude.

. . . and thank you so much for explaining about divine *Hegel*—I was enrapt and shall now see everything in terms of thesis, antithesis and synthesis. My personal thesis was the frivolous Society Girl, my antithesis is the serious-minded student *thirsting* for enlightenment, but what will my synthesis be??? No, don't answer that question, just go on telling me what churchmen think—or rather, *think.* (When people think, it might only be about the weather, but when they *think,* it can only be about things that are vital.)

Charlotte says you're a Protestant, not a Catholic, which is most confusing as I thought the whole point of the Reformation in England was that we got rid of the Catholics, said "Yah!" to the Pope and lived happily ever after as the Protestant Church of England. Why are these Catholics still around? Anyway I'm glad you're a Protestant—Protestant services are so deliciously *austere* and I've never been keen on all those flamboyant candle-lit genuflections and horrid smells which the Church of Rome finds so essential.

Charlotte also said you were a *Liberal* Protestant, which sounds so enlightened, though I'm told "Liberal" in religion isn't the same as "Liberal" in politics, which is just as well since the political Liberals are nearly extinct. Finally Charlotte said you were a *Modernist,* which sounds thrillingly wild and abandoned, like those artists who throw a pot of paint at the canvas and call the result *A Sunny Afternoon in the Bois de Boulogne.* Now, Archdeacon dear, do tell: What do all these exotic Church labels really *mean?*

By this time I was so enjoying the task of expanding her intellectual horizon that I savoured her letter for an entire week while I reflected on my reply. Finally after a friendly opening paragraph I wrote:

. . . and now let me address myself to your enquiries. The Reformation did indeed re-form the Church *in* England into the Church *of* England, but although Catholicism was greatly purged during the following decades it was never eliminated. It had a strong resurgence in the last century (the phenomenon was known as the Oxford Movement) and even today, although most of the Church is Protestant, there is a powerful, vocal and influential Anglo-Catholic minority. The pertinent word here is "Anglo." They're our own home-grown breed of Catholics, loyal to the Church of England and owing no allegiance to the Pope. However, they've become increasingly keen on the idea of reunion with Rome, a pipe-dream which I'm bound to say I believe to be not only Utopian but misguided.

This Anglo-Catholic group is known as the High Church party. Opposite them on the other wing of the Church are the Protestant Evangelicals, also known as the Low Church party, another powerful and vocal group, which unfortunately has suffered from indifferent leadership during this century. This no doubt helps to explain how the Anglo-Catholics have managed to grab power in so many important places, but the Evangelicals will rise again and put the Anglo-Catholics back in their place, of that I'm quite sure. Catholicism is fundamentally alien to the British temperament. The tradition of the stiff upper lip, the modest understatement and the horror of foreigners is incompatible with a tradition of embarrassing emotion, ritualistic excesses and the ethos of Southern Europe.

In between these two militant wings lie the middle-of-the-road moderates who constitute the majority of church-goers. The services I conduct are aimed at this majority although I do incline to Low Church practice. Certainly nothing would induce me to dabble with incense, auricular confession, perpetual reservation of the Sacrament or any other cause so dear to the Anglo-Catholic heart.

I should perhaps explain here that the Evangelicals play down the importance of the Liturgy (the centrepiece of Anglo-Catholic worship) and play up the importance of the Bible and the sermon. Non-Conformist Evangelicals (those Protestant sects which don't belong to the Church of England, such as the Methodists and the Baptists) can be fatally bibliolatrous (that is to say, they often believe every word of the Bible to be literally true) but in the Church of England, which places such a high value on enlightened scholarship, I'm glad to say that such a crude approach to religious truth is rare. Although I'm a Low Churchman by inclination I have always insisted that my religion be compatible with the best modern scholarship—and that, my dear Miss Tallent, brings me to MODERNISM.

Modernism cuts across all parties in the Church of England. It also existed in the Roman Catholic Church (in a far more extreme form, I may add, than it existed among the Protestants) but the trend was exterminated by Papal decree earlier in this century. In other words, it's as possible to be a High Church Modernist as it is to be a Low Church Modernist. Modernism is less a creed than an attitude of mind.

In short, we believe in reinterpreting Christianity in the light of modern knowledge. Consequently we welcome all scientific advances—in geology, anthropology, psychology, chemistry, physics and so on—and use them as a springboard to an expanded spiritual enlightenment. This leads, inevitably, to the expression of theological views which startle conservative people in all parties of the Church and scandalise the ordinary layman—with the result that Modernists are occasionally accused of heresy. This is usually quite unjustified. All genuine Modernists (and here I discount the eccentric crackpots who give the movement a bad name) hold fast to the Divinity of Christ, the Resurrection and the concept of Eternal Life. They are therefore orthodox believers. But exactly how Jesus was the Son of God and in what manner he was resurrected and in what sense one is to interpret "Eternal Life"—these are questions which the Modernists hold are open to constant revision in the light of modern knowledge. For example, Modernists don't believe in miracles; they don't believe in anything which contradicts the scientific order. But they still believe that Jesus was the sort of man whom people believed capable of performing miracles; they still believe in the absolute centrality of Christ to the Christian faith.

Because the Modernist movement is based on an attitude of mind and not a creed, there's a large amount of disagreement among us. Some Modernists believe that women should be ordained, for example, but in my opinion such a view is too extreme. I always take care to be moderate and sensible in my Modernism so as not to give needless offence to my superiors. It's well known that Raven's support of the ordination of women has cost him a bishopric. When extreme views are under consideration, one always has a moral duty to discern where to draw the line.

To sum up, my moderate Modernism complements the so-called Liberal Protestant theology which evolved among enlightened Victorians. I believe (and this belief chimes with Darwin's work) that the world is evolving steadily in accordance with God's purpose for mankind, a purpose which is fundamentally good and benign. I believe that sin and evil aren't as important as man's basic goodness, the goodness which is exemplified for all time by Our Lord Jesus Christ. I believe that God is immanent in this world and that the Holy Spirit is present as a spark in every member of mankind.

Because of my adherence to such beliefs I strongly disapprove of the new school of theology which is trying to displace the glory and the nobility and the intellectual quality of Liberal Protestantism with an anti-intellectual, pessimistic, degrading approach to God's creation. This neo-orthodox school (I use the word "neo-orthodox" because the theology is in some ways a barbarous reversion to old-fashioned Calvinism) is also known as the theology of Crisis (the word "Crisis" being used in a somewhat technical sense and meaning that we're all undergoing the ordeal of awaiting God's judgement). It emphasises mankind's sin and misery and says that God isn't immanent but utterly transcendent, quite unknowable by man. Meanwhile the role of Christ is played down; he merely becomes a salvation event. How repellent! Instead of the forgiveness and compassion of Christ we're offered the judgement and punishment of God; instead of the Christian message of hope we're offered a vision of hell and despair. Yet this "neo-orthodoxy" is a rising tide, thriving on the suffering and guilt produced by two world wars. God is seen not putting himself at one with us out of love and compassion but standing over and above us as He plays the stern father and metes out the punishment. All I can say is that to those of us who are revolted by the concept of stern fathers meting out punishment, this theology is utterly nauseating.

And now, Miss Tallent, if you're still conscious after my diatribe against neo-orthodoxy, I shall end this sermon by apologising for writing to you at such length. Should you, however, be interested in hearing more about Liberal Protestantism, I can describe in my next letter the thought of the quintessential Liberal Protestant of the twentieth century, Dr. Charles Earle Raven, a former Canon of Liverpool Cathedral who's currently Regius Professor of Divinity at Cambridge and Master of Christ's College. As I've already mentioned, his more extreme flirtations with Modernism are best ignored, but his general credo is one with which I find myself profoundly in sympathy . . .

I thought that having wheeled on the heavy intellectual artillery I might have reduced Dido to a bemused silence, but never was I more mistaken. Replying by return of post she embraced my cannon-fire with delight.

. . . and I can't tell you how grateful I am to you for taking the *time* and the *infinite trouble* to introduce me to this new world where I feel sure my future husband is lurking behind some Liberal-Protestant-Modernist bush! What a romantic name Charles Raven is! I feel he ought to be a hero in a novel by Elinor Glyn. Is he handsome? And how old is he? More details, please—oh, and when you write back, could you explain what difference there is, if any, between "idealism" and "Idealism" with a capital I? Liberal Protestants sound beautifully idealistic, so romantic, but on the other hand William Temple, who is said to be a Platonic Idealist (among other things), must need to be very down-to-earth and unromantic as he's the Archbishop of Canterbury and obliged to deal with all the cynical politicians. What is this Idealism which belongs to Plato? Explain, please!

What worries me is that idealists (in the colloquial sense) aren't usually successful in life and I need to marry a potentially successful husband so that my social gifts can come into full play. But on the other hand perhaps the Church is the one place where idealists can be madly successful, with the result that the episcopal bench in the House of Lords is simply littered with idealists—like that extraordinary Bishop of Chichester, George Bell, who's always saying we mustn't be beastly to the Germans who aren't Nazis, although how he expects us to separate the wheat from the chaff when they're up in the sky bombing us to bits, I really can't imagine.

Oh, how I'd love to be a bishop's wife! I'd run the episcopal palace very efficiently and organise gorgeous garden-parties for the diocesan clergy and give fascinating little dinner-parties for sixteen every week and I'd raise lashings of money for the Poor and dress very tastefully whenever I had to open a fete, and I'd wear wonderful hats when I visited the House of Lords to hear my husband speak—and I'd behave *beautifully* at Lambeth and Bishopthorpe whenever we were invited for a weekend with the Archbishops, because by that time I'd be well-educated and serious-minded and quite different from the ignorant creature I am now. I'm sure *some* future bishop *must* see my potential if only I can meet him—and I'm beginning to see him quite clearly now in my mind's eye.

I want a Liberal Protestant (*definitely* not an Anglo-Catholic or a neo-orthodox Protestant) with Modernist leanings, and he must be a few years older than me, but not *too* old, say around forty—in the prime of life—and being nouveau-riche myself I shan't mind if he's not blue-blooded so long as he speaks correctly and knows how to behave. He should be an Oxford man but a Fellowship of All Souls is not essential. (One can't have everything.) He should have a deep voice—so masculine—and preach sermons which make me want to cry (I *always* cry when I feel spiritually uplifted) but he shouldn't rant and roar. His manner should be cool, austere and dignified.

I shan't mind if he's not handsome but he must have something about him which is irresistibly attractive—deep-set blue eyes perhaps (so heroic)—or a high forehead or broad shoulders or (most scrumptious of all) a very straight firm mouth which represents a MASTERFUL NATURE. I've never seen the point of pursuing the sort of man who allows a woman to trample all over him. Men must be *men,* otherwise why bother, one might just as well live with a woman. I'm sure there must be quite a few *men* in the Church of England or else it wouldn't be such a powerful national institution, although bounders like Rollo always say that the men who are against fornication are always the ones who are incapable of it. But bounders like Rollo have no choice but to say that, have they? It's the only way they can make their weakness look like strength.

Well, Archdeacon dear, I'll stop prattling now, but do write *soon*—don't leave me in suspense for a whole week this time—and make sure you give me a few tips on how I can spot a neo-orthodox supporter at fifty paces and take immediate evasive action. Ever your devoted disciple,

DIDO TALLENT.

P.S. What is soteriology?

I phrased my reply to this last question when I was shaving. I looked into the mirror at my deep-set blue eyes, my high forehead and my straight firm mouth and thought: My dear Miss Tallent, the word "soteriology" refers to matters pertaining to salvation, a state which may well elude you if you continue to write flirtatious letters to a married man . . .

And I vowed to terminate the correspondence.

But I didn't. Instead I wrote:

My dear Miss Tallent:

I'm a clergyman, not a dictionary, so I shan't waste time defining soteriology; I shall merely ask who's been talking to you of soteriological matters! It sounds to me as if you've already brushed against a follower of neo-orthodoxy. Did he thunder that we're all "under judgement"? If ever you hear this phrase, the odds are that you're in neo-orthodox country and you should beat a quick retreat to more Liberal pastures.

Meanwhile rest assured that if I meet a Liberal Protestant with the kind of Modernist leanings which would never damage his chance of episcopal preferment, I shall unhesitatingly point him in your direction! Professor Raven, I fear, is quite unsuitable, being not only a non-starter as a bishop (see my previous letter) but far too old for you (nearly sixty). He's also a married man—and I'm afraid you really can't go around chasing married clergymen. "There's no future in that," as a clever woman bent on capturing a future bishop might say, and I think on the whole you'd be best advised to look for a husband of your own age. Men of forty nowadays are usually either married or homosexual. And now to intellectual matters. Platonic Idealism is the father of our colloquial "idealism." The Greeks believed . . .

And for a further two pages I wrote fluently on the subject of Plato's philosophy.

I was just congratulating myself on conducting this exceedingly enjoyable correspondence with such faultless propriety—a correspondence which my perfect wife never once asked to see—when my harmless epistolary friendship began to swing stealthily out of control.

I was invited by Lady Starmouth to spend a weekend at the Earl's country house.

III

"Comfort, power, the applause and wonder of men—is there any Church in Christendom, or any Christian soul, not deeply tainted with these things?"

CHARLES E. RAVEN
THE CROSS AND THE CRISIS

I

I WAS greatly surprised by the invitation. I had met the Starmouths through Alex soon after he had appointed me his Archdeacon in 1937, but they had remained mere distant acquaintances, and although Lady Starmouth had a reputation for befriending clergymen, I had always suspected she found me too dull to merit her special attention. Certainly in her presence I had found it difficult to shake off a sense of social inferiority, which made me appear shy and awkward. Yet now for some reason Lady Starmouth had decided to take trouble with me. Moreover in the same post I received a letter from the Earl himself saying that he did hope I was free to accept his wife's invitation as he was most anxious to hear me preach. Would I deliver a sermon at his local parish church? Now I was no longer merely surprised. I was amazed and excited. Lord Starmouth was one of the most influential laymen in the Church of England and always spoke on important Church matters in the House of Lords. If he wanted to hear me preach I was indeed being thrust into the ecclesiastical spotlight.

"What an opportunity!" I exclaimed in jubilation to Grace.

"It's very exciting for you—and so kind of Lady Starmouth to invite us both," said Grace, "but of course I can't possibly go."

There was a silence. We were in the study where I had been opening the morning's second post. As soon as I had read the vital letters, I had called Grace to join me.

"It's you they want," she said in a rush as the silence lengthened.

"They're just inviting me out of politeness, and it would be much better if you went on your own."

All I could say was: "You're coming with me."

"But the children—"

"You're coming with me."

"But what on earth shall I wear?"

"Buy whatever's necessary."

"But the coupons—"

"Steal them."

"Neville!"

"All right, borrow them! I was just trying to make you understand how absolutely vital it is that you come with me! It would be the height of foolishness if you evaded this invitation—Lady Starmouth would almost certainly be sceptical about any excuse you might make, and if she feels she's been snubbed, what kind of position do you think that would put me in?"

"In that case we'll have to take the children with us."

"Don't be absurd! We can't do that when the children haven't been invited! We'll have to leave them with Nora or one of your other friends."

"I don't like to impose—"

"No, but this is the one occasion where you must be ruthless—or if you really can't face tackling Nora I'll tackle Emily. I've no scruples at all about imposing on my sister in urgent circumstances."

"I always feel so awkward about asking Emily to have the children when she has no children of her own—"

"Nonsense—they'll provide a welcome diversion from that dreary husband of hers! Now listen to me, Grace. I quite understand why you should feel this weekend will be an ordeal, but it's an ordeal you're perfectly capable of surmounting—all you're being required to do is to look pretty and be polite. I'm not trying to throw you to the lions. I'm just trying to ensure you don't miss out on an exciting and worthwhile excursion. Make up your mind you're going to enjoy yourself! Why not? Why shouldn't it all be great fun?"

But Grace only said in despair: "How I wish we'd never left Willowmead!" and I heard her stifle a sob as she rushed from the room.

2

"I DIDN'T mean it, Neville—of course I didn't mean it—I just feel nostalgic about Willowmead sometimes, that's all . . ."

I had followed her to our bedroom where she had retreated to calm down, and as we faced each other we could hear the charwoman talking good-naturedly to Sandy as she worked in the drawing-room below us. Primrose was at nursery school as usual. I was supposed to be on my way to a diocesan committee meeting, and I was acutely conscious of the clock ticking on the bedside table as I was obliged to delay my departure.

"I know how much you loved Willowmead," I said, "but we've been happy in Starbridge too and we're going to go on being happy here."

"Yes, of course. I'm sorry."

"To be honest, I find the Starmouths intimidating as well. But one can't spend one's life cowering in corners just because one feels socially inferior!"

"No, of course not. Will there be a maid, do you think, to unpack our suitcases? I don't want anyone seeing my darned underwear."

"In that case I'll tell the servant we don't require help with the unpacking. Now, Grace, stop worrying yourself into a frenzy, there's a good girl, and make up your mind you're going to be strong, brave and resourceful!"

"Yes. All right. I'll try," she said, but my heart sank as her shoulders drooped.

Willing myself not to despair, I hurried off to my meeting at the diocesan office on Eternity Street.

3

STARMOUTH Court stood not, as might be assumed, near the port of Starmouth, in the south of the diocese, but eighteen miles from London in the county of Surrey; the Earl's connection with Starmouth was lost in the mists of antiquity. When we eventually arrived at our destination on a sunlit Saturday morning in July, I was just as horrified as Grace to discover not a friendly country house but a tall stout elderly mansion of forbidding proportions. Accustomed though I was to calling at the various grand houses in my archdeaconry, I had never been invited to stay the night in these places and the thought of being a guest in the Starmouths' overpoweringly dignified country seat made me feel for a moment like a fallen woman obliged to take refuge with a formidable maiden aunt.

Built high on a hillside, the house was surrounded by trees and approached by a long winding drive which strained both our nerves and the engine of the chauffeur-driven motor which our hostess had sent to meet us at the station. " 'Childe Roland to the Dark Tower came,' " I muttered to Grace before the Dark Tower was revealed as the plump Queen Anne palace. I allowed myself one quick shudder before resolving fiercely to appear self-possessed. "Isn't it exactly like the country house in a detective story?" I murmured to Grace with a heroic attempt at nonchalance. "I foresee corpses in the library, a sinister butler lurking behind the green baize door and Hercule Poirot hovering in the shrubbery!"

But Grace was too terrified to reply.

We were admitted by a stately footman to a hall the size of a tennis court. Vast pictures of men in togas were suspended from points so remote as to be barely visible. An enormous arrangement of flowers stood in what appeared to be a pseudo-Greek vase. Then I realised there was nothing pseudo about the vase. It had that dim ancient look which is impossible to reproduce, and it reminded me of countless visits to the British Museum on wet Saturday afternoons in my childhood when Willy and I, boarded out with strict Methodists, had taken refuge once a week in the sights of London.

"Nice flowers," I said casually to Grace in an automatic effort to signal to the footman that I found the hall itself too mundane to merit a comment. "Very well arranged."

I had barely finished speaking when a door banged, footsteps pattered swiftly in our direction down a distant corridor, and the next moment someone was bursting joyously into the hall. A familiar peal of laughter rang out. A well-remembered voice cried: "Welcome to Starmouth Court!" And with horrified delight I recognised my disciple.

4

"DID you know she was going to be here?" demanded Grace as soon as we were alone in the bedroom which had been assigned to us, but my stupefaction was so obviously genuine that she never doubted my denial. Moving to the window, I saw that the room was placed at the back of the house and overlooked a formal garden which unfolded upwards in a series of terraces before rolling out of sight over the summit of the hill. On the lowest lawn twin rows of classical statues eyed each other across a sward dotted with croquet-hoops. The sun was still shining radiantly, reminding me that I felt much too hot.

"She should have told me," I said as I automatically took advantage of the opportunity to remove my clerical collar. "Why on earth didn't she mention it in her last letter?"

"I suppose she thought it would be fun to surprise you." Grace was already unpacking her darned underwear before a servant could materialise, like the genie of the lamp, between her and the open suitcase.

"I don't like those sort of surprises." I began to roam around the room. The brass bedstead gleamed. Lifting the counterpane I absent-mindedly fingered the very white sheets.

"I suppose they're real linen," said Grace. "And look at those towels by the washstand! Can they possibly be linen too?"

"Must be pre-war. But expensive things always look new for years." I stared around at the room's luxury, so subtly sumptuous, so tastefully extravagant, and before I could stop myself I was saying: "I suppose you're still wishing you hadn't come."

"Oh no!" said Grace at once. "Now that the adventure's begun I'm enjoying myself—in fact I'm sure you were right and it's all going to be great fun!"

I did realise that Grace was belatedly exercising her intelligence, but I found I had no desire to consider the implications of this new canny behaviour. I merely smiled, gave her a grateful kiss and began to unpack my bag.

5

EVERYONE was very kind to Grace, who despite her tortuous self-doubts was as capable as I was of being socially adept in unfamiliar circumstances. Certainly no one was kinder than Dido, who lavished attention on her to such an extent that I was almost ignored. More than once I told myself conscientiously how relieved I was that my disciple was on her best behaviour; it seemed all I now had to do, in order to survive the weekend with my clerical self-esteem intact, was to stick close to my wife and keep my eyes off Dido's legs, which seemed to shimmer like erotic beacons whenever I glanced in her direction. I even thought in a burst of optimism that I might soon be able to write off my embarrassingly carnal preoccupation with Dido as an example of that well-known phenomenon, the middle-aged man's vulnerability to the charms of youth. However, although I was keen to reduce my feelings to a trivial inconvenience, I suspected I was still too young to be in the grip of a middle-aged malaise. Or was I? If my diagnosis was correct I could only shudder. If I was like this at forty, what would I be like at fifty? I had a fleeting picture of myself at sixty, an elderly lecher surrounded by young girls, and it was not at all a cheering vision for a churchman who had always been anxious to Get On and Travel Far.

The weekend gathering at Starmouth Court was hardly "smart" in society's sense of the word, although Lady Starmouth ensured that the atmosphere was friendly and cultivated. In addition to my disciple, who was on a seventy-two-hour leave, the guests consisted of a residentiary canon of Radbury Cathedral and his wife; a contemporary of the Earl's from the House of Lords; a bossy lady of uncertain age who worked in London for Jewish refugees and who talked of Bishop Bell with the enthusiasm women usually reserve for film stars; an etiolated civil servant from the Ministry of Information; and the Starmouths' youngest daughter, Rosalind, who had been a debutante with Dido in 1933; her husband was now serving with the Army in India. I soon felt confident that I could hold my own in this company, even with the Canon, who was at least twenty years my senior, but nonetheless I was careful to temper my growing self-confidence with a quiet unassuming manner. Alex had warned me more than once that the upper classes disliked a newcomer who was too strident.

"Whatever you do," I said to Grace as we changed for dinner on the night of our arrival, "don't mention to that bossy Miss Wilkins, who's obviously in love with Bishop Bell, that I may be having contact with German prisoners in the future at the new camp on Starbury Plain. Once one starts discussing the Church's attitude towards Germans, Bell's name's bound to come up and I don't want to get involved in any conversation which is politically controversial."

"But I thought you admired Bishop Bell!"

"Yes. Privately. But I don't want anyone thinking I'm 'soft on Germans.' "

"I'm sure no one would think—"

"Oh yes, they would! The trouble is that politically speaking Bell's dynamite. Why has he been passed over for senior bishoprics? Because over and over again he's stood up in the House of Lords to hammer away at the Government, and in consequence even though he's no pacifist people are convinced he's soft on Germans!"

"But he's not soft on Nazis, is he? The people who accuse him of being soft on Germans aren't really being fair—"

"No, but I just don't want to get into one of those arguments about whether it's possible in wartime conditions such as these to make a distinction between the Nazis and the non-Nazis in Germany—I don't want to get into any argument about the morality of saturation bombing. Of course Bell's right to champion the cause of the suffering Germans—all the Christian and Jewish refugees before the war, all the Christians and Jews now in the concentration camps, even all the Germans who are loathing every moment of Hitler's rule but have somehow managed to stay free—and of course it's absolutely wrong to say, as that ass Babbington-French says, that the only good German's a dead German, but Bell shouldn't try to tell Churchill how to run the war. It's madness, absolute madness—as well as professional suicide—and I can't support it. We've got to stay solidly behind Churchill, got to—how else are we going to survive this appalling ordeal?"

"Oh darling, I do understand and I do agree with you—please don't think I'm criticising! Where would we all be now if it wasn't for Mr. Churchill? Not at Starmouth Court, that's certain! It's just that I can't help admiring Bishop Bell for standing up for Christian values in such very adverse circumstances and at such personal cost to himself—"

"Yes, he's a hero." I moved to the window to stare out at the terraced lawns. "Charles Raven stays in his academic ivory tower and preaches pacifism," I said, "but George Bell's out there in the chaos, battling away doggedly for God in a world gone mad. I used to admire no churchman more than Raven, but now I think . . . well, never mind what I think. As I said earlier, it's best to keep quiet on the subject of the Bishop of Chichester."

Much to my surprise Grace suddenly kissed me and said: "I'm glad you admire him so much. That's the real you, isn't it?"

"Real me?" I was much pleased by this unexpected gesture of affection.

"The man behind the successful archdeacon."

"The successful archdeacon's the real me too."

"Yes, but—"

I suddenly caught a glimpse of the time. "We ought to be going downstairs," I said, trying not to sound nervous at the thought of the grand meal ahead. "Are you ready?"

We hurried down to dinner.

6

AFTER the ladies had retired from the table, Lord Starmouth abandoned his other guests to a discussion of the Desert War—now grimmer than ever after the shattering fall of Tobruk less than three weeks before—and motioned me into a quiet corner by the sideboard.

"Alex Jardine's always spoken highly of you," he said, "but perhaps now is the moment when I should confess it wasn't Jardine who prompted my wife's invitation to you this weekend."

"Then I must assume it was Dr. Ottershaw."

"As a matter of fact it wasn't him either. Ottershaw's been singing your praises for years, I admit, but I'm ashamed to say my wife and I ignored him. No, your cause has been promoted by Miss Tallent, Archdeacon."

I stifled a gasp, prayed not to blush and belatedly realised that my mouth was open. I managed to close it.

"Dear little Dido!" said the Earl, taking advantage of the fact that his advanced years gave him a license to be openly sentimental about young girls. "She showed me the letters."

This time I was unable to stifle a gasp. My mouth had sagged open again.

"*Your* letters!" said the Earl, smiling at me benignly. "I really must congratulate you, Archdeacon—what an epistolary tour de force! I particularly liked your essay on the Incarnation, complete with Professor Sanday's Modernist development of the kenotic aspect. Lucky little Dido, I thought, stumbling across a clergyman who could so ably guide her along her spiritual way."

By a mighty effort I recovered myself sufficiently to say: "I'm glad my efforts met with your approval, my lord."

"Well, as soon as I'd read the letters I said to my wife: 'I must hear this man preach!' I look forward immensely to your sermon tomorrow—and little Dido, I might add, is in a veritable fever of anticipation." The Earl sighed with pleasure, though whether at the thought of my sermon or of "little Dido" it was impossible to discern. "There's a heart of gold underneath all that flashy behaviour," he confided, "and I'm delighted she's become more serious lately. I suspect she's been very unhappy. London society's an awful business. I'm glad my daughters married quickly and didn't have to rattle about for too long . . . Now tell me this, Archdeacon: Do you think little Dido should marry into the Church? You may not have realised this, but she's set her heart on it"—that was when I finally dared to believe that Dido had been highly selective in her choice of letters—"and to be honest I can't quite see her in a vicarage. I don't think she realises how old-fashioned the Church is in so many ways and how conventional her behaviour would have to become. She'd be better off with a land-owning politician, I think—someone who has a house in London and a few hundred acres somewhere in hunting country."

"Possibly so." A still small voice was now busy whispering in my mind that with Dido at my side no ecclesiastical prize would be unobtainable, but I knew very well that this voice came not from God but from the force which old-fashioned churchmen called the Devil and which I, as a good Modernist, recognised as the dark side of my ego. I have no wish to make excuses for the dark side of my ego, but perhaps I might be permitted to attempt to justify the desire to do as well as I possibly could in my career—the desire which my critics would unhesitatingly label as an ambition quite unbecoming to a clergyman.

Ambition, like everything else in one's life, must be dedicated to the service of God. When I dreamed of preferment I had no wish merely to serve myself; I only wanted to get into a position where I could serve God to the very best of my God-given ability, and the truth was that my God-given ability was not for living on locusts and wild honey as a holy man in the wilderness. My talent was for administration. My archdeaconry ran like clockwork. My curates were trained, groomed and buffed to a high lustre. I had only to cast an eye on any diocesan department, and bureaucratic slovenliness instantly evaporated. I could put the Bishop through his paces so painlessly that he ceased to be depressed by paperwork.

Now, I'm willing enough to admit that this gift of mine is not spiritually exciting, but I submit, with all due respect, that not every clergyman is born to be a St. Francis of Assisi or a St. Ignatius Loyola. My duty was not to waste time bemoaning my limitations but to dedicate my gift, modest as it was, to God's service. Am I deceiving myself when I speculate that God was probably glad to receive it even though it was sadly lacking in spiritual glamour? I think not. After all, someone has to run the Church of England, that historic witness to the power of the Christian faith, and since in an imperfect world a Church can hardly thrive on a diet of undiluted holiness, first-class administrators must always be essential for its welfare.

In short, I felt I could justify my ambition to travel upwards in the ecclesiastical hierarchy. What I could never justify was a desire to travel that road in the company of a woman who wasn't my wife. That was utterly reprehensible and no good clergyman would ever allow himself to sink so low—a statement which was the equivalent of saying the thought had never occurred to me because I was such a good clergyman. Wiping it from my mind with shame, I resolved to forego the pleasure of making love to my wife beneath an earl's roof that night and instead spend time polishing my sermon.

Alex had once advised me that a clergyman addressing the upper classes from the pulpit should never forget that they had received, no matter how unwillingly, a good education; he had recommended including at least one well-known quotation at the start of the sermon, as they would feel clever when they recognised the words and this self-satisfaction would put them in a benign, receptive mood. Accordingly when writing the sermon I had begun with a quotation from Browning ("How very hard it is to be a Christian!"), glided into Tennyson ("Ring out the darkness of the land; ring in the Christ that is to be"), brushed against T. S. Eliot ("Each venture is a new beginning"), and bound all these lines together with one of my favourite biblical texts: "Jesus Christ is the same yesterday, today, yea and forever"—words which I always felt offered comfort, particularly in an unstable, war-torn world.

Starmouth Court stood in the parish of Leatherhead, a pleasant country town not far from the outer reaches of the South London suburbs, and the fine Norman church overlooked the valley of the River Mole, so called for its habit of burrowing underground in unexpected places. I wondered if the vicar minded when his distinguished parishioners imposed guest-preachers on him, but when he greeted me with unflinching cordiality I deduced he was more than ready to welcome a holiday from homiletics. The service began. The moment for the sermon arrived, and without wishing to brag I must confess that I made the most of my golden opportunity.

It was after lunch when I was cornered by Lady Starmouth. Having discovered that afternoon rests were permitted to guests, Grace had slipped away to our room in order to drum up some extra stamina and I had wandered outside for a stroll in the grounds. I wound up prowling aimlessly from terrace to terrace as I tried to pretend I had no desire to bump into Dido.

"Archdeacon! Just the man I wanted to see," exclaimed my hostess, eventually ensnaring me as I loafed around the rose-garden's wishing well. "Let's sit down for a moment. I want to talk to you about Dido."

"Ah!" I said. The monosyllable might have seemed unadventurous but at least it had the merit of being uncontroversial. I allowed myself to be steered to an elegant wrought-iron seat which overlooked a bed of oppressively feminine red roses.

"I really must congratulate you, Mr. Aysgarth," said Lady Starmouth, dark eyes very friendly, and bestowed upon me one of her most gracious smiles.

"Oh?" I said, dumb as any uncouth Yorkshire yokel. In panic I ordered myself to abandon these absurd monosyllables.

"Come now, Archdeacon!" said Lady Starmouth, effortlessly charming, subtly grand. "Don't pretend you don't know what I'm talking about! Of course you're well aware that Dido's in love with you, and of course you realise that I'm congratulating you on your skill in dealing with her infatuation."

"Ah!" I said again. No wonder Yorkshiremen had a dour reputation. All I needed to complete my imitation of the wooden-headed provincial northerner was a cloth cap. Furious with myself for being so crippled by shyness, I cursed the entire English class system and tried to pretend my hostess was merely one of my middle-class parishioners.

"I'm not sure I entirely agree with your diagnosis of Dido's feelings, Lady Starmouth," I said, somehow producing a casual smile, the kind of smile a clever clergyman produces when he's talking of worldly matters to a sophisticated older woman. "She's not in love with me. She's in love with what I represent."

"That's a shrewd remark and confirms my opinion that you're no fool. But Archdeacon, I think it's time someone helped you by throwing a little extra light on what could prove to be an inflammable situation. The truth is, I'm afraid, that Dido's a very naughty little girl. Oh, I concede there are extenuating circumstances—the father's a rogue, the mother's unpresentable, new money always produces vulgar consequences—but nevertheless one can't escape the fact that the Tallent children were thrown into society with only hired old crones to chaperone them, and since those three girls had no education, no breeding, no proper childhood discipline and no real inkling of how they should conduct themselves, it's hardly surprising that their social successes—based, I may say, entirely on their ability to flirt—should have resulted in scandal and tragedy. Dido's told you the whole sad story, I presume?"

"She did mention—"

"Merry's married to a compulsive gambler, Laura's dead and Dido has a reputation for . . . shall we call it mischief? She makes fools of the decent men and chases the rakes. Has she talked to you about Rollo Carlton-Blake? He's a confirmed bachelor with a penchant for loose women of the lower classes, as everyone told her years ago, but Dido took no notice of what everyone told her and I believe I know why. *Au fond* that girl doesn't want to get married, Mr. Aysgarth, and that's why, consciously or unconsciously, she falls in love with men who are either impossible, like Carlton-Blake, or unavailable, like you. I once had an American friend who was like that. She too fell in love with a very promising young married clergyman and nearly ruined him—although I'm glad to say he survived and became a bishop. Such women are dangerous . . . But perhaps you'd already reached that conclusion and were wondering how to extricate yourself?"

"I must be quite honest," I said, heart sinking as I realised I was being compelled to lie, "and say I'm anxious to extricate myself, but as a clergyman I can't help but be mindful of the fact that I might be promoting a genuine spiritual awakening by writing to her. As the Bible says, one mustn't quench the smouldering flax or break the bruised reed. Any new moral awareness should be carefully nurtured."

"Quite. That's very conscientious of you, Mr. Aysgarth, and indeed my husband said much the same thing when Dido resurrected her old friendship with Rosalind in order to cultivate our acquaintance on your behalf, but be warned and take care . . . And now," said Lady Starmouth, having completed her verbal disembowelling of my disciple, "let's turn to pleasanter subjects. What a very charming and delightful wife you have! I do hope she's enjoying herself."

Immediately I suspected that this was no new subject but merely a different aspect of a certain sinister theme. "We're both enjoying ourselves immensely, Lady Starmouth!" I said, feigning a sunny-natured innocence. "It's been the most memorable weekend!"

"How delighted I am to hear you say so!" Lady Starmouth had evidently decided that a little sunny-natured innocence of her own was now called for. "I'd heard a rumour that your wife doesn't care much for social occasions."

"Really?" I said surprised. "How extraordinary! She has a wide circle of friends, and of course her parish duties—which she performs to perfection—require her to be very sociable indeed."

"How proud you must be of her! An excellent wife is so essential for a clergyman. I once knew a very unfortunate clergyman's wife," said Lady Starmouth, again wielding her clerical memories with ruthless skill. "She spent her whole time weeping on a chaise-longue because she couldn't cope with her responsibilities. The effect on the poor husband was quite devastating, but fortunately in the end he obtained the necessary domestic help—always *so* essential for a clergyman's wife, don't you think?—and I'm glad to say they lived happily ever after. More or less." She gave me yet another of her radiant smiles and rose to her feet. "I'm reminded of your sermon this morning," she added lightly. " 'How very hard it is to be a Christian'—and how very hard, Browning might have added, it is to be a clergyman! But of course since you're a clever devout man with an admirable wife who offers you every support, I'm sure you find life far easier than some of your less fortunate brethren." And having signalled to her new protégé that she was happy to lavish approval on him so long as he had the good sense to keep his private life in order, she drifted gracefully away from me across the rose-garden.

7

THE immediate result of this scene was that I wanted to punch Alex on the nose for gossiping about me to his favourite ladyfriend, but then I calmed down and reflected that I had jumped to a conclusion which was most unlikely to be true. Devoted as Alex was to Lady Starmouth, he would hardly have disclosed to her details about my domestic troubles; any clergyman would have judged our conversation about my private life to be confidential. Reluctantly I was driven to assume that some other person—perhaps Mrs. Ottershaw, commenting on Grace's absence from the fatal palace dinner-party—had indiscreetly murmured that the Archdeacon's wife seemed to be quietly fading away at the vicarage, and Lady Starmouth had consequently made her own shrewd deductions about what was going on in my marriage. I saw clearly that she liked Grace but doubted her stamina, that she liked me but worried that I might land up in a mess, and that she disliked Dido very much indeed but was prepared to tolerate her for a weekend in order to humour her husband.

Feeling considerably shaken by this benign but bruising encounter with my hostess, I put aside all thought of a chance encounter with Dido among the roses and withdrew to the house. No one was about. Padding upstairs I glided along a thick carpet past portraits of voluptuous Georgian ladies and quietly eased open the door of the bedroom in an attempt to avoid waking Grace. But she was not asleep. To my dismay, exasperation and—worst of all—anger, I found her sobbing softly into her pillow.

I shoved the door shut. Then making a belated effort to control my feelings I slumped down on the bed beside her and said in my most neutral voice: "So the truth is you hate it here. You were only pretending to enjoy it."

I had thought such bleak statements might jolt her into a denial, but she merely nodded her head in despair as she made a futile attempt to wipe away her tears.

"And of course you're missing the children."

Another nod. More tears began to fall.

Rising to my feet I took off my jacket and hung it carefully over the back of the nearest chair; because of the heat I had changed from my archidiaconal uniform to a plain clerical suit immediately after lunch. Then I removed my collar and slumped down on the bed again. These trivial movements helped to calm me. My voice was still devoid of resentment when I said: "Well, it's no good having anything but a candid talk, is it? We've got to try to solve this problem."

Grace made yet another attempt to mop up her tears, but by this time her eyes were red and swollen. I realised it was going to be impossible for her to go down to tea.

"Now," I said, trying to take control of the situation by adopting a brisk sensible manner, "the first thing we have to do is to find out why you're so unhappy. I'm not talking about your present misery. I'm talking about the more general unhappiness which I know has been afflicting you for some time. When exactly did it all begin? Was it when we found out Sandy had been conceived and you started to worry about how you were going to cope?"

I was, of course, busy laying the foundations for an unanswerable argument that we should employ a live-in nursemaid, so I was expecting her to reply "Yes" to my question. It came as a considerable shock to me when she said: "No, this has nothing to do with Sandy. He simply complicated a situation which already existed."

I stared at her. "You're saying this unhappiness existed before Sandy was conceived in 1940?"

"Yes, I first became aware of it when we moved to Starbridge in '37, but now that I look back with the wisdom of hindsight I believe the seeds of my unhappiness were sown in 1932."

"At Willowmead? But that's impossible! You were so happy there!"

"Yes, but that's when things started to go wrong."

"But what on earth happened at Willowmead in '32?"

"You met Alex Jardine. As soon as he started taking an interest in you he was a malign influence on our lives."

I was speechless.

"I've never liked Alex," said Grace in a rush. "Never. I know you were always ambitious, but I felt he stoked up your ambition so that it blazed in all the wrong directions—"

"What on earth are you talking about? It was his sympathetic interest which gave me the confidence I needed to make the most of my God-given abilities!" I was now very shocked indeed. "My dear Grace, I can hardly believe you feel like this about Alex! He's always admired you so much and said what a perfect wife you were for a clergyman!"

"Maybe that's one of the reasons why I dislike him—I always feel he sees me as no more than an appropriate accessory, like a pair of gloves. Poor Carrie! No wonder they're unhappily married."

"But they're devoted to each other!"

"I don't think he's devoted to her at all. Think of all the times we've heard him being sarcastic when poor Carrie makes one of her stupid remarks!"

"Well, I agree there's a large amount of surface irritation, but I'm sure that underneath he's—"

"Underneath I think he's actually a rather nasty piece of work—and I'm absolutely convinced that his influence has had a disastrous effect on our marriage."

"But how can you possibly blame Alex for—"

"Very easily. It was Alex who singled you out from all the other clergy in the diocese and gave you ideas above your station—"

"*Ideas above my station?* Good heavens, Grace, which century are you living in? I'm not a Victorian servant!"

"No, you're a Yorkshire draper's son on the make—and Alex has been constantly encouraging you, bringing you to Starbridge, giving you grand ideas by introducing you to people like the Starmouths, spoiling you with that glamorous preferment which I often think quite turned your head when you were too young to know better—"

"Well, of course I know you're a cut above me socially and entitled to look down on me if you please, but I must say I find your attitude offensive and your accusations insane. But then women are notoriously irrational when they're upset, and wives are notoriously peevish when they find they can't keep up with their husbands any more—"

"*And who put us in a position where I can't keep up with you any more?* Who turned my gentle, sensitive, shy, romantic husband into someone else altogether?"

"Nobody's turned me into anything. People evolve, Grace! They don't just stand still! You can't expect me to remain as I was when we first met on the beach at St. Leonards!"

Once again she dissolved into tears of despair.

"My dearest love . . ." I suddenly realised that I too was in a state of extreme emotional distress. There was a knot of tension in my stomach and I was aware of a vague nausea which threatened to become acute. In the end all I could say in a stricken voice was: "You don't really think of me as just a Yorkshire draper's son on the make, do you?"

Still crying she shook her head and flung her arms around my neck. Eventually she managed to whisper: "Forgive me."

I suddenly felt I could not bear her misery a second longer, and wanting only to terminate this truly appalling scene I said unevenly: "I'm the one who should be asking for forgiveness. My dearest love, tell me what I can do to make you happy again—I'll make any sacrifice for your sake, I swear it."

Grace screwed her sodden handkerchief into a ball and gripped it so hard that her knuckles shone white. "Give up your archdeaconry. Give up Alex. And give up that double-faced little bitch who's bent on ruining you."

I was silenced. As I automatically took a pace backwards she raised her head to look me in the eyes. "Well, you did say," she said in a shaking voice, "that you'd make any sacrifice."

"I'm sorry but in my vocabulary 'to make a sacrifice' doesn't mean 'to commit professional suicide.' " I got a grip on myself and managed to add in a calm polite voice: "I can't resign my position as Archdeacon; I honestly believe I'm doing the work God's called me to do. As for Alex, I'm sorry, but I can't give him up; it would be the height of ingratitude after all he's done for me. I'll make an effort not to inflict him too often on you in future, but it's quite unthinkable that I should ever say to him—"

"And Dido Tallent? Don't let's pretend, Neville. I know you find her attractive. Wives always do know when their husbands' attention strays in that particular way."

"If you think for one moment that I've ever done anything wrong with her—"

"No, of course I don't think that! I've lived with you for sixteen years and I know better than anyone what a very good, devout man you still are in spite of everything—and that's exactly why this present crisis is such a nightmare. I feel you're on the brink of going to pieces in some very profound way which I'm unable to understand."

"*Going to pieces? Me?* But my dear Grace, *you're* the one who appears to be disintegrating!"

"Yes, but I'm only disintegrating because you're going to pieces! Neville, there's something dreadfully wrong here, I'm sure there is, and to tell you the truth I don't really believe our fundamental problem is my unhappiness. I think my unhappiness is just a symptom of something far more complex and sinister."

"You're raving." Turning aside from her, I replaced my collar and jacket. My Bible was lying on the bedside table. Trailing my fingers across the cover, I said: "I'm not going to pieces. There are no fundamental problems in our marriage. The only difficulty I have to resolve is how I can make you happy again, and now, by the grace of God, I'm going to work out exactly what I have to do to put matters right." Picking up the Bible I headed for the door, and it was only when my fingers clasped the handle that I added casually over my shoulder: "Of course I'll terminate my association with Miss Tallent. I can see clearly now that I've been in the wrong there, and I'm very sorry if my acquaintance with her has contributed to your unhappiness."

I made my exit. My mind was in chaos. In the hall I got in a muddle and dived down the wrong marble passage, with the result that I left the house by an unfamiliar side door. Skirting the kitchen-garden I staggered through an orchard and steered myself around a succession of high yew hedges. I was just beginning to feel like one of Kafka's characters, lost in some nightmarish metaphysical maze, when I found myself back in the rose-garden—and there by the wishing well stood my disciple, quite alone at last, dark hair combed and curled to perfection, dark eyes glowing with a bewitchingly artless delight as I found myself propelled down the grass path to her side.

"Archdeacon dee-ah!" she exclaimed, mimicking the drawing-room drawl of an earlier generation of society women. "How too, too lovely!"

"I think not," I said, reaching the well. "Miss Tallent, I regret to have to inform you—"

"What a ghastly phrase! That's the sort of jargon people in trade use when they tell a customer that some important item's going to be out of stock for six months! Now stop being so beastly pompous, Archdeacon dear, and let me tell you that your sermon this morning was quite wonderful and I was so proud of you and I felt so spiritually uplifted that I soaked two entire handkerchiefs! Isn't life absolute heaven?"

Without a second's hesitation I said: "Yes, I feel as if it's spring again after a long dull winter!" And having delivered myself of quite the most reckless remark any married clergyman could have uttered to a flirtatious young woman, I abandoned my Bible on the parapet of the wishing well and impulsively clasped both her hands in mine.

IV

"Passion cannot be eliminated: it can be kept uncontaminated, be sublimated, as the jargon of today would say."

CHARLES E. RAVEN
A WANDERER'S WAY

I

THE clasp lasted three seconds. Then, releasing her, I found myself muttering idiotically: "Sorry. Most unedifying. Thoroughly unseemly," and those adjectives, so well-worn by an earlier generation of clergymen, added an air of bathos to my horrified reaction; with a few antique words it seemed I had turned a silly slip into melodrama. Finally, to pile indignity upon indignity, I began to blush, and turning my back on Dido I grabbed my Bible from the parapet of the wishing well. I instinctively knew that my hands should be fully occupied before they succumbed to a second catastrophic urge to wander.

"Dearest Stephen!" said Dido enthralled. "Why on earth are you apologising? I can't see anything wrong with an affectionate hand-clasp between friends!"

All I could say was: "You promised not to call me by that name." I was still unable to look at her.

"Archdeacon dear, please don't be so upset! Of course I adore you passionately, but why should sex ruin our beautiful friendship? I'd never go to bed with any man unless I was married to him, and as I can't marry you, you're absolutely safe. Meanwhile you can have no possible desire to go to bed with me—how could you when your wife's so much prettier and nicer than I am?—so that takes care of beastly old sex, doesn't it, and leaves us free to enjoy our glorious romantic friendship as you guide me along my spiritual way!"

"Miss Tallent," I said, "before I met you I'd have thought it impossible that a woman should be both very sophisticated and very naive. May I congratulate you on achieving such a remarkable paradox? But I'm afraid the time has come when you must set your naivety aside."

"Oh, I adore it when you're being so stern and austere! Now, Archdeacon dear, stop looking as if you'd like to spank me, and calm down for a moment. I'm not in the least naive; I'm the last word in down-to-earth common sense. If I don't misbehave with you—and I've no intention of doing *anything* which would wreck our beautiful friendship—how can you misbehave with me? Adultery's a two-way street."

I cleared my throat. "Not entirely. Theologically speaking—"

"Oh good, I did so hope there'd be a fascinating theological angle—how delicious!"

"Miss Tallent—"

"Dearest Archdeacon, *don't worry.* I'll leave you alone now so that you can glue together your shattered nerves, and I shall keep a chaste distance from you for the rest of the weekend, but when you get home do write and explain all the theological aspects of adultery!"

"I won't have time. I'm leaving on Wednesday for my holiday in the Lake District."

"Will you send me a postcard?"

"No, that would be quite improper."

"But you'll pray for me!"

I said in a voice of steel: "I pray regularly for all the souls in my care," but to my horror I realised I was smiling at her.

"Well, so long as God's brought into the situation we can't go far wrong, can we?" said Dido, smiling radiantly in return.

"I think you'd better leave, Miss Tallent, before I really do give way to the urge to spank you."

With a laugh she danced away from me across the rose-garden.

2

COLLAPSING on the wrought-iron garden seat where earlier Lady Starmouth had declared with such incomparable style how very hard it was to be a clergyman, I clutched my Bible as if it were a life-belt and forced myself to face the unspeakable. I had fallen in love. Hitherto I had believed that only irrational women could succumb to the full force of an *amour fou,* yet here I was, collapsed in a heap, almost asphyxiated by the reek of red roses, and shivering with desire from head to toe. This was no middle-aged inconvenience. This was a passion of the prime of life. Nothing like it had ever happened to me before. I was appalled.

Automatically I started recalling my seven-year courtship of Grace, but although I had embarked on that period of my life in a fever of calf-love, my feelings had matured into a solid reliable devotion and I had never experienced the suspension of my rational faculties. On the contrary, I had plotted my marriage campaign with military precision, calculating down to the last farthing when I would be able to afford the trip to the altar, scheming how I might win my future father-in-law's consent while I was still so young, rehearsing the necessary speech to my mother until I was word-perfect. By no remote stretch of the imagination could I describe myself as having been demented with love. In fact in the light of my present madness I was almost tempted to wonder if I had ever really loved Grace at all—but that was an insane thought which only indicated the disintegration of my reason. Of course I had loved Grace. I had adored her. She had been exactly the kind of wife I knew I had to have.

"Such a fetching girl!" said my mother benignly in my memory. "So quiet and refined—*and* with a hundred and fifty pounds a year of her own! Darling Neville, I couldn't be more pleased . . ."

The memory terminated. Wiping the sweat from my forehead I pulled myself together and resolved to fight this monstrous insanity which had assailed me. Why was I loafing amidst the nauseating stench of roses and thinking of my mother? That was hardly constructive behaviour. I had to start planning how I could cover up the disaster as efficiently as a cat burying a mess, and while I was engaged in this vital task I had to pretend to the whole world—but especially to Grace—that I was my sane, normal self.

That was the moment when I remembered our forty-eight-hour second honeymoon, which was due to take place before we embarked on our family holiday. Common sense, liberally garnished with a strong instinct for self-preservation, now told me that this was not the time, in the sixteen-year-old history of my perfect marriage, to spend forty-eight hours entirely alone with my wife. My most sensible course of action was to hide from her among the children as I shored up my defences and made myself impregnable to the violent assaults of my irrationality.

Leaning forward with my elbows on my knees, I clasped my hands, squeezed my eyes shut and said to God silently in desperation: "Lord, help me, save me, protect me so that I can consecrate myself afresh to your service." Then I waited, trying not to feel as if I were whistling in the dark, but I experienced no easing of my fear and anxiety. Evidently my prayer was not going to be answered in any simple straightforward way, and at last, wiping the sweat again from my forehead, I nerved myself to return to the house.

3

"DARLING," I said to Grace as I entered the bedroom and found her struggling into an afternoon frock, "I feel I've been at fault in failing to realise how very unhappy you are when you're separated from the children. Why don't I start my task of making you happier by suggesting that we forget our little holiday alone together this week? Instead of leaving for Manchester on Wednesday we'll travel north with all the children on Saturday and go straight to the cottage."

She was pathetically grateful. "Well, if you're sure you wouldn't mind—"

"Say no more. It's settled." Having given her a kiss, I eyed the frock and said: "You don't really want to go down to tea, do you? I'll say you have a migraine."

"Well, I know I look a fright after all those tears, but I hate the thought of putting you in an awkward position—"

"That doesn't matter. All that matters is that you should be happy. Are you sure you even want to go away on our family holiday? Perhaps you'd rather just stay at home and rest."

"Don't be silly, I could never rest at home—there's always so much to be done! No, I can hardly wait for the holiday—although now that we don't have to abandon the children with Winifred I do wish it wasn't too late to alter our plans again and go to Devon as usual."

"It'll be fun to have a change."

"I'm not very good at changes," said Grace.

I thought: And not very good at fun either.

But that comment was contemptible and I despised myself for letting it loose in my consciousness.

It was then that I first began to have misgivings about our family holiday in the Lake District, but I had no premonition of disaster. I was no mystical dreamer, and as a good Modernist I didn't believe in clairvoyance.

4

NINE weeks after that fatal dinner-party at the Bishop's palace Starbridge remained intact, but Canterbury had been battered as a reprisal for the RAF's formidable raid on Cologne at the end of May. In both cities the cathedrals remained standing, monuments to hope in a world demented with the lust for destruction. Hitler, bogged down in Russia but boosted by Rommel's victorious manoeuvrings in the desert, had apparently in a fit of absent-mindedness turned over the Baedeker page which described Starbridge, but it was too soon to take our escape for granted, and meanwhile the ruins of Bath, York, Norwich, Exeter and Canterbury served to remind us of the nightmare which could still come true.

"How wonderful it'll be to escape from all thought of air raids for two weeks!" said Grace, but of course there was no real escape from the war. At the start of the school holidays, following advice from the Government, I warned the children about the dangers of playing with long metal tubes, metal balls with handles, cannisters which looked like thermos flasks, and glass bottles of every description. It seemed unlikely that we would come across unexploded bombs in the Lake District, but the Luftwaffe sometimes jettisoned their cargo in unexpected places, and I felt nowhere in England was completely safe.

Meanwhile on a more mundane level Grace had been struggling with the bureaucratic regulations attending the issue of the new ration-book which was to replace at the end of the month the three ration-books already in use. Rationing was on the increase. The children were aghast to hear that the supply of sweets was about to be limited and as soon as the older boys returned from school they rushed out to splurge their pocket-money on tuppenny-ha'penny blocks of ration-chocolate in defiance of the slogan ONLY ASK FOR IT IF YOU REALLY NEED IT. Neither Grace nor I had the heart to stop them. All chocolates and sweets were being removed from the automatic machines, and at fetes and fun-fairs sweets were forbidden to be donated as prizes. The heavy hand of war-time government was closing upon us ever more tightly for the big squeeze. SAVE BREAD, we were exhorted, and given fifty different ways of serving potatoes. IS YOUR PURCHASE REALLY NECESSARY? we were repeatedly asked, and when we arrived at the station to begin our journey north the first poster we saw was the Railway Executive Committee's stern directive: DO NOT TRAVEL. I at once felt guiltily that we should have stayed at home after all.

To my dismay I discovered that in a new burst of austerity the restaurant car had been withdrawn from the train, but fortunately Grace—perfect as always—had foreseen this danger and packed a picnic-basket. The children alleviated the tedium of the journey by guzzling biscuits, which for some reason were one of the few foods still in plentiful supply.

I mention these details of life on the Home Front not merely to underline the essential dreariness of the war, punctuated as it was for us by the almost inconceivable horror of random murder by travel guide, but to show that I was living in an atmosphere of austerity and repression which drove better men than I to seek refuge in the insanity of a grand passion. I'm not offering an excuse for myself, and I'm certainly not suggesting my madness had its origins in a two-ounce sweet-ration and a shortage of bread, but when deprived in one area of life human beings tend to compensate themselves in another, and if a fully accurate picture of my crisis is to be drawn, an explanation of my insanity must include the drab stress of existence on the Home Front.

A clergyman with a wife and five children can seldom afford the luxury of taking his family on holiday to a hotel, and even when the children were fewer in number I had found it less awkward as well as more economical to rent a neat, clean, spacious cottage near Woolacombe in Devon for our annual sojourn by the sea. I had discovered this idyllic retreat while exploring the advertising columns of *The Church Gazette,* and when in May I had embarked on a search there for a cottage in the Lake District, it had never occurred to me that I might not repeat my earlier success. Having spotted an advertisement which lyrically described an appropriate haven for my large family, I had written without a second thought to the owner to secure a booking.

When we eventually arrived at this idyllic retreat after an exhausting journey on an erratic train, a bone-jolting excursion in a decrepit bus and a muddy walk up a lonely lane, I realised in rather less than three seconds that I had brought my family to a rural slum. The key lay under the front door-mat, just as the landlord had promised, but no other facility matched my expectations. Fortunately, since it was summer, the evening was light; the prospect of being obliged to master oil lamps and an old-fashioned kitchen range was bad enough, but in the dark it would have been intolerable. I can never understand why people become dewy-eyed and sentimental about the past. Life without gas, electricity and decent plumbing must have been one long unromantic round of time-consuming inconvenience.

Primrose, stupefied by tiredness, began to wail that she was hungry. Christian, after a speedy reconnaissance, reported: "There appears to be no lavatory. Shall I start digging a hole in the garden?" Grace said: "I think I have a migraine coming on," and sank down on the nearest chair. Sandy, who had been asleep in her arms, was woken by this abrupt manoeuvre; he promptly started to scream. James said: "I don't want to go to the lavatory in the garden," and Norman commented gloomily: "I wish we were in Devon." Setting down the heavy suitcases which I had been carrying, I dredged up my last ounce of strength, tossed off a quick prayer for divine support and prepared to perform any miracle not contrary to the laws of physics.

Grace was ordered to lie down on the moth-eaten material which covered the sofa. Christian was dispatched to make a second attempt to find something which resembled a lavatory. Norman and James were sent upstairs to make the beds. Primrose was given an apple, left over from our picnic lunch, and put in charge of Sandy. In the picnic-basket I also found a half-eaten roll which I stuffed into Sandy's mouth to keep him quiet. Then having assembled some logs from a pile which I found outside the back door, I lit the kitchen range with the aid of an old newspaper which I found on the filthy floor of the larder. As I morosely watched the feeble smouldering of the logs I tried not to remember that a mere week ago I had been dining in the height of luxury at Starmouth Court.

"I'll make some tea," said Grace, struggling nobly from the sofa.

"No, you stay exactly where you are." I filled the kettle, found the ration we had brought with us and unearthed a teapot from a cupboard which stank. Meanwhile Christian had returned to report the existence of a privy and Norman was shouting from upstairs that there were no sheets but plenty of blankets. We appeared to be making progress.

"Take the suitcases upstairs and start unpacking," I said to Christian. "Do Sandy's first."

"That infant smells as bad as the privy," remarked Christian, who was fastidious.

"Why do you think I told you to unpack his bag first? We need a clean nappy." I had taken a plate from the cupboard and was now busy extracting some Spam from a large tin.

"I'll find the nappy," said Grace, making a new effort to struggle to her feet.

Sandy started to roar again.

"I simply can't understand," observed Christian languidly, "why infanticide isn't more common."

"What's infanticide?" said Primrose as Christian and Grace trailed away upstairs together.

"Baby-killing, my love." I opened two large cans of baked beans just as the kettle showed signs that it might one day come to the boil. Sandy was still roaring but when I gave him a baked bean he spat it out. Turning back to the table I found that the Spam was being investigated by a mouse. Without thinking I snarled: "Bugger off, you bally blighter!"—a response which avoided blasphemy (just) but was hardly a fitting exclamation for a clergyman. In a paroxysm of rage I hurled a spoon, but the animal merely frisked down the table-leg and scampered to safety across the floor. Primrose screamed. Sandy stopped crying and immediately began to chant: "Bugger, bugger, bugger!" with zest. (Why is it that small children have such an unfailing talent for picking up bad language?)

Seconds later Christian, Norman and James, all waving nappies, clattered down the stairs to inform me that Grace had had to rest again as she was feeling faint.

"Well, don't just stand there waving nappies as if they were Union Jacks! Get some cotton wool and the talcum powder—and some lavatory paper might be useful too, if one can judge by the smell—"

"There isn't any lavatory paper," said Christian.

"Nonsense, there must be."

"I don't feel very hungry," said Norman, eyeing the Spam. "This conversation's putting me off my food."

"Rubbish—stop being so feeble!" I said with a robust good humour which bordered on the saintly. "Is that the spirit which built the Empire?"

"Daddy," said Primrose, "I think the mouse went to the lavatory on the table."

"Bugger, bugger, bugger!" shouted Sandy.

"I think I'm going to be sick," said Norman, bolting for the back door.

"Who taught Sandy to say 'bugger'?" demanded Christian in delight as he searched the kitchen cupboards for lavatory paper.

"Daddy, did you hear me? I said: 'I think the mouse—' "

"Yes, my love. Pass me that rag hanging by the sink, please."

"Neville." Looking up I saw Grace, white as a winding-sheet, in the doorway. She was carrying the cotton wool and the talcum powder. "I'll change Sandy."

"Very well," I said, deciding that this was the moment when I would be ungrateful if I continued to refuse my wife's noble offers of help, "but afterwards you're to go straight to bed—and let's hope there are no bed-bugs."

"I simply can't understand how *The Church Gazette* could have allowed—"

"It's not the fault of *The Church Gazette.* One can't expect them to inspect all the properties they advertise. The fault was mine for not immediately realising that 'old-world charm' meant 'no modern conveniences.' "

"Gaudeamus igitur!" cried Christian, flourishing a roll of toilet paper.

"Christian, stop behaving like a precocious undergraduate and stir the baked beans. James, go outside and see if Norman's finished being sick."

"Is Norman ill?" said Grace alarmed.

"Daddy," said Primrose, "what are bed-bugs?"

"Bugger, bugger, bugger!" shouted Sandy with zest.

Grace reeled. "Sandy! Christian, did you—"

"No, Mother, not guilty, absolutely not. I say, these beans look a bit odd—"

"Here's Norman," said James. "I think he might be dying."

"I feel terrible," said Norman, looking like death.

"It's always so metaphysically interesting," mused Christian, very much the Winchester scholar, "when feelings so precisely mirror appearances."

"Shut up, you great big beastly brute!" yelled Norman.

"ENOUGH!" I barked as Grace started swaying in the doorway. "Grace and Norman—go to bed at once before you both pass out. Christian, make the tea. James, start spooning out the baked beans. Primrose, bring over those plates from the dresser. Sandy—" I sighed and reached for the toilet paper. There were times when even I, a devout clergyman dedicated to preaching the joys of family life, was obliged to admit that being a husband and father could leave a lot to be desired.

5

"WHY can't Sandy learn to do without nappies?" asked Primrose later when the Spam and baked beans had been consumed. "I gave up nappies when I was much younger than he is."

"All babies are different, my love."

"You may think you're clever," said Christian to Primrose, "but I walked, talked, gave up nappies and translated the *Iliad* well before my first birthday."

"Show-off!" retorted Primrose, who was a girl of spirit.

"Did he really, Daddy?" said James worried.

"No, of course not!"

James, who was nine, had begun to realise that he was not so clever as his older brothers, and I knew he was mortified that he never came top of his class. Unlike Christian and Norman, he would never lighten my financial burdens by winning a Winchester scholarship, but I thought in the end he would be happy enough; he was popular with his contemporaries and keen on cricket. In some ways he was the son with whom I felt most at ease. His sunny nature made him restful and his normality provided a soothing contrast to the intellectual pyrotechnics displayed by his more gifted brothers. In my judgement he was on course to becoming a thoroughly decent, presentable young man and I was very pleased with him. So much for James.

Primrose, now sitting next to me in her privileged position as the Only Daughter, was approaching her fifth birthday and would one day, I thought, prove to be a brilliant conversationalist; already she was fascinated by language and never missed an opportunity to expand her vocabulary. Since for a woman intelligence is less important than looks, I spent much time worrying that she might wind up a blue-stocking, and it was with relief that I noted she showed signs of turning into a delectable blue-eyed blonde. I foresaw a splendid career ahead of her as a wife and mother, a prospect which filled me with paternal pride. So much for Primrose.

Sandy, now dozing against my chest, was going to be very clever, perhaps even as clever as Christian. When he was not indulging in his fondness for vulgar language he was capable of stringing together sentences of extraordinary quality for a child who was still little more than a baby. His latest masterpiece, delivered that day on the train, was: "Peter Rabbit has great sartorial elegance but I prefer the coat worn by Benjamin Bunny." Of course Christian had taught him the phrase "sartorial elegance," but Sandy's remarkable achievement lay not only in pronouncing the words but in using them correctly. I judged a Winchester scholarship inevitable and was already basking in delight. So much for Sandy.

Norman, now upstairs as he battled with his malaise, was twelve years old and engaged in a non-stop contest to prove he was as clever as his older brother. If James was the son with whom I felt most relaxed, then Norman was the son with whom I could most obviously sympathise; I too had spent my childhood in a non-stop contest with my older brother. It was a contest which I had won but which I suspected Norman was destined to lose, although he remained far too clever to give me cause for anxiety. He never failed to receive glowing school reports which made me sigh with satisfaction. So much for Norman.

Finally there was Christian, now sitting opposite me at the far end of the table. What can I say to convey the unique quality of this, the most extraordinary member of my family? I could never write "so much for Christian" at the end of a brief description of him, because no brief description could convey more than the bare bones of his personality. Perhaps I can best capture the aura of glamour he exuded by stating that Christian was the idealised son which men so often dream of fathering but so rarely ever do. Christian was the self I would like to have been, a genetic miracle, my own self glorified. Exceptionally clever, blessed with the gift of reducing every classics master he encountered to a stunned admiration, talented at games, popular with his contemporaries, he was fifteen years old, still growing and evidently destined to be not only charming, witty and accomplished but tall, dark and handsome.

I regarded him with a deep, fierce, utterly private devotion which I was quite unable to articulate. I could be demonstrative with Primrose because men were allowed to show affection towards their daughters, but with my sons I had a horror of indulging in any behaviour which might be judged sentimental. The kindly authority I exercised had never included barbarous physical punishment, but no matter how much I wanted to demonstrate my affection I was unable to do more than produce an air of mild good will. In Yorkshire we don't wear our hearts on our sleeves—and perhaps too I could never quite forget Uncle Willoughby declaring in 1909 that a sentimental father who slobbered over his male offspring was the kind of fool who inevitably wound up in an early grave.

"Daddy . . ."

I returned to 1942 with a jolt. "Yes, James?"

"After the war ends, what will happen to the newspapers? There won't be any more news, will there?"

"There'll be blank pages edged in black," said Christian, "to mark the utter cessation of journalism. But who says the war's going to end? As far as I can see it's all set to go on for ever."

"Nonsense!" I said roundly. "Think of Napoleon! Once he attacked Russia he was finished—the British Army merely had to mop him up at Waterloo."

"I wish the British Army would start mopping up Rommel in the desert."

"Daddy," said Primrose, "why aren't you in the Army?"

"The Bishop said he couldn't spare me from my work in Starbridge. Not all clergymen are called to serve God in the Army, even in wartime."

Christian said suddenly: "Do you ever regret abandoning your pacifism after Munich?"

"Sometimes. I still believe pacifism is intellectually consistent with Liberal Protestantism, but unfortunately Herr Hitler doesn't leave much room for intellectual consistency."

"I'm beginning to think it's Liberal Protestantism which doesn't leave much room for intellectual consistency. How can you play down evil and maintain your optimistic view of the universe when you're confronted with a catastrophe like Nazism? I mean, what do you *do* with someone like Adolf Hitler? You can't simply pat him on the head, cite the compassion and forgiveness of Christ and say cosily: 'Go thy way and sin no more!' "

I was much taken aback. I had to remind myself that fifteen-year-old adolescents were notorious for questioning their parents' views. "I'll tell you exactly what you do with someone like Hitler," I said abruptly. "In practical terms you fight him. And in spiritual terms you pray for him and remember that there's a divine spark in every human being."

"But isn't that hopelessly idealistic? Isn't that out of touch with the reality of the evil going on here? Try talking to the Jews about Hitler's divine spark!"

"Idealism is also a reality—the reality to which we must all continually aspire."

"Yes, but—"

"Christian, I've had a long hard day, I've wound up in a hovel and quite frankly I'm not in the mood to discuss theology. Can we continue this debate later?"

"I'm sorry, I just wanted to have a real conversation with you for once."

I stared at him. "But we always have real conversations!"

"No, they're usually about Latin and Greek and how well I'm doing at school."

"Well, what's so unreal about all your splendid successes?" I stood up with one arm encircling Sandy and held out my free hand to Primrose. "Bed-time, my love," I said to her, "and let's hope that tomorrow morning after a good night's sleep we'll find our holiday taking a turn for the better."

"It could hardly get much worse," said Christian.

But he was wrong.

6

NORMAN'S condition showed no improvement the next morning. Grace—perfect as always—had remembered to bring a thermometer, and when we discovered he had a high fever I trekked to the nearby village in search of a doctor. Influenza was diagnosed. Grace was obliged to spend most of her time caring for the invalid. The weather was not only wet but cold. The younger children quickly became fractious.

It was on the fifth day after our arrival, just as Norman's condition began to improve, that Grace fainted. Rushing upstairs in response to Norman's frightened yell for help, I found she had collapsed on the bedroom floor.

"I haven't felt well for some time," she whispered later, "but I was afraid you'd think it was the last straw if I couldn't cope."

When the doctor returned he ordered her sternly to stay in bed. Afterwards he told me that she had probably made matters worse by ignoring all the signs that she had caught Norman's influenza.

But Grace did not have influenza. She had caught a chill after being soaked on a shopping expedition—it could never have happened in

Devon, where the village shop stood next door to our cottage—and now she was suffering from pneumonia.

At eleven o'clock that night she began to have difficulty with her breathing. On arrival the doctor took one look at her and said: "She must go to hospital at once." He made no attempt to summon an ambulance. He drove us to the hospital at Keswick in his own car. I remember thinking what a blessing it was that Christian was old enough to be left in charge at the cottage.

Soon after she was admitted to hospital she became delirious and the pneumonia was finally diagnosed. I telephoned her sister Winifred in Manchester. To my great relief she at once offered to come to my rescue. I was unable to leave the hospital, and although Christian was capable of taking charge of four children for a short time I could hardly leave him without assistance for more than twenty-four hours.

The day passed. Winifred arrived and could barely bring herself to leave the hospital. I had to remind her sharply that if she wanted to help her sister she should attend to the children. Winifred cried but left. More time passed. The sympathetic nurses offered me cups of tea but I could hardly drink. Eating proved quite impossible.

For some time Grace was unconscious, but in the evening when the sun was setting far away in the other world beyond the hospital walls, she opened her eyes and said clearly: "I can't go on. But I must. She'd never care for the children."

For a long moment I was so appalled, so overpowered by my guilt and my shame, that I was unable to speak. Then leaning forward I clumsily clasped her hands as if I could somehow infuse her with strength, and stammered: "You mustn't say such things. You mustn't even think them. I love you and no one else but you, and *you're going to live.*"

She died a minute later.

V

"Passion may be dangerous, but for all that it is the driving-force of life . . ."

CHARLES E. RAVEN
A WANDERER'S WAY

I

INSTINCTIVELY I knew that my best chance of maintaining an immaculate self-control was to organise the chaotic aftermath of the tragedy with the efficiency of the born administrator. I dealt with the hospital personnel. I made the necessary urgent telephone calls. I drew up a list of the other essential matters which required my attention. I prepared a short speech to deliver to my children and memorised it; I even bought extra handkerchiefs to mop up all the tears.

After dealing with the children I dealt with the local vicar, who called in performance of his Christian duty, and I dealt with Winifred, who by this time was well-nigh prostrated by her shock and grief. Having drafted the notices for *The Times* and the *Daily Telegraph,* I wrote the innumerable necessary letters and decided which of Grace's favourite hymns should be included in the funeral service. I was ceaselessly active. Sleep was shunned as far as possible because I was afraid of what might happen when I could no longer control my thoughts. From past experience I knew that if one wanted to preserve one's sanity in adverse circumstances one had to ring down the metaphorical curtain in one's mind in order to hide the horrors which had taken place onstage, and how could one be sure of keeping the curtain down once sleep had impaired one's ability to play the stage manager?

After a while I realised that the curtain was trying to rise even when I was fully conscious, and I became engaged in a deadly struggle to keep it in place. It tried to rise when Christian stammered: "How could God have allowed such a dreadful thing to happen?" and although I embarked on an answer I found I was unable to complete it as I would have wished. I did manage to say: "In a world where nothing bad ever happened we'd be mere puppets smiling at the end of manipulated strings," but then the curtain began to rise in earnest and I could not speak of the great freedom to be, to love and, inevitably, to suffer which made us not unfeeling puppets but human beings forever vulnerable to tragedy. Instead all I could say was: "We'll talk about it later," as I struggled to nail my curtain to the ground.

But no sooner was the curtain back in place than Winifred was exclaiming in a burst of detestable feminine emotion: "Neville, you don't deserve this—you were such a devoted husband, and everyone always said what a wonderful example you and Grace were of a truly Christian marriage!"

Once more the curtain started to rise and once more I managed to grab the hem before it could sail out of reach. I said woodenly: "Tragedy's so difficult to discuss, isn't it? Better not to try," and with a mighty effort of will I heaved the curtain down, but I was to have no respite. The curtain was developing a sinister life of its own.

"Are you sure Mummy's happy with Jesus?" said Primrose. "No matter how nice Jesus is, I think she'd be happier with us," and a second later my nurse, Tabitha, was saying in 1909: "Your Pa's gone to heaven to be with Jesus." Then in my memory I heard Willy cry outraged: "How dare he!" while Emily asked: "When will Jesus let us have him back?" A world had ended then and a world had ended now, the new tragedy eliding with all my most terrible memories as the curtain began to go up and up and up . . . But I hung on to the hem with my last ounce of strength and doggedly refused to let go.

The funeral service was held at St. Martin's-in-Cripplegate before the private interment at the cemetery, and when the Bishop himself offered to help I was spared the task of finding another clergyman to take the service I would have been unable to conduct. The ancient church, originally founded for the benefit of the workmen who were building the Cathedral, was packed with mourners, and the small graveyard too overflowed with those wishing to pay their respects.

The Bishop was superb. Dr. Ottershaw had his episcopal shortcomings; as his Archdeacon I knew them better than anyone, but he was a good, decent man, and in his goodness and his decency his Christian message of hope lightened the darkness which must always surround the mystery of suffering. There were no sentimental clichés from Dr. Ottershaw, only profound religious truths expressed with exquisite simplicity, and I felt not only relieved but grateful that my children were at last able to hear the message which my fear of emotional breakdown had prevented me from giving them.

It occurred to me that my disciple would have soaked at least one handkerchief as she listened to the Bishop, but of course I could not allow myself to think of Dido.

I glimpsed her before the service and she spoke to me afterwards, but only the briefest of conversations was possible. After the exchange of greetings she merely said: "I'll write, I promise. I was too upset to write before," and as she disappeared I saw her eyes shone with tears. Perhaps she was merely feeling emotional in the wake of Dr. Ottershaw's address, but perhaps too she was temporarily overcome with all manner of ambiguous feelings.

After the concluding rites in the cemetery I continued to deal with everyone who required my attention until at last, much later, I found myself alone with my brother and sister in the vicarage kitchen as my curtain once more tried to rise. I was struggling fiercely with the hem, but to my terror I realised it was sliding out of my grasp. I thought: I mustn't look at the stage, can't look, won't look, no one can make me look. Then I suddenly realised I had spoken the words aloud. As Willy and Emily looked at me appalled I muttered: "Sorry. Mind wandering. Very tired," and covered my face with my hands.

Emily said drearily: "I'll make you some tea."

"For God's sake, woman!" exploded Willy. "He's already drunk enough of your tea to float Noah's Ark! Neville, where the hell's the bloody whisky?"

"There isn't any. I don't drink spirits."

"Well, all I can say is it's about time you started!"

"Really, Will!" said Emily scandalised. "What would Mother say if she were alive!"

I said: "I don't want to talk about Mother."

"Neither do I," agreed Willy. "Let's keep the old girl buried six feet deep or else I'm going to hit the bottle in the biggest possible way."

"Really, Will!" said Emily again in her primmest voice. "How can you talk like that after what happened to Father!"

I said: "I don't want to talk about Father."

"Good God, Em, you don't believe all that bloody rubbish about Father dying of drink, do you? That was just a vile slander put out by Uncle Willoughby!"

Leaping to my feet I shouted: *"I don't want to talk about Uncle Willoughby!"* But then I collapsed in my chair and once more covered my face with my hands.

Willy said: "I'm going to the off-license to buy some whisky."

Emily said: "I'm going to make tea."

Recognising their desire to offer comfort, I was soothed by their careful avoidance of emotion, and after a while I thought I was strong enough to drag down the curtain again. But I was wrong. I was so weak that I glanced at the stage first, and there waiting for me in 1909 was Uncle Willoughby, rich, robust and ruthless as he hitched up his coat-tails to warm his backside at the parlour fire. ". . . and I'll not say one word against your father, poor miserable idle stupid fellow that he was, because it's not right to speak ill of the dead, even when a weak selfish thoughtless fellow with a wife and three children has the intolerable effrontery to die in penury. So all I'll say is this: If you two lads want to save yourself from hell and damnation—"

"Here's your tea, Nev," said Emily in 1942.

"—if you two lads want to save yourself from hell and damnation," bawled Uncle Willoughby, outshouting her in 1909, "and save yourselves from the miserable fate of winding up a failure in a coffin before you're forty, you'll work and you'll work and you'll work until you've dug yourself out of this shameful black pit, and you'll never forget—never as long as you live—that there's only one road to salvation and that's this: You've got to go *chasing the prizes* if you want to stay out of the coffin—you've got to go *chasing the prizes* if you want to be happy and safe—you've got to go *chasing the prizes* in order to Get On and Travel Far . . ."

"Poor Nev," said Emily in 1942. "You can shed a tear if you like. I'll look the other way and afterwards we can pretend it never happened."

"For God's sake!" I shouted and blundered out of the kitchen into my study. Willy arrived five minutes later with the whisky and banged on the door until I let him in.

"Em driving you round the bend? How her husband stands all that tea I don't know. What a mystery marriage is, but of course I'm just a bachelor schoolmaster who observes society's mating customs from afar . . . Do you remember when you said to me on the beach at St. Leonards all those years ago: 'I'm going to marry the perfect girl and have the perfect family and live happily ever after'? I'd never even considered getting married, and yet there you were, seventeen years old, with that misty look in your eyes, the look of the dyed-in-the-wool romantic, the look Father always wore when he read us 'The Charge of the Light Brigade'—"

"Shut up and give me some whisky."

"But my dear Neville, I speak only in admiration! How many other romantic idealists have the guts and the drive to make a success of such a notoriously difficult venture as marriage? It was a tremendous achievement, and nothing can ever take that away from you, not even this appalling tragedy—"

"Shut up, Will—shut up, *shut up,* SHUT UP!"

He shut up, looking shocked, hurt and considerably puzzled. Left on my own I drank three large tots of whisky, stumbled upstairs to bed, and for the first time since Grace's death I slept for eight unbroken hours.

It was a merciful release from my torment.

2

THE next day I sorted out the messages of sympathy into separate heaps, refilled my fountain pen and selected the letter which lay on top of the most important pile. It read:

Archdeacon dear,

I'm very, very sorry—she was so lovely and so *good* too, which is rare because many people who look lovely aren't good at all, quite the reverse as we all know, but she was very good, especially to me at Starmouth Court, though I think she did find me a little puzzling and indeed I expect I would have been puzzled too if I'd been in her shoes, which is why I so admired her for being so quiet and serene, qualities which always seem quite beyond my reach. But perhaps it's *because* I'm so noisy and restless that I deeply admire someone who possesses the virtues which I know I shall never have, and I did so admire Mrs. Aysgarth and envied her too, I confess, because she had so much and I had so little, I mean so little of what really matters, but of course she deserved to have so much and I deserve very little really, as I know all too well. I'm glad that even though she died young she had so much, my Laura did too, and in fact it's not the length of life but the quality that counts, isn't it? Of course it's terrible for those left behind, but it seems to be one of the hardest truths of life that suffering can in the end have beneficial results and certainly I know that was true in my case, because if Laura hadn't died I'd still be frittering my time away aimlessly and it was her death which made me see my life in a new light. But I must stop now because sympathy letters should be short and this is already much too long, so I shall just say that I send you my deepest, *deepest* condolences, and of course I shall say lots of prayers for you, though I'm not very good at praying yet, but I firmly believe more things are wrought by prayer than this world dreams of, as Lord T. says, and I'm sure you agree.

Ever your most devoted disciple,
DIDO TALLENT.

I read this communication three times before deciding that any attempt to answer it immediately would be most unwise. Then I examined the next letter. It came from Lady Starmouth, who had written:

My dear Archdeacon,

Permit me to send you a word of the most heartfelt sympathy as you endure your tragic bereavement. Your wife was clearly a most exceptional woman, and I shall always regret that I did not take advantage earlier of the opportunity to know her better, but at least I can treasure the memory of her at Starmouth Court. Please let me know at once if there's anything I can do to help.

After doodling on the blotter to make sure the ink was running smoothly from my pen, I wrote:

My dear Lady Starmouth,

Thank you so much for your kind, thoughtful letter. The bereavement is indeed devastating. Grace and I were married for sixteen years and were acquainted for seven years before our wedding day, so I'm sure you will understand that I find it impossible to imagine life without her. Originally, I confess, our relationship was a mere youthful romance, but by the grace of God this immature affection was translated into a rich, rewarding married life which brought us both an unflawed happiness. For so many years the sun shone brightly upon us, and even now that night has fallen at last I shall remain always profoundly grateful for those unclouded skies from which the light shone so radiantly for so long.

This letter was not, as might be supposed, a cold-blooded exercise in hypocrisy. It was a method of alleviating emotions which were genuine but so complex that they could not be accurately expressed at all. It is also a fact that when all emotion is suppressed in public, writing a florid letter in private can act as a catharsis. I recalled how in adolescence I had been shy with my mother, whom I seldom saw, but how in my letters to her I was able to compensate myself for this failure in verbal communication by writing with a stylish fluency. Remembering my mother I thought how she would have enjoyed my letter to Lady Starmouth. She had always savoured the old-fashioned epistolary convention which permitted naked sentimentality to be lavishly expressed when bereavement was under discussion, and I thought that Lady Starmouth, despite her sophistication, would remember her Victorian youth and savour the convention too.

Feeling greatly fortified after this stylised emotional blood-letting, I decided I was now capable of attending wisely to my disciple, and pulling a fresh sheet of paper towards me, I wrote without hesitation:

My dear Miss Tallent:

It is hard to express on paper how deeply your letter affected me, so I hope that next time you have leave I shall be able to see you in order to express my gratitude in person. Meanwhile I can only thank you from the very depths of my being for your unstinting sympathy, your kind thoughts and your most welcome prayers.

Yours sincerely,
N.N.A.

I read this letter through twice. Then madness gripped me. Tearing the letter in two I grabbed a fresh sheet of paper and wrote:

Dear Dido,

Your letter was a lifeline. How soon can we meet? Can you return to Starbridge immediately without risk of being court-martialled for desertion? I need to see you urgently.

Yours,
STEPHEN.

But of course this reckless piece of lunacy had to be burnt at once in the ash-tray. Finally I wrote:

My dear Miss Tallent,

Your letter meant a great deal to me and I thank you for it with all my heart. Is there any chance that you might be able to return to Starbridge in the near future? I don't want to tempt you into going AWOL, but I'd so very much like to see you. This letter comes with all the usual good wishes and blessings from your mentor

N.N.A. ("S").

She was on my doorstep by noon of the following day.

3

"I PAUSED only to twist the authorities around my little finger," she said as I led her into the study and closed the door, "but I got the leave so you needn't worry about me being AWOL. Gosh, you look completely ship-wrecked! What can I do to save you from drowning?"

Insanity finally triumphed. "Marry me," I said, and took her in my arms.

"Stephen!" She recoiled. "My God, what are you saying?"

"But you can't be surprised! You must have known!"

"Known what?"

"Known I'm in love with you!"

"But you can't be! And even if you are, you can't possibly say so, not now, not so soon after your wife's death!"

"Well, I'm saying it. I love you—and since you said at Starmouth Court that you were passionate about me—"

"But I didn't mean it! I mean, I didn't mean it in that way! I mean—oh God, what did I mean, what the hell's happening, this situation's plunged right out of control—"

"But Dido—darling—"

"Now look here, Archdeacon dear, this simply isn't playing the game. *I'm* the one who has to be burning in a fever of unrequited love! *You're* the one who has to be implacably austere and deliciously unobtainable!"

"I don't like that game any more. I'm tearing up the rules."

I thought she was going to faint but she merely collapsed on the nearest chair. In a shaking voice she said: "I don't play any other game."

"Never mind, you'll soon learn the new one. After all, you did say you wanted to marry a clergyman—"

"Yes, but for God's sake, not a widower with five children—I'm not completely insane even if you are!" Making a great effort she jumped to her feet, looked me straight in the eyes and said bluntly: "It's not on. I'm very sorry, I know it's all my fault and I've behaved abominably, but you've got to understand that I shall never marry you, *never,* not even if I live to be a hundred."

There was only one answer to that. It was not an answer any clergyman should have given, but the scene had stripped aside my clerical mask to expose the rough, tough, dogged Yorkshireman beneath. "You little bitch," I said, "I'm going to marry you even if it's the very last thing I ever do." And as the violent excitement blazed through every particle of my being, I saw her as the prize which I could never have endured to lose.

4

IT will be clear by this time that I was in a disturbed mental state, so I shall surprise no one when I now disclose that I was mad enough to marry her. It took me over two and a half years to lure her to the altar, but in the end I got what I wanted, and in the meantime what a splendid chase this prize offered me—so stimulating, so enthralling, so nerve-racking and so addictively exciting! I chased and I chased and I chased, many times rebuffed and cast down but never for one moment abandoning hope, and ahead of me danced my prize, weaving this way and that, now drawing closer, now haring for cover, but finally allowing me to flog her down the finishing strait towards matrimony as both her early demobilisation from the Wrens (arranged, of course, by her influential father) and her thirtieth birthday loomed on the horizon of 1945.

It would be too wearisome to recount our bizarre courtship in detail, so I shall recall only one incident which will illustrate both the staying-power of my obsession and the stranglehold of her fear of marriage. I had been chasing her for a year when she summoned me to London to meet her father. Naturally I assumed this invitation boded well for my future, but when I was confronted by Mr. Tallent, a bumptious City shark the size of a minnow, I soon realised my mistake.

"If you want to marry Dido for her money, you're wasting your time," he said, speaking with an accent in which genteel Edinburgh wrestled with the Glasgow slums. "She's got no money of her own and the marriage settlement won't give you a penny."

"How very kind of you to inform me of your financial plans for her," I said with a truly Christian self-restraint, "but I'm motivated by love, not money."

"Then you're a fool!" said this charmless individual, baring some yellow teeth and regarding me with contempt. "She doesn't give a damn about you—you ask her about Harry Harland!"

As soon as I was alone with Dido I took his advice, and immediately she burst into tears. "I told Father to put you off," she wept, "but I never meant him to go that far!"

"Well, he did go that far and nothing could put me off. What's all this about Harland?" I demanded, imagining some flirtatious incident in a nightclub with this heavily decorated fighter pilot—indeed as it turned out Mr. Tallent himself had imagined no more than this—but to my horror Dido now confessed that the incident had resulted in the loss of her virginity.

I said: "You pathetic, muddled-up, wretched little girl. How can you endure to wallow in this revolting emotional mess when you could be loved and cherished as my wife?"

"But Stephen, I did it all for you!"

"You *what?* I'm sorry, either I'm hallucinating or you're certifiable. Did you actually say—"

"I thought I couldn't face marriage because I was frightened of sex, so I said to myself: Well, if I take the plunge at least I'll know where I stand—and now I do know where I stand: in perpetual chastity. Oh Stephen, you've got to stop chasing me, you've absolutely got to, because I can never marry you now that I've discovered sex is so awful—and it *was* awful, honestly it was, I hated every minute—"

"Well, of course you did, you idiotic little fool! If you lie on your back with your legs apart and let some stranger romp all over you until he violates not just the most private part of your body but the most private recesses of your inner self, how can you expect to be other than revolted? But what's all that half-baked disgusting behaviour got to do with us? What's that got to do with marriage? What's that got to do with going to bed with a man who loves you and who would treat you with reverence, with tenderness, with—"

"Don't, don't, don't!" shrieked Dido, almost hysterical with remorse. "You're making me feel I want to curl up and die!"

"That won't be necessary. All you have to do to wipe out this incident is walk down the aisle with me."

"Oh Stephen, you're so wonderful, so perfect, so patient, so noble that I think I really will marry you after all—"

"When?"

"Oh, very soon—but not just yet . . ."

And so it went on.

Meanwhile it was hardly surprising that the people who cared most about my welfare were nerving themselves to persuade me that marriage with Dido would be a disaster.

"You can't seriously want to marry this woman," said my brother Willy. "Archdeacons and society girls just aren't designed by God to mix without bursts of lewd laughter erupting on all sides—think of all the 'said-the-bishop-to-the-actress' jokes! I simply don't understand this grand passion of yours. How could you even consider marrying a woman who's the exact opposite of your perfect Grace?"

"It's because Grace was so perfect that I've got to marry someone utterly different. How could I tolerate a second-rate Grace who could do nothing but remind me of how much I'd lost?" I said logically enough, and when Willy remained dissatisfied I concluded that a confirmed bachelor would never understand the glorious compulsion which had enslaved me.

My next critic, however, was very far from being a confirmed bachelor. Alex Jardine, taking me to dine in London at the Athenaeum, said bluntly: "You can't possibly marry that woman, Neville. It's out of the question. She'll ruin you."

We were drinking sherry before taking our places in the dining-room; after Alex had delivered his opinion, my first instinct was to drain my glass and smash it. I did overcome this impulse to behave like a Cossack, but it cost me a considerable effort to say in a mild voice: "Aren't you rushing to judgement, Alex? You hardly know Dido at all."

"I know enough to realise you're taking the most appalling gamble with your future. Obviously there's a strong sexual attraction going on which is annihilating your common sense, and I can only pray to God that you haven't already slipped up in the worst possible way."

I was appalled. In fact I was so shocked that for a moment I could only wonder if I had heard him correctly. Then I realised that not only had I heard him correctly but that I had been insulted in a manner which, since we were both clergymen, was quite beyond toleration.

I heard myself say: "You can't seriously believe I'd behave in any manner which represented gross misconduct."

"Such things do happen."

"Yes—to the clerical failures, but not to people like me! How can you sit there and even *think* that I'd—"

"I'm sorry." Belatedly Alex realised he had gone too far. "I'm afraid that as a bishop I encountered the clerical failures, and even now I'm retired I tend to believe the worst on the grounds that the worst is usually true."

Again I was appalled. "What a very cynical and unattractive attitude! And how profoundly un-Christian!"

"Listen, let's just forget I ever said—"

"Oh no, I'm not letting you off the hook as easily as that! Now look here, Alex. I'm getting very tired of your habit of jumping to conclusions on the minimum of evidence, and when those conclusions also happen to be insulting, I think it's time someone pointed out a few home truths to you. Don't you realise that this rushing to judgement is actually rotten counselling? What happened to that bishop who used to pride himself on his pastoral care?"

Alex went white. At first I thought he was furious. Then I realised he was shattered. "I'm sorry," he said numbly. "I suppose I'm too involved in your life. I've long thought of you as a son."

"Well, I'm not your son and I won't tolerate you passing judgement on me like some autocratic Victorian father. You've absolutely no right to interfere in my affairs like that!"

Now I was the one who belatedly realised he had gone too far. "No right?" repeated Alex as the colour flooded back to his face. "Did you say I had *no right?* I may not be your father, but who made you Archdeacon? *Who made you what you are?* What other bishop on the bench would have offered such a preferment to a draper's son from Yorkshire?"

"I don't deny you've been very good to me, Alex. All I'm saying is—"

"I suppose now that I'm just a retired bishop, someone who can no longer further your career, you feel I can be rebuffed and discarded! Well, all I can say is that you'd better take care you don't wind up among life's losers—a young clergyman who ignores his mentor's advice usually comes to a sticky end!"

"And who are you to talk of losers?" I demanded, finally throwing all restraint to the winds. We were tucked away in a secluded corner of the room, but I was aware of the distant heads turning as I sprang to my feet. "During the five years you spent at Starbridge you succeeded in upsetting every other bishop in the House of Lords—why, you even insulted the Archbishop of Canterbury!—and when your ill-health forced you to retire, the Church of England's collective sigh of relief equalled the velocity of a hurricane-force gale!"

Alex jumped up so violently that he overturned his glass of sherry. "No man talks to me like that!"

"Then it's about time someone tried! And while we're on the subject of you winding up a loser, why the deuce have you frittered away your retirement scribbling an autobiography—which never gets finished—in between visits to London to drink too much at the Athenaeum? I know you've got a heart complaint, but surely there was no need for you to be quite so idle! Why haven't you preached the occasional guest-sermon—or offered to help out in a neighbouring parish where the vicar's absent in the Army? Even our *bête noire* Jon Darrow had the grace to do that!"

"Obviously we've come to the parting of the ways," said Alex in his bitterest voice. "I'd wish you well, but I fear I'd be wasting my time. It's quite clear you're hell-bent on ruining yourself." And he walked out of the room.

Within minutes I was regretting my violent verbal assault, but although I later wrote more than once in an attempt to repair our friendship, he stubbornly refused to reply.

5

"MY dear Archdeacon," said Lady Starmouth just before the engagement was announced, "I wonder if I might take advantage of my numerous years of seniority and talk frankly about a matter which you may well prefer not to discuss. I refer, of course, to your attachment to Dido."

By this time Lady Starmouth had been my devoted benefactress for over two years. She had found me a paragon of a housekeeper and a saint of a nursemaid, both possessing not only experience of clerical households but a remarkable tolerance of my inability to afford lavish salaries. She had invited me regularly to Starmouth Court; she always called at the vicarage whenever she was in the Starbridge area, and she had persistently introduced me to a succession of eligible church-going women who were all quick to proclaim their devotion to children. This benevolence was by no means unprecedented, since Lady Starmouth was renowned for her kindness to clerical protégés, but the fact that I was not the only pebble on the Countess's privileged beach hardly altered the fact that I was under an obligation to listen to her, even when she declared herself on the brink of proffering unwelcome advice.

"I know what you're thinking," she said pleasantly. "You're afraid I'm going to echo Alex Jardine's opinion that marrying Dido would be disastrous for your career, but in fact I don't agree with Dr. Jardine. Dido may be . . . shall we say eccentric? But she's no fool and she does have this ambition to be a successful clerical wife. Why shouldn't she realise this ambition if she marries an able man who's devoted to her? No, I concede her effect on you may be beneficial. But I'm less optimistic about her effect on your children."

"Dido shares your doubts, Lady Starmouth. For some time now she's been using the children as an excuse to avoid the altar, but I'm personally convinced that the duties of a stepmother in this case wouldn't be too arduous. After all, the older boys are away at school for two-thirds of the year, and since Sandy and Primrose have their nanny—"

"All children require an appropriate amount of care and dedication from their father's wife," said Lady Starmouth, "and I very much doubt whether Dido has the ability to meet such a challenge. Her background militates against her—think of that pathetic mother in Edinburgh and that frightful father in London! In Dido's world if you've neither the time nor the desire to care for children properly you palm them off on someone else and hope to be relieved eventually of your responsibilities by a series of useful marriages."

"But Dido's by no means indifferent to children—in fact she's very keen to have children of her own—"

"Of course—she'll see them as little mirrors reflecting her own success. But Grace's children? They'll simply be mirrors reflecting the rival she'll never quite manage to forget."

I said at once: "Dido doesn't seem to see Grace as a rival."

"If she's convinced you of that she's been very clever—or maybe she hasn't yet faced up to the reality which will be waiting for her if she marries you. *I* was a second wife, Mr. Aysgarth. I know all too well how easily first wives can be idealised, not only by their husbands but by their numerous friends as well, and it can be very hard to live in the shadow of a paragon. Dido may well profess to admire Grace, but I suspect that deep down her attitude borders on jealousy, resentment and dislike."

The silence which followed this statement lasted until Lady Starmouth added abruptly: "You could do better for yourself, Archdeacon—and better for your children too. Think on what I've said and ask yourself if you don't have a duty to look elsewhere."

Naturally I promised her I would reconsider my position. Then I plunged straight back into the pursuit of my prize.

6

IT might be thought that my work would have suffered from my obsession, but in retrospect I can see that between the summer of 1942, when Grace died, and the spring of 1945, when I remarried, I reached my zenith as an archdeacon. Possibly the sublimation of an inflamed sexual desire produced the unprecedented energy which I channelled into my work at this time; as a Modernist I can never ignore the theories of psychology, but personally I look askance at psychologists who produce a sexual explanation even for an innocent act such as tieing one's shoelaces. The truth was that I was violently in love, even when Dido was at her most intolerable, and this peculiar form of insanity made life so relentlessly thrilling that I approached my work with a zest generated not (with all due respect to the Freudians) by physical frustration but by mental euphoria.

I'm not claiming that my genitals were unaffected by this mental intoxication; a grand passion combined with an enforced chastity hardly results in a eunuch's detachment. But I had no hesitation in resuming the habits of adolescence in order to maintain a tolerable degree of tranquillity. So much rubbish has been talked in the past about this sort of behaviour that rational statements by clerics are almost nonexistent, but personally I believe masturbation need be no more sinful than contraception. It entirely depends on the intent of the perpetrator. If one adopts contraception merely to neutralise the risks of fornication, then of course it must be wrong; if one adopts it to preserve one's wife's health, then it must be right. A similar distinction can be made between masturbating in order to avoid a healthy relationship with the opposite sex and masturbating to save oneself from sliding into dementia while battling towards the altar, and if anyone thinks I'm behaving like a Modernist heretic when I state this fundamentally moral opinion, all I can say is: too bad.

Did I spend much time thinking of Grace while all this feverish activity was going on? I did not. One of the most useful aspects of my grand passion was that it blotted out all I could not bear to remember. On the first anniversary of my bereavement I forced myself to go alone to the cemetery and lay flowers on the grave, but I found the experience so unendurable that although Nanny took the children to the grave occasionally, I never accompanied them. At first the children mentioned Grace's name often, but this spontaneity ceased when they discovered I was unable to talk of her. I had to remove her photograph from my study. I sent our double bed to the Red Cross and slept on the divan in my dressing-room. I could never even enter the bedroom we had shared. Once I heard Nanny say to Primrose: "It's the grief," but she was wrong. It wasn't grief which paralysed my tongue and put parts of the vicarage out of bounds. It was the guilt I was unable to face.

Fortunately grand passion and hard work created a continuous diversion from past tragedy, and soon the war became another welcome distraction as the tide began to turn against the Nazis. After the fall of Tobruk came the victory at El Alamein. After the losses of D-Day came the capture of Berlin. It was then, as Churchill entered the bunker of his adversary and sat at last in Hitler's battered chair, that my hidden ministry began to take an unprecedented amount of my time, the ministry I seldom mentioned because I feared it might taint my career: my work among the German prisoners, bitter and despairing, cynical and demoralised, at their camp on Starbury Plain.

The camp had been opened early in 1943 to house officers graded as C (Nazis) and C+ (Super-Nazis); contact with British civilians was forbidden. However, after the Normandy invasion in 1944 the huge influx of prisoners meant that the camp had to be reorganised. The Super-Nazis were sent north to Caithness, officers were admitted from Grades B (seemingly neutral but possibly still Nazi) and A (Pro-Allies), and a contingent of Other Ranks (all grades) was also admitted to act as orderlies. Still no contact was permitted with British civilians, but after the lynching of a Grade A man it was admitted that the Grade C's were out of control, and a second reorganisation took place.

Three Grade C's were hanged for their part in the lynching, while the culprits who escaped the gallows were shipped off to Caithness. Then a new commandant was appointed to run the camp, and by chance he happened to be not only a devout Christian but a friend of Dr. Ottershaw.

Colonel Laker was immediately faced with the fact that there were no qualified German priests or pastors among his prisoners. These pre-war clergy, serving in an atheist army, had been unable to be chaplains in any acceptable sense, but once in the camps many of them proved keen to revert to their calling. However at Starbury Plain the intake of prisoners had never included a Catholic priest, and of the four Protestant pastors one had died soon after admission, one had been sent to Caithness after the riot, one had had a nervous breakdown and one had lost his faith. As Colonel Laker remarked to Dr. Ottershaw during a visit to the palace, the flock was quite untended. A usable German pastor had been applied for, but sane, devout non-Nazis were highly prized by their captors and the commandants tended to hang on to them. In the interim (proposed Colonel Laker) could the Bishop possibly send an English clergyman who could hold a service for the Grade A's and the few Grade B's who might deign to turn up? (It was assumed no Grade C would go near an English clergyman.) War Office permission had been sought, and in these difficult circumstances a refusal was not anticipated.

Since the other Archdeacon, Babbington-French, was still saying that the only good German was a dead German, I was asked, just as I had always feared, to play Daniel in this den of German lions.

I hated it. I did my best, but my best seemed abysmal, and I found it hard to bear the humiliation of having my weakness for pastoral work so brutally exposed. Here I could no longer hide behind my talent for administration; it no longer mattered that I was a successful archdeacon, because now I was in a situation which required a missionary, someone with the guts to fight for Christianity right in the front line. There were times at the beginning when I used to be physically sick before I visited the camp. Could any reaction have been more cowardly and inadequate? I despised myself. Later I fought off the nausea but used to shiver from head to toe. Revolting! I continued to despise myself. Later still I conquered the shivers and stopped wasting emotional energy despising myself, but I went on thinking what hell it was to be quite such a failure. I felt as if my nose was being repeatedly rubbed in the mud.

Eventually to my relief a new German pastor turned up, but he proved useless and Colonel Laker out of kindness transferred him to Featherstone Park, the camp which had just begun to specialise in retraining the German clergy; after their years as Nazi soldiers even the good men tended to be disorientated and demoralised, no matter how much they wanted to return to their calling. Again the camp on Starbury Plain was without a pastor. The Commandant asked me to keep calling. The Bishop asked me to keep calling. The War Office extended my pass. There was no way out.

I slogged on.

After a while I got involved with the men and didn't mind so much. The Grade A's in fact became very civil and as the war drew to a close the Grade B's began to abandon their sullen neutrality. Finally when the war ended I found myself even talking to the Grade C's, not only the ones who tried to commit suicide but the ones who went mad, clinging to the belief that the German surrender was a lie, a product of the Allies' propaganda machine. But as the British pored over the photographs of the cheering crowds in Whitehall, of the Royal Family on the balcony of Buckingham Palace, of the great London landmarks floodlit after six years of darkness, of the service of Thanksgiving at St. Paul's, all the Germans were shown pictures of their ruined cities, the captured U-boats, the vast enclosures of prisoners and the surrender at Lüneburg Heath. Arrangements were also made for them to see film of the concentration camps. The Grade C's said the film had been made in Hollywood. The Grade B's were silent. Only the Grade A's, it seemed to me, could make any attempt, no matter how inadequate, to articulate the sheer pulverising horror of being German in that May of 1945.

"So it's finished," said my favourite, Hoffenberg, a very plain young man, awkward and ungainly but with a quick mind which deserved a university education. "Führer, Fatherland, Fantasy—all finished, nothing left, nothing but ruins and shame and guilt and hopelessness—no, don't try to console me, Mr. Aysgarth! We're in the darkness where your Christian light doesn't shine, and there's no Englishman alive who could possibly understand how we feel."

I said only: "Aren't you forgetting there's one Englishman who always understands? Who wants to go to Germany as soon as possible to preach the Christian message of hope in the ruins of Berlin? Who's dedicated himself to the task of helping the German churches take their place in a reconstructed Europe? Who speaks out again and again for suffering people, regardless of their nationality, in a world ravaged and brutalised by war?"

Hoffenberg shed a very small, very pathetic tear. I hated this side of my ministry. The sight of a man overcome by emotion always makes me want to bolt in the opposite direction, but of course I stayed with Hoffenberg, and at last I heard his simple answer: "Who else but the Bishop of Chichester? Who else but George Bell?"

By 1945 Bell was the most famous churchman in Europe. He was the man whom the politicians found intolerable but whom no civilised democracy could afford to silence; he was the voice of conscience and humanity, the voice of an idealism which no horror could ever obliterate and no evil could ever destroy. Passed over for the Bishopric of London in 1939, he was rejected for the Archbishopric of Canterbury when William Temple died unexpectedly in 1944. "Bell should go to Canterbury," I had said to Dr. Ottershaw, but we had both known it would never happen. Bell had disqualified himself long since by criticising the Government whenever they found it politic to ride roughshod over Christian principles in the pursuit of victory, and in the February of 1944 he had driven the final nail into the coffin which contained his hopes of future preferment. With a courage which I had found almost inconceivable he had risen to his feet in the House of Lords to condemn the Government's policy of saturation bombing and remind the nation yet again of the other Germany which existed beyond the swastikas: the Germany of the persecuted, the suffering and the innocent. Bell was doggedly anti-Nazi, but no one was more mindful that not all Germans were Nazis and that Nazism itself was transcended by the brotherhood of man.

"Bell's wasting his breath," I said tersely to Dr. Ottershaw after Bell had committed professional suicide by condemning the policy of saturation bombing. "No one wants to be reminded of the other Germany—when one country's fighting another country to the death it can't afford to see the enemy as anything but an evil monolith."

"Then isn't it all the more important for our moral survival," said Dr. Ottershaw gently, "that someone should remind us innocent people are dying in Germany as well as in England?"

But I was too confused about Bell to reply. Indeed sometimes my feelings seemed so intolerably complex that I could not even read his speeches in *The Times.* However—and this was very strange—I found I could always talk about him to my Germans. After all, whenever I entered that camp I ceased to be the successful Archdeacon obliged to avoid discussions of controversial bishops, and as I struggled, just like any other ordinary unknown chaplain, to communicate with my flock I would use Bell as a Trojan horse to penetrate the hostile citadel of their minds. Here at last I could confess my admiration for Bell's courage; here at last I no longer had to suffer in agonising silence whenever he was battered by the forces of antagonism which he inevitably unleashed.

"Here's a great man speaking for humanity!" I would declare with passion to my Germans, although later that same day I could only bring myself to say offhandedly to Dr. Ottershaw: "It's such a pity Bell will never be more than Bishop of a dull little town in Sussex."

"Ah!" said Dr. Ottershaw at once. "But all the persecuted victims of the Nazis care nothing for the internal politics of the Church, do they? They can't spell Canterbury and they've never heard of York, but every one of them's heard of Chichester—and every one of them talks of George Bell." He paused before adding mildly: "It's a question of values, isn't it? Whenever I read one of George's speeches I can always imagine him saying to himself like Luther: 'Here I stand! I can do no other.' "

"Of course—better that he should stand up for his beliefs and remain in Chichester than keep his mouth shut and go to Canterbury," I said at once, anxious that my superior should not find my values wanting, but privately, to my shame, I hoped I would never be trapped in a position where I had to pass up a great prize in order to echo the famous words of Martin Luther. I knew then exactly why Bell could wreck my equilibrium with such ease. It was as if he held up a mirror to me, and whenever I glanced in that glass I saw how far I fell short of his outstanding spiritual power. This insight was so painful that sometimes I longed to smash the glass by whole-heartedly condemning him in public, but I never did. Outside the camp I merely continued my policy of keeping silent about him as far as I could while I struggled with my conflicting emotions, and towards the end of that May in 1945 it was a relief to turn aside from him at last in order to concentrate on my marriage.

By V-E Day the preparations for my wedding were well advanced. I had expected war-time shortages to reduce the dimensions of the society wedding which Dido demanded, but her detestable father, reaching deep into his pocket and using his influence to surmount the difficulties caused by rationing, confounded me by plotting a celebration of almost pre-war sumptuousness. I could sense his relief that his youngest daughter was finally getting off the shelf, but I became increasingly worried about the prospect of a flashy wedding and feared it might raise disapproving eyebrows among the churchmen who mattered. Finally I was so concerned that I confided my anxiety to Dr. Ottershaw.

"But my dear Neville," he exclaimed warmly without a second's hesitation, "how can anyone hold you responsible for the fact that Dido's local church happens to be St. Mary's Mayfair? And how can anyone expect you to restrain Mr. Tallent from running wild afterwards at Claridges?"

This generous approach to the revels reassured me, but as soon as I had stopped worrying about the churchmen who mattered, I found myself worrying—not for the first time—what my children would think of their father's extraordinary transformation into a society bridegroom.

It was a subject which greatly disturbed me.

7

SINCE my first meeting with her, Dido had always taken care to stay away from Starbridge during the school holidays. At first I had not realised this absence was deliberate; because of war-time circumstances it was hardly surprising that our long courtship had been conducted mostly by letter. Later, when I realised she was avoiding the children I had raised the matter with her, but she had always insisted that the meeting should wait until we became engaged. She had reasoned that because the children were deterring her from agreeing to marry me, any meeting would affect her ability to consider the problem with rational detachment.

At first I accepted this decision but when I came to suspect that Dido was merely using the children as an acceptable excuse to postpone marriage, I realised that her determination to avoid a meeting was rooted in her fear of failure: she was afraid the children would compare her unfavourably with their mother and dislike her. I sympathised with this fear, which did indeed represent an unpalatable reality, so I never attempted to force a meeting, but when we became engaged in early March I at once invited her to the vicarage to see the younger children. Sandy was the one child she had met, since he was young enough to be always at home during her rare visits to Starbridge, but Primrose, who was now approaching her eighth birthday, attended a day school in the Close and had been easier for Dido to avoid.

The meeting appeared to be a success. Dido departed in good spirits and Sandy commented graciously that it would be nice to have a real mother again, just like everyone else.

"She won't be your mother," said Primrose, "and besides, everyone knows stepmothers are always perfectly horrid."

My heart sank. This was exactly the reaction Dido and I had both feared. "I'm surprised you should say that, Primrose," I said, knowing I could not let the remark pass without censure but taking care to use my mildest voice. "Since Dido was so anxious to be friendly, I think you're being a little unkind."

Primrose, unaccustomed to any word of criticism from me, promptly burst into tears. But worse was to come. The next day, before visiting James at his prep school in Salisbury, I travelled to Winchester to break the news of my impending marriage to Christian and Norman. I took them out to lunch. Naturally I had planned the entire meeting with military precision. The main course was allocated to a conversation about life at school. Then as soon as I had given the order for pudding to the waitress, I embarked on the speech which I had carefully prepared and memorised. For perhaps thirty seconds all went well. Then the metaphorical curtain tried to rise. If I had been one of those misguided people who believe in spiritualism I would have thought that Grace's ghost had joined us at the table.

I broke off. The two boys, curiously alike in their resemblance to my father, regarded me with an unflawed politeness. Somehow I managed to drag the curtain down again but to my fury I could feel myself blushing. "Good heavens, what a hash I'm making of this!" I exclaimed, trying to hide my agonised confusion beneath a burst of jovial bonhomie. "The truth is I'm so excited that I hardly know whether I'm coming or going!"

They both smiled courteously and waited in silence for me to continue.

"Well," I said, "possibly you may be quite surprised that I wish to remarry. In fact you may well be very surprised indeed. But it's really better for a clergyman to be married."

"You've already said that, Father," said Norman.

"Ah yes, so I have." I finally found the correct place in my script. Taking a deep breath, I declared: "Nothing, of course, will ever alter the fact that your mother and I enjoyed sixteen years of the most perfect married life. In my eyes she was the most wonderful woman in the world—and that explains why I now feel I must marry someone quite different. I wouldn't want my second wife to impinge in any way on such cherished memories."

They continued to look at me in silence. Then Norman stole a glance at Christian and Christian idly began to examine his fingernails.

"Dido has many fine qualities," I said as I watched Christian's expressionless face, "and she's very anxious to be friends with you. It is my earnest hope—" I broke off again. That sounded too pompous. Unfortunately prepared speeches so often do. "I hope very much that you'll like her," I resumed rapidly. "She may feel a little awkward with us all at first, but I know I can rely on you boys to act like gentlemen and try hard to make her feel at home in our family."

"Of course, Father," said Christian. Abandoning the examination of his fingernails, he turned to Norman and said: "Well, what are we waiting for? We must behave like gentlemen and offer Father our best wishes."

"Oh yes," said Norman. "Yes, of course."

"Thank you," I said. "That's very good of you both." But in the small, deadly pause which followed I heard Christian complaining in my memory about the unreality of our conversations.

I made a great effort. Looking him straight in the eyes, I said: "You should take it as a great compliment to your mother, Christian, that I find I can no longer live without a woman in my home."

"Oh, I quite understand that living without a woman must be very awkward for a clergyman."

I suddenly felt much too hot. "I'm not talking about sex."

"No, of course not. You never do."

I started to sweat. As the knot of tension began to thicken in the pit of my stomach I somehow managed to say in my most neutral voice: "I don't thunder on the subject of sex like a Victorian paterfamilias because it's my firm belief that if a boy's been given a Christian upbringing and set a good example he should be able to work out for himself exactly where he stands on matters relating to personal conduct. Now—" I had run out of breath. I had to pause for air. "Now, if I may return to the subject under discussion, I was saying—"

"You were saying that Mother is quite irreplaceable but you've made the decision to replace her."

I was finally silenced.

"Well, that's fine," said Christian, effortlessly self-possessed. "We wish you well and we're quite willing to be friends with Miss Tallent. But just don't expect *us* to treat her as a substitute for Mother. Mothers, unlike wives, are quite irreplaceable."

I realised the conversation had to be terminated at once. "I don't think you quite understand my point of view, Christian," I said as the waitress arrived with the pudding I knew we would be unable to eat, "but I trust I'll be able to clarify it later. Meanwhile may I say how much I appreciate your willingness to accept the situation in a friendly spirit and how convinced I am that everything's going to work out well in the end."

We toyed with our pudding. I made another short speech about the wedding. Both boys nodded at intervals and assumed expressions of courteous interest. At last, as Christian began to examine his fingernails again, I paid the bill, took the boys back to school and escaped.

Fortunately I had my car with me, and so despite the fact that I was wearing a clerical suit I was able to smoke a cigarette as soon as I could halt in a secluded spot. Winchester was not too far from the diocesan border and so there had been no extravagant use of extra petrol coupons. As I smoked I tried to work out why Christian had upset me so much. Perhaps I merely resented the fact that my talent for debate, a talent which had earned me the nickname of "The Sledgehammer" long ago at the Oxford Union, had been used against me with such a devastating result. "You were saying that Mother is quite irreplaceable but you've made the decision to replace her . . ." That was demolition work at its best, a sledgehammer's tour de force. One had to admire his forensic skill, but on the other hand Christian was not supposed to pound my carefully crafted speeches to pieces, just as he was not supposed to make awkward remarks about sex. Christian was supposed to be perfect. Christian *was* perfect, but if he was perfect why had he deliberately made me look hypocritical and foolish? I felt psychologically bruised in a way not easy to define. I only knew I felt upset when my prizes deviated from my expectations and assumed an unauthorised life of their own.

I lit a second cigarette as I made a new attempt to regain my equilibrium. Was I in fact such a hypocrite as Christian had made me appear? No. I had genuinely loved Grace. The fact that after many years of marriage I had begun to outgrow her (or so it now seemed) could not in any way invalidate the reality of all the happiness we had shared. Thus although I was now in a new phase of my life, a phase which required a wife like Dido, I could talk without hypocrisy of the cherished memories of my first marriage.

This concept of the new phase, as I suddenly realised, was the key to rebutting Christian's implied criticisms. The fact was that I had become a different person. As the old Neville I could say with perfect truth that Grace had been irreplaceable, but as the new Neville I could talk without difficulty of replacing her. Contrary to what Christian had supposed, I was not being hypocritical. I was merely trying to express a peculiarly complex truth. Paradox demolished, problem solved. Heaving a vast sigh of relief I stubbed out my cigarette and reached for the ignition key.

Yet halfway back to Starbridge I thought: Why, after all those years of marriage, did I change into someone else? And why did I change into the person I've apparently changed into? And why did this stranger decide that he had to have a wife like Dido, who in so many ways is such an unsuitable wife for a clergyman?

I had to stop the car again, and as I lit my third cigarette I suddenly saw my obsession as others saw it—as extraordinary, as incomprehensible, as utterly out of character. It was at that moment, nearly three years after my first meeting with Dido, that it finally occurred to me to wonder what, underneath all the tempestuous trappings of grand passion, was really going on.

No answer presented itself.

Then it occurred to me that in fact I was more than two persons. I was the old Neville, the new Neville and the Neville who was now standing outside them both and wondering whether I was demented. It also occurred to me that the new Neville had not arrived in the world out of the blue at the Bishop's dinner-party, but had in fact been around for a long time, living with the old Neville, while the third Neville somehow kept the peace between them. But who exactly was this third Neville who sat smoking a cigarette in a secluded corner of the diocese and regarding the new Neville and the old Neville with detachment? And with these three Nevilles all milling around in my consciousness, who on earth was "Neville" anyway?

It was time to pull down the curtain before the men in white coats arrived to remove me to the nearest lunatic asylum. Morbid introspection was an activity I always found inexcusable; I entirely disapprove of people wasting time by agonising over themselves when they could be out in the world making themselves useful, and besides, I was convinced that so long as I went on working hard and winning the prizes nothing too dreadful could happen to me. The more prizes one collected the more secure one felt, and now that one of the greatest prizes I had ever encountered was finally within my grasp, I was sure I stood on the brink of unparalleled happiness and good fortune.

Six weeks later I married Dido at St. Mary's Mayfair and the grand disaster of my second marriage began.

8

I HAVE now reached the point in my life when I almost committed adultery. Well, perhaps I haven't quite reached it. But I hardly think, in the light of what I have already written, I shall surprise anyone when I reveal that the honeymoon was a catastrophe. Dido was unable to face consummating the marriage and I was unable to decide what to do next. A clergyman can never justify rape, no matter how desperate he feels on his honeymoon, but so desperate did I become that I even considered rape as a serious possibility. Fortunately reason gained the upper hand and I realised our marriage would have no chance of survival unless she gave herself to me of her own free will. Dido might chatter blithely about her approval of masterful men, but I thought she would be shocked to the core and permanently alienated from me if I were to demonstrate the dark side of a masterful masculine nature.

In shame I stopped brooding on violent solutions and told myself I should see the consummation of the marriage as yet another prize, something to be won by guile, not grabbed by brute force. Immediately I felt better, and I was still telling myself I would succeed in bringing the honeymoon to a triumphant conclusion, when Dido ran away.

We had been staying at a smart Scottish hunting lodge on her father's estate, but as the tension between us increased, the lodge's romantic isolation had become so oppressive that Dido had suggested we withdraw to Edinburgh. The day after our arrival I had left the hotel early in order to attend the Sunday celebration of Holy Communion, and on my return I had discovered her disappearance. On the bedside table I found a note which read:

Darling Stephen,

I've gone to stay with Merry for a few days in order to sort myself out. Please *don't* try to follow me because I can't think—I mean *think*—when you're breathing non-stop passion all over me. I'm afraid that our marriage wasn't one of your brighter ideas, was it? I should never have said yes, but you went on and on and on at me until I was too exhausted to say no. Do you think we could possibly agree to have a quiet tasteful little annulment and part good friends?

Love,
DIDO.

I sent her a telegram which declared: ABSOLUTELY NOT UNDER ANY CIRCUMSTANCES WHATSOEVER STOP I ADORE YOU STOP STEPHEN. Then I took the train home to Starbridge, announced to the world that Dido was visiting her gravely ill sister in Leicestershire, and tried to work out how I could save myself from ruin.

9

I WAS halfway through my third whisky—or was it my fourth?—when the telephone rang. I pounced on it. I was expecting a call from my sister-in-law.

"Hullo?" I said hopefully into the mouthpiece.

"Neville, it's Alex. Thank God you're back from your honeymoon."

I was so disappointed not to hear Merry's affected society drawl informing me that Dido was coming home that at first I failed to register the identity of my caller.

"Alex Jardine," he said as the silence threatened to become embarrassing, and added with his familiar caustic humour: "I know we haven't been on speaking terms for two years, but I hope I wasn't flattering myself when I assumed you'd remember me."

"My dear Alex!" Belatedly I struggled to pull myself together. "Forgive me for being so slow—what a welcome surprise to hear your voice! How are you?"

"Well, as a matter of fact I happen to be dying. I trust you're not similarly inconvenienced." He paused, but when I was too shocked to reply he added tersely: "You won't have forgotten how I hate the telephone, so let's keep this conversation brief. I'm sorry about that idiotic quarrel. I need to see you urgently. I've only got a month to live—perhaps even less—and there are matters which have got to be discussed. How soon can you come to Stoneyford?"

Without a second's hesitation I said: "I'm on my way."

VI

"I am not easily shocked: school and the classics and a normal curiosity and, I hope, an abnormal imagination had given me a wide acquaintance with aspects of life and sex usually taboo: facts are facts, and I have no wish to run in blinkers."

CHARLES E. RAVEN
A WANDERER'S WAY

I

MY promise that I would leave immediately for Alex's house at Stoneyford proved to be too optimistic; I was short of petrol coupons, there was no convenient train at that hour, I had to delegate various matters to my curates, my housekeeper had to be warned of my impending departure, and the younger children had to be reassured that although I was disappearing into the blue for the second time in two weeks I would only be absent for a day. It was not until the morning after Alex's telephone call that I was finally able to walk to the station and catch the fast train to Oxford.

By this time I was in such a muddle about Dido that even Alex's imminent death could almost be welcomed as a diversion. I was conscious of an enormous relief that I could temporarily ring down the curtain on my private chaos, and as I began to grapple with the knowledge that Alex was approaching the end of his life it occurred to me to wonder if his autobiography was finished. Then suddenly I was certain not only that he had completed it but that in consequence he had come to regard death as preferable to an empty life. Again the mystery of his misspent retirement confronted me, and sensing that I was on the brink of unravelling a tragedy which was as enigmatic as it was profound, I began to grieve at last for the friend I was to lose.

2

I SAW her as soon as I walked out of the station. She was sitting in the driving-seat of a black Morris and smoking a cigarette wedged into a black holder. From a distance it was impossible to tell she was my age, forty-three; she looked a sophisticated twenty-eight, cool, aloof and infinitely alluring. I was reminded at once of Greta Garbo in *Ninotchka.*

When she saw me she wound down the window and produced the famous chilly smile which had broken the chaplains' hearts in the old days at Starbridge when she had been employed as Carrie Jardine's companion, the smile which had prompted less susceptible males to refer to her as "the ice-maiden." Cocooned by my perfect marriage, I had judged Lyle Christie—Lyle Ashworth as she now was—to be a virgin engaged in a discreet passion for Carrie, but now, with my perfect marriage finished and my emotions rubbed raw by Dido's preposterous behaviour, I saw with blinding clarity that this *femme fatale,* gleaming in her smart white belted raincoat, was no stone-cold lesbian. Her wavy dark hair had a hot reddish tinge. Her eyes, which one of my former curates had called "soulful" and another had described as "sultry," were the colour of rich, luscious, utterly sinful dark chocolate; I was at once reminded of that golden moment in my youth when during a visit to the cinema I had watched Clara Bow oozing "It" as I sank my teeth into a sumptuous peppermint cream.

"Hullo," she said casually in a voice which would have stopped Attila the Hun dead in his tracks. "Get in."

I got in. As I closed the passenger door I managed to say lamely: "What a surprise!"

"I arrived yesterday. Carrie sent me a *cri du coeur* which I couldn't ignore."

"I'm glad to hear it. Considering Carrie treated you as a daughter I always thought your determination to prolong the estrangement was a great pity."

She had been on the point of turning the ignition key, but now she paused and gave me a look which would have turned steam to ice. "Do you usually dish out stinging criticism to someone who's in the midst of doing you a favour? If you can't be civil you can damn well get out and walk!"

"I'm sorry, I—"

"Anyway we ended the estrangement back in 1942. Dr. Jardine came to see me. I thought you knew."

"Yes, I did. Look, I do apologise—I'm afraid I'm rather on edge at the moment—"

"Later I met Carrie in London and made up the quarrel with her as well. I admit that until yesterday I hadn't seen either of the Jardines since 1942, but what with the ghastliness of war-time travel and my reluctance to leave the children—"

"Are the boys well?" I said, hoping to change the subject.

"I believe the word is 'high-spirited.' If I didn't have Nanny I'd be in a lunatic asylum."

We set off. She drove well, very well for a woman, and conveyed an impression of fluent ruthlessness which I found curiously exciting. I found myself casting surreptitious glances at her small fine-boned hands as they caressed the steering wheel and at her small elegant feet as they massaged the pedals. Her ankles and wrists were exquisite.

"How's your wife?" she said at last.

"Fine. Any news of your husband?"

"None." Her voice was bleak.

"I'm very sorry." Ashworth, taken prisoner at the fall of Tobruk, had been transferred from one camp to another in 1944 and since then there had been no word from him.

After a short drive we reached Stoneyford. It was an unspoilt village, picturesque and compact, and the Jardines lived in a small Georgian house opposite the church. Lyle halted the car at the gate, and as we walked up the flagstone path through the front garden the elder of the two Ashworth boys opened the door. He was about seven years old, small and fine-boned like his mother but without her good looks. He had dark hair which stood up in the wrong places and eyes the colour of pale mud.

"Hullo, Charley!" I said with a smile. "I didn't realise you were here!"

"Mummy was able to bring me because I'm not sick on trains as Michael is." He beamed at me. I had never formed the habit of calling regularly on the Ashworths, but occasionally when I was visiting their area on business I looked in as a courtesy, and I had had a soft spot for Charley ever since he had confided to me that he wanted to be a clergyman when he grew up.

"Carrie's pottering in the back garden," said Lyle to me. "We'll leave her for the moment. Come in and see Dr. Jardine straight away." She glanced at her watch. "He's timed his drugs so that he'll be at his best now."

"What exactly—"

"Cancer of the stomach. This way, please." Leading me into Alex's study she announced abruptly: "He's here, Bishop," and withdrew at once to the hall.

A very old man, shrunken and faded, a waxen wraith of his former self, was sitting in a high-backed armchair by the fireplace. As always he was dressed in smart clothes, but now the material of his expensive suit hung on him in folds. I found it almost unbearably distressing that in a dogged attempt to cling to the debonair stylishness which had marked the high noon of his episcopate he was again wearing a carnation in his buttonhole.

"Alex." There's little room for social pleasantries when a man's dying. Clasping his dry cold hand in mine, I sat down silently at his side.

"My dear Neville," he said, "how very good it is to see you again and how very kind it was of you to respond so quickly to my summons."

"I wish you'd sent for me earlier."

"I fooled myself into thinking I'd get better. Now let's not mention the quarrel—let's just put it behind us and make the most of this lucid interval of mine. There are certain things I have to tell you—no, don't be alarmed! This is no deathbed confession. We'll leave that sort of fandango to the Papists. But I want to ask a favour of you, and you won't understand my request unless I explain one or two mysteries first."

"Mysteries?"

"Well, let's start with the mystery which I know has troubled you—the mystery of my idle retirement. The truth is I couldn't have worked as a clergyman in any capacity. I'd lost my faith."

I stared at him. Automatically I said: "I don't believe you."

"Oh, I've recovered it during these last months of illness! Let me hasten to assure you that you haven't been summoned to minister to an unbeliever, but back in 1937 I felt I was an apostate. There was no heart trouble. I resigned because it was morally, not physically, impossible for me to continue as a bishop."

But I could only shake my head. "No," I said. "No, that's not credible. You had the kind of religious sincerity which can't be faked. If you'd lost your faith I'd have known."

"I tell you I lost it! And I tell you that you had no idea!"

"But I was so close to you in 1937—"

"We know so little about even those who are closest to us," said Alex. "We're all mysteries to one another—and often we're profound mysteries to ourselves."

"That's not true." I was at once deeply disturbed. "I know myself through and through—and you know me through and through as well—"

"No," said Alex. "I realised as soon as you embarked on your pursuit of Miss Tallent—Mrs. Aysgarth, I should say—that I knew nothing about you at all. However, let's keep to the subject under discussion. I'm telling you that I lost my faith and you've got to accept that this is true."

"But why did you lose it, Alex—*why?* I'm sorry, I do want to believe you, but—"

"I discovered that the Modernist road leads eventually into a void. If you pursue certain radical approaches far enough you end up with nothing—and that, of course, is why the Roman Catholics suppressed Modernism so brutally. They knew it was the gospel of the Devil, not the gospel of God."

With shock I realised he was mentally unhinged, although whether this was as the result of his illness or of a spiritual breakdown or of the two combined, it was impossible to discern. As I struggled to beat back my horror I could only protest feebly: "Alex, surely you're not going to start talking like a nineteenth-century Evangelical!"

"Oh, I know there's no room for the Devil in that cosy ivory tower which the Modernists inhabit! But the Devil exists, I know that. He's a force. Evil's a force, sin's a force—and we're all tainted by that force, we're all sinners, we're all under judgement—"

"Alex, this is the neo-orthodoxy of Karl Barth! I can't believe a Liberal like you could have succumbed to Crisis Theology!" But as I spoke I was remembering that his father had undergone a mental breakdown which had assumed the form of a rabid fundamentalism, and abruptly I realised I had to alter my course. It was futile to expect someone who was not only dying but mentally impaired to conduct a rational argument. Adopting my most soothing voice, I said: "Well, never mind all that. I'm only relieved that by the grace of God you've managed to regain your faith, and I do urge you not to become so obsessed with sin that you overlook the forgiveness Christ grants all sinners who repent."

"If you respond to my request I'll finally be able to believe myself forgiven."

"What request?"

"That brings me to the second disclosure I must make. Are you ready? Brace yourself. It's about Lyle. She's my daughter."

"Your daughter?" I could only assume he was raving.

"Oh, for heaven's sake stop looking at me as if I'm certifiable!" cried Alex with such a healthy irritation that I was at once driven to doubt my diagnosis of insanity. "She was the result of a final fling I enjoyed not long before I was ordained—the woman was already engaged to a soldier named Christie but he was away somewhere in the Army and we were at one of those Edwardian house-parties where everyone visited everyone else after the lights were out—"

"My God." It says much for my stupefaction, as I started to believe him, that I forgot to substitute the acceptable exclamation "My goodness." "So that's why—"

"That's why there was such a strong bond between Lyle, Carrie and me. That's why Lyle stayed with us for ten years and why we always regarded her as a daughter. That's why we became so fatally possessive, an ill-assorted childless couple who had always longed for a child to unite them—"

"Yes, I see. Yes, of course—it all makes sense now. So when Ashworth wanted to marry Lyle—"

"We behaved atrociously, unable to bear the thought of being on our own again after enjoying a happy family life which had so miraculously alleviated our unsatisfactory marriage. In the circumstances was it surprising that Ashworth leapt to the conclusion that our emotional dependence on Lyle was thoroughly unwholesome and that we should keep out of her way in the future?" Alex sighed before adding unexpectedly: "The irony of it all was that I liked Ashworth so much. I only wish I could believe now that he'll come back from the war, but I don't think he will—and that leads me on to my big request. Neville, if he doesn't come back, could you see that those children are all right? Boys need a father. I'm not so worried about the little one, Michael—I can see him gliding successfully through life, just as Ashworth himself did before the war—but Charley . . . Charley's temperamental and sensitive, and life won't always be easy for him. If I knew there would be a man he could rely on—someone who'd give him a helping hand whenever life became intolerably difficult—"

"Say no more, Alex. I'll do all I can for both those boys, I promise."

"But especially Charley—"

"Especially Charley, yes."

Alex slumped exhausted into the depths of his chair. "Then he'll be all right," he said. "Thank God." And he added in a whisper: "That's a sign. That's forgiveness at last. 'Lord, now lettest thou thy servant depart in peace.' "

I leant forward, unsure if he wanted me to assume a professional role. "Alex, I know you made that remark about leaving deathbed confessions to the Papists, but would you like me to—"

"No, I won't ask you to celebrate Communion. The sands of time are running out on this interview, and it would be better to communicate later when I'm not distracted by pain . . . But perhaps the General Confession wouldn't be inappropriate in the circumstances."

"Of course." I gave him the lead of "Almighty and Most Merciful Father," and then we recited together the beautiful words from the Book of Common Prayer. Afterwards when I had pronounced the formal words of absolution and benediction, I saw Alex was greatly moved.

"I feel justified now," he said, using the word in its technical religious sense. "I've got the faith to believe that by grace I stand right with God. Call the nurse for the morphia—no, wait! How selfish I've been, thinking only of myself . . . How's your wife?"

"Oh, she's fine. Absolutely fine."

"And you're happy?"

"Couldn't be happier!"

"I was so frightened that you'd marry the wrong woman, just as I did. Such a mistake, my stepmother Ingrid always said it would be a mistake . . . You remember me talking of my stepmother, don't you? My father didn't really love her. It was my mother he loved, and after she died he only wanted a housekeeper who'd go to bed with him. Ingrid told me once how hurt she'd been when she finally realised that . . . Oh, how I loved Ingrid! She protected me from my father, got me an education, made sacrifice after sacrifice for my sake . . . but then the truest love thinks nothing of the self. Looking back now I can see so clearly how much she meant to me, just as I can see so clearly how in my eyes she reduced all other women to mere sources of sexual satisfaction. So she was a malign as well as a benign influence on my life—but that's a reflection of the existence we live on earth, isn't it? Beneath all the goodness lies the malignant force of evil . . . Poor Neville, I'm embarrassing you again—put yourself out of your agony by calling the nurse to put me out of mine!"

After the injection had been administered I helped him lie down on the makeshift bed in the corner of the room, and when the nurse had departed he said casually, as if the pain had already begun to ease: "And talking of Ingrid, I must just issue a word of advice about my autobiography: Don't bother to read it. It's all true and yet it's all false, a preposterous literary paradox. I never disclose how much I loved Ingrid. I never disclose that my marriage was a failure. I never disclose my true relationship with Lyle. I never disclose how much I hated my father for driving my elder sister mad with his incest. I never disclose—"

"*Incest!* I'm sorry, obviously I misheard you. For a moment I thought you said—"

"I did. He committed incest with her over a period of months when Ingrid was keeping house for me at the start of my career. After my sister was admitted to an asylum Ingrid found out what had been happening and went back to him before he could start on my younger sister. Oh, nobody knows the half of what goes on in people's lives, all the sin and the suffering, the mess and the misery, the souls screaming and writhing in an endless hell of dereliction and pain—"

"But Alex—"

"Oh, I'm sorry, I forgot. You have to have your happy ending with everyone living in perfect bliss for ever more. My God, no wonder Karl Barth moved in after the First War to grind the Liberal Protestants into the dust! There's something almost criminal about such innocent idealism when the whole world's screaming in agony!"

"My dear Alex, no Liberal Protestant would deny that terrible things go on in this world, but"—I was so shocked I hardly knew what I was saying—"but one must never give up hope, never—the hope that we can work for a better world—the belief in Christ the Redeemer—the knowledge that God was in Christ reconciling the world to himself, the knowledge that suffering can be commuted and transformed, the knowledge that all sin and evil can be overcome—"

"Oh, yes, yes, yes," said Alex impatiently, "that's all true too."

"But when the Liberal Protestants and the neo-orthodox Protestants oppose each other so violently, how can their theologies both be true?"

"All the most profound truths lie in paradox—and death itself is a paradox, the end yet the beginning, all quite indescribable but all utterly real—another paradox—and in the end the ultimate reality—that ultimate prize, as you might say—lies beyond myth, beyond metaphor, beyond symbol, beyond analogy, beyond words, beyond the breath of life itself . . . Ah, the morphia's working at last, it takes longer to work nowadays . . . Sometimes when it works I see Ingrid. She's a symbol, of course, a symbol of Love, of Christ, of God . . . so in the end even the hallucinations are real—another paradox—and where there's paradox there's eternity, because beyond all the paradoxes lies the eternal truth." He closed his eyes. Then suddenly he said very clearly: "Oh God, how we all lie to one another!" and sighed with a profound resignation.

They were the last words I ever heard him say. It seemed such a bizarre final statement from such a famous fighter for truth.

3

WHEN I emerged from the study Carrie Jardine was waiting in the hall. To my relief she was calm; she thanked me for coming, asked after Dido and said she did so hope the weather had kept fine for the honeymoon. Fortunately before this banal conversation could be prolonged we were interrupted by her current companion, a bossy female called Miss Jenkins, who announced that the gardener wanted to know where to plant the new rose-bush. Escaping into the drawing-room I found Lyle, gliding around in a slinky black frock and a pair of very high-heeled shoes. Forgetting Garbo in *Ninotchka,* I began to toy with my memories of Marlene Dietrich.

"Well?" she said, halting abruptly. "How did it go?"

"Fine," I said, but then realising that this comment could only sound ridiculous in the circumstances I added: "But of course he's in a bad way and sometimes he didn't make much sense."

"Did he tell you about me?"

"Yes." I felt embarrassed enough to look away. "That was the one point in the conversation which rang true. But as for the rest . . . To be frank I found it hard to judge where fantasy ended and truth began."

"What's so unusual about that? If you ask me we spend most of our lives floating about in a fog of illusion and very rarely glimpse reality at all."

I was still so shattered by the interview that I found myself unable to control my impatience. "That's a well-known point of view, I admit," I said curtly, "but in my opinion it's grossly exaggerated. I for one don't spend most of my life floating around in a fog. I move clear-eyed through a well-defined landscape."

"Yes, I always did think you were revoltingly smug beneath that prim exterior. How that nice first wife of yours put up with you for all those years I really can't imagine."

I was so stunned, not only by the insults but by the spectacular nonchalance with which they were delivered, that for a moment I was speechless. Then I said: "It's a pity that as a clergyman I can't call you by the name you deserve," and walked out, slamming the door.

Having paused in the hall to take three deep breaths to restore my equilibrium, I plunged into the dining-room in the hope of downing a quick drink before lunch, but my plan to raid the sideboard was foiled. The little boy was sitting at the dining-room table. He was writing with a much-chewed pencil on a large sheet of notepaper.

"Hullo," I said, trying not to sound annoyed. "What are you up to?"

"I'm writing to Daddy. Just because the Germans won't let him answer our letters any more, it doesn't mean he can't read them. I'm telling him I've got a Union Jack to wave when he comes home."

"Ah." There was a pause while I forgot the bitch in the drawing-room and focused my full attention on the child before me. I felt as if I were seeing him for the first time, and I could now clearly detect the resemblance to his grandfather. It lay not only in the wide mouth but in the eyes, which were no longer, so it seemed to me, the colour of pale mud but of dark golden sand.

"I've got the best daddy in the world," said Charley, writing busily, "and when I grow up I want to be just like him."

This remark, curiously moving in its extreme innocence and passionate sincerity, reduced me to silence. I could only wonder if any of my boys had ever paid me such a compliment when talking to a stranger. Certainly none of them had yet expressed an ambition to be a clergyman. I kept hoping Christian would bring up the subject but he never did, and suddenly I felt jealous of Charles Ashworth as I stood looking at his son. A second later the envy had vanished, swallowed up by my non-combatant's shame that I should be safe in England while Ashworth was lost in Europe, and at once I found myself praying fiercely that he might still be alive.

Returning to the hall I met the bitch as she emerged from the drawing-room.

"Still in a huff?" she enquired. "I thought Christians were supposed to turn the other cheek when they were insulted."

"Are you having the insufferable nerve to lecture me on my Christian duty?"

"Oh, for the love of God, stop being so priggish and stupid! Haven't you any sensitivity at all? Can't you, a clergyman—a *clergyman,* for heaven's sake!—see that I'm absolutely *in extremis* and make allowances for me?"

"I'm sorry, I—"

"Oh yes, yes, yes, you're *in extremis* too—we're all *in extremis*—so let's have a truce and at least make *some* effort to behave as if we're not both itching to slap each other!"

It suddenly occurred to me how much I would enjoy administering a hearty slap. Very quickly, killing the fantasy at birth, I said mildly: "Any chance of celebrating the truce with a quick drink before lunch?"

"There's claret and sherry on the dining-room sideboard—help yourself. I'd better go and rescue Carrie from that ghastly companion."

Little Charley scampered into the hall. "Mummy, read my letter to Daddy and see if you like it!"

Instantly I made a second beeline for the decanters on the dining-room sideboard. I had just realised that I was starting to think the unthinkable—and the unthinkable, of course, was that Lyle was very much prettier than Dido and, at this tormented stage of my life, at least ten times more desirable.

4

AFTER lunch Lyle drove me back to the station at Oxford. We travelled in silence. It was only when she halted the car that she said: "By the way, did he mention that he wants you to conduct the funeral? The request's in his will."

I was greatly taken aback. Unless the circumstances are exceptional, a clergyman should avoid conducting the funerals of those closest to him. Apart from the obvious fact that his own grief will impair his ability to conduct the service professionally, he will be in no fit state to offer an adequate pastoral sympathy to the mourners.

"I personally think it's a rotten idea," Lyle was saying, "and quite unfair on you, but the trouble is he's drifted apart from the clerics he used to know, he doesn't get on with the local vicar and he's obsessed with the idea of having what he calls 'a decent Protestant funeral.' You know how opposed he is to Anglo-Catholicism, and he feels you're the one man he can trust to do the job properly."

"Poor Alex."

"Yes, one can only hope for his sake that the funeral's sooner rather than later . . . Oh, and if you'd find it more convenient to stay overnight in Stoneyford after the funeral, don't waste money on a hotel. There'll be room for you at the house."

"Thanks. That'll please my bank manager," I said and managed to extract myself from the car without offering her my hand, but once physical contact had been avoided I felt I could afford a smile. "Sorry about all the friction," I added. "Nice seeing you again. Good luck"—I remembered just in time that I was a clergyman—"and God bless you."

"Thanks. 'Bye." She roared off, leaving me inhaling a cloud of exhaust fumes.

On the train I resolved that as soon as I knew the date of the funeral I would book a room at a hotel in Oxford, but then I thought of my overdrawn bank account, my sheaf of unpaid bills and my bank manager's increasingly lugubrious expression. I also pictured myself after the funeral: worn out and fit only for an early night. Why was I so hell-bent on locking myself up in a hotel in order to preserve my admittedly dog-eared but fundamentally indestructible chastity? I didn't even like the bitch, and besides I was incapable of gross misbehaviour because good clergymen never behaved grossly. In shying away from a hospitable invitation I was being both idiotic and irrational; in fact I could only conclude, as I resolved not to waste money on a hotel, that poor Alex's unhinged disclosures had driven me too to the brink of lunacy.

5

AS soon as I walked through the front door of my new home in the Close I looked hopefully around the hall for a glimpse of luggage, but there was no suitcase in sight, and upstairs in the main bedroom, which faced the Cathedral, no one lay arranged in an attitude of repentance on the virgin double bed. Returning downstairs I grabbed the telephone in my study and put through a call to Merry in Leicestershire.

"Stephen! I was going to ring you this evening—look, it's going to be all right, but she still needs more time. Can you keep saying I'm dying or is everyone starting to get suspicious?"

"No one suspects anything at the moment, but—"

"Thank God. Now don't despair—I've been hammering away on your behalf and I'm sure I'm going to win. When I threatened to betray her to Father she had to face up to the fact that if she makes a mess of this marriage she'll be labelled a complete and utter failure for the rest of her life by all the people who matter—my dear! The hysterics! She can't bear the idea of Father thinking her a failure, although why she should still care what he thinks I've no idea—personally I've long since given up all hope that he would ever see his daughters as anything but amusing little second-rate sons, but there we are, we all have our dreams, and if Dido wants to dream that one day she'll be as good as our brothers in Father's estimation, who's to say she's not entitled to her fantasy? Anyway, Stephen, keep telling everyone I'm at death's door, and I'll do my best to shovel her onto the train to Starbridge some time within the next week."

Having concluded the call I poured myself a stiff whisky to celebrate this news, but after a while I realised I was thinking not of Dido but of Alex and his extraordinary revelations. I was wondering how far the heavy doses of morphia had undermined his grasp of reality.

The curtain in my mind twitched as I thought of drugs, and for a second I heard my mother whispering in fear to Uncle Willoughby about the laudanum taken by my father, but then the curtain dropped abruptly, just as it always did when I found myself recalling that horrifying snatch of dialogue I had overheard, and I was able to think of Alex again. Surely the story of incest had been a drug-ridden fantasy! Terrible things could happen in families—as I knew all too well—but if Alex had been telling the truth, then not only did my experience of domestic tragedy bear no resemblance to his but the likeness suggested by our impoverished backgrounds was an illusion. I felt as if Alex had at a stroke rewritten my past relationship with him. I had believed that he was a man with whom I could identify myself, yet now it appeared he was someone who had come from a different planet.

As I thought of my own planet the curtain drifted idly upwards, but for once I made no attempt to stop it; the memory was benign, and in recalling it I could blot out the tragedy which had later overtaken us all. I saw my father opening one of the Beatrix Potter books; Willy and I could both read, but we enjoyed our father's evening visits to the nursery so much that we pretended we barely knew our alphabet. He liked to read to us. Sometimes we all acted the story and then we would wind up laughing so loudly that my mother, lying on her chaise-longue downstairs with her volume of Browning, would bang crossly on the ceiling with her walking-stick. "Your Pa's such a card!" our nurse Tabitha would say, laughing with us. Being illiterate she shared our pleasure in hearing my father read aloud.

Once when Willy and I had been washed, scrubbed, stuffed into our nightshirts and presented for our daily kiss, my mother had remarked to my father: "Don't you think those boys should be applying their brains to something more intellectually edifying than Miss Potter's anthropomorphic fantasies?" but my father had answered: "Time enough for that later," and winked at us. Later I had asked him: "What's anthropomorphic?" and he had said laughing: "Peter Rabbit in a blue coat!"

My father liked rabbits. He liked all animals. He was constantly filled with wonder by God's creation. "Look at the wild-flowers!" he would say to us on those fine summer Saturday afternoons when he took us for walks. "Look at the birds! And look how even the town looks beautiful from a distance, blending into the background of the hills . . . It's all a unity, you see. The things that we can touch—the landscape, the flowers, the animals—and the things which we can only hold in our minds—Beauty, Truth and Goodness—they're all a manifestation of God, all a unity, all one." Later he added: "It's a good world and getting better all the time. A very clever gentleman called Darwin proved that scientifically. Other very clever gentlemen, who should have known better, became upset and started saying science aimed to destroy religion, but of course they were wrong. Science is just another lens through which we look at God—and all the lenses are a unity. Beyond their dissimilarities they're all one."

My father had been speaking before the First War, when Liberal Protestant optimism was at its zenith, but I thought he would have clung to his religious interpretation of evolution despite mankind's twentieth-century regression into the barbarism of international tyranny and bloodshed. "Evolution demands wear and tear, even occasionally devastation and destruction," he had once said, "but as it's written in the Bible: 'All things work together for the good for them who love God.' " I tried to picture him abandoning his optimistic creed and sinking, like Alex, into a pessimistic outlook which so perfectly matched the pessimistic mood of the modern age, but I could only imagine him recoiling in horror, and suddenly as I pictured my father clinging to his cherished beliefs, I felt sure Alex had been lying when he had said he had lost his faith.

I examined my memory of the interview with care. I could accept, though with repugnance, that he might now feel genuinely drawn to express his faith in a morbid and depressing form of Protestantism; since his father had succumbed to a similar spiritual aberration it could be argued that in a time of stress the tug of heredity might have pulled Alex off the theological rails. I could also accept that he had spoken the truth about Lyle; that particular revelation certainly made sense of various minor mysteries, and although I knew Alex would never have fallen into any gross error since his ordination, I could well imagine him being tempted to sow a wild oat or two as a very young man. I could even accept that he might have been telling the truth about the incest, for unnatural evils did undoubtedly occur and Alex had always said his family life had been a nightmare. But what I could not accept, when all was said and done, was that he had ever been wholly estranged from his faith.

I knew more than most people about the nature of Alex's faith. Since I had been his protégé, we had had numerous theological discussions and he had spoken frankly to me about spiritual matters. His faith was Christocentric, based on a firm belief in the past, present and future reality of Jesus Christ as God Incarnate. As an intellectual churchman with Modernist leanings he might tinker with various theories about the Jesus of history; there would be various doubts, a benign agnosticism on certain matters, perhaps even an unorthodox theory or two. But no scholarly speculation on Christ's humanity would alter his opinion of Christ's divinity; or in other words, nothing would weaken his allegiance to the Christ of Eternity, the unique form of metaphor, mystery and timeless truth in which God had uniquely chosen to reveal himself to mankind. In Alex's opinion this vision of the Eternal Christ, born of the Jesus of history but transcending the mere historical life which could never be fully known, was indestructible unless someone proved beyond all doubt that Jesus had never existed. No serious scholar doubted Jesus' existence and probably no serious scholar ever would. So how had Alex's particular brand of Christological faith been demolished?

Of course loss of faith did happen among churchmen, but it was not a disaster which happened every day and it was never an overnight phenomenon. There would inevitably be a period of doubt coupled with an increasing inability to work properly, but I had seen no sign of such symptoms in Alex during 1937. Moreover, such a rock-solid faith could hardly have been lost without a good reason, and I could see no sign either, as I examined my memory, of a fateful event which might have acted as a trigger.

I surveyed my conclusions. I had apparently reasoned myself into believing either that Alex had woken up one morning in 1937 and experienced an irrational brainstorm, or that he was lying. Neither theory was plausible, but if one assumed that the latter possibility was fractionally more credible than the former, one was immediately confronted by the mystery of why he should have invented such a story. It would seem he felt compelled to give me an explanation for his idle retirement; he had evidently been disturbed by the bewilderment I had expressed during our quarrel, and now it seemed he was anxious to provide an explanation which would stop me from jumping to certain conclusions. But what conclusions was I supposed to be jumping to? It was true I might conclude he was a lazy clergyman who had behaved badly, but I thought Alex would much rather I judged him guilty of sloth than guilty of apostasy. Reluctantly I was driven to conclude that the theory of the big lie raised more mysteries than it solved. But this conclusion, on the other hand, did not prove my theory was untrue.

I tried to hack my way deeper into the conundrum. If the heart condition had been a fiction and the lost faith a lie, what was the real explanation of Alex's refusal to do any church work after he left Starbridge? And—most baffling of all—why had he resigned his bishopric? I had to admit that apart from a loss of faith I could think of no reason which was remotely plausible. Since his retirement it had indeed occurred to me that he might be drinking more than was good for him, but back in 1937 he had had this weakness well in control. So there was no possibility that he might have felt morally obliged to resign because of alcoholism. Adultery, of course, was out of the question. It was beginning to seem after all that I would have to accept the explanation of the lost faith—but if I did it would be only because an alternative theory had proved untenable.

I suddenly felt I wanted to talk to Alex again. After all, my faith too was Christocentric in a Modernist mould; I too tinkered adventurously with the Jesus of history while I held fast to the Christ of Eternity. If Alex could declare in all sincerity that the Modernist road led into a void,

I wanted to know exactly how he had come to hold such a deeply disturbing opinion.

I decided I had no choice but to pursue the matter further at the earliest opportunity, but unfortunately I soon learnt that this was a mystery which was destined never to be unravelled. Two days later I received a telephone call from Lyle to say that Alex had died that morning, peacefully, in his sleep.

6

ALEX had requested in his will that I should on no account deliver a eulogy at the funeral, but he had asked me to address the congregation for five minutes on a text which I felt was consonant with his life and work. I thought hard about this task. Alex's favourite text had been: "I am not come to call the righteous but sinners to repentance"—words which unfortunately had a neo-orthodox ring nowadays, although Alex had always interpreted the passage in a manner which illustrated the Christian message of hope. I was certainly willing enough to preach on the theme that no matter how unworthy one was, there remained always, through Christ, the opportunity for a new life, but nevertheless I could not help but balk at that text. The word "sinners" had such a gloomy ring, and since most mourners find the funeral service deeply depressing, the least a clergyman can do to alleviate their distress is to inject a shot of optimism into the address.

Finally, after reflecting on Alex's stormy life which had been made smooth by his dying belief that he was "justified by faith," I turned to St. Paul for inspiration and was unable to resist selecting the famous text: "For I am persuaded, that neither death nor life, nor angels, nor principalities, nor powers, nor things present, nor things to come, nor height, nor depth, nor any other creature, shall be able to separate us from the love of God, which is in Christ Jesus our Lord."

I wanted to drive to Stoneyford because I felt that travelling by car would be less of a strain than travelling in a dirty, inevitably delayed train, but I knew I could ill afford the petrol-coupons. Fortunately, however, the diocesan office succumbed to a fit of nostalgia, and as a mark of respect to the former Bishop of Starbridge they eased my way to his funeral by allocating me some of the coupons kept for ecclesiastical emergencies. On the fatal day I reached the village in good time, forced myself to eat lunch at the local inn and ruthlessly avoided all alcohol. Then I called at the Jardines' house to leave my overnight bag and spend a short time with Carrie. Lyle was there but not her sons; disapproving of children attending funerals, she had made a quick trip home in order to leave Charley with Michael and the nanny.

I withdrew to the vicarage. There I was greeted sympathetically by the vicar, who had the supreme tact to abandon me as soon as he had escorted me to the vestry. I had already calculated that I would need to spend at least half an hour in solitude to drum up the necessary strength, and as soon as I was alone I willed myself to study my selected words from Romans, review my sermon and pray. No clergyman could have been more disciplined, and at last, confident that I could perform my task in a manner which would have satisfied Alex, I left the vestry to await the mourners.

I was an old hand at surviving the unspeakable.

7

THE sermon began. I'm no flamboyant preacher who seizes the audience's attention by the sheer force of his personality, but I know how to hit hard from the pulpit. My "sledgehammer" technique is employed; I set up a theme—in this case the Christian message of hope in the face of death—and slam the congregation over the head with it from half a dozen different angles. I try to be utterly calm, faultlessly logical and powerfully persuasive. As my Oxford tutors always used to say, I would have made a good barrister.

" '. . . who against hope believed in hope . . .' " As I punctuated the sermon with quotes from Romans, I thought of the hope that Alex had regained at the end of his life, of the hope that the world needed to regain after six years of war, of the hope that the Liberal Protestants still cherished for the evolution of a better world, of the hope that sprang from the loving, forgiving, compassionate teachings of Christ, teachings which the neo-orthodox converts were so ready, in their pessimistic rantings, to pass over. But then suddenly—was it halfway through the sermon?—I remembered that St. Paul had not, in his writings, stressed the teachings of Jesus. He had preached on the meaning of Christ crucified, and the next moment, quite without warning, my memory was regurgitating his words: "For all have sinned, and come short of the glory of God."

I stopped speaking but my memory, as if driven by an unseen force, hammered on. I tried to think of Jesus' compassionate words about the forgiveness of sins, but in my mind's eye I saw the other Jesus, the stern

Jewish prophet who had warned: "Repent! For the kingdom of Heaven is at hand." I shuddered. The church was packed, for Alex had been famous in his day and people had journeyed to the funeral from all over England. As the silence lengthened I stared at my congregation in panic until by a miracle I caught sight of Lady Starmouth in the third row. The glimpse saved me. I knew I could never afford to make a fool of myself in front of Lady Starmouth, and as my iron will revived, my survivor's instinct flogged me back on course. I had to refer to my notes but I completed the sermon fluently, and for the remainder of the ceremony, every harrowing moment of it, I was well in control of myself.

It was not until afterwards that I wondered what my bizarre moment of dislocation could mean, but it seemed wisest to write the mystery off as a consequence of emotional stress and think no more of it.

That alien image of Jesus as a stern religious leader, exhorting people to repent of their sins, would take me straight to the heart of neo-orthodox country, and that was a road I was determined never to travel.

I rang down the curtain.

8

BY six o'clock that evening Carrie, Lyle, I myself and the companion, Miss Jenkins, were alone at the house. Carrie and her companion had just retired upstairs. I was sinking exhausted into the depths of the drawing-room sofa.

"Whisky?" said Lyle tersely.

"I didn't think Alex kept spirits."

"I bought some."

"Congratulations."

Carrie, escaping from the companion, fluttered into the room just as the whisky had been rescued from the dining-room sideboard. "Lyle dearest—"

"What's that wretched Jenkins up to now?"

"She keeps talking about dinner and I can't cope. If only there was some way of getting rid of her for twenty-four hours!"

"There is. Leave her to me." This was certainly the ruthless spirit which had ruled Starbridge's episcopal palace in the thirties. "Help yourself to whisky, Neville, while I sort this out."

Miss Jenkins was informed that she had to stay the night at the inn where I had had lunch. She tried to protest but Lyle was resolute, and as soon as the victim had slammed the front door in rage Carrie shed a tear of relief. "Dearest Lyle, I can't think how I've managed without you all these years . . . Now what shall we do about dinner? I can't quite decide—"

"Leave it all to me, darling. Lie down upstairs and I'll call you when the meal's ready."

Carrie retreated, shedding another tear of relief, and five minutes later I found myself sitting at the kitchen table with a large whisky-and-soda. It was my third. (The eviction of the companion had taken some time.) Lyle, peeling potatoes at the sink, was attended by a tumbler of gin-and-tonic the size of a small goldfish bowl.

"Can I do anything?" I offered vaguely after a long silence.

"What can you do? You don't strike me as being the domestic type."

"You'd be surprised. I can make tea, cook eggs, serve up Spam, heat baked beans and change nappies."

"You're right. I'm surprised."

"Grace needed help sometimes."

"If I'd had five children I'd have needed a padded cell. Why don't you darken up that whisky of yours? It looks a bit pale."

"Well, I thought I'd better go carefully because I don't usually drink whisky—although now and then—"

"Quite. This is definitely now-and-then time. Oh, and do smoke. I expect you do that now and then too, don't you? Well, take off your collar and start puffing."

"Take off my collar?"

"Doesn't the Church still disapprove of clergymen smoking cigarettes when they're in uniform? My husband always took off his collar," she said, speaking very fast, "always." And the next moment, dropping the potato peeler, she burst into tears.

Automatically I sprang to my feet and moved over to her. "Sorry—too much gin," she whispered, still shuddering with sobs, and collapsed abruptly against my chest.

Supporting her with the efficiency of a robot and the outward emotion of a wooden plank, I prayed feverishly for the sexual responses of a eunuch.

"I was so sure he was dead," she wept, "and I'd decided I couldn't hope any more, I'd run out of hope, but then when I heard your address at the funeral, when I heard you saying the word *hope* over and over again, I wondered if it could be some sort of sign telling me Charles was still alive—oh, if only he could come back! I could transform the marriage now, I know I could—" She broke off uncertainly, dashing away her tears, but the hesitation lasted no more than five seconds; the impulse to tap the source of hope was too strong.

"The marriage wasn't altogether a success," she said rapidly. "I was so mixed up about a past love—there was a broken engagement in my twenties—and although I did love Charles I couldn't show it properly—in bed, I mean—and then we used to sort of act and I'd become so frightened, frightened that he'd get fed up and stop loving me—and all the fear only made things worse—but now, having been separated from him for three years and missing him more and more every day, I know that if he comes back everything will be all right, I've been set free at last and we can finally be happy. But if he's dead—oh, I couldn't bear it! I keep thinking: *Surely* I've been punished enough for all my past sins—I mean, for not loving him properly—"

I said gently: "I never think talk about sin is very helpful. It tends to enhance a guilt which can be destructive. Why not think of yourself instead as someone who was impaired, not able to love properly, but who now by the grace of God has been cured? Think of Christ as a healer, not as a stern teacher meting out punishment!"

I'd lost her. As she made a gesture of impatience and drew away from me I sensed that the fragile line of communication, established so unexpectedly by my sermon, had been broken.

"Oh yes, yes, yes!" she said irritated. "I know all those sort of arguments! Dr. Jardine—well, I suppose I can refer to him as Alex, can't I, now that you know I'm related to him—Alex used to trot out that Liberal stuff *ad nauseam* in the thirties. But Charles used to say that although the Liberals tried to sluice away the problem of sin, the problem refused to go down the drain and disappear into the sewer—it was always clambering up the pipe back into the sink. Charles moved right away from Liberal theology before the war. He was fascinated by Barth and Hoskyns. People used to say to him: 'How can you, a doctor of divinity who's made his name as a church historian, flirt with a theology that downgrades history?' But he used to answer: 'History deals with sin and evil. How can I believe they're capable of being sluiced neatly away down the drain with a good dose of Liberal disinfectant when all the evidence of history tells me this isn't true?' Charles had faced up to sin and evil. He was so good, so brave, so *Christian*—oh, no words of mine could ever describe how wonderful he was to me, and if I never see him again . . ." She could say no more. Leaning against the sink, she covered her eyes with her hands and shuddered again beneath the weight of her grief.

Cursing my pastoral inadequacy, I abandoned my gentle approach and grabbed my oratorical sledgehammer in a last-ditch attempt to provide help. "You don't know you'll never see him again," I said. "You can't know that you'll never see him again. And you won't know that you'll never see him again until the telegram arrives from the War Office. Of course you dread he's dead, but what does that dread actually mean? It doesn't mean he's dead. It means you're human. Don't let your terrible torment drive you into making false assumptions and treating them as hard facts. The first hard fact here is that your husband is missing. The second hard fact is that the camps are still being liberated—which means he could still turn up. And the third hard fact is that to give up hope in these circumstances would be irrational, inexcusable, unwarranted, unedifying and absolutely unjustified. Don't do it."

"Gosh!" said Lyle. I had recaptured her. With great relief I watched as she dashed away her tears again, grabbed her glass and took a large gulp of gin. "What a curious mixture you are!" she said unexpectedly. "Tough as nails on the one hand and all soggy romantic Liberalism on the other! It's as if you're two separate people."

"Liberalism need be neither soggy nor romantic. Modernists like me are usually very down-to-earth, keen to ring down the curtain on all the outdated theological concepts which have no relevance to the present age—"

"That's all very well, but supposing the things you label outdated turn out not to be outdated after all? And how does ringing down a curtain achieve anything except an artificial interval in the continuing drama onstage? Can Act Two ever be entirely unrelated to Act One? And how do you know Act Three won't revert to the themes of Act One and negate the themes of Act Two altogether?"

"Well, of course the difficulty in using metaphors is that they can be twisted into a symbolic—"

"Oh God, he's going to give me the Modernist lecture on symbolism. Where the hell's the bloody gin?"

"Here. Are you sure you want another?"

"Oh, shut up and have some more whisky! Sorry, I don't mean to start biting your head off again, but if you only knew the state I'm in—"

"I promise you I do understand—"

"Oh no, you don't! You've absolutely no idea of the extent of my private agony here—"

"—and you have absolutely no idea of the extent of mine! My honeymoon was a disaster, my marriage appears to be a catastrophe and I feel like climbing the walls."

As soon as the words were uttered I looked appalled at my empty glass but Lyle said at once: "Don't worry, I'm discretion personified. Have another drink."

"Thanks." I helped myself to Scotch. I was still so unnerved by my reckless honesty that I decided to drink the whisky unadulterated.

"Presumably you're practising what you preach," said Lyle, watching me over the rim of her replenished glass of gin, "and refusing to give up hope."

"Of course. But unfortunately that doesn't stop me wanting to climb the walls."

"Neville, I honestly don't want to be rude to you any more, but I've got to ask the obvious question: Why on earth did you marry her?"

"I'm beginning to wonder. Sex, I suppose."

"Bloody sex! Nothing but trouble."

"You mean you don't like it?"

"I mean I'm mad about it. That's why I said it's nothing but trouble."

"I'm mad about it too. But in my opinion it's worth the trouble," I said, and suddenly found that my arms were sliding around her waist at the exact moment that her hands were gliding around my neck. We had each set down our glasses as soon as the word "sex" had entered the conversation.

Ten seconds later—or it might have been fifteen; I'm never very numerate when engaging in a sweltering kiss—I recoiled in a burst of sanity and sagged panting against the table. Unfortunately I then returned to madness and knocked back my neat whisky in a single gulp. Or was I in fact being brilliantly clever? Perhaps I was. Grabbing the whisky bottle, I slopped another stiff measure into my glass.

"Sorry," I mumbled at last. "Gone berserk. No offence meant."

"None taken. So that's what goes on beneath that virtuous exterior—how exciting! Do you go berserk often?"

"Only with my wives."

"Lucky Dido!"

"Unfortunately she doesn't seem to be too keen."

"Then she must be either mad or a lesbian."

"Maybe she's both. That would be a challenge, wouldn't it? I must have my challenges," I said, knocking back the Scotch. "I must have my prizes to chase."

"What prizes?"

"I was speaking metaphorically. Ringing down the curtain, chasing the prizes—it's all a unity, as my father used to say, all one. Here, give us another kiss."

"Is that a metaphor too?"

"Everything's a metaphor," I said, pinning her against the wall, and started to tug off her clothes.

Lyle suddenly said in her iciest voice: "This is rape. Let me go at once, please."

"I don't rape women, I'm a clergyman."

"Well, if it's not rape it's indecent assault. Stop it this instant or I'll scream the house down!"

"Oh no, you won't! Don't try to pretend you don't want it just as much as I do!"

"Well, of course I want it!" she shouted. "But not with you!"

That was the moment when we finally lost control. I gave her a disgusted shove that sent her off balance, she deliberately pulled me down on top of her, and after that there was no more talk of rape or wanting someone else. In fact there was no more talk at all. We were like two starving prisoners suddenly presented with a square meal. Sheer excitement and a ravenous greed ignited an appetite so overpowering that all civilised behaviour was suspended. We were merely two bodies consumed by irrationality as we grabbed and clawed and heaved and sweated our way towards a steamy satisfaction.

I was eventually saved, just as I had hoped, by the Scotch. My bemused body, revved up by lust on the one hand but soused by neat whisky on the other, failed to respond to the crucial order, and I was aware of thinking: Thank God! even as I muttered: "Bloody hell." That was when I realised my personality had split cleanly in half, and I knew—every instinct of the born survivor told me—that I had to weld those two halves together to stay sane.

Rolling away from Lyle I slammed into one of the table-legs and in a strange gesture thumped the floor very hard three times with my clenched fist. Perhaps I was trying to channel the anger out of my body, the anger with Dido for humiliating me, the anger with Lyle for pretending I was someone else, the anger with myself for violating the moral code which I had long since vowed to uphold. I felt I wanted to go on the rampage, breaking crockery, smashing windows, even picking a fight and beating someone up. The violence of my anger frightened me, and in my fear I at last regained my self-control.

Crawling upright I levered myself to my feet and tossed off some more whisky to ensure I stayed impotent. By this time Lyle had also groped her way to her feet. I was aware of her silently slipping into her knickers as I wordlessly buttoned my fly.

At last I said: "This never happened."

"Don't worry, I've kept worse secrets."

"There was in fact no adultery," I said. "None. No adultery without penetration. Law of England. So technically nothing happened. Nothing at all—which means we can ring down the curtain and forget about it."

"Suits me. I've always been faithful to Charles. If I'd given way now, just when he might be about to turn up, I'd never have forgiven myself."

"That sounds as if you've started to hope again!"

"What else could I do after you'd made that speech? I felt as if I'd been attacked by a verbal pneumatic drill! Oh God, why on earth, having started to hope again, did I—"

"You didn't. It never happened."

"I suppose I was temporarily insane, all that stress, all that gin—"

"It never happened."

"No, of course it didn't, you're right, it never did."

We stared at each other. Then I turned away and headed rapidly for the door with the bottle of whisky tucked under my arm. "Well," I said, "I'll skip dinner if you don't mind. Not hungry. In fact I'm rather exhausted. Think I'll have an early night."

I escaped. For one long moment I stood shuddering in the hall. Then I retired to my room and drank myself into unconsciousness.

VII

"It may be argued that a working parson . . . is not afraid to face the facts and knows the power of the latent motive and the perversions of the sexual instinct. He has studied the works of Dr. Havelock Ellis and has learnt something from Freud and Jung . . ."

CHARLES E. RAVEN
THE CREATOR SPIRIT

I

A HANGOVER is always distasteful. A hangover combined with horror, guilt and self-loathing is hell on earth. As I tried to pray and failed, tried to analyse my appalling behaviour and failed, tried to ring down the curtain on the disaster and failed, I felt as damaged and degraded as if I had been defrocked.

What shocked me almost as much as the breakdown of my sexual discipline was the drinking. Having turned to whisky after Grace's death I had allowed the innovation to become a habit because I had been confident that I would be able to keep my regular doses at a harmless level. The whisky had become a useful aid to maintaining my enforced celibacy, and it had also been a welcome treat after a hard day's work in the diocese. But now, after the inevitable bout of vomiting, I realised I would have to take myself very firmly in hand. There must be no more whisky—and absolutely no more indecent assaults on sex-mad sirens who ought to be required by law to keep at least fifty yards from all clergymen not called to the celibate life.

Having sluiced away the vomit in the bedroom's basin, I tried to read the morning office, but the words failed to register. Rigid with shame I applied myself to less elevated tasks, and eventually, shaved, shod, clad and feeling like death, I opened my bedroom door. Outside on the floor I found a tray bearing a glass of water and a jar of Epsom salts; the sex-mad siren had evidently undergone a miraculous conversion into a paragon of womanly understanding. Faint with gratitude, I dosed myself, visited the lavatory and staggered downstairs.

Somehow I reached the dining-room where Lyle, pale but composed, was arranged tastefully behind the coffee-pot. I guessed that her composure, like mine, had been obtained with the aid of Epsom salts. Meanwhile Carrie, looking fresh and even cheerful, was talking about nothing with her usual aplomb. I was reminded of the steady, monotonous sound of a dribbling tap.

". . . and they say rationing's going to get worse, but my neighbour has this wonderful Polish cook—a refugee, of course, but *so* clever with coupons and she can make a real English boiled pudding now, although plenty of people don't like boiled puddings, Alex always hated them, but then Alex didn't like any pudding much except that marvellous summer pudding Cook used to make at the palace—and talking of summer, what a mercy that the weather was so fine yesterday . . ."

On and on she droned while Lyle and I toyed with cold toast and drank black coffee, but at last it dimly dawned on me—rather late in the day for a clergyman, but better late than never—that this non-stop verbal haemorrhage might indicate a wound which needed dressing with something that resembled pastoral care. I made a great effort. To attempt pastoral care while labouring under a hangover seemed a hideous distortion of my calling, but I knew I must at least try to be kind to this pathetic little old lady who was so bravely trying to pretend nothing was wrong.

"I'm sorry your brother's accident prevented him from attending the funeral, Carrie," I interrupted when his name suddenly cropped up in the monologue, "but I'm very glad he's invited you to live with him. No doubt he's been lonely since his wife died—and of course you'll be lonely too without Alex. I shall worry less about you now that I know Colonel Cobden-Smith will be keeping you company."

"Dear Neville!" exclaimed Carrie, touched by the notion that I might be worrying about her. "How very kind you are! People who say you're so cold and reserved don't really know you, do they? They can't see it's only shyness. I'm sure Dido will be so good for you—all that vivacity—so different from poor Grace who was prone to melancholy. Alex could never bear it when I was melancholy, it irritated him so much, and I'm sure clever men like you and Alex should marry clever women to keep them amused, clever men soon get tired of someone who's just a pretty face. Oh, I couldn't bear it when Alex got tired of me, I'd have done anything to make him happy—well, I did do everything, and when I think of all I did—"

"Darling," said Lyle, "we'll talk about all that later."

"It's all right, dear, I was only going to say how ghastly it was for me when he invited his stepmother to live with us at the end of her life—"

"Ingrid doesn't matter now Alex is dead."

"Alex may be dead but I'm still alive, aren't I, and sometimes I feel so angry and muddled when I look back over my marriage—"

"Carrie—"

"Sometimes I think: Oh, if only there was someone who'd listen while I pour out my heart—"

"There is. Me. After Neville's gone we'll have a long talk and a good cry and then with any luck we'll both feel better. Now, darling, why don't we go into the drawing-room and listen to that nice man who plays the records on the wireless? He's always so soothing that he's bound to cheer you up . . ."

They departed for the drawing-room. I drank another cup of coffee and toiled upstairs to pack my bag. When I returned to the hall Lyle was waiting.

"Say goodbye to Carrie," she said, "and then I'll come out to the car with you. There's something I forgot to ask."

I knew I should stay longer. I knew I ought to be listening while Carrie poured out her heart. But I knew too that at that moment I was too disabled to provide the help she needed. As we said goodbye all I could do was promise to pray for her.

"Dear Neville!" she said again, so pathetically grateful for this painfully conventional assurance that I realised she had not consciously intended a plea for my help earlier. "How can I ever thank you for all you've done?"

I was so crippled by guilt that I could barely stumble outside to my car. I even forgot that Lyle wanted to talk to me; before I glanced through the open front door and saw her waiting at the gate I had already wasted time searching for her.

"What's this question you forgot to ask?" I said, unlocking the car and heaving my bag into the back seat.

"Who will you talk it over with? Or in other words, who's your spiritual director?"

I stared at her. "Why do you want to know?"

"I've got this horrid feeling you may have the same spiritual director as my husband, and I simply couldn't bear you telling Jon how I've behaved."

"Jon who?"

"Jon Darrow of the Theological College."

"*Jon Darrow?* That ecclesiastical buccaneer? Good heavens, nothing would induce me to confide in an Anglo-Catholic ex-monk who combines the arrogance of Napoleon with the showmanship of Houdini!"

"Thank God. If I ever thought Jon would find out about last night—"

"No one's going to find out about last night."

"But what about your spiritual director?"

"I don't have a spiritual director. I'm a Protestant, not an Anglo-Catholic."

"Charles isn't an Anglo-Catholic either, but he believes very strongly in the importance of—"

"Well, naturally I've always had an older clergyman with whom I can discuss my work. At the beginning of my career my older clergyman was Bishop Hargreaves, after 1932 he was Alex, and nowadays he's Bishop Ottershaw."

"But don't you find it rather inhibiting to discuss personal problems with your boss?"

"What personal problems?" I got into the driving-seat, slammed the door and wound down the window. "Goodbye—and good luck. I'd apologise except there's nothing to apologise for as it never happened."

"Quite." She was gazing at me with an expression of wonder tinged with concern. "But I'm beginning to think that you're the one who needs the good luck."

"All I need is will-power and common sense," I said abruptly, starting the engine. "God helps those who help themselves." Then having delivered myself of this latest masterpiece of optimism, I drove off, still feeling like death, into the next stage of my crisis.

2

IT was noon when I reached Starbridge but on entering the Close I turned not west towards my new home but east along the North Walk. At the far end stood St. Anne's Gate, the entrance available only to pedestrians as they slipped in and out of the vast walled domain of the Cathedral. Parking the car I walked through the gateway, crossed the main road beyond the walls and entered the Crusader Hotel in pursuit of refreshment. I felt unable to face returning home and picking up the threads of my archidiaconal life until I had been fortified with another dose of caffeine.

Having given the order to the lounge waiter, I visited the cloakroom to sort out various symptoms of discomfort in my outraged intestines and dashed some cold water over my face before daring to look in the mirror.

I looked very pale and very sober. Reassured that death's door was receding I returned to the lounge and dumped myself in the nearest armchair.

Triumphing over my hangover meant that I was at last able to *think,* as Dido would have put it, instead of merely to think. I was no longer worried about Lyle; it was in her own best interests to keep quiet. But although I might succeed in ringing down the curtain with my usual masterly efficiency, I knew I had an absolute moral duty to establish why I had wound up in such an appalling mess.

It was no good merely telling myself my behaviour had resulted from the strain of the funeral and a surfeit of whisky. These factors, though not without significance in my journey over the brink of decency into lunacy, were mere irritants, exacerbating a situation which already existed. My sexual frustration was probably a more crucial factor than the strain and the drink; any man who returns from his honeymoon with his marriage unconsummated is bound to be in an unstable state. Nevertheless I felt I had to look past my sexual frustration too in order to perceive the complex problem beyond. Why, after all, had I returned from my honeymoon with an unconsummated marriage? Because I had married Dido, even though it had been patently obvious that she had profound psychological difficulties which included sexual frigidity. And why had I married her? It was no use now, at this stage of the game, to plead feebly that I was the victim of an *amour fou.* That explained nothing, and as a good Modernist I had to believe in a rational explanation.

Of course a psychologist would probably have jumped to the conclusion long since that I was a masochist, one of those unfortunate creatures who obtained sexual thrills from being maltreated by women. But the trouble with this theory was that it bore no relation to my private fantasies, which usually (since I was a good clergyman) I managed to suppress. In other words, I knew very well that if Dido and I were locked up naked together with a couple of unspeakable toys, it certainly wouldn't be me who'd wind up chained to the bedpost and begging to be whipped. Every instinct told me that I was very far from being a masochist, but if I wasn't a masochist, why on earth had I married Dido after all her appalling behaviour during our tortuous courtship? I ADORE YOU, I had declared in my recent telegram, and since I still wanted her I could only suppose this must be true, but if I wasn't a masochist, how had this unlikely adoration managed to survive?

It was all very well to tell myself (romantically) that I was endowed with inexhaustible patience, outstanding tenacity and a truly phenomenal Christian charity; it was all very well to tell myself (cynically) that I had to adore her in order to save the marriage and rescue myself from ruin.

But what in heaven's name, I asked myself in all honesty, was really going on? Even if I pleaded that I had fallen victim to the thrill of a challenge and the euphoria of chasing a first-class prize, I would still have to ask myself why I, a born survivor, had wound up taking such a suicidal course of action.

I began to feel frightened by my ignorance, but fortunately I was diverted by the arrival of my coffee which resembled not the familiar dishwater but some pre-war nectar of the gods. Evidently the Crusader Hotel was still celebrating V-E Day. I looked hopefully for sugar-lumps of pre-war dimensions but was disappointed. Even the Crusader had its limitations. Nevertheless the coffee was perfect, and by the time I was halfway through my first cup my brain was ticking over much more briskly. I could see now that it was futile to waste time wondering how I could have got into such a mess. The only important matter to be resolved was how on earth I was going to get out of it. I was almost certain that Dido would eventually return to me, but the time had come to decide what I was going to do when she turned up once more on my doorstep.

Ignoring the fact that I adored Dido (whatever that might mean), I considered the problem with a scrupulously rational detachment. A divorce was out of the question for a successful clergyman who wanted to remain a success, but could I perhaps pursue Dido's suggestion of an annulment? I could not. An annulment would quickly be transformed by the gutter-press into a society scandal, and no clergyman who featured in a *News of the World* scoop ever survived in any worthwhile professional sense no matter how innocent he might be. Besides, I hardly wanted the entire diocese twittering about the poor Archdeacon who was too weak to consummate his marriage. I shuddered convulsively. What a nightmare! But at least I now knew beyond all doubt that I had to make the marriage work—and if the marriage was going to have any hope of working, it somehow had to be consummated.

I forced myself to confront the hideous possibility of a continuing non-consummation. If—when—Dido returned to me, she would be coming back primarily to still the gossiping tongues and there was no guarantee she would be able to surmount her repulsion. Moreover—and now I was really peering into the bottom of the sexual snake-pit—even if she did eventually consent to let me attempt intercourse, I might find she was physically unable to complete the act because of her mental revulsion. I had heard of such cases; I had dipped into my Freud and my Jung and my Havelock Ellis. Obviously my most sensible course of action was to coax her to consult a psychiatrist, but how long would all the inevitable therapy take? And how much longer could I continue without sex in these exceptionally frustrating circumstances when it was quite obvious that my chastity belt was buckling at the seams? If I was in a mess now, what kind of a mess would I be in after six months or—God forbid—a year? Utter despair suddenly overwhelmed me. Unable to finish my coffee I leant forward, my elbows on my knees, and buried my face in my hands.

I was not alone in the lounge. Two old ladies were whispering away in the far corner and a red-faced individual who might have been a retired Army officer was tucked into a chair with *The Times,* but none of these people had taken any notice of me. I was wearing a clerical suit, not my archidiaconal uniform, so I was easy enough to ignore; laymen expect Starbridge to be littered with clergymen circling the Cathedral Close in the manner of planets orbiting the sun, so even when I made my gesture of despair, burying my face in my hands, I hardly thought any observer would rate my behaviour worthy of a second glance. But I was wrong. After a moment I became aware that someone had stepped between me and the sunlight, which was slanting through the nearest window, and when this unseen body failed to remove itself I realised in alarm that I was being watched.

Whipping aside my hands I saw to my horror that a very tall man was towering above me with an expression of concern on his face.

It was my diocesan *bête noire,* Jon Darrow.

3

I SHOULD perhaps be fair (always such a difficult exercise when describing a man one dislikes) and state at once that Darrow was in his own peculiar way a most successful clergyman. He had a distinguished record as a chaplain during the First War. He was still remembered at Starmouth Prison, where he had worked after leaving the Navy. Later he had pursued a remarkable career as an Anglo-Catholic monk in the Fordite Order, and in the 1930s he had acquired a reputation as an accomplished spiritual director. I was certainly prepared to concede that Darrow had his gifts, but the trouble was that some of these gifts of his were, to put it kindly, unconventional. He was supposed to be a psychic—or so everyone whispered, and he never bothered to deny the rumors. I had heard people exclaim naively: "Darrow foresaw Pearl Harbor!" as if that proved his paranormal powers beyond doubt. All I can say is that with my own ears I heard him prophesy confidently at a dinner-party that General Rommel would never take Tobruk. Tobruk fell a month later.

So much for men who pose as psychics, and so much for Mr. Jonathan Darrow.

However although he dabbled on the fringes of the absurd, there was nothing absurd about his personality and it would have been the greatest mistake to write him off as a harmless eccentric. He was arrogant, obstinate, ruthless and troublesome. In 1940 he had bounded out of his monastic Order (it was even rumoured that his call to leave had been manifested in a dream which he had had the nerve to describe as a vision) and having tossed aside his monk's habit he had bounced back into a clerical suit in order to pursue a new career in the Starbridge diocese. Unfortunately he chose to invade my archdeaconry, which soon showed signs of dissolving into chaos; he started to indulge in parlour-tricks which he insisted on performing in church. (He was going through a faith-healing phase, and as far as I could discover he did everything except tell fortunes.) Poor Dr. Ottershaw used to reach automatically for his indigestion tablets whenever Darrow's name was mentioned—as it often was, by me, in our discussions of diocesan problems.

At last in 1942 Darrow showed signs of adjusting to the world he had so flamboyantly re-entered, and he was recruited, as I have already mentioned, to teach at the Theological College in the Cathedral Close. Of course he wound up running the place. The principal had a breakdown, the vice-principal dropped dead and Darrow elbowed his way past the surviving staff to grab the reins of power. The surviving staff even seemed pleased. The students—the ordinands, I should say, since they were all hoping to be ordained—were thrilled. One either loathed Darrow or one loved him, and a great many people were so dazzled by his devout Anglo-Catholicism and his powerful personality that they never noticed the buccaneering adventurer who lurked alongside the image of the formidable clergyman which Darrow so successfully projected. He was in his sixties but prided himself on his youthfulness. After leaving the cloister he had even been reckless enough to marry a woman twenty-eight years his junior and beget a son—but of course it would never have occurred to Darrow in his arrogance that marriage and procreation are hardly dignified activities for a clerical gentleman of advanced years.

As I now saw him towering above me in the lounge of the Crusader I wanted to emit a loud groan and run a mile in the opposite direction; I hardly felt capable of conducting a conversation, no matter how casual, with my *bête noire* when I was in such a debilitated state. At the same time I could not help but see the black humour embedded in the situation. Lyle had made it clear that the one man I should avoid while I was recovering from my folly was Jon Darrow, yet here he was, the famous spiritual director, vibrating with curiosity as he noted my uncharacteristically despairing posture and hovering at my elbow as if hungry for a confession. My immediate reaction was: Let him starve. I entirely disapprove of clergymen of the Church of England who call themselves "priests," prefer to be addressed as "Father" and amuse themselves by playing God in the practice of auricular confession. It always makes me want to bawl: "No Popery!" at the top of my voice and behave in a manner quite unbecoming to an archdeacon.

"Oh, hullo," I said to Darrow in my best polite voice. "Fancy seeing you." Unfortunately my best polite voice failed to come up to standard. I succeeded only in combining a wooden courtesy with a complete lack of enthusiasm.

"Are you all right?"

"Absolutely fine, couldn't be better. And you?"

"Splendid, thanks. Mind if I sit down?"

I did mind—intensely—but anxious to create an air of nonchalance, I said sociably: "Go ahead." During this exchange of banalities I suddenly remembered Evelyn Underhill—or was it her mentor, Baron Friedrich Von Hügel?—writing that there was no need to search for a spiritual director because when the time was right a suitable director would always appear. By no remote stretch of the imagination would Darrow ever be the right spiritual director for me, but I began to wonder if this meeting, far from being a heavy-handed jest of God, was in fact an obscure divine lifeline. "God helps those who help themselves," I had said to Lyle with a Yorkshire pig-headedness worthy of Uncle Willoughby, but the truth, as I had realised just before Darrow's arrival, was that I had reached the stage where I appeared to be beyond self-help. I was now experiencing a strong desire to confide in some wise stranger who could view my problems with detachment and offer first-class advice, but how was I to find such a paragon? The answer was: through Darrow, whose extensive work as a spiritual director would almost certainly have brought him into touch with the wisest churchmen in England. I began to frame a careful question in my mind.

"J. H. Ryder of *The Church Gazette* is giving me lunch here," Darrow was saying. "He wants information for an article about the post-war hurdles for theological education—how we intend to cope with the large new influx of ordinands and so on."

"Oh yes?" I had to stifle yet another impulse to run a mile in the opposite direction. Ryder, a Cambridge graduate, was one of the most influential ecclesiastical journalists in the land. In addition to his regular centre-page articles in *The Church Gazette,* the newspaper which had a large circulation among moderate churchmen, he wrote free-lance pieces on theology for *The Times.* He was also, like so many journalists, an incurable gossip. The last thing I wanted was Jack Ryder speculating why the Archdeacon of Starbridge was looking like death and slumped over black coffee in the lounge of the Crusader Hotel.

"If Ryder's about to arrive I'd better pull myself together!" I said, making what I could only regard as a brilliant move to explain the situation with casual good humour. "I'm sure I looked wrecked. Yesterday I buried my mentor, Bishop Jardine."

"Ah, I see. I did think, in fact, that you looked somewhat distressed . . . Are you saying you actually conducted the service?"

"It was what he wanted."

"How very harrowing—and it's difficult too, isn't it, when one loses one's mentor. One feels quite alone, with no one to confide in."

Tiresome old conjuror, prying away, throwing out unexpected statements which by sheer chance happened to be extraordinarily accurate. "Well, as a matter of fact," I said, looking vaguely out of the window as if the subject were quite unimportant, "I was just pondering on that. I'm not in the market for a spiritual director, but if you could think of a wise old man I could chat to occasionally, perhaps you'd let me know."

"Someone outside the diocese?"

I froze. If I said yes, he might jump to the conclusion that I had a deep dark secret. I could never have told anyone who knew me that life was currently a trifle awkward; a stranger from beyond the diocesan borders was essential.

"Well, yes, obviously it would be better if you found someone outside the diocese," said Darrow, serenely answering his own question before I could become flustered. "I'm sorry, I wasn't thinking clearly. Within the diocese you have your important role to maintain, and important roles can be inhibiting."

Immediately I suspected him of trapping me; he had asked a loaded question to which he already knew the answer and had then gauged my inner confusion by noting the quality of my embarrassed silence. I seethed with rage but managed to say with a studied lack of concern: "I really don't care if the man's in the diocese or not. It's all the same to me."

"Would you consider a Fordite monk?"

I repressed a shudder. "I'm sorry," I said. "I don't want to sound like a tub-thumping Evangelical, but I couldn't take the Anglo-Catholic ambience."

"Would that be so intrusive if you only visited him for the occasional chat?"

"Well, maybe not, but I must have someone who's normal—I mean, someone who's lived a normal life, been married, had children and so on."

"I'd been married, had children and so on before I became a Fordite monk."

"Quite." I seemed to be getting in a mess. Detestable old magician, tieing me up in knots! Fury overwhelmed me again.

"It's all right—I'm not taking offence!" said Darrow smiling at me. "Many people feel that a celibate can't be expected to discuss certain problems adequately. It's a mistaken opinion, but not an unusual one."

"I don't have those sort of problems." I glanced at the glass doors which divided the lounge from the foyer, but there was no sign of deliverance in the form of Jack Ryder. I wanted to leave but I was too afraid Darrow would think I was running away.

Darrow said suddenly: "I think you should meet Aidan Lucas."

"Who's he?"

"The Abbot of the Fordites' Yorkshire house. If you were to go to Ruydale to see him—"

"Oh, I could never go back to Yorkshire."

In the silence that followed I realised not only that this automatic reaction had in some mysterious way ripped open a hole in the fabric of my personality but that Darrow was now peering with intense interest into the gap. In rage I embarked on some hasty repairs.

"Well, you know how it is, I daresay," I said, faultlessly casual. "I'm a self-made man, and self-made men can't go back to the world in which they no longer feel at home. It's a very well known syndrome."

"Ah yes," said Darrow. "Of course."

I looked at him suspiciously, but although I could discern no trace of scepticism in his manner I felt driven to underline what I had said. "I've rung down the curtain on Yorkshire," I said. "I'm a great believer in ringing down curtains. It's no good picking over the past. One must apply oneself to the present and keep one's eyes firmly fixed on one's future goals."

"Very commendable," said Darrow, "but the trouble with those sort of curtains—the ones that hide the past—is that they tend to develop such an unfortunate habit of going up at the wrong moments."

My immaculate nonchalance shattered. "What utter rubbish!"

"Is it? But if the present is only the past continuing, and if, as Mr. Eliot writes, all time is eternally present, then ringing down the curtain on the past is actually a metaphysical impossibility."

Monstrous, meddling old charlatan, hitting me over the head with mystical claptrap! It took me a vast effort to grab hold of my temper again, but I somehow contrived to reply in a colourless voice: "If you'd been born and bred in Yorkshire, you'd understand that when one travels south, becomes a southerner and thrives in a southern world, it's psychologically easier to adjust to one's new self by ringing down the curtain on the past. I'm sorry, Darrow, but it's quite obvious we don't talk the same language."

"Aidan Lucas was born and bred in Yorkshire," said Darrow. "He once travelled south, became a southerner and thrived in a southern world. He'll talk your language. Would you like me to write you a letter of introduction?"

I was livid that I had been outmanoeuvred. "Darrow, I told you right at the start of this conversation that I didn't want to see a monk! Why don't you listen properly?"

"Oh, I listened!" said Darrow mildly. "I heard not only every word you said but every word you couldn't bring yourself to say. Ah, here's Ryder at last! Come along, Aysgarth, stop looking as if you'd like to punch me on the jaw and act the Archdeacon for *The Church Gazette.*"

In walked Jack Ryder, a bright-eyed, bustling individual, bursting with eagerness to spot any deviation from the clerical norm.

"Hullo, Father," he said, shamelessly awarding Darrow his Anglo-Catholic title. I knew very well that Ryder was a staunch Protestant, but some journalists will do anything to curry favour once they scent a good interview. "Oh hullo, Archdeacon! Coincidence! You didn't see me, but I was at the back of the church in Stoneyford yesterday. Thought I'd just pay my parting respects to a bishop who always provided such good copy—and of course the *Gazette* wanted a paragraph or two for the Friday edition." He turned beaming to Darrow. "The Archdeacon preached an absolutely first-class sermon, Father, to a packed congregation which included six bishops, three deans, two professors of divinity and a gaggle of fellows from All Souls. I foresee great things ahead for our friend Aysgarth!"

"Well, as it happens," said Darrow blandly, "I've just been asking myself if Aysgarth might be on the brink of interesting times."

I ignored this masterpiece of sinister ambiguity. Thanking Ryder for his generous compliments, I wished him a pleasant lunch, bid Darrow a firm goodbye and finally escaped from the hotel.

4

AS I opened the front door of my home I saw the suitcases in the hall and realised that one aspect at least of my crisis had been eased. The last remnants of my hangover dissolved; I was conscious of a vast relief.

"Stephen!" As I closed the front door she rushed out of the drawing-room and hurtled into my arms. "Oh Stephen!" She began to shower me with kisses.

"Hullo," I said. "Nice to see you. Staying long?"

"Through all eternity!"

"Oh, fine." I gave her a peck on the cheek and started to toil up the stairs.

"Darling, can you ever, ever forgive me?" She was bobbing along feverishly in my wake.

"I might."

"Stephen, I simply adore it when you're so deliciously cool and austere!"

"Oh yes?" I plodded across the upstairs landing into the bedroom.

"Yes, it's so madly sexy. I want to pin you against the nearest wall, rip off all your clothes and rape you. Or at least . . . Can women rape men? I suppose they can't."

Entering the bedroom, I dropped my overnight bag on the floor, leaned against the nearest wall and said: "They can try."

"Stephen, how thrilling—you're about to set a new trend in seduction!"

"No, to be honest I'm about to pass out. Are you going to pin me against the wall and rip my clothes off or do I merely collapse in an unviolated stupor on the bed?"

"Poor darling, did Alex's funeral exhaust you? Merry said I should have gone with you, but you know how bad I am at funerals, and . . . oh Stephen, can you ever forgive me for being such a dreadful failure on the honeymoon? Merry said that if you hadn't been a clergyman you'd have beaten me up and tossed me over a cliff, and I do realise that I've behaved absolutely dreadfully, but you see, I've been in such a ghastly muddle and when I'm in a ghastly muddle I can't *think,* it's as if some sadistic demon's strangling my brain—"

"Dido," I said, "I can forgive you for everything except for prattling away at the wrong moment. If you can't bring yourself to rape me, would you like me to rape you?"

"But if you're on the point of collapsing in a stupor—"

"I appear to be experiencing a miraculous revival."

"Darling, how simply too exciting, but does this mean you've genuinely forgiven me for being so absolutely frightful?"

"Apparently."

"You're not secretly loathing me and wishing I was dead?"

"Not yet."

"You really do still love me?"

"I adore you."

"Oh Stephen, you're so wonderful, so compassionate, so patient, so—"

"Dido, do you really want me to beat you up and throw you over a cliff?"

"No, Archdeacon dear, I want you to make mad passionate love to me from dusk till dawn."

I laughed. Then leaning forward I grabbed my prize before she could once more slip through my fingers, and pounded hell-for-leather down the finishing strait to victory.

5

AFTERWARDS I thought: Is that all there is? And I wondered incredulously how I had managed to whip myself into such a fever of desire for so long. I could only reflect blankly that after the chase for a prize, victory was so often an anticlimax; as soon as the glow of satisfaction began to fade, one was left wondering what to do next, and never did my glow of satisfaction fade faster than after the ludicrous and pathetic consummation of my second marriage.

Because of my recent excessive consumption of alcohol I was hardly at my sexual best but at least I was still capable of taking trouble over the preliminary rituals. Conscientiously I made the required effort but I was wasting my time. Dido wriggled or stiffened until at last she exclaimed in an agony of impatience: "Oh Stephen, do get on with it and stop fussing around!" How I did manage to "get on with it" after this insensitive exhortation had further undermined my debilitated physical state must remain forever a mystery. I could only conclude I had the constitution of an ox, the hide of a rhinoceros, the stamina of a Byronic hero and the obstinacy of a Yorkshire village idiot.

I managed to keep going for a couple of minutes, but then succumbed to the lingering aftermath of the whisky, the lack of practice and Dido's obvious longing for the torture to finish. Lighting a post-coital cigarette I asked myself whether, despite the consummation, there was any conceivable hope for our marital future. As far as I could see, any affirmative answer to this question would be pushing my Liberal Protestant optimism far beyond the bounds of credibility.

Meanwhile Dido was chattering away in the artless fashion which I had once judged so delectable and now found so dreary. "I've done it, oh Stephen, I've done it, thank God, oh my goodness, what a dreadful hurdle, but now we can settle down and live happily ever after—because of course we *will* live happily ever after, I shall become absolutely *sizzling* at sex and satisfy you utterly, just as a successful wife should, and God knows no one deserves to be satisfied more than you do. Oh Stephen darling, how can I ever thank you for being so kind, so patient, so—"

I suddenly had a revelation. I saw that Dido's artless prattle might be a behavioural mirror-image of Carrie Jardine's monotonous monologues; behind the apparent normality might lie an abnormal grinding pain.

"Just a minute." I handed her my cigarette to keep her quiet and lit another for myself. Then I said in a firm but not unfriendly voice: "Let's get this straight. I think it's time we established, for better or for worse, what on earth's going on. I believe that you only married me because you felt that (a) spinsterhood and a successful life were incompatible, and (b) once you were thirty and still unmarried, failure would be staring you in the face. Now, am I right or wrong?"

"Well, I suppose you're right, more or less, but Stephen, I would never have married you if I hadn't admired and respected and adored you! I'd have married someone else."

"Who?"

"Well . . ."

"There wasn't anyone else, was there? Not by that time. You'd overplayed your hand, the hand which dictated you had to be hard to get, and I was the only admirer still on offer."

"True—but that doesn't alter the fact that during the time you spent chasing me I came to adore you!"

"I believe you're sincere when you say that. But I put it to you that your use of the word 'adore' tends to be highly idiosyncratic."

"Oh darling, do stop behaving like prosecuting counsel! 'I put it to you'—honestly! What a phrase!"

"I knew you didn't love me in the conventional sense," I pursued, riding roughshod over this uneasy protest. "At least I was a clear-eyed romantic. But my mistake was to believe that when you kept exclaiming: 'I adore you,' those words meant more than: 'I'm grateful to you for getting me off the shelf.' I honestly thought that you were fond enough of me to come to love me later."

"But I was—I am!"

"Again, I believe you're sincere when you say that, but I'm now convinced that you haven't faced up to the fact that the way things ought to be in our marriage has as yet no relation to the way things really are. That's why this whole sex business has been such a nightmare for you. Sex in marriage is the place where one hits rock-bottom reality, and so long as rock-bottom reality has no connection with the romantic froth you're trying to pass off as the truth, you're going to be buckling at the knees with horror whenever you catch sight of a double bed."

"But Stephen—"

"Let me now tell you what I think is really going on beneath your romantic froth. I think you find me quite amusing in an odd sort of way. I'm sure you're genuinely grateful to me for sticking to my guns and marrying you. However I doubt that you respect and admire me much; I think it's far more likely that you despise me for putting up with your bad behaviour for so long, but on the other hand, I suppose there's always the possibility that you might admire my fanatical determination to get what I want. You find the fact that I'm a clergyman mildly stimulating (all that black cloth—so erotic!), but you feel it's a bore that I can't ride to hounds, talk horses with you and lead a fast social life. Nevertheless you probably appreciate the fact that I'm not a fool. As acquaintances go I can be classified as passable, but as a husband I'm a disaster. I'm not tall, dark and handsome; I'm not rich, well-bred and well-connected; the earth never moves for you when I enter a room and—let's be quite frank—if I fell under a bus tomorrow you'd soon recover from your bereavement. Carlton-Blake was the one you loved and it's my bet you love him still. You'd leave me tomorrow if he asked you to—but of course he never will, and that's a brutal fact which I suspect you still, subconsciously, can't bring yourself to accept. So exactly where do you now find yourself? I'll tell you: in hell. You're utterly miserable, married to a man you don't love. You feel trapped, defeated and despairing. You may pat yourself on the back for crawling off the dreaded shelf, but the truth is you've wound up flat out on a filthy floor."

I stopped speaking. I had never before made such a long speech to Dido and received no interruption. Silence enfolded us. Then she flung down her cigarette in the ash-tray and burst into tears.

I remained unmoved. All I said was: "I'm right, aren't I? That's the truth. That's the way things really are."

On and on she wept but finally I heard her whisper: "I suppose I'll never be a successful wife now. I must give up all hope."

At once I experienced an electrifying enlightenment. *"Give up all hope?"* I shouted, making her jump. "Don't be ridiculous! This is where the fun really begins!"

She was so amazed that she forgot her tears. "What on earth do you mean?"

"I've managed to marry you. I've managed to go to bed with you. But there's still something left to win. My dear Dido," I concluded, radiant with relief as my disastrous situation was once more transformed into a delectably addictive challenge, "I've now got to win your heart, mind and soul—your love's my new prize!"

Of course I was mad as a hatter.

6

"YOU'RE mad!" said Dido, laughing through her tears, and added: "But you're very splendidly mad and I think perhaps I do love you after all."

"Never use the word 'love' unless you really mean it, please. Otherwise how will I know, when the time comes, that you mean what you say?"

"Can I go on using 'adore' in my special way, meaning a deeply grateful approval?"

"Yes, but not too often." Greatly invigorated, I sprang out of bed and started pulling on my clothes. "What's for lunch? And why hasn't Sandy battered down the door and demanded to see me?"

"He and Nanny had lunch early and went down to the river to feed the swans. Oh darling Stephen, do you really think I can still be a success even though I've wound up flat out on a filthy floor?"

"Of course. I'm going to haul you up inch by inch."

"But how?"

I paused in the act of tieing my shoe-laces and took a quick hard look at possible strategies. "The first problem to solve is sex," I said briskly. "We must reach a *modus vivendi.* Now, I'm reluctant to force you into a regular performance when it's clear that at present this is the last thing you want, but on the other hand, I think that the more you do it the easier it'll get. I'm not suggesting we should hammer away every night, but if you can grit your teeth sufficiently hard to stand sex twice a week, I suspect your disgust will quickly be eroded by boredom—and boredom is easier to deal with than repulsion."

"I hope I don't grind my teeth into stumps. Maybe they'd have a better chance of surviving intact if I drowned myself in gin beforehand—can we have sex at set times so that I know when to hit the bottle?"

"Good idea. Spontaneity can wait till later. Shall we say Wednesdays and Saturdays?"

"Stephen, I can't tell you how much I admire you for being so wonderfully practical about all this—"

"Then don't bother. Focus your mind instead on our next problem, which is reproduction. Let's forget all the romantic drivel we spouted on the subject before the wedding and discuss the matter realistically. Can you face a pregnancy yet or shall we wait till you're less miserable?"

"Oh, but I must have a baby as soon as possible! Then everyone will think the marriage is a success!"

"Never mind 'everyone' for the moment. Let's just concentrate on you. Do you really want to bear the child of a man you don't—as yet—love?"

"But darling, we can't hang around waiting for me to become besotted with you—that could take years! No, I must have a baby, preferably on or before our first wedding anniversary."

"Are you sure you've got over your fear of childbirth? I know the doctors say there's no reason why you should follow in Laura's footsteps, but were you being completely honest when you said you no longer had any qualms about embarking on a pregnancy?"

"Well, I'm sure most women experience the odd qualm or two before setting out on a journey which might just end in death, but—"

"The qualms aren't overpowering. Very well, that's settled—we'll have a baby as soon as possible. Now my next most pressing problem is that I'm starving. Do you have any further questions or can we adjourn to the dining-room?"

"I've only one more question, Stephen darling, and that's this: You've spelt out with the most beautiful candour what I truly think of you, but what do you truly think of me?"

"I'm mad about you."

"Honestly?"

"Well, I must be, mustn't I? Why else would I have wound up in this extraordinary marriage?"

"Darling!" exclaimed Dido, flinging her arms impulsively around my neck. "If only you knew how guilty I feel about this ghastly crisis!"

"Crisis?" I said. "What crisis? The crisis is over—ring down the curtain! I've no doubt at all that we'll eventually succeed in living happily ever after!"

Was ever optimism more misplaced?

The real crisis, the most terrifying crisis I had ever faced in my life, was now moving stealthily towards me behind the curtain.

VIII

"Repression is no good."

CHARLES E. RAVEN
A WANDERER'S WAY

I

I HARDLY think it necessary to recount in detail the remainder of my journey to the bottom of the black pit which came to symbolise my second marriage. For a while we limped along with the aid of good intentions, resolute play-acting and sexual intercourse twice a week, but soon Dido was prostrated by pregnancy and suffered a wide variety of ills, real and imaginary, which effectively secured her a separate bedroom. In between numerous cold baths I worked feverishly in my archdeaconry and somehow managed to convince myself that once the pregnancy was over, all would eventually be well.

I felt exasperated by Dido's collapse but I tried hard to beat back my anger and drum up some sympathy. I knew she had lost her nerve and grown convinced, despite the doctors' assurances, that she was destined to follow Laura to an early grave. After a while I myself began to wonder if something would go wrong, but instinct told me that this speculation could lead to dangerous thoughts so I resolutely turned my mind elsewhere.

In order to cope with this grinding marital difficulty I found myself reverting to the romantic charade of my courtship, that long-running drama which at the time had seemed to vibrate with sincerity but which I now found rang so unpleasantly false. There was comfort in acting. One could escape from one's tormented self and become someone else, someone stylised, someone who moved within marked limits which could be ruthlessly controlled at all times. Day after day when I returned home from work I would sit by her chaise-longue in the drawing-room and exude a doting patience while she wept and called me an angel and swore I was much too good for her. We enacted this scene tirelessly, as if not just our sanity but our lives depended upon it, and soon we became polished performers.

"Do you still love me, Stephen?"

"Darling, don't you realise by now that my love is utterly indestructible?"

"Oh Stephen, you're so noble, so splendid, so loyal, so—"

"No, no, you're so brave, so courageous, so—"

How we managed to dredge up such a collection of empty adjectives never failed to amaze me.

As the drama slid inevitably into melodrama I found myself experiencing that curious phenomenon of *déjà vu,* moments when I was convinced that our melodrama had all been played before—as no doubt it had, on stage, by various nineteenth-century actors. Since Dido had now become a Victorian heroine, wilting neurotically on a chaise-longue, and since I had been translated into a Victorian hero, radiating a sexless high-mindedness, it was hardly surprising that my trusty memory should occasionally be nudged by the sheer volume of all the Victorian clichés which were declaimed.

Once I asked Dido if she too was experiencing the *déjà vu* phenomenon, but she shook her head. "I adore those peculiar hiccoughs of memory!" she added. "I'm sure we've all lived before in another life. Why doesn't the Church believe in reincarnation?"

I tried to explain but she lost interest so I gave up. All that now interested her was her ill-health. She had lost interest in theology, lost interest in Church affairs, lost interest in her sadly unsuccessful attempts to create a smart social life for herself in her new surroundings. After our reunion she had made great efforts to be a dazzling ecclesiastical wife, calling on everyone in the Close and organising a succession of extravagant dinner-parties, but the inhabitants of the Close, conservative and cautious in their ways, distrusted this London flamboyance almost as much as my bank manager distrusted my ability to pay for it.

Money was a problem. Dido had expensive tastes. Fortunately her villainous father had given her an allowance which covered her general maintenance (clothes, hair, cosmetics, little sorties into antique shops) but unfortunately the money was settled, just as he had threatened, in a manner which ensured I could never touch a penny of it, and the expense of keeping Dido did not end with her general maintenance. I had to move house; Dido argued that anyone who was anyone in Starbridge lived in the Close. However I need hardly add that the real reason why Dido could not live in the vicarage—and the real reason why I agreed to move—was because neither of us could face living with Grace's ghost. Every room of the vicarage seemed to be impregnated with memories of her, and although her name was never mentioned I knew that both Dido and I had to escape from the stage on which the drama of my first marriage had been played.

I made arrangements to lease from the Dean and Chapter the house which had belonged to General Calthrop-Ponsonby (recently deceased) on Canonry Drive. Dido managed to squeeze money out of her father for the refurbishment, but a larger house meant greater expense, and soon I found myself burdened with financial demands I was ill-equipped to meet. Old Tallent had bought the twenty-year lease for us as a wedding present but I could hardly look to him to pay the ground-rent or the rates. In the end I wangled a housing allowance from the diocesan funds, but the Board of Finance was cool and I was informed frankly that the concession had only been made because the Bishop had interceded on my behalf. I felt I was sailing much too close to the wind. How I was going to pay for a new child remained uncertain, but I was praying for a girl who would be cheap to educate.

Meanwhile my other children, who knew nothing of my financial gymnastics, were entranced by their new home which faced the west front of the Cathedral. Built in mellow brick, wreathed in ivy and set in a large garden, the house exuded "character," that ambience so beloved by estate agents. The older boys were also quick to see that the house represented a step up the social ladder.

"Can we have people to stay?" inquired Norman. "It'll be easier now we don't live in a mere vicarage."

I said severely: "That's a snobbish remark, Norman," but Christian only retorted: "If you take the trouble to send us to one of the top public schools, Father, you can hardly be surprised if we show revolting tendencies to prefer Jacobean mansions to Victorian vicarages. But isn't that all part of Getting On and Travelling Far?"

Christian's inclination to make snide remarks showed no sign of decreasing, but I was so relieved by his decision to respond with charm to Dido's attempt to be friendly that I was prepared to turn a blind eye—and a deaf ear—to the less attractive aspects of his adolescent behaviour. However once Dido had been reduced to the role of the ailing Victorian heroine, she had neither the time nor the energy to play the delightful stepmother. The older boys were affronted by the abrupt cessation of her good humour; Sandy was hurt when she complained he made too much noise. Only Primrose, gratified to receive evidence that Dido really was as beastly as stepmothers are always supposed to be, remained tranquil.

I took care to explain to my children that Dido was ill and frightened, but privately I was angry with her for playing with their affections in such an irresponsible manner, and I had a hard time keeping my anger hidden as we conducted our increasingly unreal conversations.

But I was reaching the end of that phase in which I was able to keep my marital problems at bay by acting. In the May of 1946, a week before our first wedding anniversary, Dido went into labour, and twelve hours later at Starbridge Hospital I was informed that the child would have to be sacrificed if Dido's life was to be saved.

2

I SANCTIONED my child's murder and waited. Unfortunately I was unable to wait in solitude. Having rushed to Starbridge as soon as Dido telephoned to announce the onset of labour, my sister-in-law was now weeping intermittently at my side. A smart-as-paint society woman, larger than Dido but equally svelte, she had been steadily grating on my nerves for some time.

I wanted a drink but knew a clergyman could hardly go in search of whisky when his child was being murdered and his wife's life was at risk. At intervals I tried to pray but my mind was in such chaos that I could only etch empty banalities on my consciousness. It seemed a long time before I was at last informed that Dido had survived and that her prognosis was good.

"Thank God!" sobbed Merry with a typically vulgar lack of control.

My informant, who was the chief gynaecologist and obstetrician at Starbridge Hospital, then tried to explain what had gone wrong but I found I could barely understand him. I heard various words but they evoked no emotional response. I only knew I had to listen and occasionally nod my head as he paused for breath amidst his seemingly disconnected phrases.

". . . impossible to predict beforehand . . . very rare but such things do happen . . . severe haemorrhage . . . had to act quickly . . . did try to save the baby, but lack of oxygen . . . umbilical cord twisted . . . could only have survived in a brain-damaged state . . . difficult labour . . . wife's terror, anaesthesia required so early . . . forceps . . . blood transfusion . . . very sorry indeed." He finally stopped speaking.

At once Merry shouted: "I think this hospital should be bloody well sued for negligence!" and rushed out of the room.

The doctor, exhibiting a magnificent sang-froid, as if hysterical females were a mere trifling occupational inconvenience, raised an eyebrow and uttered a disapproving "T-t-t!" before adding firmly: "I assure you, Mr. Aysgarth, that everything possible was done."

I nodded again, unable to grapple with the concept of medical negligence, and the doctor pursued with his professional smoothness: "Your wife's still heavily anaesthetised, but I'm sure you'd like to see her, wouldn't you?"

I had no idea. However since the question seemed to require an affirmative answer, I tried yet another nod and was promptly guided upstairs to a room where Dido was lying motionless. I was reminded at first of the wax dolls which my sister Emily had played with long ago, but then I found myself remembering my other sisters, Beatrice and Enid, who had failed to survive infancy. They too had resembled wax dolls as they lay close to death in their cradles. My mother had produced five children, one a year, in an orgy of parturition which had ceased only after a series of miscarriages.

Taking a deep breath I averted my eyes from Dido's corpse-like appearance, said: "Ah yes. Very nice," and swiftly retreated to the corridor. Then I realised I had uttered an idiocy. "Sorry," I added to the doctor as he rejoined me. "Not quite myself. All rather a shock." I was privately telling myself that now was hardly the moment to start thinking of my mother, whose death not so long ago in 1941 had so profoundly distressed me.

The doctor was still murmuring soothing platitudes when the ward-sister appeared and asked me with a genuine sympathy if I wanted to see the baby.

"The baby?" I wondered if I had finally gone mad. "But I understood it was dead."

"Yes, but sometimes parents wish to—"

"No, thank you." I had to lean back against the nearest wall in order to ensure I remained standing. How could I possibly face the child whose murder I had sanctioned? But perhaps it was my Christian duty. Another wave of horror assailed me. I was the Archdeacon of Starbridge. I had to do the right thing. Only demented laymen blundered around without caring whom they shocked.

"Tomorrow," I said with a great effort. "I'll see it tomorrow."

The sister nodded as if she quite understood my decision, and said that when I returned to the hospital the almoner would be available to discuss the arrangements. I almost said: "What arrangements?" but realised just in time that they would relate to the corpse. I reflected with relief that babies born dead could be disposed of without fuss. The very thought of organising a funeral was intolerable.

Eventually I emerged from the hospital and retreated to my car where

I found Merry snuffling in the passenger seat. I managed to say in my most neutral voice: "Feeling better?" but unfortunately my neutrality inflamed her.

"*Better?* No, I bloody well don't, I feel simply too devastated for words! Why didn't you give that doctor hell? Why did he put darling Dido through such agony? Why didn't he damn well do a Caesarian?"

"Because your favourite Harley Street lounge-lizard agreed with that poor bastard you've just savaged that a Caesarian wouldn't be necessary! Now will you kindly stop flouncing around like Bette Davis on an off-day and behave like something that resembles an English lady?"

"Stephen!" Merry subsided into a shocked silence. It was only when we reached the house that she said: "You've got a very hard streak in your nature, haven't you? I always thought you had. It's that mouth of yours. It shouts *Brutal!* every time you set it in that thin straight line."

I did not trust myself to reply. Entering the study, I slammed the door, plucked the whisky bottle from its home behind the Oxford Dictionary and poured myself a triple measure. I was just raising the glass to my lips when Merry knocked on the door.

Instantly I whipped the glass out of sight behind my desk. "Yes?" I shouted.

"Stephen"—as she came in I saw she was carrying an envelope—"I'm sorry, I should have been making allowances for you. After all, I'm sure the last few hours were torture for you as well as for me, so for God's sake let's have a truce now and stop screaming at each other . . . Do you have any whisky?"

"No, I don't usually drink spirits. What's that envelope you're holding?"

"It's a letter Dido wrote two weeks ago and sent to me for safekeeping. She wanted me to give it to you if she died."

"Well, she hasn't died. Tear it up."

"*You* tear it up," said Merry, cross that her winsome apology had failed to flush out a whisky bottle. "It's your letter, not mine. Anyway she could still die. Laura died of that embolism four days after she gave birth."

"Dido's not Laura. Dido's going to live," I said to myself levelly after the door had banged shut. Picking up the letter which Merry had flung down, I eyed it without enthusiasm. I was hardly in a mood to enjoy reading Dido's characteristic epistolary drivel, but nevertheless I was aware that beneath my antipathy a powerful curiosity was stirring. In fact I was probably incapable of destroying any woman's letter unread. I always thought of letters from women as little prizes, gratifying and delicious, a just reward for my faultless behaviour, and as soon as this piece of self-knowledge floated into my mind I found myself recalling all the white envelopes which had cascaded into my life for so many years, the letters from St. Leonards-on-Sea.

I was thinking of my mother again. Pouring myself a second whisky I slit open Dido's pale blue envelope and unfolded the letter within.

"Darling Stephen," I read.

> If I die (and I think I will) I want you to know that since our ghastly honeymoon you haven't wasted your time by being so wonderfully good and kind and loving to me. I used to think there was nothing else for me to do but die tragically in childbirth as it would solve all my terrible problems, but as I told you once I'm not the suicidal type, and anyway now you've made me want to live—although of course God's will is almost certainly that I should die as a punishment for being so awful for so long. But I want to live because love really does conquer all, and dearest, dearest Stephen, I felt I had to write you this letter because I couldn't possibly die leaving you in ignorance of the *Great and Glorious Truth*—which is not only that you love me (a true miracle) but that *I have come to love you.* No, I'm not fibbing, not exaggerating, not pretending—I mean every word I say and I'm saying yes, you've done it, you've succeeded, you're victorious—YOU'VE WON YOUR ULTIMATE PRIZE! Death really does concentrate the mind, just as Dr. Johnson said, and now I can see so clearly that you're the most wonderful man I've ever met. No man has ever cared for me as you have—you've made me feel I really am worth something after all, and I'm convinced now that with the help of your love I could overcome my troubles, but if I never get the chance to put matters right, just remember that you did indeed win me completely, exactly as you always wanted. Darling Stephen, this letter comes to you with eternal love from your utterly devoted
>
> DIDO.

I finished the letter. I finished my whisky. And I finished my long descent into the black pit of my second marriage. As I finally hit rock-bottom I had no choice but to face the terrible truth: I no longer wanted her. My ultimate prize had become the ultimate nightmare. I was trapped in an empty marriage with a woman I despised and detested, trapped in a marital horror which could last another thirty years, trapped on a tightrope where one false step could terminate my career in the Church, and as I stared appalled at the new world in which I found myself, I saw that the wasteland stretched ahead of me as far as the eye could see.

PART TWO

UNDER JUDGEMENT

Most people have, at some time or another, to stand alone and to suffer, and their final shape is determined by their response to their probation: they emerge either the slaves of circumstance or in some sense captains of their souls.

CHARLES E. RAVEN
A WANDERER'S WAY

IX

I do not want to approach the subject in any morbid or sentimental mood, but it is my full conviction that until men and women individually have been into hell they are not mature.

CHARLES E. RAVEN
THE CROSS AND THE CRISIS

I

IT was very silent in the wasteland, very cold and dark. I thought how strange it was that hell should be conventionally depicted as hot and noisy, an inferno of leaping flames and screaming souls welded together in a ceaseless roaring activity. I also thought how strange it was that the Modernists could attempt to slough off hell by defining it as an antiquated concept which could have no meaning for twentieth-century man. Hell was dereliction in the wasteland—the wasteland in which the soul was imprisoned when God was absent, the wasteland where there was no convenient exit marked SALVATION and no convenient signpost directing one to the spiritual presence of Christ.

I realised then that the formulae by which I lived my life were no longer working. The sword of my Liberal optimism had shattered. I had thought the horrors of the atomic bomb and the concentration camps had already tried my Liberalism to its limits, but it had survived by insisting that these evils had been an aberration in mankind's steady evolution in accordance with God's plans. I had of course been aware that I stood at a privileged distance from those who had suffered so grossly in the war, but I had told myself that this gave me the necessary detachment to squeeze the horrors into my theory of atonement: God had achieved an at-one-ment, putting himself at one with suffering humanity through the sufferings of Christ so that all evil might be overcome and mankind made whole, reconciled and redeemed by God's love. It had never occurred to me that I could find myself in a situation where God appeared to be not at one with mankind at all but utterly absent, utterly remote and utterly transcendent. Even during the most difficult moments of my childhood I had always been convinced that God was on my side, rewarding all my hard work and good behaviour with well-deserved prizes. The world might often be harsh but it was rational, and because it was rational it was safe and good. God was in Christ, reconciling the world to himself. Or as Browning, the favourite poet of the Liberal Protestants, had written: "God's in his heaven— All's right with the world."

But now God was in his heaven, I was in hell and there was no at-one-ment, no sign of Christ. I was cut off from my sources of spiritual strength, absolutely alone. My instinctive reaction, as always, was to put everything right by chasing the next prize, but the only prize in sight was the prize I had won, the prize which was now poised to destroy me, and I did not see how I could survive.

I was suddenly so frightened that I had another triple whisky. That calmed me. I tried to think clearly. What did I do next? I had no idea. Slowly I realised that I would have to find someone who would tell me what to do. At that point my administrator's brain woke up, groped its way through the fog of panic and fastened on the problem as if it belonged to someone else. When a clergyman sat around drinking triple whiskies and telling himself he was finished, he could be classified as having broken down, and when a clergyman broke down in the Starbridge diocese there were fundamentally two courses of action open to his superiors. If he was exhausted but still *compos mentis* we dispatched him to a clerical establishment called Allington Court in Devon, a hotel which had the facilities (peace and quiet, a chapel with daily services, a warden experienced in counselling) to double as a convalescent home for clergymen who needed a rest. On the other hand, if the sufferer was no longer able to function normally in the world, we carted him to the Fordite monks at Starwater Abbey. The Fordites, who were Anglican Benedictines, had a good reputation for refurbishing battered souls.

It seemed obvious that I was far beyond being helped by a little holiday at Allington Court, and anyway I could hardly wander off to Devon when my wife was ill in hospital. But I shuddered at the thought of the Fordites. Although the monks lived in my archdeaconry, the Abbey was a small independent state where my writ failed to run. The Fordites might operate within the Church of England but they formed a private organisation which answered only to the Archbishop of Canterbury. The Bishop of Starbridge, who was officially appointed their "visitor," called on the monks every year but he had no power over them, and I, as the Archdeacon, had not only no power but also no obligation to make any visits. After my appointment in 1937 I had called as a courtesy to introduce myself to the Abbot, but I had been so horrified by the stench of incense in the chapel and the appalling plaster statuette of the Virgin Mary in the visitors' parlour that I had never returned except to unload the occasional unfortunate colleague who was undergoing a breakdown.

I thought that the monks could probably cope with me if I were to pay them a quick visit (a long visit was out of the question, of course, as tongues would start to wag), but could I cope with them? I thought I might if I could shelter beneath a cloak of anonymity, but a number of the monks would inevitably remember me; when I delivered my demented brethren I hardly dumped them on the doorstep and scuttled away in my car. I shuddered as I thought of the monks gossiping behind my back, and automatically I reached again for the whisky bottle.

At last it occurred to me that I could not continue to sit at my desk, drink whisky and shudder at the thought of the Fordites. I had to find someone who would tell me how to survive, and when one stood in the wasteland one could hardly afford to be fussy. One just grabbed the best man available and prayed for deliverance.

It was then that I remembered Darrow, the former Fordite monk. He had never lived at the Starwater house but since his return to the world he had visited it regularly, and without doubt he would know the best men there. If Darrow were to arrange an interview for me by telephone I could avoid being assigned to someone I knew, and then I would have the chance to be anonymous.

I stood up. There was no more time to waste. Carefully I put the whisky bottle to bed behind the Oxford Dictionary and carefully I hid my empty glass in a drawer of my desk. Steering myself outside, I crawled into my car and after five attempts managed to shove the key into the ignition. Was I too drunk to drive? No, but possibly the police might not agree with me. Would there be any police patrols around at three o'clock in the morning? Not once I was clear of the city. Could I drive the twelve miles to Darrow's home at Starrington Magna without having an accident? Certainly, and if anyone tried to stop me I'd punch him on the nose.

I chugged down Canonry Drive at a speed approaching two miles an hour. It seemed hard to see where I was going but at last I realised I had forgotten to switch on the headlights. How absent-minded! I stopped the car in order to find the switch. No point in searching while I was driving—silly to try to do two things at once. The lights blazed on, full headlights, no black-out—thank God for the end of the war!—and then as the darkness miraculously dissolved I saw ahead of me the gates of the Close, shut and locked, just as they always were between eleven at night and six in the morning.

That was when I was forced to acknowledge that I was either mad or drunk or both. How could I have forgotten such an elementary fact of life in the Cathedral Close? I did have a key to the gates, but the realisation that I was drunk and/or mad made me pause to reconsider what I was doing. Then I realised not only that I was incapable of driving to Starrington Magna but that I could hardly turn up unshaven, distraught and reeking of whisky on Darrow's doorstep at some extraordinary hour of the morning.

Struggling back to the house I abandoned my car and retreated to my study to have another big think, but in fact my next task was now so obvious that thinking was unnecessary. I had to make myself presentable. Doggedly I dosed myself with Alka-Seltzer. Painstakingly I crept upstairs, washed, shaved without cutting myself (no mean feat) and put on clean clothes. At last, satisfied that I looked no worse than any other clergyman who had almost lost his wife in harrowing circumstances, I returned to my study, drank tea, chain-smoked and waited for the time to pass.

I tried to calculate when Darrow would arrive at the Theological College. He would have to arrive before eight, when the students and staff gathered in the chapel for Matins. Pulling down my copy of Bradshaw from the bookshelf I looked up the early trains from Starrington Magna and discovered one which reached Starbridge at seven thirty-five. The station was ten minutes' walk from the Close. By a quarter to eight Darrow would be striding through the front door.

I glanced at my watch. Then slipping out of the house for the second time that morning, I entered the Cathedral churchyard and began to plough across the vast sward to the Theological College by St. Anne's Gate.

2

HE had just arrived. As I entered the principal's office he was hanging up his hat.

"Oh hullo, Darrow," I said as if I had encountered him by chance at a garden-party. "Sorry to descend on you at such an early hour. Can you spare me a moment?"

"Of course." He gave me a smile, the wintry one which combined the maximum of courtesy with the minimum of warmth, and indicated the two chairs placed at the small table by the window. "Sit down."

"Thanks." As we both seated ourselves I embarked on the essential preliminary explanation of my haggard appearance. "Excuse me if I look a trifle battered," I said, "but I've been up all night. My wife had the baby but it was born dead."

"I'm most extremely sorry." His sincerity took me aback. I had expected a polite expression of sympathy, not a manifestation of genuine concern. "Was it a boy or a girl?"

I stared at him. To my horror I realised he had asked a question I was unable to answer. No one had told me the baby's sex and I had never enquired. I had been too busy wanting to sweep the corpse under the nearest rug and ring down the curtain.

"No doubt you were so distressed about your wife that you weren't able to focus on the child at all," said Darrow, skilfully glossing over my embarrassed silence as he realised what had happened. "That would be a very normal reaction in the circumstances."

I said stiffly: "It wasn't possible for me to see the child last night. I shall see it today. You needn't think I'm not aware of my Christian duty."

"I wasn't thinking of your obligation to perform a Christian duty. I was thinking of your need to come to terms with your bereavement."

"What bereavement? For a father a baby born dead is a baby that never happened. Only the mother, who's carried the child for nine months, can feel any emotion which could be classified as bereavement."

Darrow made no comment but looked concerned.

"You needn't worry!" I said dryly. "I haven't come to sob on your shoulder about my private misfortunes! I merely told you about the disaster because I wanted to explain why I'm looking a trifle frayed at the seams."

"I see," said Darrow. "So you're all right, are you?"

"Absolutely fine."

There was a pause while I belatedly realised I had boxed myself into the most implausible corner. How could I conceivably have been so stupid as to say I was absolutely fine? He would be thinking me a monster of callousness, unmoved by the dead baby and my wife's brush with death. Feverishly I tried to present myself in a more Christian light.

"Well, as a matter of fact," I said, "to be absolutely honest, it really has been rather a harrowing twenty-four hours. But of course I don't want to bore you with all the gruesome details."

"Bore me as much as you please."

"No, no, no, it's really not necessary. It was just . . . well, to be perfectly frank, it was rather an awkward situation. They had to sacrifice the baby to save my wife. Later I was told that they had in fact tried to save it but that even if it had been born alive it would have been hopelessly damaged. So of course that makes it easier for me to come to terms with . . . what happened. The decision. My decision. They had to ask me, you see. Just a formality, they already knew what they wanted to do, what had to be done. But nevertheless . . . it really was rather awkward."

"Very."

"But I mean, what else could I have done? If a doctor turns up and says: 'Your wife will die unless such-and-such is done,' one's moral duty is to save one's wife and sanction such-and-such. I know I made the right decision, because no other decision could possibly have been made. But all the same, I can't help wishing that I hadn't been put in a situation where that kind of decision was required."

"A great ordeal."

"Yes. I suppose so. Yes, that was what it was. An ordeal." I seized on the word with relief. Now that the mess had been placed in a definitive category it could be filed away safely behind the curtain. "Well," I said, taking a deep breath and preparing to turn to other matters, "so much for all that. Now—"

"I'm so very sorry, Aysgarth."

"What? Oh, thanks. Nice of you. Well, I really mustn't waste any more of your time by dwelling on—"

"In the circumstances it's fortunate you don't consider yourself bereaved. If you had to deal with grief as well as all the horror and anger, the situation would be well-nigh unendurable."

"Anger?"

"You said you wished you hadn't been put in a position where that terrible decision was required."

"Oh, I see. Well, it's no good agonising about it now, is it? What's done's done. Now if you don't mind, we'll put all that aside and turn to the reason why I've come to see you. I—"

"Ah, I've got it!" Darrow exclaimed suddenly. "You're trying to ring down the curtain! I remember you telling me last year in the Crusader how devoted you were to your curtains, but Aysgarth, has it never occurred to you that occasionally a curtain really ought to be allowed to stay up?"

"If I want to ring down the bloody curtain I'll bloody well ring it down!" I yelled, suddenly overpowered by the urge to ease my mounting tension by channelling it into verbal violence, but immediately the words were uttered I realised—too late—that in giving way to aggression I had swung fatally out of control. I began to panic. Clutching the edge of the table I tried to dredge up a manner which could pass for normal. "Sorry,"

I muttered. "Bad language. Disgraceful behaviour. Not quite myself at the moment. Got a small problem—very minor—quite apart from all this business, and that in fact is why I'm here. Can we stop discussing irrelevant matters now and finally get down to business?"

"Of course," said Darrow. "I'm so sorry I diverted you."

The apology steadied me. I felt calm enough to adopt a casual offhand manner. "I won't bore you with the details of this little problem," I said. "It's not particularly important, but it occurred to me that it might be useful if I had a short talk—about half an hour would do—with one of the Starwater Fordites. Is it possible for you to arrange such a meeting for me? I'd do it myself, but some of those monks know who I am, and . . . well, I know it sounds absurd, but—"

"You want to be anonymous. That's not absurd. That's natural—and sensible too. If you're looking for detachment, the last person you want is someone who exclaims: 'Ah, good morning, Archdeacon!' as soon as you enter the room."

I was greatly reassured. Speaking with renewed confidence I said: "That's why I thought I'd ask for your help. If you can tell me the names of the best men at Starwater I can tell you the ones I don't know, and then—"

"Can you get to London for a few hours?"

"London! You mean the Fordite headquarters?"

"It would solve the anonymity problem and it would save you a trip to Yorkshire. Do you remember me talking to you in the Crusader of Aidan Lucas?"

"Are you saying—"

"I'm saying you're in luck. He's in London, convalescing after an eye operation."

And that was the moment when I glimpsed, far away across the wasteland, the faint outline of the signpost inscribed SALVATION.

3

"IS he seeing visitors?"

"He saw me last weekend. I think he'd see you. He can't read much at present and he finds visitors a welcome diversion."

The outline of the signpost to Salvation faded as I suffered another bout of panic. "The trouble is I don't think I could spare the time at the moment to go to London. I've got a lot of work on hand, and—"

Darrow, who had somehow managed to maintain a mild, tranquil manner from the start of the interview, suddenly decided that a radically new approach was required. Without warning he blasted into the attack. "My dear Aysgarth," he said, "shall we abandon this soothing fiction that your problem is just another little awkwardness which can be glossed over with half an hour's tea and sympathy at Starwater Abbey? I know exactly how you feel about the Fordites! You wouldn't even consider seeking help from them unless you'd hit rock-bottom hard enough to crack cement. Now stop flaunting that lethal Yorkshire pride, stop flourishing those idiotic Yorkshire understatements and stop falling over yourself to prove to me that you're the toughest archdeacon in Christendom!"

At once I was released from the panic-infested muddle which had been exacerbated by his sympathy and concern. Almost gasping with relief I waded straight into the attack.

"You want me to collapse in a heap on your carpet, I suppose!" I shouted. "That would give you great satisfaction, wouldn't it—you'd be delighted to see your old enemy vanquished! But I'm not the kind of clergyman who has nervous breakdowns, I'm not the kind of clergyman who makes a mess of his life, I'm not the kind of clergyman who—"

"You appear to be the kind of clergyman who's in urgent need of spiritual first aid, and if you'll now give me the chance I'll—"

"Oh, go and play the wonder-worker to all your doting disciples! My problems are no business of yours!"

"That's exactly where you're wrong. I have a duty to the Church—and to Dr. Ottershaw, our superior—to see you don't crack up and create a first-class scandal. You've been drinking, haven't you?"

"I'm not obliged to answer that! I'm answerable only to my Bishop, not to arrogant ex-abbots like you!"

"So be it," said Darrow, rising to his feet and moving to the telephone on his desk. "I'll ring Dr. Ottershaw."

I gasped. Then I jumped up, grabbed the receiver from his hand, slammed the instrument back in its cradle and stood guard over it.

"Aysgarth, short of murdering me you can't stop me speaking my mind eventually to the Bishop if I choose to do so! Now stop flailing around in panic and try to take in what I'm about to say. I'll leave Dr. Ottershaw in ignorance of your truly appalling condition if you put yourself in my hands and do exactly as I tell you."

"But—"

"Aysgarth, do you want to survive this crisis or don't you?"

"What a damn silly, time-wasting, half-baked question!"

"Then sit down again in that chair and let's try to stop you bleeding to death before you reach Aidan's operating table in London."

4

I HAD just collapsed in my chair when there was a knock on the door and Jennings, the vice-principal, looked in.

"Excuse me, Jon—oh, good morning, Archdeacon!—but I just wanted to make sure you were here. It's almost eight o'clock." As if on cue the bell in the chapel began to toll for Matins.

"I'd be grateful if you'd take the service for me, Frank. There's an urgent matter I have to discuss with the Archdeacon."

That disposed of Jennings and Matins. Darrow was now free until the service of Holy Communion—"Mass," as he usually called it in his Anglo-Catholic fashion.

"The first thing you must do," he said as soon as Jennings had left the room, "is list your morning's engagements so that I can cancel them. What were you planning to do after this interview?"

"Obviously I must go home, break the news about the baby to my younger children—the older boys are away at school, of course—and embark on my day's work. I must see my curates at nine, Dr. Ottershaw at ten—and then at eleven I have a diocesan committee meeting about—"

"When will you return to the hospital?"

"They told me not to go back before noon. So as soon as the committee meeting finishes I must go to the hospital, see my wife, see the almoner, see the baby—" I stopped. A long silence followed. Then from a long way away I heard my voice say: "I can't face it."

"Can't face seeing the baby?"

"No, that's all right. I'm not bereaved so I won't feel anything. I can endure the baby. It's my wife I can't face."

"Can you tell me why?"

"None of your damned business."

"You feel guilty, perhaps? Guilty that she's suffering through bearing your child?"

"Oh, stop making wild guesses and trying to pass them off as psychic insights!"

"Maybe you feel guilty because you wish the baby was alive and she was dead."

I sprang to my feet. My chair keeled over. In a shaking voice I said: "You *sinister* magician! Go to hell—I'm walking out!"

"Aysgarth"—in a flash he was barring my path to the door—"do you really want to destroy yourself? You've got to face your wife this morning and I've got to help you do it. I can cancel the curates, the Bishop and every diocesan committee meeting on Eternity Street, but I can't cancel your wife."

"I tell you I can't see her—I can't—"

"You must. If you don't turn up at that hospital this morning the scandal's going to begin. Your marriage is already the most discussed partnership in the diocese. Possibly it's the most discussed marriage in the Church of England—it's not every day an archdeacon marries a society girl—and any adverse gossip about the two of you now is going to be picked up and magnified. Then the gutter press will rush in, and do I really have to spell out what will happen if the more unscrupulous journalists decide your marriage has run aground? Aysgarth, you've got to get it into your head that you're absolutely on the brink of catastrophe and one false step could send you over the edge into the abyss!"

It was impossible to argue with him; that indeed was how I myself saw my crisis. Hardly aware of what I was doing I turned aside from the door and moved to the window. With horror I saw the outline of the Cathedral was blurred.

"All the familiar landmarks are disappearing," I said. "How can I find my way when there are no landmarks?" I waited for an answer but Darrow was silent, and now the Cathedral was a mere haze of light and shade, as indistinct as an Impressionist painting. Fearful of showing any trace of weakness, appalled at the thought that I might betray unacceptable emotion in the presence of a man I disliked, I once more resorted to rage to keep an unbearable truth at bay.

"Why am I being tormented like this?" I shouted, and as I spoke I slammed my fist down on the surface of the table. "Why has this happened to me?"

Darrow at once threw me a lifeline by implying that the torment could be eased. "Aidan will help you discern the answer to that question," he said, "but at present you're quite beyond discernment. Now, Aysgarth"—I was aware of him moving back to the table—"you must try to be still. In your distress you're making so much noise that you wouldn't hear a communication from God even if He were transformed into an anthropomorphic deity who could thunder instructions to you in impeccable BBC English. The way forward at this moment, I assure you, is not to thrash around making a noise. What you have to do is to listen—to listen to the silence and be calm."

I blinked rapidly, pretended to rub a fleck of grit from one eye and collapsed yet again at the table. Meanwhile Darrow was moving his chair so that he could sit closer to me. The silence lengthened but eventually I felt strong enough to look at him. He stared back. He had an angular face with prominent cheekbones, a tough jaw and a high forehead. His eyes were a peculiarly clear shade of grey, and I knew, as I noted their clarity, that he was trying to will me into a calmer state. Damned witch-doctor! He thought of himself as a healer, of course, like Christ. He would. I seethed with irritation as I contemplated such arrogance, but the next moment my mind had forgotten Darrow's shady parlour tricks. The image of Christ, having drifted so idly into my mind, was now expanding; I found I was thinking of him moving among the sick, the oppressed, the tormented; I imagined him saying: "Your faith has made you whole."

"It's all a unity," I said. "It's all one." It took me a moment to realise I had spoken my father's words aloud, and in confusion I tried to gloss over this apparently irrelevant quotation. "I mean *I* want to be all one," I said, "and not torn apart by my troubles."

"You want to be whole."

I froze. "Why use the word 'whole'?"

"Why not? It was a word favoured by Our Lord, wasn't it? Whenever he moved among the sick—"

"Quite." I wrote off the apparent synchronisation of our thoughts as a coincidence and finally managed to relax.

"Feeling better?" said Darrow.

To my surprise I realised that I was. Grunting a cautious assent I stole a furtive glance at the Cathedral and found to my profound relief that the outline was clear.

"Very well," said Darrow, satisfied that I was no longer trying to climb every wall in the room, "let's try and build up your strength for this crucial interview with your wife. I'll find you a corner where you can snatch a few hours' sleep."

"But what on earth are you going to say to—"

"Leave everyone to me—I'll deal with them. All you've got to do is deal with yourself by recuperating as far as possible from your sleepless night—and before you try to argue, may I remind you that the care of your health is a religious duty," said Darrow austerely in the kind of voice which made it plain that no further argument was possible.

I saw no alternative but to allow him to lead me from the room. Once Darrow started dealing with people he was like a tank; I felt as if I'd been mown flat. Trudging along in his wake I was taken upstairs to a bedroom which belonged to an absent ordinand and told to lock myself in as soon as I was alone.

"You think he might come back?" I said confused.

"No, he's attending a funeral in Birmingham. I was merely worried in case a zealous cleaning-woman chose to wander in with her duster

. . . Well, don't just stand there, Aysgarth! Take off your shoes and collar, adopt a horizontal position on that bed and at least make an effort to rest even if you can't manage to sleep. I'll come back at half-past eleven with some food, and at quarter to twelve we'll leave for the hospital."

"You're coming with me?"

"Of course. Did you really think I'd leave you to face this nightmare alone?"

"But your work—your classes—your appointments—"

"I'll deal with them. No need for you to worry."

"But I really can't disrupt your life like this just because I'm currently a little under the weather—"

"Aysgarth, will you kindly stop pretending this dire emergency is a mere passing inconvenience?"

He left. Locking the door obediently, I shed my shoes and collar, lay down on the bed and prepared myself for three hours of tormented solitude.

But I slept.

5

I SLEPT, and into my dreams walked Uncle Willoughby, shouting: "This is a dire emergency—and this is where you start to pay!" I knew he wanted to kill me with the bloodstained axe he held in his hand, but I ran away from him, I ran all the way home, I ran upstairs to the nursery, where I picked up the sledgehammer which was lying beside a cradle filled with dead babies, and as the door of the room burst open I smashed his skull to pulp. I smashed and I smashed and I smashed but suddenly I realised with horror that my victim wasn't Uncle Willoughby. It was my mother. In terror I knew I had to cover up my mistake, I knew I had to pound the corpse to pieces so that I could sweep it under the rug and ring down the curtain, but the body refused to disintegrate and the moment I stopped wielding my sledgehammer it began to come back to life. In panic I tried to raise the sledgehammer again but now it was too heavy for me to lift, and as I wrestled futilely with that leaden weight I suddenly became aware of Uncle Willoughby creeping up behind me and swinging back his axe and—

I sat bolt upright, gasping and sweating, to find myself in the little bedroom beneath the eaves of the Theological College. Beyond the window the sun was still shining on the Cathedral from a radiant cloudless sky.

After a while it occurred to me to glance at my watch and to my relief

I saw it was almost time for Darrow to arrive. I felt ready for action. No more idle dozes and ridiculous nightmares. The moment had come to face the next stage of my ordeal.

In despair I tried to imagine how I could survive my visit to the hospital.

6

"LET'S try to decide what approach you're going to take with your wife," said Darrow, offering me a Marmite sandwich and a tall glass of water. "The key to surviving a difficult interview is to be well prepared. Are you capable of saying something as mundane as: 'Darling, I'm so sorry you've been through this terrible experience but thank God you're still alive,' or would even that be too much for you?"

"No, I think I could manage that. But I don't think I could manage it for very long."

"Could you last five minutes?"

"I might. It depends on her. If she's well enough there'll be no difficulty because she'll quickly take over the conversation."

"If she's not well enough to talk much there's still no difficulty, because the nurses won't let you stay long. I'll tell you what I'll do. I'll see that whatever happens you're hauled out after five minutes. If you feel you can't last that long, say that you have to go to the lavatory and I'll make sure a nurse will be waiting to terminate the visit when you get back."

I said in despair: "How in heaven's name am I going to get through the next thirty years of married life?"

"Don't think of the next thirty years. Just concentrate on getting through today."

"I simply don't understand how I could have wound up like this—"

"Don't think of that either—all speculation can wait till later . . . When did you first realise your marriage was a mistake?"

"Some time ago, but I thought I could make it come right so long as I had a prize to chase. So long as she was capable of being converted into a prize, I was fine."

"You mean you finally gave up trying to convert her?"

"No, I mean I finally won her completely."

"And then you didn't want her any more?"

"Well, there was nothing left to chase, you see, and there's not much you can do with a prize after you've won it except keep it on the mantelshelf—and sometimes that's fine, of course, sometimes one gets great pleasure and satisfaction from keeping a prize on the mantelshelf to remind one of one's luck in possessing such a perfect object, but the trouble with Dido is—"

"She's very far from being a perfect object. Yes, I do see. A most baffling dilemma . . . And how long have you been chasing the prizes?"

"Oh, forever. It's the way to get on, isn't it? It's the way to stay out of the pit."

"What pit?"

"The failure pit. The one where the coffin is."

"Failure equals death? Winning the prizes equals life?"

"Yes. But—" I broke off. My memory was regurgitating the famous declaration of Jesus according to St. Matthew: "He that findeth his life shall lose it and he that loseth his life for my sake shall find it." Covering my face with my hands I said in horror: "I've won everything I've ever wanted—but I've lost all the way along the line."

"Not quite."

"But I've wound up in the pit—I'm alongside the coffin—"

"But not in it."

"Yes, but—"

"You're going to fight your way out of that pit, Aysgarth. You're going to escape from that coffin."

"I don't see how I can ever—"

"Put on your collar and shoes, dust yourself down and fix your eyes resolutely on survival. Survival's your new prize. Start chasing."

Reaching for my collar without another word, I began to drag myself painfully to the starting-line for my next race.

X

"It might be impossible to make sense of life: life was not worth living until the attempt to do so had been made."

CHARLES E. RAVEN
A WANDERER'S WAY

I

"DARLING Stephen—"

"Dido—my poor little love—"

"Oh Stephen, I feel so useless, such a failure, not even able to produce a proper baby—"

"All that matters is that you're going to be all right."

"I could still die of post-partum complications—"

"But you won't. I absolutely forbid it," I said, and smiled at her as I gripped her hand.

"Oh Stephen, I love you so much—I wrote you a letter—"

"I've read it. Darling, I thought it was the most beautiful letter any husband could ever receive."

"You were only supposed to read it if I died!"

"Yes, but isn't it nice that you're still alive to hear me tell you how wonderful it was?"

We laughed. The interview was zipping along with the quick-fire verve of an *I.T.M.A.* script, each character trotting out the type of lines which the audience had come to expect, but I felt as if the script was shaking in my hands, and in my memory I heard Alex saying again and again: "How we all lie to one another!"

"Darling Stephen!" Dido was saying passionately. "If only we could pretend this whole disaster had never happened! You won't believe this, but just before you arrived they tried to show it to me. *It.* The dead body. My dear! Can you *imagine* anyone being quite so insensitive? I started screaming straight away. Merry was right—I should have had the baby in London and not in this provincial medical dustbin—well, I *would* have had it in London if I hadn't been so worried that people would say I was an awful wife, leaving you on your own all over again. I'm sure that if I'd been in a nice smart London clinic they wouldn't have tried to push a corpse under my nose when all I wanted was to pretend my dreadful failure never happened . . ." And she began to cry.

At once I seized the opportunity to ring the bell for the nurse. The ward-sister appeared, took one look at her patient, who was now sobbing uncontrollably, and said to me: "We're as well as can be expected but it's only natural that we should still be very upset."

Dido shrieked: "That's the one who tried to rub my nose in the corpse!" and began to scream.

The sister advised me without expression to cut short my visit. Giving Dido a quick kiss I declared I adored her and fled.

Darrow was outside in the corridor. He was talking to a large woman of the type who can always be relied upon to arrange the flowers in church each week.

"Aysgarth, this is the almoner, Mrs. Collins." He gave her the smile he kept specially for women. Mrs. Collins simpered. Darrow, my personal tank, was once more carrying all before him. "Mrs. Collins has offered to take you to see the baby before we sort out the paperwork."

"Ah yes." After the scene with Dido I felt that even seeing a dead baby could be ranked as a pleasure. "Thank you, Mrs. Collins."

The woman expressed the usual words of sympathy before leading the way downstairs. Outside the main building we crossed a lawn which unexpectedly sloped to the banks of the river. In Starbridge the river was forever turning up in unexpected places; it not only looped around the town but also, with the aid of a tributary, twisted through it so that one was never far from the water. One was never far from the Cathedral either. Beyond the flowering cherry trees which flanked the river-bank, beyond the chimney-pots of the distant buildings, I could see the spire shimmering against that dazzlingly cloudless sky.

On the other side of the lawn the almoner took us into an unnamed modern building and opened the first door on the left of the hall.

"I'll wait here," said Darrow, planting himself by the nearest wall.

I followed the almoner into a room where a little lump lay under a blanket on a table.

"I'll wait with Father Darrow outside," said the woman in the hushed voice people reserve for churches, and to my relief I found myself abandoned.

The door closed. I eyed the blanket. No one was watching. I didn't have to look underneath. I made up my mind not to look, but then I remembered Darrow. If I failed to look, he would know. I had no belief in telepathy, of course, but I knew he would ask a prying question, gauge my reaction and put two and two together before I could even say "white magic." The thought that he now knew exactly how I felt about Dido was enough to make my blood run cold. He would tell no one, I was sure of that, but the very fact that he knew suddenly seemed unbearable. I suffered a violent urge to escape from him before he could uncover my lack of paternal feeling towards the corpse, but I knew very well that I needed my personal tank, flattening every obstacle in my path, if I was to survive.

Thinking of survival reminded me of the little lump to whom survival had been denied. Gritting my teeth, I raised the blanket and took a quick look. The baby was very small, very ugly and very dead. I dropped the blanket but then realised I still had no idea of the child's sex. I had to find out. Supposing the almoner were to uncover my ignorance as we wrestled with the paperwork? What would she think of such crass indifference to my own flesh and blood? I shuddered from head to toe.

Reluctantly I raised the blanket again, but the baby was encased in a cloth which I could not bring myself to unwrap. By this time I was feeling so nauseated that I noticed the corner basin with relief. What *was* this room? Why hadn't the baby been left in a side ward until I had been through the farce of viewing the body? And why, after Dido's bout of hysterics which had preceded my arrival, had the baby been whipped out of her room and dispatched straight to the mortuary? Was an autopsy to be performed? Or was the removal merely in accordance with regulations about dead bodies in hospitals? I had no idea. No doubt Mrs. Collins would enlighten me later, but meanwhile here I was, standing in a building which must be a mortuary and staring around at a room which seemed to be specifically for viewing corpses. But if the room had really been set aside specifically for the viewing of corpses, who was the fool who had painted the walls such a repulsive shade of yellow?

I vomited neatly into the corner basin. That made me feel better, and as I sluiced away the mess I made a new resolution to behave in an orderly Christian fashion. Returning to the corpse I noticed there was a little label attached to the cloth. The inscription read: AYSGARTH (MALE). I was looking at my son.

Folding my hands I closed my eyes and tried to pray. As a Protestant I disapproved of prayers for the dead, but I thought I should pray for forgiveness for my part in his death. Unfortunately I seemed quite incapable of an *ex tempore* prayer. I decided to embark on the Lord's Prayer instead, but seconds later I realised I was reciting the General

Confession. Obviously I was on the point of climbing the repulsive yellow walls. How could any clergyman in his right mind decide to recite the Lord's Prayer and wind up halfway through the General Confession? Perhaps in my guilt I had subconsciously decided that the plea "forgive us our trespasses" in the Lord's Prayer was inadequate. Or perhaps the aberration was merely further proof that I was thoroughly worn out.

In despair I wished I could sense the presence of Christ. Then I would be in command, infused by the power of the Spirit, and all would be well. It occurred to me then that if Jesus had been physically present he would have picked up the corpse, and the baby, transformed by love, would have been beautiful. Nerving myself to clasp the bundle I held it in my arms, but the child remained ugly.

As my despair deepened I said aloud to my unnamed flesh and blood: "Sorry. Awful mess. Better off where you are." But as I spoke these idiotic words I thought of him being "with Christ," as the symbolic saying goes, in some dimension of ultimate reality which lay far beyond the scope of the human imagination to conceive, and suddenly I saw Jesus clearly in my mind, not the effeminate romantic of those sentimental Victorian paintings and not the magnetic leader I usually pictured, but an idealised version of my father, who had loved children and who had transformed the bleak hills above Maltby into a paradise when he had taken us for walks on those summer afternoons long ago. And when I glanced down again at the corpse I saw it was no longer just a dead body but a person—and not just any person but someone special, as special as all the other grandchildren whom my father would have loved if only he could have lived to see them, and as I remembered my father's love the vile repulsive room became suffused with light, my despair was smoothed away and for a single moment my wasteland was transformed, just as the Yorkshire countryside had been transformed long ago when my father had been alive and I had walked with him in paradise.

I said aloud: "You'll be all right now," and when I spoke I heard not the idiotic utterance of a demented man but a symbolic communication with my father's grandson, a unique individual whose memory would be valued and cherished. Putting the baby back in his resting-place, I stood motionless for a long moment as I grieved for all that had been lost. Then drawing the blanket for the last time across that unforgettable face, I walked abruptly from the room.

2

IN the hall I said to Darrow before he could speak: "I don't want to talk about it." Then I noticed the almoner's absence. "Where's Mrs. Collins?"

"Gone on ahead to her office."

We went outside. The sun felt hot after the chill of the morgue. The grass was a radiant green.

"I can deal with Mrs. Collins once you've signed the forms," said Darrow. "You can wait in the car."

"Thanks." Keeping my gaze firmly on the main block of the hospital ahead of us, I said: "There's to be no anonymous disposal. He's not to be swept under the rug."

"I'll make that clear to her."

"And he's to have a proper birth certificate. He's not to be passed off without a name just because he was born dead."

"What name should I give?"

"Arthur. And if there's no space on that piece of paper they allocate to stillborns, the name must be written in the margin or on the back. He's to have a proper name and a proper funeral and a proper grave and a proper headstone with 'Arthur' on it."

"I'll organise the undertakers. Don't worry, Aysgarth, everything will be arranged exactly as you wish. Just you leave it all to me."

3

AS we drove away from the hospital Darrow said: "Congratulations. You appear to have survived that ordeal surprisingly well."

"Curiously enough, seeing Dido wasn't as difficult as I'd feared. That was just another exercise in fantasy. It was seeing Arthur that nearly finished me off. That was reality."

"It was important that he should have become real to you. One can't surmount a painful experience unless one first faces it directly."

I considered this statement with care. Then I said: "I daresay I shall always feel some degree of guilt, but it'll be a guilt I can live with because I know now he's all right. And the very fact that I know this means I'm forgiven." This obscure assertion sounded oddly familiar, and again I experienced the *déjà vu* phenomenon which had been haunting me for so long. In an effort both to clarify my feelings to Darrow and to grope in my memory for the prior image which had made the words so eerily familiar, I said slowly: "When I saw him he became special and the alienation caused by guilt dissolved. It was like the automatic working of a law of science."

"Ah, you Modernists!" said Darrow. "Always so ready to worship at science's altar! Why can't you just say that love has the power to cast out misery and generate forgiveness? Or if that's too direct for you, why not merely say: 'God was in Christ, reconciling the world to himself'? Why drag in science?"

"We belong to different generations, Darrow."

"Yes—and mine was the one infatuated with scientific advances! I'd have thought that your generation would have recovered from that love affair by now, particularly after Hiroshima."

I suddenly identified the missing half of the *déjà vu* experience: Alex had used almost identical language in expressing his relief that I would be keeping a benign eye on his secret family if Ashworth failed to come home. He had seen the easing of his anxiety about Lyle's boys as a sign of God's forgiveness. They, like Arthur, would be "all right." He no longer needed to worry about them. They had become a symbol of God's saving grace and atonement.

"By the way," I said abruptly, thinking of Lyle, "how's Charles Ashworth?"

"Much better. He's going to spend some time with me later this week."

"It's a miracle he's alive. I never thought he'd come back," I said, for Ashworth had survived not only the prison camp where he had spent the months following the fall of Tobruk, but the concentration camp to which he had been transferred in 1944 after aiding fellow-prisoners to escape. Once he had passed through those gates he had sunk to the status of a missing person, unable to write letters and beyond the reach of the enquiries made by the Red Cross. In 1945 after the liberation of the camp he had been obliged to spend some time in a military hospital, but now he had been discharged and Lyle, leaving her temporary home in Starvale St. James, had resumed her married life in Cambridge. I thought of little Charley, shining-eyed, waving his Union Jack. Amidst all the bereavement I encountered as a clergyman it was heartening to hear of a family who had not hoped for a reunion in vain.

"What made you ask about Charles out of the blue like that?" said Darrow curiously as I drove under the archway into the Close.

I could hardly talk about Alex's secret family and my guilty memories of Lyle. "You mentioned Hiroshima," I said, "and I thought of the prisoners of war in the Far East, able to come home as the result of the bomb. Then I thought of the POWs in Europe." In an effort to change the subject I asked: "What happens now?"

"Drive to the College, please. You can leave your car there and come home with me for a few hours. I've made all the arrangements."

I boggled. "You're not working this afternoon?"

"By a fortunate coincidence I'd already arranged to take the afternoon off. I'll tell you about that later."

"But what about *my* work? I'm supposed to be making a visitation at—"

"So your senior curate informed me. It's been cancelled."

"Well, in that case perhaps I should stay at home and catch up on my other work. Quite apart from the usual pile of letters which have to be answered, I've got to write a homily for a wedding next Saturday, a sermon for Sunday Matins, a draft report for the diocesan committee on—"

"There'll be time for all that later—the weekend's still a long way away. I'm sorry, Aysgarth, but I'm not letting you out of my sight at the moment. It's too dangerous. You might start drinking again."

"I must say I find that a most offensive statement!"

"Are you going to pick a fight with me? Save your energy and just accept that you've been removed from circulation for twenty-four hours!"

"Twenty-four hours?"

"After you've passed the afternoon with me at Starrington Magna you'll take the five-thirty train to London to see Aidan and spend the night at the Fordite headquarters. Everything's arranged," said Darrow, and dimly I grasped how relieved I was that he was still playing the tank in his characteristically high-handed fashion. Some unexpected emotion stirred within me. For a moment I was unable to identify it. Then I realised it was gratitude.

Feeling weak and confused but improbably *compos mentis,* I began to drive down the North Walk to the Theological College.

4

NO sooner had I turned into the North Walk than I spotted the vast black Rolls-Royce waiting for us outside the College entrance. This magnificent motor, which I had long secretly coveted, belonged to Darrow's second wife, the wealthy landowner whom he had swept to the altar soon after he bounced out of his monastery in 1940. It was typical of Darrow that he had wound up marrying a Rolls-Royce and a manor house in addition to a woman twenty-eight years his junior. Darrow never did anything by halves. He usually managed to avoid flaunting the Rolls and was careful to stress how much he enjoyed bicycling (like many men of his generation he had never learnt to drive), but there were times when he commandeered the motor and brazenly left it lying around in the Close to scandalise the inhabitants. Clergymen are just not supposed to swoop around in chauffeur-driven Rolls-Royces. Dr. Ottershaw used to cringe whenever a sighting was reported to him.

"I sent for the Rolls to save time," said Darrow airily. "I have an appointment at home with an architect at quarter-past three."

"I see," I said dryly, parking my car a respectful six feet from the Rolls's noble bumper.

The ancient chauffeur crept out of the front seat and raised his cap. I wondered how fit he was to be in charge of a car, and as I slumped onto the sumptuous upholstery I tried not to eye the steering wheel with longing.

"What's all this about an architect?" I said in an attempt to divert myself from covetous thoughts.

"I wanted to talk to you about that." As the motor glided away from the curb Darrow said to the chauffeur without raising his voice: "Can you hear me, Jarvis?" but there was no response. "Poor old boy!" said Darrow, although the chauffeur was probably only a few years his senior. "He's very deaf, I'm afraid, but at least we can talk in privacy. Now let me explain how I've managed to take you out of circulation for twenty-four hours. I've told everyone you're conducting an urgent enquiry into my new plan for the Theological College, an enquiry which obliges you to stay overnight at Starrington Magna. The Bishop was a little startled to hear I had a plan, but I told him I'd explain everything later."

My heart sank. I feared the worst. I only hoped Mrs. Ottershaw had replenished her husband's supply of indigestion tablets.

"Might I be so bold as to ask," I said, "precisely what plan you have in mind, or am I to be kept temporarily in ignorance, like Dr. Ottershaw?"

"That's up to you. We don't have to discuss the matter today if you don't feel like it."

"It sounds like a splendid diversion from my troubles. Keep talking."

The Theological College was in fact a private institution which should have been independent of the diocese, but since its nineteenth-century endowments had long since depreciated in value it had turned increasingly to the diocese for financial support and was now firmly under diocesan control. The Bishop was always a member of the Board of Governors, and the Archdeacon of Starbridge was obliged, as the Bishop's henchman, to keep an eye on the place. I began to suspect my eye was about to be sorely tried.

By that time, the May of 1946, the College was facing the problem of accommodating all the men who had received a call to the ministry during the war and who were now free to embark on their training. In an effort to meet this challenge Darrow, I was now informed, had conceived the idea of opening a temporary extension of the College at his home and had invited an architect to call that afternoon to estimate the cost of converting the unused east wing into a suitable habitation for the ordinands. It was typical of Darrow that he should have engaged an architect without bothering to consult the Bishop, but Darrow was an old hand at riding roughshod over Dr. Ottershaw.

I was unable to stop myself saying: "The diocesan funds may well be unable to afford such a scheme—wouldn't it have been better to present your idea to the Bishop before roping in an architect?"

"But how can the Bishop and I have a useful discussion unless I have some idea of the expense involved?"

"I take your point, but the conversion of the building would be only one of many expenses. How are you going to provide for these new residents? You'll need extra domestic staff, extra—"

"Those are the expenses I can calculate without seeking professional help, and naturally I shall allow for them when I draft my proposal."

His casual arrogance never failed to set my teeth on edge. Realising that I was yet again being obliged to deal with an attempt to create havoc in my archdeaconry, I reflected that he was incurably addicted to playing a lone hand. He would dream up an idea, implement it without consulting anyone and then be both amazed and offended when those in authority failed to be convinced that his pipe-dream was a manifestation of the Holy Spirit. I thought of his faith-healing phase and shuddered. I could still see an ashen Dr. Ottershaw reaching for his indigestion tablets.

"And what does your wife think of your plans to requisition her family home?" I enquired, blissfully oblivious of my own troubles by this time and unable to resist the temptation to lunge straight at the jugular vein. "I suppose she sees it as a nice little retirement job for you."

"Retirement?" Darrow was scandalised. "Who said anything about retirement?"

My worst suspicions were confirmed as I realised he was planning to slip into his favourite role: the wonder-worker. "My dear Darrow," I said, "this may surprise you, but you can't possibly be in two places at once. Either you run the Theological College or you run the extension—assuming the diocese can afford it—but you can't do both! However, since you're now nearer seventy than sixty, I quite see that this may well be an appropriate moment for you to step down from your present position and—"

"Age is quite irrelevant!" Darrow was now outraged. "Anyone would think, to hear you talk, that I was going to be seventy tomorrow! In fact I've only just celebrated my sixty-sixth birthday, I'm extremely fit and I'm more than capable of supervising—with the appropriate delegation of authority, naturally—both the College and the extension."

I gave up and spent the rest of the journey plotting the advice I should give to the Bishop. It's not easy when a clerical buccaneer like Darrow goes on the rampage in pursuit of a power-mad pipe-dream. In fact it's enough to make strong archdeacons weep.

I was still meditating on this magnificent diversion from my troubles when the Rolls reached the parish of Starrington Magna and purred down the main street of the village. Beyond the last cottage lay the Manor, tucked away behind the high brick wall which encircled the grounds. The house was large but not nearly so grand as Starmouth Court, and even poor Grace had been able to enjoy her visits there. Although Anne Darrow was very much a member of the county aristocracy, her unpretentiousness, her sincerity and her down-to-earth common sense had combined to put Grace at ease, with the result that an unlikely but genuine friendship had been formed. Anne was Primrose's godmother; Grace and I had been guests at Anne's small, quiet wedding in 1940. Liking her as I did I could only wish she had married someone other than Darrow.

The Manor appeared to have grown out of the soil like some eccentric species of vegetation, an illusion created by the fact that the colour of its pale golden bricks blended so pleasingly with the lawns, shrubberies and trees which surrounded it. As the Rolls drifted up the drive I saw a child's tricycle parked on the gravel sweep in front of the main entrance. Beyond the steps leading up to the porch the front door stood open, instantly creating the atmosphere of a tranquil country life. For a moment I imagined the tricycle's owner, growing up in such idyllic surroundings but only realising years later what a paradise he had enjoyed when he had been too young fully to appreciate his good fortune.

"How's your boy?" I said civilly to Darrow. As I was to be his guest I had decided it was time to make amends for my assault on his jugular vein.

"Fine, thanks." Darrow, who had not only children but grandchildren from his first marriage, was never loquacious on the subject of his progeny, but whenever the subject of this latest offspring was raised he seemed to vibrate with pride. I supposed that any man who had achieved fatherhood at an advanced age was entitled to be proud of himself, but I still felt that procreation was an unsuitable activity for elderly clerics.

As we emerged from the Rolls the child came out of the house to meet us. He was not yet four but was sturdy and tough, with thick fair hair and eyes the colour of flint. He was rumoured to be a terror at tea-parties, but at that moment he looked mild enough. He was carrying a huge tabby-cat which appeared to be in ecstasy. The purring was clearly audible as we advanced towards the porch.

"Hullo," said Darrow. "How well you're carrying William! Is Mummy in?"

The little boy shook his head and impulsively offered Darrow the cat.

"We're late for lunch," said Darrow to me as he accepted the offering, "so my wife probably decided she couldn't wait for us. She's very busy at the estate-office at the moment." Entering the hall he nodded towards the room on his right and added: "Have a seat in the library while I tell Cook to take the food out of the oven."

He and the boy went off hand in hand, the cat still purring in the crook of Darrow's arm, and the child's nanny came through the green baize door to meet them as they headed in the direction of the kitchen. Retiring obediently to the library, a chaotic room where dusty Victorian volumes on field sports fought for wall-space with glass cases of stuffed fish, I reflected that what I wanted most at that moment was not a seat, as Darrow had offered, but a drink. Fortunately before leaving the house that morning I had taken the precaution of filling a small cough-syrup bottle with whisky, and now, whipping the bottle out of the inside pocket of my jacket, I quickly unscrewed the cap. I was on the point of taking a hefty swig when Darrow crept into the room and caught me red-handed.

"A makeshift hip-flask," he said. "I thought so."

I said in my flattest voice: "You told me you were going to the kitchen."

"I delegated that task to Nanny. If you'd care to give that bottle to me, Aysgarth, I'd be delighted to look after it for you."

"That's quite unnecessary, thank you. If you think I need to abstain at present, then I'll abstain."

"I'm relieved to hear that abstention's so easy for you, but nevertheless I'd feel happier if the bottle was in my care."

I could keep my temper no longer. "How dare you imply I can't control my drinking!"

Darrow walked to the nearest wall of books, plucked out a Bible in the manner of a magician producing a white rabbit from a hat, and dumped the book on the writing table in front of me. "Put your hand on that and swear you haven't been drinking far too much lately."

I grabbed the Bible, stuffed it back on the shelf and blazed into the hall with my bottle. There was a cloakroom under the stairs. Striding to the basin, I poured the whisky down the drain while Darrow watched. "There!" I said, thrusting the bottle into his hands. "So much for your theory that I'm incapable of abstaining whenever I choose!"

Darrow rinsed the bottle thoroughly, sniffed it to make sure no whiff of whisky remained and finally dumped it in the wastepaper basket below the basin. All he said was: "Ready for lunch?"

Rigid with rage and shame, I followed him in silence to the dining-room.

5

DARROW pronounced a brisk grace, poured me a glass of water and said: "We won't talk while we eat. A conversation would encourage you to pretend this is a mere social occasion, and I think we need to cut down ruthlessly on your opportunities to act as if nothing's amiss. The incident with the bottle shows that your inclination to deceive yourself remains strong."

"Oh, for heaven's sake let's forget the wretched bottle!" I said, and felt pleased that I had managed to avoid an obscenity. Regaining control over my language meant that I was stronger. I hoped Darrow had noticed. As I attacked the shepherd's pie on the plate before me I savoured the pungent aroma of minced lamb and admired the crisp thatch of mashed potatoes. To my surprise I found that I was hungry.

Eventually an elderly maid tottered into the room with a bowl of stewed apples and a jug of real custard; the Darrows' cook had access to the eggs hatched on the Manor's home farm. When I had scooped up every morsel on my plate I eyed Darrow speculatively and tried to decide if he would seethe at the sight of a cigarette. I was beginning to feel as if I had been consigned to the care of a formidably strait-laced nanny. At last I demanded: "Are you going to get upset if I smoke?"

"You can smoke so long as you don't drink."

"How can I drink when I've poured away my whisky?"

"Well, we do keep wine and spirits in the house."

I stared at him. "You think I'm an alcoholic, don't you?"

"The word 'alcoholic' is like the phrase 'nervous breakdown,' " said Darrow. "It arouses all sorts of emotional reactions, none of which are very helpful. No, of course I don't think you're the sort of drinker who reaches for the brandy bottle every morning when he wakes up! If you were, you'd have got into trouble long ago. But I do think you might be the kind of drinker who would find it useful to know that I've noted the levels in the decanters on the sideboard and that I'll know at once if you filch a tot when my back's turned."

I lit a cigarette. Then I said in my pleasantest voice: "Why is it that I keep wanting to punch you on the nose? It's such an embarrassing urge for a clergyman!"

To my astonishment Darrow at once said with great seriousness: "That's a very interesting question—in fact I wonder if you realise just how interesting it is. The obvious answer, of course, is that we've always been incompatible and the stress of the present circumstances is exacerbating that incompatibility, but I have a hunch there's a great deal more going on than that. Naturally we must allow for the fact that you feel humiliated because someone you dislike is seeing you when you're vulnerable, and naturally we must allow for the fact that you're so horrified by what's happening to you that you're trying to cover up your horror with a display of pugnacious behaviour. That's all obvious. But why is it that when you have your back to the wall you only seem capable of hearing advice when it's couched in aggressive terms? You may find this hard to believe, but I don't usually behave like a sergeant major with men who are in distress. Yet although I adopted my customary serene manner at our first conversation earlier today, you were never fully at ease until I was telling you brutally in my toughest voice that you'd hit rock-bottom hard enough to crack cement. You liked that. You responded with gusto. For the first time I felt I was really getting through to you. Tough talk is obviously the only language you can understand when you're frightened, but why? Was there perhaps someone long ago who taught you to survive by giving you a series of verbal batterings which called forth an aggressive but life-saving response?"

I was amazed. Then to my extreme annoyance I also realised I was impressed. But of course I didn't want Darrow knowing he had impressed and amazed me. Summoning up my most irritated manner I retorted rudely: "Oh, go and set up a fortune-teller's tent in the Cathedral churchyard! I'm sorry, Darrow, I know you're a very able man in many ways, but I can't stand it when you play the magician and try to mind-read. It always makes me want to—"

"Punch me on the nose. Quite. Was it your father who applied these verbal batterings?"

"Certainly not! My father was the gentlest, kindest, mildest—"

"Then perhaps it was your mother."

"Don't be absurd! No woman gives *me* verbal batterings. My mother was a highly intelligent and exceptional woman who doted on me."

"And did you enjoy being doted on?"

"Well, of course I did!"

"Why 'of course'? It doesn't necessarily follow at all. Some people find it oppressive to be doted on."

"I'm not sure what you're getting at, Darrow, but you seem to be completely off course. I wasn't able to see my mother often, but over the years we conducted a most entertaining correspondence which we both enjoyed enormously—and if you want to make some sort of Freudian capital out of that, I'll—"

"—punch me on the nose, yes. This conversation's beginning to resemble one of those old-fashioned ballads with a recurring chorus. I hesitate to prolong it, but there's one discrepancy which puzzles me. I remember hearing that you'd had a tough childhood, yet this delightful father and this doting mother would suggest a family paradise. Was the talk of a tough childhood exaggerated?"

"No, my father died bankrupt when I was seven and the home was broken up. My brother and I were sent away to be educated, given a series of miserly hand-outs and told we could either Get On or Go Under."

"That's tough talk indeed," said Darrow, "and may I ask who it was who did the talking?"

"No, you may not! I'm sick of you behaving like Sherlock Holmes in a dog-collar. It makes me want to—"

"Yes, yes, yes—full chorus followed by the final chord." Darrow tossed his napkin aside and stood up. "I'll show you to a bedroom where you can rest while I see the architect."

"If you don't mind," I said, making a Herculean effort to be civil, "I'd prefer to go for a stroll in the grounds. After all, I did spend a large part of the morning in bed."

"So you did. Very well, perhaps I'll step outside with you for a moment. That sunshine looks inviting."

Leaving the house by a side door we strolled across the lawn towards the shrubbery which bordered the woods. The air was warm, the garden peaceful. Aware of my irritation declining, I found myself recalling with reluctance the extraordinary deductive skill Darrow had shown earlier.

Finally, after a period of prolonged hesitation, I was unable to resist saying fascinated: "Darrow, how far do you follow Freud? For example, if a man confessed to you that he'd dreamt he'd bashed his mother to pulp, how would you interpret such a dream?"

"That would depend on the mother—and it would depend on the man. I wouldn't follow Freud slavishly—in fact I might well not follow him at all."

"Is there any chance, would you say, that the dream could be entirely meaningless?"

"If dreams are part of the brain's way of sorting itself out before the next bout of consciousness, then one can argue that even the most absurd dream has its purpose and is therefore not without meaning. However, perhaps the question you're really asking is: When does a dream, absurd or otherwise, become significant in any study of a disturbed psyche? I confess that not being a psychiatrist, I wouldn't bother about dreams much unless they either recurred or caused particular distress—or both."

"But if the man were to tell you that he had indeed been caused particular distress by this dream about his mother—"

"I think I'd ask if he still felt distressed. You know what happens even with the worst nightmares: you wake up in a sweat but within sixty seconds you're laughing at the absurdity."

"And if the man said he did still feel distressed—"

"Then I should probably conclude that the dream was significant. But that wouldn't mean the significance was necessarily of crucial importance."

"But wouldn't it inevitably mean that he wanted to murder his mother?"

"Oh, I don't think so," said Darrow vaguely. "He might be harbouring a death-wish against someone else and be using his mother as a substitute—perhaps the mother's already dead, a situation which would allow him to discharge his violent feelings in the knowledge that they could do her no harm."

"Ah!" I felt myself relax.

"Or alternatively he might feel irritated by all females and be using his mother as a mere symbol for womanhood. Or he might feel violent towards himself and be projecting the violence onto the first person who entered his head. There are in fact numerous possible explanations, but without knowing more about the dreamer it's impossible to come to any firm conclusion about the dream."

"Yes, I see. Yes, of course." Having been so impressed by his perception of Uncle Willoughby's malign presence in my life that I had been tempted to test his skill further, I now felt so impressed by his authoritative comments on the puzzle I had posed him that I was tempted to confess the nightmare was mine. Tentatively, fearful that I might regret the admission but unable to resist the opportunity for further reassurance, I said: "*I'm* the dreamer. I had the nightmare this morning when I was dozing at the Theological College."

"Oh yes?" said Darrow, assuming a tone of mild surprise, as if the idea had never occurred to him. I realised then that I had been naive in thinking I could fool him so easily. "And do you, in fact, still feel upset about the experience?"

"No, not now I understand what was going on. Obviously I was just using my mother as a substitute for Dido. So that's all right."

"Is it?"

"Oh yes—I was only so upset because I couldn't bear the thought of feeling violent towards my mother."

"You mean you can bear the thought of feeling violent towards your wife?"

"No, no, no!" I said exasperated. "I don't feel violent towards anyone! Of course I don't want to kill Dido any more than I wanted to kill my mother; I just want her to get out of my life and be happily married to someone else, that's all. So it seems the dream was symbolic. What I was really wishing dead was the marriage, and my violence was all tied up with my emotional distress about the baby. When I'm emotionally distressed I often want to take a swing at someone to relieve my feelings."

"So I've noticed. And do you?"

"Do I what?"

"Do you ever take a swing at anyone?"

"Good heavens, no, of course not! Clergymen just don't do that sort of thing!"

"Oh, I don't know," said Darrow, falling back on his vague manner again. "I don't see why a clerical collar should have an infallible power to neutralise violent feelings, particularly when the violent feelings are usually the result of something that happened long before the man ever thought of being ordained."

"Are you trying to tell me you've actually counselled violent clergymen?"

"Well, I admit I don't run across such people every day, but I do remember a couple of wife-beaters."

"How disgusting! Women should be put on pedestals and reverenced. How on earth did you deal with such perverts?"

"As with all distressed people," said Darrow, "one has to locate the source of the distress in order to heal the wound in the psyche." He glanced at his watch. "I must go back indoors to await my architect. I probably shan't have time for tea, Aysgarth, but I'll arrange for it to be served to you in the library at four."

"Thanks." I watched him walk across the lawn and disappear into the house. Then still savouring my relief that the nightmare had a plausible explanation which I found neither sinister nor upsetting, I embarked on a stroll through the woods.

6

AT four o'clock I returned to the library and drank two cups of tea but found I could eat nothing. Anxiety was gaining the upper hand again. I was aware of a strong desire to sink myself in my work so that I would have no time to dwell upon my crisis. Meanwhile the thought that I would soon be on my way to London for soul-surgery (I hadn't forgotten Darrow's metaphor of the operating table) had become so chilling that I now wondered if I might find myself unable to step on the train. Abandoning my tea-cup, I headed outside again in a fever of agitation and prowled around the side of the house to the back lawn.

To my relief I saw that Darrow was sitting on the garden seat; I felt I needed another dose of first aid. The child was standing nearby, but at that moment his nurse called his name from the house and he ran off across the lawn. Darrow half-rose to his feet, then sank back on the bench and rubbed his eyes as if they had been dazzled.

"Has the architect left?" I said seconds later as I too sat down on the garden seat.

"What? Oh, the architect. No, I showed him around and then left him alone to make his calculations." Plainly his thoughts were elsewhere.

It was so unlike Darrow to be *distrait* in his manner that I said sharply: "Are you all right?" but at once he pulled himself together.

"Yes, fine—I was merely experiencing one of those curious moments when one feels a scene has all been played before."

"What a coincidence! I've been dogged by that phenomenon for some months now. I believe the scientific explanation is that one half of the brain is functioning slightly ahead of the other."

"It really is amazing," said Darrow mildly, "what you Modernists can bring yourself to believe. Even the most incredible scientific theory is dutifully swallowed whole! Has this phenomenon been attached to any particular set of circumstances in your case, or has it occurred at random?"

I hesitated. "At random, I think." But I was uncertain. "To be honest I've never paused to reflect on the experiences or try to classify them."

"That's interesting. I'd have thought a man like you would have been studying the phenomenon with care and ruthlessly analysing it for the rational explanation. Is this perhaps a somewhat unpleasant experience—sinister, even—which you try to blot out as quickly as possible?"

"I don't think so. I don't know. I really hadn't thought about it." I glanced at my watch. "What happens next?"

"In five minutes' time Jarvis will drive you to Starbridge station to catch the London train. Are you ever able to identify the missing half of this *déjà vu* experience, or is the whole phenomenon consistently shrouded in mystery?"

"I identified a missing half this morning." I thought of how I had unconsciously borrowed a thought-form from Alex. "But in my opinion, if such an identification is possible it's not a genuine case of *déjà vu*. It's merely a straightforward coincidence which doesn't defy the laws of probability. By my definition the *déjà vu* sensation occurs when you feel certain that the *exact* scene has been played before—and yet at the same time you know that this can't possibly have happened."

"In my opinion," said Darrow, rising to his feet, "the most likely explanation is that the scene really has been played before, but not exactly. It's the exactness which is the illusion, not the scene itself. The scene itself is genuinely familiar." And without giving me the chance to reply he added: "You must be off, Aysgarth—and by the way, I forgot to tell you earlier that there's an overnight bag for you in the boot of the Rolls. Jarvis collected it from your sister-in-law before he met us at the College this afternoon."

So my personal tank had even mown down Merry. Unable to imagine such an achievement I demanded: "What on earth did my sister-in-law say when she heard you were purloining me for twenty-four hours?"

"She offered to be purloined in your stead. We got on rather well."

Mute with admiration I allowed myself to be led around the side of the house to the drive, and it was only when I saw the waiting motor that I recovered my wits sufficiently to say: "I've been a fool and asked you nothing about Lucas."

"That doesn't matter. He'll tell you all you need to know."

"But there are numerous questions I'd like to ask—"

"Why? Aysgarth, when a drowning man sees a life-belt floating past him does he waste time musing: 'Where did this come from? Why is it coloured red and white? By what scientific principle will it contrive to keep me afloat?' "

"I'm not drowning at the moment. I'm treading water and I want to know why you're so certain Lucas can help me. Is it merely because he's a Yorkshireman?"

"No." Darrow paused to trace a small circle on the gravel with his foot as if he were engaged in some complex calculation, but eventually he made the decision to enlighten me. "I'm not sure how much you know about my career as a monk," he said, "but after three months as a postulant at the Grantchester house I was judged impossible to train and removed. The late Abbot-General then decided on a kill-or-cure policy of kicking me up to Yorkshire for a fresh start, and when I arrived at Ruydale I was in a state similar to the state you're in now: angry, frightened, rebellious and above all deeply unhappy. Yet within five minutes of my arrival I'd been soothed, tamed and given hope for the future. 'How courageous of you to want to stay in the Order despite your recent adversity!' said Aidan, installing me in a comfortable chair by the fire and ordering hot soup. 'What dedication! I'm sure I shall find it a privilege to be your Abbot!' " Unexpectedly Darrow laughed at the memory before exclaiming with affection: "Wily old fox! His words may sound phoney now as I repeat them, but I assure you that at the time I could only think: Here's someone who really cares."

"I thought abbots were supposed to be simple holy men, not diplomats oozing a serpentine cunning."

"Aidan has his simplicity—and his holiness; but he's a clever man at managing people and he knows exactly how to use that special skill." Darrow moved forward again across the gravel sweep of the drive. "By the way, I assume you do know where the Fordite headquarters is?"

"It's that miniature version of the Carlton Club just north of Marble Arch. How on earth can the monks still afford to live there?"

"Tax-free status and adroit financial management. Personally I've always thought that house represented a luxury which was quite inexcusable, but the Abbot-General, like his predecessor, can't resist the temptation to vie with the Archbishop at Lambeth."

I said uneasily: "I met the Abbot-General briefly when he visited you here in '41. I suppose I'm unlikely to see him now and even if I did he probably wouldn't remember me, but if he were to hear my name—"

"I never gave it. I did speak to him when I arranged your meeting with Aidan, but I stressed your need for anonymity."

"So when I arrive—"

"Just tell the doorkeeper that you've been sent by Father Darrow to see Father Lucas."

"And when I come back—"

"Get in touch with me straight away and I'll try to provide the necessary post-operative care."

I was unable to stop myself saying in despair: "Supposing the operation's a failure?"

"There's no question of failure, Aysgarth. Don't you remember? Survival's your new prize. How could you bear to lose it by feebly giving up the ghost on the operating table?"

No further argument was possible. Achieving a stiff smile, I mumbled: "Thanks for the first aid," and clambered clumsily into the Rolls to begin my journey.

7

TO my surprise my spirits rose as soon as the train swung out of Starbridge at the start of the ninety-minute journey to London; escaping from home enabled me to forget for a brief interval the horrors of the present and the prospect of worse horrors to come. I had a deep affection for London, scene of my adolescence and of my first successful attempt to Get On by working hard at school. I liked not only the mindless bustle of metropolitan life, as the city flexed its muscles day and night, but the intellectual excitement emanating from the bookshops, the museums, the art galleries, the theatres and the concert halls. The dirt, the noise and the smell might be detestable, particularly the smell of unwashed bodies, but I had long since accepted the fact that my early poverty had given me an unquenchable thirst for luxury, and I refused to feel guilty just because I had received no call to serve God in the slums.

But as I glanced down from the train that evening upon the mean streets which flanked the approach to Waterloo Station, I did feel a twinge of discomfort that throughout my career I had unobtrusively managed to avoid the urban poor. I knew now, after my months of working among the German prisoners, that it was not so much the deprivation which repelled me but the fear that my limited pastoral skills would be exposed. This was a bleak piece of self-knowledge, and certainly in my present state I was hardly strong enough to dwell on my inadequacies as a clergyman, so to cheer myself up I thought of Geoffrey Fisher, now Archbishop of Canterbury, a man who was neither a spiritual leader cast in a heroic mould like George Bell, nor a brilliant philosopher-politician like the late William Temple, but a capable administrator, just like me. The post-war era was the grey, unglamorous age of the administrators as they toiled over reconstruction; it would be my age if only I could survive to enjoy it, but thoughts of survival only drew me back into the heart of my present ordeal and reminded me that even the faint outline of the signpost marked SALVATION was liable to fade whenever my despair became overwhelming.

London looked more crucified by war than ever, blackened, battered, blitzed, a war-horse ripe for the knacker's yard. In an attempt to beat back my increasing depression by making a reckless gesture of extravagance I ignored the signs to the underground and took a taxi over the new Waterloo Bridge. Beyond the river Somerset House slumbered in the hazy sunshine, and glancing east I could see the dome of St. Paul's, miraculously preserved from destruction and silhouetted against the smoky May sky.

"What number, guv?" shouted the taxi-driver when we eventually hurtled up the Fordites' street north of Marble Arch.

"It's the big house down there past the bomb-site."

"The place where they wear black-and-white fancy dress? What's a respectable C. of E. clergyman like you doing at a nasty R.C. place like that?"

I had insufficient energy to explain that the Fordites formed part of the Anglo-Catholic wing of the Church of England and owed no allegiance to Rome. "I'm paying a social call," I said, "on an old man who's recovering from an operation."

"Very good-natured, I'm sure," said the taxi-driver as the car screeched to a halt in front of the brick wall which separated the house from the street. "But then you can always rely on the C. of E. padres to behave like gentlemen."

I tipped him lavishly to reinforce his benign attitude to the Church, and as he drove away with his traditional English bigotry intact, I turned to face my destination. The wooden double-gates, set snugly within the high wall, were wide enough to have admitted a Victorian carriage and appeared to be firmly closed. However when I tried the handle the right-hand gate swung open. I stepped into a cobbled forecourt, and immediately I saw the doorkeeper's head framed in the hall window as he inspected the intruder. Shutting the gate behind me I took a closer look at the house, which I had never before seen at close quarters, and noticed that although the stucco facade had been chipped by the force of the bomb which had exploded nearby, the walls had recently been repainted. This spruce appearance set the house apart from the shabby city in which it stood and created the bizarre illusion that I had entered a world in which the war had yet to take place.

"Good evening, Father," said the doorkeeper, revealing the hall beyond the threshold as I reached the steps of the porch. "Can I help you?"

I loathe being addressed as a Catholic priest. My Protestant hackles immediately rose and it took me a great effort to say in a civil voice: "Mr. Jonathan Darrow's sent me to see Mr. Aidan Lucas." No one was going to catch *me* using the title "Father"—or indeed the pre-Reformation title of "Abbot." In my opinion Henry VIII had been entirely right to abolish the monasteries.

"Ah yes, you're expected," said the doorkeeper unctuously. "Please come in."

Angry, irritated, rebellious, sulky, guilt-ridden and shamefully nervous, I summoned all my will-power and crossed the threshold into the other wing of the Church of England.

8

THE house had once been the principal residence of the Order's founder, a certain Mr. Horatio Ford, who had acquired immense wealth in various shady ways before embracing Anglo-Catholicism (then being launched by the Oxford Movement) and donating his ill-gotten gains to the Church of England in order to make an edifying end. Enrapt not only by the High Church spirituality but also by the nineteenth-century aesthetic mania for idealising medieval life, he had stipulated that the Church should use his fortune to found a monastic community called the Fordite Order of St. Benedict and St. Bernard. This shameless piece of self-advertising had probably prompted the remark, long enshrined in Church folklore, that Ford had included St. Bernard in his title not because he had wished to honour the founder of the Cistercians but because he had wanted to immortalise his favourite dog.

From this ignorant and vulgar seed a learned and ultimately distinguished organisation had grown. It was very English, in that peculiar style so beloved by foreigners in search of our eccentricities, but despite its idiosyncratic ways it was neither ineffectual nor ludicrous. I personally think it's quite wrong for a bunch of devout men to waste their time reviving a medieval way of life when they could be out in the modern world working for Christ in the same manner as any other Christian, but even I, the staunch defender of Henry VIII's monastic policy, had to admire the Fordites' dedication to scholarship, a dedication which placed them firmly in the Benedictine tradition.

There were four houses in the Order. At Starwater Abbey in my archdeaconry the monks ran a famous public school, while at the Grantchester house near Cambridge the monks had cultivated a connection with the University by specialising in retreats for undergraduates. The London headquarters also offered retreats and was rumoured to be a haven for the leading men of the Church who wished to recharge their spiritual batteries in comfort. Only Ruydale, isolated on the North Yorkshire moors, followed a Cistercian rather than a Benedictine tradition by fostering a formidably ascetic way of life, and Darrow always claimed that this was the most spiritual house in the Order. But then Darrow would. It was at Ruydale that he had acquired his reputation as a spiritual director. He had been Master of Novices there for six years before becoming the Abbot of the Grantchester house in 1937.

Since Darrow, famous for his austere tastes, had expressed disapproval of the London house, I was confident that I would find much to admire and I soon discovered that my confidence had been justified. The house was an exquisite architectural treasure, lovingly maintained and imbued with an air of subdued luxury which I found most seductive. The visitors' parlour, into which I was shown, contained a Persian carpet, antique furniture and even a discreet chandelier. The pictures, all of religious subjects, glowed subtly in the dim light and reminded me of the remoter rooms of the National Gallery, one of my favourite haunts on wet winter Saturday afternoons during my adolescence. To my relief I noted that unlike the visitors' parlour at Starwater, the room flaunted no tasteless statuette of the Virgin Mary.

"I won't keep you a moment, Father," said the doorkeeper, abandoning me in this soothing oasis, and I sat down on the edge of a chair, but within seconds I was pacing around the room. What was I going to say? What in fact could possibly be said? How could Lucas unlock the mystery of my dilemma and tell me why my life had gone so wrong? And most vital of all, how, short of waving a magic wand, could he make it possible for me to live with Dido for the next thirty years? I suddenly realised that the whole pilgrimage was a waste of time, just another of Darrow's hare-brained inspirations. There would be no more than a cosy chat waiting for me, a dash of professional sympathy, a few clever remarks and finally, no doubt, some florid form of Anglo-Catholic benediction which would set my teeth on edge.

"Would you come this way, please, Father?" The soapy-voiced doorkeeper had returned to fray my nerves again. Following him reluctantly down a corridor, I was ushered into a room furnished only with a table, two chairs and in one corner a nasty-looking Catholic concoction which I supposed, since it reminded me of a shrine, I could dignify by the name of "oratory"; a prie-dieu had been placed in front of a miniature altar which coruscated with a crucifix, candlesticks and cloth-of-gold brocade. My Protestant soul shuddered, but before I could lose my nerve altogether I heard the doorkeeper say to someone in the passage: "Your visitor's waiting, Father Abbot," and the next moment I was face to face at last with Aidan Lucas.

XI

"Examination of acts of sin, however classified, is valuable as leading on first to the discovery of sinful motive and then to the recognition of a sinful state."

CHARLES E. RAVEN

THE CREATOR SPIRIT

I

DARROW'S reference to a wily old fox had produced an image in my mind of a hunched old man with a cunning expression, but the man before me bore no resemblance to this traditional picture of the Machiavellian conspirator. He looked a trifle frail, no doubt as the result of his recent sojourn in hospital, but he was still straight-backed, still curiously ageless in that manner peculiar to people who have unusually fair complexions; such pale, almost translucent skin seems less prone to the wrinkles and pouches of old age. His left eye was covered with a white dressing thin enough to allow him to wear without difficulty the glasses which his faded blue right eye apparently demanded. It was hard to estimate the exact point in old age which he had reached, but I guessed he was in his mid-seventies, ten years older than Darrow.

At first glance he gave the impression of being quiet and unobtrusive, not a man who would stand out in a crowd, someone who might have been a retired schoolmaster living in a cosy suburban villa with his books and his memories, a keen gardener, perhaps, someone who enjoyed listening to the cricket broadcasts on the wireless, a very English man, polite, decent and unremarkable. Yet this was the Abbot of Ruydale, the toughest house in the Order. He had dictatorial control over a wide variety of men, supervised the running of the Ruydale estate and maintained a spartan monastic rule. Here was no retired schoolmaster accustomed to book-lined studies and a companionable wireless, but an active leader accustomed to silence and austerity, a man who had stepped far beyond the conventional boundaries of clerical life in the Church of England in order to live in a manner which most churchmen would have found intolerable.

"Good evening," he said politely. "I'm Aidan Lucas. There's no need for you to tell me your name. Shall we sit down?" He had a BBC accent, just like mine, the sort of accent acquired after hours of secret rehearsals in locked bedrooms. Immediately I wondered about his background, but I knew I had to overcome my curiosity before I gave the impression of being a deaf-mute.

"It's good of you to see me at such short notice, sir," I said. "I'm sorry to impose on your convalescence."

"There's no imposition—and no need to call me 'sir.' " Effortlessly he had pinpointed the one significant word in my remark, deduced that I had been unable to address him as "Father" and was now busy smoothing away my discomfort. "Since you've stepped out of the world in order to see me," he said, "why don't we agree to abandon the worldly conventions and call each other by our Christian names?"

"Sounds sensible." As we moved to the table I found my glance falling again on the ornate oratory. Why did decent clergymen ordained in the Church of England have to adopt these Papist flourishes? I thought of the Protestant martyrs of the Counter-Reformation and felt indignant.

"Florid, isn't it?" said Lucas, instantly noting the direction of my disapproving gaze. "We do things better up in Yorkshire." And he smiled at me.

So Darrow had disclosed the name of my native county. Well, why not? Making a great effort I tried to relax but found I was still too nervous to return the smile.

"May I suggest you sit with your back to that corner? Then it won't distract you."

I sat down as directed and clasped my hands together on the table. As I tried to keep the clasp loose, I was tempted to hide my hands in my lap but thought I might then look even more tense, sitting bolt upright in my chair. I found I was desperate to maintain an air of untroubled normality.

Lucas was watching me. "Which Christian name would you like to use?" he said.

I nearly fell off my chair. "How do you know I use more than one?"

"You've just told me." He laughed before adding: "Sometimes people prefer to withhold their Christian names as well as their surnames. I merely wanted to signal to you that you could pick a name at random if you wished."

"Oh, I see." I tried to respond but found the subject was so complex that I was unable to decide where to begin. I was behaving like a deaf-mute again. I tried to pull myself together. "My first name's Norman," I said. "That was my father's choice. But after the christening my mother decided that she preferred my second name, so everyone called me Neville until 1942. Then I met my second wife. She decided to call me Stephen."

"And who are you at the moment?"

"I don't know." That sounded as if I was certifiable. In panic I told myself that I really couldn't sit in a nasty little cell which reeked of Popery and declare to an Anglo-Catholic monk that I didn't know who I was. That would be letting the Protestant side down in an intolerably humiliating manner. "I wanted to be Stephen," I said. "When I remarried last year I wanted to ring down the curtain on Neville and begin an exciting new life, but somehow that hasn't happened. Stephen's just my wife's pipe-dream, a fantasy in clericals. I'm still Neville—I don't want to be, but I can't escape into Stephen. Neville won't let me go." I was still talking like a maniac. In a paroxysm of embarrassment I muttered: "Sorry. Idiotic. Not making any sense at all."

"Oh, there's no need to apologise!" said Lucas, taking my idiocies in his stride. "I know all about having two names. I was Victor in my youth. I took the name Aidan when I became a monk, but it was by no means a smooth transition from one identity to another."

That was the moment when I forgot the oratory behind me and overcame any desire to behave like a deaf-mute. "Did Victor completely disappear?" I said. "Or did he and Aidan blend?"

"It was a little more complicated than that. Aidan was actually a synthesis of two warring Victors."

That was the moment when I forgot I was talking to an Anglo-Catholic in a room which shouted CONFESSIONAL from all four walls.

"Two Victors!" I exclaimed. "And fighting each other!" Cautiously I groped my way forward to the next question. "But wouldn't you say it was abnormal to have more than one identity?"

"It can certainly create abnormalities if the essential unity of the personality is impaired. But in fact a lot of people juggle different identities and continue to think of themselves as one person who wears a variety of masks. That's very common. Think of the managing director who roars like a lion at the office and becomes meek as a lamb once he crosses the threshold of his home. He wears one face for his staff, one for his wife—and yet a third, perhaps, for his mistress."

I was unable to resist asking: "Have you ever been married?"

"No."

"You remained unmarried through choice?"

"No. Let's not waste time on guessing games," said Lucas kindly. "I didn't marry because the lady in question was married to someone else and there was no hope of a divorce. I lived in sin for six years. That was in my atheist phase. Later I became a Christian, then a slum-priest and finally a monk. That disposes of my past history, satisfies (I hope) your curiosity and enables us to turn back to you, a far more interesting subject."

Acute embarrassment made me incoherent. "I'm sorry—none of my business—intolerably impertinent—"

"Nonsense! Everyone who meets a monk for a confidential conversation has a right to wonder how far the monk can be expected to respond to his confidences. Indeed it's often helpful if a monk's been married. When Jon Darrow was counselling visitors to Ruydale he used to make great capital out of his early marriage."

Before I could stop myself I said: "Darrow would make capital out of anything." Then I muttered in a fresh bout of embarrassment: "Sorry. Darrow and I aren't very compatible. But of course he's a good man."

Lucas said wryly: "Jon's not everyone's cup of tea," and as he smiled I recognised the Yorkshire inflection in that homespun phrase, a faint whisper of a forgotten world far away.

On an impulse I said: "What part of Yorkshire do you come from?"

"My parents ran a boarding-house in Scarborough."

"Scarborough! We went there once for a holiday. I was very young but I remember walking by the sea with my father. It seemed like paradise . . . but then everything seemed like paradise, before my father died."

"That sounds as if you're describing the first phase of your life."

"Yes, that was when I was the Neville who belonged to my father, the Neville who lived in—do you know Maltby?"

"It's near Huddersfield, isn't it?" I could hear the Yorkshire accent clearly now. He had pronounced "Huddersfield" with the long *u*.

"It's an ugly town," I said, "but it's surrounded by some beautiful countryside, and my father used to take us for walks there."

"How old were you when he died?"

"Seven. He died bankrupt. Then my uncle took charge of the family."

"Was that when the second phase of your life began?"

"Yes, that was when I became the Neville who belonged to Uncle Willoughby, the Neville who lived in London, where my brother and I were sent to be educated. My uncle had connections there and arranged for us to attend the City of London School. It had a good reputation then in a modest way—probably it has an even better reputation now—but of course it was no Eton or Harrow. However, my uncle thought we'd have a better chance of Getting On in London than in Yorkshire, and we didn't disappoint him. We both went up to Oxford, and it was there that I received my call to be a clergyman."

"Not quite what your uncle had in mind for you, perhaps."

"No, but that didn't matter because he then ceased to play any part in my life and a third Neville was born. But this Neville wasn't a synthesis of the two previous Nevilles. They wouldn't blend. What Neville Three did was to encircle them so that they could stand side by side in harmony. That worked well enough for a time, but finally—"

"They began to fight?"

"I'm not sure what they began to do, but Neville Three began to have difficulty keeping order. In the end I found myself continually ringing down the curtain in my mind to blot them out, but the curtain kept trying to go up at the wrong moment."

"Very exhausting. And to whom did Neville Three belong? If Neville One belonged to your father and Neville Two belonged to your uncle—"

"Oh, Neville Three belonged to my mother."

"What about your first wife?"

"She belonged to me. She first met me when I was Neville Two, but she never saw that side of me during the seven years before we were married. I was always Neville One then with Grace, gentle and romantic like my father. Even after we were married, when I was Neville Three, I always felt most comfortable with her when I was being Neville One."

"And your mother—is she still alive?"

"No, she died in 1941."

"And whom do you belong to now?"

"Well, I thought I'd become Stephen—who of course would belong to my second wife. But the terrible thing is—and this is why I'm here—I've just realised that I don't want my second wife any more and I can't imagine how I'm going to live with her for the next thirty years. I've gone very, very wrong somewhere, but I've no idea how it's happened. All I know is that I've ended up in the most appalling wasteland and my whole career in the Church is in jeopardy."

"Your career in the Church?"

"Yes, I'm actually rather successful—"

"And what about your life of service to God?" said the Abbot of Ruydale. "That surely is more important than any career in the Church."

I felt exactly like a dog which had been prancing along at the end of a leash, only to be brought up short by a sharp shocking tug. "Ah yes," I said. I even had to pause for breath as if I had been winded. "Yes. Well, I still feel called to serve God to the best of my ability as a clergyman. When I spoke of my career in the Church I merely meant—"

"In what way do you feel called to serve God as a clergyman? Is it your way? Or His way?"

"My way is His way. I mean, His way is my way. I mean—"

"Which Neville is it who's called to serve?"

"Neville Three. Well, Neville One as well—and Neville Two, I can't do without Neville Two—"

"You say you're in a wasteland. Who led you there?"

"No one. That's why I simply can't understand how I could have wound up like this—"

"Was it God who led you there? Or was it the Devil?"

I shifted, deeply embarrassed, in my chair. "I'm sorry, I'm a Modernist. I find all talk of the Devil rather—"

"The Devil doesn't care whether or not you're a Modernist. You can't ring down the curtain on the Devil by waving the word 'Modernist' around like a magic wand."

"Well, of course I recognise that evil exists, but—"

"What about sin?"

"Sin?"

"Sin. S-I-N."

"Yes, well, of course sin exists too, as we all know only too well, but I never think it's very helpful to harp on it. Most people are good and decent and try to do what's right. They may have their minor faults, but—"

"You're describing yourself, I think. But which self?"

"Neville Two. No, Neville Three, who tries very hard to be a good man—although I admit he makes mistakes occasionally, little slips—" I suddenly felt hot as I remembered Lyle.

"So what you're really saying is that none of the Nevilles is responsible for your presence in the wasteland. You're saying: 'The prisoners at the bar plead innocent!' "

"Prisoners at the bar?"

There was a silence. I stared at him, and as he stared back, exuding a formidable air of authority, I realised he was experimenting, just as Darrow had experimented earlier, by switching from a mild to a tough approach in order to gauge the most effective way of communicating with me. Automatically I tried to dredge up a fighting response. "Why should you imply I'm on trial?"

"We're all on trial. We're all sinners. We all stand at the bar and await God's judgement."

I leapt into the attack. "I'm surprised to find someone like you dabbling in that kind of Protestant neo-orthodoxy! I may be a Protestant but I'm a Liberal Protestant, and in my opinion—"

"There you go again, pulling down the curtain and trying to hide behind theological labels!" With a speed which took me aback he then sloughed off his stern manner and became sympathetic again. The experiment had been concluded, the results noted and a new strategy planned. I was beginning to feel like a lump of clay in the hands of a skilled artist. "It won't do, you know, lad," he said regretfully, and as he spoke he slipped still deeper into a Yorkshire accent. "Neither Barth nor Calvin possesses any patent on discussions of sin and judgement. Christians were debating those particular matters long before anyone dreamed up the title Crisis Theology and started talking about neo-orthodoxy."

"Yes, but if you ignore the Liberals' emphasis on the forgiveness and compassion of Christ—"

"Who said anything about ignoring it? But what use are the forgiveness and compassion of Our Lord unless you repent? And how can you repent unless you frankly acknowledge you're a sinner and try to understand why you've sinned?"

"I'm sorry," I said. "I just have no sympathy for this kind of talk. It's alien to my intellectual approach to God."

"And what about your spiritual approach?"

"Now look here, Mr. Lucas—"

"Ah yes, you're going to get angry with me, aren't you? I thought you would. Getting angry would make you feel better, give you a chance to expel all the difficult emotion, a chance to ease the pain . . . The pain's very bad, isn't it?"

"What pain?"

"The pain you keep behind the curtain." Without warning he clasped his hands and bent his head in prayer. To my astonishment I heard him say in a firm voice: "Lord, grant me the power to help this man and ease the suffering which has crippled him."

In the ensuing silence the concentration behind the prayer seemed almost tangible. My astonishment was rapidly succeeded first by embarrassment and then by a confused emotion which I found hard to identify. I could only think, as Darrow had thought before me: Here's someone who really cares.

Lucas let his hands fall and looked me straight in the eyes. In the same firm voice he had used for the prayer he said: "It's a question of facing the pain."

"What pain?" I said again, but this time I was making a genuine effort to understand. "The pain of the past? Or the pain of the present?"

"It's all one."

I gasped. Time suddenly began to run backwards, like some bizarre stream cascading uphill, and as my father moved silently to my side my voice whispered: "It's all a unity. It's all one."

Some moments passed before I realised I had covered my face with my hands. Panic assailed me. I had to pull myself together, show no sign of weakness, drum up some aggression to protect myself. How had I wound up in this repulsive confessional situation? Why was I letting this old man manipulate me in the manner of a cat dedicated to unravelling a ball of wool? How dare he unmask me as vulnerable and how dare he treat me as if I was sick? Nasty, meddlesome, interfering old monk, slipping into a Yorkshire accent to slide under my skin . . . I was convulsed with rage and shame.

"I'm calling a halt to this monstrous interrogation," I said strongly, but to my horror my voice shook. "I refuse to answer any more questions!"

"Now, isn't that fortunate!" said Lucas without a second's hesitation. "I was just thinking you needed a rest from my tiresome prying, and I'd decided to do something I would never normally do in this situation. I'm going to talk about myself. Not at all good practice for a counsellor, but your case interests me so much that I believe a touch of unorthodoxy would be justified. But before I begin, may I offer you the olive branch of peace in the form of a cup of tea?"

"No, thanks," I said shortly, but in fact I hardly knew what I said. I felt as if all my rage and shame had been soaked up by a piece of blotting paper which was now being lightly tossed into the wastepaper basket. I groped for words but could find none. I groped for a new attitude to adopt in place of the rage and shame, but I seemed to be in an emotional vacuum. All I could do was sit passively in a docile silence. Dimly I began to realise I was being tamed.

"Well, if you're quite sure you don't want tea," Lucas was saying, "relax in your chair and I'll tell you the story of the two Victors who became Aidan. It won't take long but it'll give you a rest, and perhaps—who knows?—you may even find it instructive."

Wily old fox. Clever, cunning, perspicacious old masterpiece. Bound hand and foot by my curiosity, tranquillised by the benign warmth of his manner, I could only wait, a willing prisoner, for him to spin the parable which would bring me closer to the truth.

2

"I HAD a happy time as Victor One," said Lucas, embarking on his narrative with an air of casual good humour. "We weren't a religious

family but my parents were decent hard-working people. We used to go to church once a year to hear the Christmas carols. I believed in God until I was fifteen, when I decided it would be smart to be an agnostic. Agnosticism was all the rage in those days, and I liked to think of myself as being modern and clever. I'd won a scholarship to the grammar school and so of course I had a very good opinion of myself.

"My ambition was to go south, but my parents weren't wealthy and I knew I'd have to make my own way. After leaving school I worked on the local newspaper, and within five years I'd reached London. The *Daily Standard* has been dead for a long while now, but back in the nineties it was one of the biggest newspapers in Fleet Street.

"I was a great success in London—such a success that I decided to forget ingenuous provincial Victor One. That was when I became Victor Two, the sophisticated man-about-town. No more God, of course. God was for provincials. And no more agnosticism. Agnosticism was just for intellectuals too weak to chuck away religion entirely. I was an atheist, untrammelled by all the old superstitions. Then finally in 1901 I was appointed a special correspondent and sent out to Africa to cover the Boer War.

"Well, that was the end of my deluded masquerade, as I daresay you can imagine. That was when I realised my life in London had nothing to do with reality at all. When I went to South Africa God destroyed my ignorant self-absorption and showed me such horrors that I knew I could never be the same again.

"I didn't actually see much fighting. It was mostly guerilla warfare anyway. But what I saw were the concentration camps. The British invented them, you know. It suits us now to forget that, but at the turn of the century I discovered that the greatest nation on earth, a nation which called itself Christian, was destroying innocent people on a massive scale. I wrote my horrifying dispatches. I sent report after report. But not one word was published and eventually I was recalled.

"I remember shouting at my editor: 'You're refusing to expose a very great evil! You're condoning a sin against humanity!' But he just said: 'You're talking like an Evangelist, Vic, ranting away about evil and sin! Take yourself off to the seaside for a fortnight's holiday and then we'll put you to work on a nice cheerful subject like the Royal Family.'

"I resigned. My mistress couldn't understand it. 'Why are you making such a fuss about the people in these camps?' she said. 'They're only Boers.' That was when I knew I could never be intimate with her again. I left her—and then I realised I had to leave London too, so I took the train to York. I was obliged to change trains there, but I never did go on to Scarborough. Victor One was there to meet me at York station, and when he led me through the streets to the Minster, Victor Two was vanquished at last and I saw the new life I was being called to lead.

"I was eventually ordained—but I didn't live happily ever after. Victor Two, who had been vanquished but not, unfortunately, destroyed, kept tugging at my sleeve, and in the end I decided that I'd have a better chance of slaying him once and for all if I battled with him on his home ground. So I returned south to London and worked in an East End mission. It was the heyday of the Anglo-Catholic work in the slums, and I felt I could use the power of Anglo-Catholicism as a suit of armour which would protect me from Victor Two whenever he laid his corrupting hand on my sleeve.

"I worked and I worked and I worked until at last—inevitably—my health broke down under the strain and I was sent here, to the Fordite headquarters, to recuperate. That was when Aidan was conceived. I met the man who was shortly to become the Abbot-General—you've probably heard of him: Father Cuthbert Darcy. He died in 1940. He was an extraordinary man. At the end of his life he became very tyrannical and difficult, but when I met him in 1907 he was at the height of his powers, a man of great intelligence, remarkable charm and an uncanny intuitive perception into spiritual dilemmas. He was the monk assigned to help me find my spiritual way again. We used to sit in a little room, just like this one, and face each other across the table, just as you and I are facing each other now, and engage in battle after battle.

"We battled because I didn't want to face up to the truth; one never does when the truth is very painful. 'Why were you working so hard?' Darcy would ask over and over again. 'Why did you have to drive yourself day and night until you collapsed with exhaustion?' And over and over again I insisted: 'Because I wanted to serve God.'

"But that wasn't true. It was myself I'd been serving. Working so hard that I had no time to think—that was my way of pulling down the curtain on truths I couldn't face. Finally Darcy said: 'It's a question of facing the pain.' 'What pain?' I said, but I knew. It was the pain of knowing good people could do evil deeds. But I said to Darcy: 'I'm not responsible for the camps in South Africa! The responsibility belongs to the Government—it's got nothing to do with me!' Darcy just raised an eyebrow and said: 'Whom do the Government represent?' And when I started to protest he said: 'We all share in the guilt of man's inhumanity to man. We all stand at the bar and await God's judgement.'

"At once I said: 'How can I be on trial? I'm a good man. Of course I've made mistakes in the past—little slips—but now I'm a priest and I know that by the grace of God I'm forgiven.' Darcy just leant back in his chair and said: 'Then why are you now in hell?'

"I fought him and fought him. On and on we battled. And then gradually as he took me through my past life I saw all the sins I'd never faced. I was forced to recall how I'd cut myself off from my parents, never bothering to write to them. I was forced to recall the husband whose wife I'd taken. I was forced to recall all the selfish acts, all the casual cruelties I had committed in the pursuit of my ambition. Worst of all I was obliged to confront my shortcomings as a priest: the bouts of irritation towards my colleagues, the contempt and revulsion which lay behind my ostensibly noble behaviour towards the poor, the endless temptation to blot out my restless boredom by resorting to fornication . . . A good man? Outwardly perhaps. But inwardly? And as I began to see myself as a good man capable of evil deeds I realised that the concentration camps were only a manifestation on a huge scale of the disorder which has the power to cripple each human soul. It was all one. Evil was an ever-present reality, a reality which Christ had conquered, and when I asked myself how I could best attempt to master that reality myself, it became clear to me that I had to live in imitation of Christ; I knew then I had to be a monk.

"However, it's most important to stress at this point that I didn't succeed in becoming Aidan merely by adopting a way of life which would be unsuitable for most priests. I was able to become Aidan first by facing the pain and then by transcending it so that I could finally serve God as he wished me to serve him, in honesty, with humility and by faith. Then as soon as I started serving God and stopped serving myself, the second Victor lost his power over me, and once my fear of his power was dead I found I could forgive him at last for leading me so far astray. In practical terms this meant that I could unify my personality; Victor One was able to embrace Victor Two and live with him in harmony—or, to express the matter in the familiar religious way, I felt that God had forgiven me for my sins by showing me the way forward into a new life, and once I knew I was forgiven I could be at peace with myself at last."

He stopped speaking. It was very quiet. Neither of us moved. After a while I found I was staring at the thickening twilight beyond the window. The room was unlit, so there were no reflections in the glass, and even if I had been able to see his mirrored image I would have looked away. At last he said in the manner of a kindly teacher explaining a sum to a child who had forgotten his arithmetic lesson: "It's a cycle. You sin. You go down into hell. You're under judgement. You face the pain. You acknowledge your sins. You repent. You're led out of hell. You're shown the way forward—and the way forward signifies forgiveness as well as the chance to begin a new life, by the grace of God, in faith and in hope and in charity. Birth, death, resurrection . . . yes, it's all a cycle, isn't it, a timeless cycle far older than Christianity, but of course Christianity is a divine manifestation of eternal truths." He began to stand up.

I said at once in alarm: "You're not going?"

He smiled reassuringly. "I thought you might like a short interval to enable you to ponder on what I've said."

"Oh, I see." I struggled to form an opinion on the proposal.

"Perhaps you'd like me to show you to your room so that you can unpack your bag and rest for half an hour."

"Oh, but we mustn't waste time! I've hardly begun to tell you yet about my problems, and—"

"You've told me a great deal. And perhaps the problems which you think are your problems aren't really your problems at all."

"But the main problem's absolutely unmistakable! How am I going to—"

"You'll never be master of your future until you're master of your past."

"But the past isn't a mystery as the future is!"

"Isn't it? In that case shall we postpone the interval so that you can tell me more about your background?"

"The postponement won't last long. In a nutshell this is just the story of a Yorkshire boy who made good, married the perfect wife, fathered five perfect children and embarked on a perfect career. Of course that's a highly condensed summary, but nevertheless it's the truth, pure and simple."

"Oh yes? You remind me of the time many, many years ago in London when I saw a play by Mr. Oscar Wilde called *The Importance of Being Earnest.* At one point in the first act the young hero declared: 'That's the whole truth, pure and simple!' Whereupon his friend commented: 'The truth is never pure and rarely simple.' " Lucas sighed before adding: "I fear poor Mr. Wilde spoke from experience."

I laughed but I remained wary. I knew any relaxation in my defences could be dangerous. Cautiously I said: "Exactly what do you want to know about the past?"

"I want to know more about the three Nevilles—which means, if I've understood you rightly, I want to know more about your parents and your uncle."

"Well, that's easy," I said, anxious to create the impression that I could ring up the curtain without batting an eyelid. "But be warned! A lurid story in the best tradition of Victorian melodrama is now about to unfold . . ."

3

"I WAS born in 1902," I said, "so I'm an Edwardian, but all the main characters in this drama were Victorians. I'll just run through the *dramatis personae* for you: my father was the tragic hero, my mother was the noble heroine and my Uncle Willoughby was the villain of the piece. Then there are the minor roles: my brother Willy, who became the misogynist schoolmaster (he was called after Uncle Willoughby, of course—my mother insisted on that), my sister Emily, who became the spinster daughter but eventually married a shoe salesman, and Tabitha our nurse (a splendid cameo role, this), who was the illiterate working-class Yorkshirewoman with a heart of gold. Finally there was me. I was a latter-day Oliver Twist, the orphan who asked for more.

"My brother Willy and I were as close as twins, but he had poor health and couldn't keep up with me, even though he was a year my senior. My mother had poor health too, but that was because she had so many pregnancies. My father and Emily were often ill. However, I've always had the constitution of an ox. My mother used to say that in health I resembled Uncle Willoughby.

"Uncle Willoughby was my mother's brother. His full name was Herbert Willoughby Stoke, but he never used the name Herbert because he thought it was too ordinary. Uncle Willoughby always liked to stand out from the crowd. His father was just a clerk up at the mill, but Uncle Willoughby became manager and wound up Mayor of Maltby. He was always clever with money, speculating in business ventures, and became well-heeled when he was still quite young—he actually owned his big house: that was very rare in those days. He married well too. His wife was a solicitor's daughter with two hundred a year of her own—a real lady who pressed wild-flowers and painted water-colours and kept a piano in a room she called a drawing-room.

"My mother thought she was an awful bore. 'If Ella shows me one more dead flower I'll scream!' she'd say. My mother thought that drawing, painting, playing the piano—all the traditional feminine accomplishments—were a complete waste of time. She used to read—but not the books women were supposed to read; she despised the novels from Mudie's Library. She read history, philosophy and poetry. The only novelist whose work she would consider skimming was George Eliot. She was interested in politics, always read *The Times.* People thought she was very eccentric, but my father adored her and so did Uncle Willoughby. She and Uncle Willoughby used to discuss politics together. They were both Liberals, although my mother used to flirt with socialism, women's emancipation, all that sort of thing. My father wasn't interested in politics but he and my mother used to discuss poetry. My mother couldn't talk about literature with Uncle Willoughby because he didn't read much. Too busy making money.

"My father couldn't make money. He inherited a thriving business from his father, but his heart wasn't in it. It was a draper's shop, a large one—he employed six people—and it stood on the best corner of the High Street. The family had lived over the shop, but when my father came into his inheritance and knew he could afford to marry, he took a detached house on the edge of the town. The house had an acre of garden with a real lawn and real flower-beds—I mean, it wasn't just the conventional vegetable patch or hen-run or pasture for the goat—and inside the house (*inside,* not outside) there was a real lavatory which flushed. Uncle Willoughby insisted on that. He said my mother could hardly be expected to reduce her standard of living, and as she'd been living in his house before her marriage, that standard was high. I think he was probably the first person in Maltby to have an inside lavatory. He got it because he heard all the gentlemen had them in the South.

"To make sure my mother was comfortable, my father employed a cook and a maid-of-all-work—and Tabitha, who took care of the children while my mother lay on her chaise-longue before, during and after her pregnancies and read her highbrow books. Willy and I grew up thinking ourselves very grand. We had no idea that by southern standards we were all dirt-common, but we didn't really understand about the South. I was five when I finally realised that Yorkshire was part of England and not vice versa.

"But I was telling you about my father. He was a tall, good-looking man with a delicate look and a nervous temperament. He suffered from asthma. And he suffered from moodiness. When he was happy he was very, very happy but when he was gloomy he was morose. Normally we only saw the happy side, but at the end of his life he used to drink and then he'd be silent and withdrawn.

"I believe he was a profoundly religious man but was never comfortable with the simple-minded bibliolatrous Non-Conformism which ruled Maltby. We all went to chapel dutifully every week, but once my father took Willy and me to a Church of England service in Huddersfield so that we could hear the liturgy. My mother was very shocked. 'You'll wind up a Papist if you're not careful!' she said. 'Liturgy indeed! Whatever next?' But my father just said: 'It was so beautiful.'

"That's what he used to say when he took us for walks in the hills. 'It's all so beautiful!' he'd say, and he'd talk about Beauty, Truth and

Goodness and how all was sacred, all was one in God. 'It's all a unity!' he'd say. 'It's all one!' I suppose he was really a pantheist, although he wouldn't have had the education to realise that pantheism, when pushed to its limits, has nothing to do with Christianity at all. Perhaps it would be kinder not to call him a pantheist but simply to say he possessed to an intense degree what Rudolf Otto called *Das Heilige,* a sense of the holy.

"Was there ever a man less suited to run a draper's shop?

"Anyway, there he was, living far beyond his means in this expensive house and mishandling his business, when suddenly death intervened and we found out he was bankrupt. Uncle Willoughby stepped in to clear up the mess. All the servants were sacked, Tabitha was sent to the workhouse without even being given the chance to say goodbye to us, the house was reclaimed by the landlord, and the bailiffs took possession of its contents.

"Willy and I asked Uncle Willoughby if he'd lend us the money to buy back our toys from the bailiffs, but he wouldn't. He just said: 'You won't need toys where you're going,' and shovelled us off to a spartan boarding-school run by Methodists. It was Dickensian—first cousin to Dotheboys Hall. If Willy and I hadn't had each other, I think we'd have died or gone mad. We were even boarded out there for the holidays. We felt we had no home any more, no family, nothing. My mother did write to us, but she only said she was praying we were learning to become Christian gentlemen. We wrote and begged her to rescue us, but she didn't. She said later that Uncle Willoughby had intercepted our letters.

"This nightmare went on for a year. Then the situation changed. My mother was advised to go south for her health, and she wound up in rooms with my sister Emily at St. Leonards-on-Sea. Uncle Willoughby then decided that we should be educated in London—not just because London was the best place for anyone who wanted to Get On but because we'd be near enough there to the South Coast to visit my mother without incurring too much expense. The visits took place three times a year but they could never last long because there was no room set aside for us; we had to take it in turns to sleep on the horse-hair sofa in the parlour, and whoever didn't have the sofa slept on the floor.

"In London we were boarded out with a doctor and his appalling wife, both Primitive Methodists, both friends of Uncle Willoughby, and eventually attended, as I've already mentioned, the City of London School. We were given no pocket-money on a regular basis, just the occasional hand-out. 'That'll teach you how to survive!' said Uncle Willoughby. 'Either you Get On or you Go Under, but don't expect *me* to lift a finger to help you if you wind up a failure like your father!' So we knew we had to Get On.

" 'You'll be grateful to me one day!' said Uncle Willoughby. I can see him now, a tough stout little man with a pugnacious chin and angry blue eyes. 'I'm teaching you how to win wealth, fame and success—all the prizes that make life worthwhile! You've got to go chasing the prizes,' said Uncle Willoughby, 'if you want to make sure you survive.' Oh yes, I can see him now, very smart in his expensive suit, his gold watch-chain glinting on his paunch; Uncle Willoughby the survivor, Getting On, Going Far.

"I won a scholarship to Oxford and Willy joined me a year later—his schooling had been interrupted by a long bout of glandular fever. Uncle Willoughby paid his fees, but in fact he'd lost interest in Willy by that time. *I* was the blue-eyed boy. He was in ecstasy when I won my scholarship. 'You'll be a real gentleman now,' he said. He was misty-eyed. 'I couldn't be prouder,' he said, 'not even if you were my own son.' He'd married soon after my parents' wedding but he had no sons, only three ghastly daughters. 'You'll read for the bar later and go into politics!' he said. 'And just you make damned sure you wind up Prime Minister!' He was so carried away by the thought of this ultimate prize that he even forced himself to part with five pounds. 'Mustn't spoil you,' he said, 'but you deserve a generous present.' Mean old devil, he could never bear to be parted from his brass . . .

"I read Greats up at Oxford and enjoyed my time there very much. The only blot on the landscape was Uncle Willoughby who seemed to be constitutionally incapable of leaving me in peace—and I knew why. The old devil was living vicariously through me; I was now leading the life he hadn't travelled far enough to lead, so whenever he had the chance—which seemed to be all too often—he'd be chugging south from Yorkshire to see me.

"Well, I was just getting very fed up with these constant visits when I received the biggest possible diversion: my call to be a clergyman.

"I must say straight away that I'm not a mystic and I haven't a psychic bone in my body. But this call wasn't the quiet kind, the gradual evolution which most people seem to experience. This was the road-to-Damascus call, the blinding light coming out of the blue. I heard that Charles Raven was preaching in Christ Church Cathedral and I knew at once that I wanted to hear him.

"By that time I was used to the Church of England—I'd been attending services regularly for some time. After all, if one wanted to Get On up at Oxford one didn't go trekking off to a Methodist chapel in the wrong part of the city. One pretended one was Church of England, born and bred—and I enjoyed doing that; it seemed a pleasant way of rebelling against my chapel upbringing.

"I'd heard of Raven. I'd been told he was an electrifying preacher but I knew nothing about his theology. I didn't know he was a biologist who took an evolutionary view of Christianity, supported the Modernists and stood in the forefront of Liberal Protestantism. But as soon as he started to speak I became aware that his thought was curiously familiar to me—I didn't quite feel that I'd heard it all before, but I felt he was repeatedly jogging my memory.

"Then it happened. He was talking of the principle of evolution in nature and applying it to the evolution of mankind towards the Kingdom of God, when all of a sudden he stopped in mid-sentence. He flung out his arms—Raven has a whole series of dramatic pulpit gestures—and he appeared to look straight at me with those brilliant eyes of his and he cried: 'It's all a unity! It's all one!' And then I saw the light which had shone on St. Paul.

"The world—the world of Neville Two—Uncle Willoughby's world—ground to a halt. I was back on the moors again as Neville One and my father was there with me—I could actually see him—and Christ was there too, I knew he was—there on the Maltby moors, there in Christ Church Cathedral, there standing shoulder to shoulder with Charles Raven, and it was all a unity, all one—and then as I experienced that unity, Uncle Willoughby's world was rent from top to bottom, like the curtain in the Temple when Christ was crucified, and I saw the way back at last into that paradise which had been lost.

"Well, it wasn't easy telling the old villain that his dreams of calling on his nephew the Prime Minister at Ten Downing Street weren't going to come true, but the next time he came pitter-pattering south to see me I told him without mincing my words that I was going into the Church. One didn't mince words with Uncle Willoughby. One called a spade a spade and looked as aggressive as possible. That was the only way to win his respect.

"At first I thought he'd have apoplexy, but then he said: 'That's a fine palace the Archbishop of York has at Bishopthorpe—and I shan't have to journey so far to see you in my old age!' The old rogue! I was livid that all he could think of was Getting On and Going Far. The spiritual implications of my decision completely eluded him.

"It was then that I lost my temper and . . . well, we had the most almighty row. I suppose it had been brewing for a long time. I don't think I need describe it in detail. Suffice it to say that afterwards we never met again.

"My mother said she was delighted that I'd decided to be a clergyman. That surprised me because she too had dreamed of Downing Street, but as soon as Uncle Willoughby disappeared from my life my mother seized the chance to move closer to me. We'd always corresponded regularly, but now the correspondence changed; it became sharper, wittier, more affectionate. My mother had a great gift for letter-writing—in fact I began to enjoy her letters so much that I made the effort to visit her more often at St. Leonards. After a while I realised that although my mother was hopeless with small children she came into her own once they were grown up. I found myself bathed in approval and affection. 'Darling Neville!' she would exclaim. 'So charming, so clever, so attractive and so *good*—what have I done to deserve you?' I suppose this sort of dialogue should have seemed revoltingly sentimental and silly, but it didn't. In fact I have to confess I lapped it up. I hadn't been petted and pampered like that since the days when Tabitha looked after me.

"I was a little nervous when I announced my engagement to Grace after a long courtship, but I needn't have worried. My mother wasn't a fool and she knew when she was well off—she knew Grace was the kind of daughter-in-law who would never give her any trouble, and besides she could see as clearly as I could that Grace was the perfect wife for a clergyman. Grace was devout, beautiful, intelligent, kind, generous, sensitive, unselfish—and always so feminine, always conforming so exactly to the image of the ideal woman. 'Such a delightful girl!' said my mother. 'I'm devoted to her!' When she said that, I remember I felt so relieved. I didn't want to marry anyone who would have roused my mother's jealousy. That would have driven a wedge between us. My mother had been very jealous of Uncle Willoughby's wife even though she'd despised her for all those pressed wild-flowers.

"In 1938, when I'd been married for twelve years, my sister Emily finally managed to get to the altar and Mother had no one to look after her any more. Grace and I discussed the situation, and when Grace was quite perfect, saying our Christian duty was plain, I asked Mother to come to live with us. 'Darling Neville!' said my mother. 'How often I've dreamt of living with my favourite child! How happy we'll be, discussing literature, politics and theology every day—I can hardly believe my good fortune!'

"Well . . . You can guess what happened, can't you? It was a disaster. My mother and I . . . she . . . I . . . no, I can't quite explain it, but we didn't get on. For a long time we pretended we did—we used to have the most appalling phoney dialogues. 'Neville darling, how wonderful, how devoted, how noble, how *Christian* you are . . .' 'Darling Mother, how adorable of you to say so, but of course I'm only following your example . . .' Ugh! Yes, our conversations became quite unreal and eventually . . . Well, she was being much too possessive with me and much too beastly to Grace and in the end I had to draw the line. At least . . . to be absolutely candid . . . there was a little dust-up. A tiff. But fortunately Emily came to the rescue and bore Mother away to her home in the South London suburbs. Mother and I were reconciled soon afterwards, of course, but somehow the relationship was never quite the same again, and after she died . . . After she died I felt very, very upset. I adored her, you see. And she adored me. But we shouldn't have tried to live under the same roof. That was a mistake.

"She died in the September of 1941 and Grace died in the August of 1942. It was a most difficult year for me, and when Grace died I . . . well, it's hard to explain, but it was so terrible when she died that I felt all I could do was pull down the curtain and not think of her any more—but that doesn't mean I didn't love her. On the contrary it was because I loved her that I couldn't bear to think about her after she died. I had to pull down the curtain, had to . . . And after I'd pulled it down I began to court the lady who last year became my second wife.

"She led me quite a dance, but I never gave up. I chased and I chased and I chased because she was such a prize, you see, such a prize, and once I was chasing the prizes again I felt safe and secure, in control of my life, winning . . . And I did win. I won my prize. I won everything I'd ever wanted—and then I found I didn't want it any more. Obviously it's once more time to ring down the curtain, but this time there's no curtain waiting to be pulled down. I'm saddled with her indefinitely and how I'm ever going to stand it God alone knows . . . But that's the future. I'm digressing. You only wanted to know about my past, and that's it, I've finished. That's the truth, pure and simple."

Sinking back in my chair I took a quick look at the old boy across the table. His one visible eye bore a kindly expression. I managed to stifle a sigh of relief, but as the silence lengthened I couldn't resist asking: "Well? Have I told you all you wanted to know?"

"Oh dear me, yes," said Lucas. "I like your truth, pure and simple, very much. I always had a weakness for Victorian melodrama. But alas! I fear Victorian melodrama has very little to do with reality."

My heart thudded in my chest. I sat bolt upright in my chair. "What the deuce do you mean? Are you implying—"

"Yes, I'm afraid I am. It's a lovely yarn, lad, but you'll have to do a little better than that."

"Are you calling me a liar?"

"I hope I wouldn't be so ill-mannered. But let's lean on this pure simple truth for a moment and see if it doesn't keel over—let's take another look at your Uncle Willoughby, the stage villain, the character everyone loves to hiss as soon as he walks onstage. Brutal, avaricious, worldly, ugly, fierce—I think you'd agree, wouldn't you, that by using these adjectives I'm not misrepresenting him?"

"Certainly I'd agree! He was a monster and I detested him!"

"Yes, but during the course of your narrative I repeatedly received the impression that what you said about him bore little relation to what you actually felt. I think," said Lucas in his gentlest voice, "that contrary to all you've said, you were really very fond indeed of your appalling Uncle Willoughby."

XII

"No man, be he lawyer, doctor, priest or poet, can correctly describe the real history of another . . . The little events that determine the growth of the soul, the secret memories that colour his mentality, the hidden springs from which arise his motives and his actions, these no friend however intimate can fully know."

CHARLES E. RAVEN
A WANDERER'S WAY

I

I FELT as if someone had slid a skewer straight into the centre of my memory. Instantly the past started to swing out of control and I knew I had to drag down the curtain, but I was paralysed. All I could do was stare at Lucas in the manner of a man hypnotised by a serpent.

"And now let's lean on this pure simple truth of yours again," he was saying calmly. "Let's take another look at your father, the tragic hero—who occupies far less space in your narrative than your wicked uncle. Curiously enough it's not his heroic qualities you emphasise. After a passing reference to his good looks, you talk of his delicate health, his nervous temperament, the lack of education which encouraged his nature-mysticism to veer towards pantheism. The picture you draw is of an ineffectual romantic, and finally you conclude with a bitterness which you're quite unable to conceal: 'Was there ever a man less suited to run a draper's shop?' I suggest that you actually feel a profound ambivalence towards this man. After all, what really happened when you were seven? He left you, didn't he? He left you destitute and vulnerable—in fact it was he, not your uncle, who broke up your happy home."

I leapt to my feet. My voice cried: "I deny every word you say!"

"Very well, let's move on to your mother, whom you rather surprisingly label the noble heroine. Here we have a woman who is apparently content to abdicate her parental responsibilities and—"

I shouted: "No man insults my mother in my presence!" and walked out.

Slamming the door so violently that it shuddered on its hinges, I blazed down the passage to the hall. Only the sight of the doorkeeper brought me to a standstill. "Can I help you, Father?" he asked as I hesitated, and at once, unable to control myself, I exploded: "Yes—you can stop addressing me in that distasteful fashion! I'm no Catholic priest—I'm a Protestant Archdeacon!"

"I'm so sorry, Archdeacon, I had no idea."

This immaculate courtesy in the face of my extreme rudeness I found so unbearable that I wanted to hit him. The impulse frightened me. Obviously I had to remove myself from the house before I committed some horrifying atrocity, but even as half my mind was urging me to abandon my pride and run, the other half was ordering me to conquer this humiliating desire to bolt and stand my ground.

I was still dithering when a large, grand monk glided into the hall with a sheaf of papers in his hand. He had thick silver hair which needed cutting, horn-rimmed spectacles parked on the end of a Roman nose, and a cool, snooty air of authority. The repulsive jewel-studded cross on his chest immediately reminded me of the Pope. With a sinking heart I recognised the Abbot-General, Francis Ingram.

He said casually to the doorkeeper: "If anyone calls I'm not available—except to the Archbishop, of course." Then he became aware of me, cowering in the mouth of the corridor which led to the guest-wing of the house. Holding my breath I prayed he would experience no twinge of recognition, but my prayer went unanswered. I should have remembered that the most able men in managerial positions train themselves to remember faces.

"Good evening," he said pleasantly to me. "Forgive me—I'm sure we've met, but I can't quite place you."

"This is the Archdeacon, Father," said the doorkeeper in a disastrous attempt to be helpful, and almost at the same moment Lucas said behind me: "It's Jon's visitor. I'm about to show him to his room." As I spun round I saw he was carrying the overnight bag I had forgotten.

Meanwhile the Abbot-General, prompted by the word "Archdeacon" and no doubt recalling memories of his visit to Darrow's diocese in 1941, had remembered who I was and was busy glossing over my identity. "Ah yes, of course—welcome to our London house!" he said sociably. "I'm delighted that you have the opportunity to meet Father Lucas!"

I managed to utter the words: "Thank you, sir," but I was appalled by the loss of my anonymity. Ingram would know every bishop on the bench and might feel it his duty to be lukewarm in the future when I was considered for a major preferment. Word would then get around that I was unsuitable. I wondered what Darrow had said to him when my visit had been arranged. "I have a clergyman here who—" No, Darrow never used the word "clergyman" unless he was among rabid Protestants. "I have a priest here who's gone off the rails and needs urgent attention . . ." Despair overwhelmed me. I felt as a drowning man must feel when he realises that the water has closed for the final time over his head.

"This way," said Lucas gently, piloting me back into the guest-wing towards some distant stairs.

As soon as we were alone I blurted out: "The Abbot-General recognised me," but Lucas remained tranquil.

"I assure you that's of no consequence. He'll treat the matter as he would treat information disclosed to him in the confessional."

"But what can he possibly be thinking? An archdeacon seeking anonymity—"

"We receive distressed visitors from all ranks of the Church. If Father Abbot-General's paused long enough to think twice about your presence in his house, I dare say he's respecting you for having the humility and good sense to seek help from an older priest."

I was sufficiently reassured to wipe the sweat from my brow with a steady hand. Then as we reached the top of the stairs I realised he was still carrying my bag. "Here, I'll take that," I said, grabbing it. "I'm sorry, I'm treating you as if you were a porter."

"And I'm afraid I treated you as if you were a novice who wilfully refused to make an adequate confession. I apologise for upsetting you."

My voice said: "I was going to walk out. I would have walked out if the Abbot-General hadn't appeared."

"Yes. But you would have come back."

"Would I?"

"Of course. You're not the kind of man who throws in the sponge. You're a fighter—and it's your fighting spirit which is ultimately going to save you. You'll think of your Uncle Willoughby shouting: 'Get On or Go Under!' and you'll battle on in pursuit of the prize of your spiritual health."

"That was Darrow's verdict. I suppose a sick man should find it comforting when two specialists agree on a hopeful prognosis, but I'm beginning to feel as if I'm at death's door."

"You may have to die before you can live again."

Subtle old serpent, feeding me the Christian message of hope by reminding me of Easter! Tightening my clasp on my bag I forgave him for his horrific assault on my equilibrium and allowed him to lead me on down the corridor towards the light at the far end.

2

THE room which had been assigned to me was furnished with a table, two wooden chairs, a chest of drawers, a wardrobe and a bed which, I discovered to my relief as I sat down on it, had a comfortable mattress; I felt in no mood at that moment for the ascetic life. On the chest of drawers lay a Bible and a Prayer Book. There were no pictures on the walls but a crucifix hung by the bed. Like the Abbot-General's pectoral cross, the crucifix made me want to bawl: "No Popery!" at the top of my voice. Why was I being smitten by this disgusting urge to behave like a Cromwellian iconoclast? I was quite capable of exercising charity towards Catholicism in both its English and its Roman forms, even though I disapproved of it intellectually. I could only suppose in alarm that the anxieties of the present had induced me to regress to the Non-Conformist, bitterly anti-Catholic atmosphere of chapel society in Maltby.

"I'm going to arrange for some tea and sandwiches to be brought to you while you rest for half an hour and meditate on our dialogue," said Lucas, pulling down the black blind over the window. "It's very important that you should be well-nourished; you need the strength to stoke up your fighting spirit."

It says much for my addled frame of mind that I almost answered: "Yes, Father." Instead I said: "All right," but that sounded much too grudging and unfriendly. Finally I succeeded in uttering the words: "Yes, sir," and looking respectful.

My inability to call him Aidan, as he had suggested, must have been very obvious; my confused mental state was no doubt equally plain to a skilled observer. Murmuring "There, there!" as if I were an unhappy small child, the old boy patted me reassuringly on the shoulder and said: "If you want any help while I'm gone, just go to the top of the stairs and shout: 'Peter!' That's the guest-master. He'll look after you."

I nodded. The old boy gave my shoulder another pat and padded away. The door closed. I was alone.

I did try to reflect on what had happened, but it was too frightening so I stopped. I could only sit on the edge of the bed and wait numbly, just like an unhappy small child, for him to return and take charge of me again.

3

TEN minutes later the guest-master brought me two rounds of cheese sandwiches, an apple and a large pot of tea. I was aware of him giving me a shrewd, speculative look as if he were trying to calculate how likely I was to start climbing the walls.

"Would you like a spot of company while you wait for Father Abbot to return?"

"No, thanks. I'm fine." That disposed of the guest-master. I embarked on the task of forcing myself to eat but I was still toying with the second sandwich when Lucas returned.

"I believe I have most of the information I need," he said, sitting down opposite me at the table. "There are only a few more questions which must be asked tonight before we adjourn. Then tomorrow morning after I've had the chance to think and pray, I'll offer you my opinion and make suggestions for the future."

"Tomorrow morning I have to return home."

"And so do I. We'll meet at five-thirty." Lucas evidently considered this suggestion raised no problems, but when he saw my expression he added kindly: "I'll ask Peter to wake you at five. I expect you're worried because you haven't brought your alarm clock."

Unable to think of a reply I sank my teeth into the remainder of my second sandwich and wondered what suggestions about the future could possibly be made.

"Now let's deal as quickly as we can with these final questions," Lucas was saying. "First of all, would I be right in thinking that your second wife is somewhat different from your first?"

I stopped eating. "Yes," I said. "She is."

"Would you go so far as to say they were really startlingly dissimilar?"

I abandoned the sandwich. "Yes," I said. "I would. But what made you think—"

"Your second wife is a clever young woman, perhaps, very charming and original, with a flair for writing fascinating letters?"

"How *on earth* did you know?"

"I have a theory, based on what you told me about your mother and your first wife. Now, Neville, you may find my next question hard to answer, but I do beg you to respond as accurately as possible. When were you first attracted to your second wife?"

There was a long, long pause which I found I was unable to end.

"Since you implied that you started courting your second wife fairly soon after your first wife's death," said Lucas, "it seems reasonable to assume you met her when your first wife was still alive."

"Yes." I began to arrange the crumbs on my plate into a pattern. "I first met Dido," I said at last, "in the May of 1942."

"And you were immediately attracted? Could one possibly deduce from this," said Lucas, not waiting for me to answer the question, "that at the time you were a little dissatisfied with Grace? Forgive me, I know I'm touching on difficult, painful matters, but I'm only anxious to obtain information which will allow me, by the Grace of God, to help you."

I stopped arranging the crumbs into a pattern and began to sweep them into a neat pile with my forefinger. After a while I said: "I was a little restless. But I tried to beat it back. I loved Grace."

"I understand. Now, can you look back and pinpoint the moment when the restlessness began? Was it around the time in 1938 when your mother came to live with you?"

"Oh no!" I said at once, relieved that I could at last speak with confidence and look him straight in the eye. "That disaster actually united us. No, the marriage only started to get awkward after our fifth child was born in March 1941. We'd only—" I bit back the word "planned" on the grounds that it might upset an Anglo-Catholic. "We'd only hoped for four children. The fifth wasn't entirely a welcome surprise."

"So the restlessness began after March 1941. Directly after?"

"No." Again I could speak with confidence. "Newborn babies aren't usually much trouble. They just sleep most of the time. Sandy didn't start to wear Grace out until he was six months old, sitting up and demanding constant attention, and it was when she was worn out that I became aware of feeling restless."

"That takes us to the September of 1941, doesn't it? And in the September of 1941, you said earlier—"

"My mother died. Yes," I said. "That's when it all began, I can see that clearly now. Grace told me she was too exhausted to go to the funeral, she couldn't bear to leave Sandy, didn't want to take advantage of her best friend's offer to look after him—and so on and so on. I remember looking at her and thinking: I don't need a dull dreary wife like you any more. That horrified me, of course, because it was such a terrible judgement, so unfair, in fact quite unacceptable. Grace was so perfect, you see—"

"Such a prize."

"Yes, such a prize, and prizes have to be perfect because if they're not perfect they wouldn't be prizes any more. So long as Grace was a prize I could feel happy and secure, but once she ceased to be a prize—"

"You didn't want her."

"But I did! I adored her and she adored me and we had this perfect marriage—"

"No, that's not quite right, is it, Neville? That was the drama you were playing on stage. But reality—as indeed you admitted a moment ago—lay elsewhere."

"Well, of course I'm not denying there was a little awkwardness—"

"No, Neville. That's not quite right either, is it? I'm afraid you're going to have to come down off that stage. This was no 'little awkwardness.' You fell in love with another woman, didn't you, when your wife was still alive."

"Well, yes, but nothing happened! I fought against the attraction! I concede that I was in love with Dido, but I swear there was no impropriety!"

"No, that's not quite right either, Neville, is it? I'm sorry, but we really do have to face this other drama that was taking place off stage. If you fell in love with another woman while your wife was still alive, there was impropriety."

"But all I did was clasp her hands once and tell her I felt as if spring had arrived after a long dull winter! All right, I know that was idiotic, but—"

"It was wrong."

"But it was only a little slip!"

"It was a sin."

"Oh, for heaven's sake! I did my best to be good and decent—"

"You mean you went through the motions of being good and decent. But the truth was, wasn't it, that you were harbouring adulterous thoughts and wished that you could have carnal knowledge of this woman within the only context available to you as a priest: marriage. And this desire in turn must mean, mustn't it, that there were times when consciously or unconsciously you wished you were a widower—"

"That's a monstrous accusation!"

"You mean it's painful. Yes. Sin always is."

"But I didn't do anything, I didn't hurt anyone—"

"No? Are you telling me your wife died in ignorance of your so-called 'little slip'?"

I said: "I'll not talk about this. I refuse to discuss this any more. I won't discuss it, I won't, I absolutely refuse—"

"No, it's much, much too painful, isn't it? It's a torment. It's a nightmare. But Neville, in the end you've got to screw up all your courage and face this pain. The road to repentance doesn't lie, you see, in ringing down the curtain on the sin you can't bear to face."

I lost control of myself. Springing to my feet, I shouted in fury: "My repentance is between me and God! I don't have to approach God through a clergyman—through a *priest*—like you! I'm a Protestant, not a bloody Catholic, and I'll not tolerate any manifestation of Catholicism—no confessionals, *no celibate priests playing God,* NO DAMNED MONKS TALKING DAMNED RUBBISH—NO BLOODY POPERY, NOT IN MY LIFE, NOT NOW, NOT EVER!"

During this chaotic speech I had broken down, blundering from the table and slumping onto the bed, but I knew that this time there could be no running away; I was far beyond an escape which could have been achieved by rushing out of a room. I had no clear idea at first why I had sunk into emotional disintegration. All I knew was that the wasteland had suddenly become pitch dark. I covered my face with my hands as if I could protect myself from the horror I could not name, but as the tears streamed past my fingers I realised what had happened. I had been almost annihilated by the pain I had just faced. I thought of my Grace, that innocent victim who had been so wounded by my infidelity that she had been drained of the will to live, and at last the river of guilt which I had suppressed for so long burst its banks. In the flood that followed, Christ was absent, God had turned away His face, and I felt I could only drown in my grief and my shame.

Then someone sat down on the bed beside me; someone stepped into my wasteland to share my agony; someone made the darkness endurable. Automatically I reached out for his hand. It was there, waiting, and as his fingers closed on mine I knew that Christ, the resurrected Christ, not the Jesus of history but the Christ of Eternity, had moved through the closed door of the room to be again at one with his disciples. He was contained in the compassion which now encircled me and in the sharing of the suffering. My tears ceased. My pain eased. A great stillness seemed to blend with the silence.

After a long while I said: "I'm so frightened of failing, and sin means failure. But I won't be Going Under, will I, if I now call my mistakes sins?"

"No, Neville, you won't be Going Under. You'll be Getting On."

"And the prize I have to win now isn't merely survival, is it? It's the new life where I'm finally set free to serve God instead of myself."

"That's it. That's when you'll be Going Far."

After an even longer while I said: "I'm not much of a clergyman. My sermons tend to resemble legal arguments. I'm awkward at pastoral work. I try to avoid the poor. I think too much about cultivating the people who matter. In fact although I'm so successful I'm really rather a failure. That's a paradox, isn't it?"

"If you pursue the truth far enough you always wind up in the land of paradox. You reach a point where the apparent truth divides into two opposing truths, and then you have to try to reach beyond them to grasp the ultimate truth, their synthesis."

"Raven doesn't approve of that type of Hegelian dialectic. He sees all truth as a unity."

"Hegel's synthesis could be Raven's unity. Who knows? Most ultimate truths lie beyond words altogether."

"That, I know, is how Catholics justify their use of elaborate ritual." I blew my nose before saying: "Sorry about all the Protestant bigotry. Disgusting. Don't usually behave like one of Cromwell's statue-bashers."

Lucas said with a wry, dry humour which I could immediately appreciate: "That's all right, lad, we're all bigots here. Cuthbert Darcy used to refer to the Church of Rome as 'Our Fallen Sister.' " Releasing my hand, he rose to his feet. "Sometimes I think the Church of England's little short of a miracle," he said idly. "Anglo-Catholics, Evangelicals, the whole range of worshippers between the two extremes—it's a wonder we all coexist as we do."

"We manage it because fundamentally we're a unity."

"But couldn't one equally well say we manage it because we're a disunity, Catholics and Protestants opposing each other in a continuing dialectic which results in the synthesis of the Church?" He allowed me no time to reply but merely added over his shoulder as he moved to the door: "I'll be back at half-past five. If you need help at any hour of the night, knock on Peter's door—number ten at the top of the stairs—and he'll fetch me."

"I'll be all right now."

"Yes, I believe you will. Good night, Neville. God bless you."

He left, the wily old fox padding back to his lair to recuperate from his latest adventure in the tangled spiritual thickets which beset his territory, and I was left exhausted but not without hope on the cross of my guilt and my pain.

4

THE guest-master woke me at five and returned with tea ten minutes later to make sure I had kept my eyes open. By the time Lucas arrived I was fully dressed in my clerical suit and reading the office. This semblance of normality pleased him. "Maintaining a familiar routine is important," he said. "Comfort as well as strength can be derived from such discipline . . . Did you sleep at all?"

"Not much. I hope you did. I felt worried afterwards that I might have tired you, so soon after your operation."

"If I could still be classed as an invalid I wouldn't be going home today." He smiled as he sat down opposite me at the table. "Now let's start thinking about you again. First of all I'm going to explain what I believe is going on—but let me stress that you're under no obligation to agree with a single word I say. I venture an opinion not because I want to impose a theory on you but because I want to help you understand the suggestions I shall be making about the future. Since these suggestions spring from my interpretation of your crisis I can hardly expect you to understand them until you first grasp the essence of my interpretation."

"I understand. But of course I'm very anxious to hear your theory and I promise I won't go storming out if I don't like it."

"Splendid, but let me now help you keep calm by begging you not to take what I say too literally. Great difficulties arise when one tries to express complex truths in words, and although there may be several valid ways of describing what's happened to you, none of them will be exact because we're not dealing with a mathematical equation. Father Ingram, the Abbot-General, who's twelve years younger than I am and very much cleverer, would talk the language of modern psychology. Jon Darrow, who's also twelve years younger than I am and far more heavily endowed with psychic powers, would probably use the ancient symbolic language of mysticism. I'm just an ordinary old dog who doesn't know any fancy tricks, so I shall fall back on the commonplace literary device of the metaphor, which we successfully employed yesterday when we talked of your personality as if it were a trio of people, the three Nevilles. Now, so long as we remember that we're using a method which is an inexact way of describing a complex truth, I don't think we'll go too far astray. The biggest danger about techniques which employ metaphor, symbolism and analogy is that sometimes people mistake these devices for hard facts and get tied up in knots."

"I understand. You'll be painting an impressionist picture, not taking a photograph, so I mustn't get upset if some details are missing or distorted."

"Precisely. In fact only God is in a position to take a photograph because only God can ever know the whole truth about any human being and the circumstances surrounding his life. But what I can do here is to illuminate what we do know in such a way that what we don't know becomes more sharply defined. Then once we grasp what we don't know you'll be in a better position to reach beyond the paradox to the ultimate truth which is hidden from us." He smiled before adding: "And there you see how words break down under the strain of expressing complex matters! I'm not saying that you'll ever know the whole truth, which is God's truth. I'm saying that you may have a good chance of grasping that part of the truth which God has made available for you to know."

"The truth which should be accessible but which I'm at present too muddled to discern?"

"That's it. Now—" The old boy leant back in his chair, removed his spectacles and began to polish them on the skirt of his habit. His casual, relaxed manner was very soothing. "Let me tell you what I think has happened. For the first seven years of your life—very important years, as any Jesuit will tell you—you were Neville One, living in a benign world dominated by two loving adults, your father and your nurse Tabitha. This was an excellent start in life, although it might be worth noting that from infancy you would have been aware of two contrasting types of women, the simple motherly soul and the remote complex blue-stocking.

"Then your father died, Tabitha disappeared, your mother became even more remote and your uncle made it plain that if you wanted to survive you had to become just like him; in other words, Neville Two had to reject his father. This you did most successfully, but as you grew up, Neville One, who had never quite died but had merely been locked up, began to rattle the bars of his prison. You became very tired of Uncle Willoughby. Like most young men you wanted to assert yourself and become independent of those who had authority over you, so when you heard Professor Raven declaring: 'It's all a unity! It's all one!' it was hardly surprising that Neville One was spurred to break out of jail. And once he was free you were able to re-establish your loyalty to your father, whom you saw as a profoundly religious man.

"Now it's Neville Two's turn to be locked up, but after a while you find you can't live without him after all. He's the one who knows how to survive and flourish. He can't be consigned to prison, but how is he going to run in harness with Neville One when they're so incompatible? This is a very difficult problem, but you solve it by binding the two Nevilles together and enfolding them in a new identity. They're still separate—a merger is impossible because of the acute dissimilarity—but at least they're contained harmoniously within Neville Three, who's emerged into the world to keep them trotting smoothly in tandem.

"The arrival on the scene of Neville Three has a most unexpected result. Your mother, who's been very much on the fringe of your life all these years, now discovers that this new Neville is irresistible, a miraculous manifestation of her husband *and* her brother, those two gentlemen who were so dissimilar that it would have seemed to her impossible that they could ever be combined in one person. You've got rid of Uncle Willoughby by this time, but nature abhors a vacuum; you've always had a focal point in your emotional life, and even now you're a grown man you find you still need this powerful presence, the audience which can be guaranteed to applaud your dazzling performance whenever you step on stage.

"It's easy to deduce that you feel compelled to give this dazzling performance because you want to win the love, attention and security which were all so brutally wiped from your life when you were seven years old, but in fact I suspect this compulsion preceded your father's death. You had a brother close to you in age, someone with whom you were inevitably in competition from the cradle onwards. I'll wager you've always felt this need to produce a strong performance for the people who matter and thus prove your superiority not only to them but to yourself.

"But we must return to Neville Three, who has just discovered the ideal new audience: his mother, who not only bathes him in doting approval but cheers him on as he goes chasing the prizes. Obviously this relationship gave you the most enormous emotional satisfaction—why else would you have been so careful to marry a woman of whom your mother couldn't help but approve? Of course you loved your wife for her many admirable qualities, but you did mention that the desire to please your mother was not entirely absent from your mind. And what kind of woman could your mother be expected to tolerate? Why, an educated and refined version of Tabitha, a motherly soul who knew her place and offered no rivalry. Interestingly, you said you met your wife when you were Neville Two, so even in those days, it seems, when your mother was so remote, she was still immensely important to you.

"Now we reach the point in your life when things start to go wrong. Your mother comes to live with you and the move is a disaster. A fifth child arrives. Your perfect wife begins to show worrying imperfections. However, you survive all these setbacks without too much trouble; you merely readjust your identities, putting Neville One on a short leash and giving Neville Two, the expert in survival, a free rein. In the circumstances this is an understandable move, but the result is that Neville Three becomes dislocated. He's no longer containing Nevilles One and Two in harmony. Neville Two's setting the pace, and Neville Two, when all's said and done, hasn't much idea of what being a clergyman is all about.

"Then in September 1941 comes the event which finally blows your multiple personality wide apart: Your mother dies. Can Neville Three live without her? Indeed, can any of the Nevilles live without their special audience cheering them on as they give their magnificent performances on stage? Your father, your uncle, your mother—they're all gone now, and for the first time in your life you have to define yourself as you really are as you stand alone before a deserted auditorium. In other words, you can't be any of the Nevilles any more because each Neville was a creation of—or perhaps I should say a response to—one of those three all-important older figures. You realise there has to be a Neville Four—or possibly someone equally new, a Stephen—to complement this radically different phase of your existence, but as soon as you're aware of this you realise you can't possibly give birth to your new personality on your own. You need another powerful emotional presence who can act as a midwife—not someone like Grace, who was a mere adjunct of the earlier Nevilles, but someone very original and fascinating, a strong personality, someone who'll cheer you on as you go chasing the prizes—someone, in fact, just like the lady who becomes your second wife.

"But in the confusion following your mother's death, you've made a fatal mistake. Contrary to what you suppose, your solution won't turn you into Neville Four or Stephen, because all you've actually done is resurrected Neville Three by putting another woman in your mother's shoes. So you wind up back with Neville Three, repeating the relationship with your mother, repeating the relationship which should be at an end—and Neville Three's long been seriously unbalanced, dominated by the worldly Neville Two. As the pressures mount this imbalance increases and eventually you reach the point where your multiple personality is in danger of disintegration. You've somehow managed to get the personalities back in harness, but Neville One barely exists, Neville Three is no more than a facade and Neville Two is out of control, chasing the wrong prizes on a road which spirals inexorably downwards into hell.

"Now, Neville, I can't stress too strongly that this picture I've painted is *not the whole truth.* It isn't even the whole of that part of the truth which God has made accessible to you. But do you feel it's a recognisable representation of what's been going on in your life? Or do you feel I've created a fantasy which has no relation to reality?"

But I only said: "How do I make all my identities a unity? How can they all become one?"

5

LUCAS seemed to relax; perhaps he had been afraid I would balk at his theory and put myself beyond the reach of the help he planned to offer. "Very well," he said, leaning forward on the table, "we'll now push the theory to its logical conclusion, which is this: If the three Nevilles are reflections of the three vital figures in your past, the way to unite the Nevilles is to harmonise those three figures—and this is where we get to the point where having described what we do know, we try to describe what we don't know."

"Meaning—"

"Meaning we must look beyond the melodramatic figures you presented earlier and ask ourselves what these people were really like. I know nothing beyond the rudimentary descriptions you've given me. You must inevitably know more, but there are bound to be great gaps in your knowledge. All we can assume for certain, given your fragmented warring personality, is that you're not at peace with any of these people and that only by understanding them will you be able to forgive them and live in harmony with their memory."

"But I understand them very well!"

"Do you? Then answer me these questions: What was really going on in your parents' marriage? Why did she marry him and why did he marry her? How did your uncle fit into their relationship? How did your mother succeed in keeping the peace between these two very different men who both, so you say, adored her? What did your uncle's wife think about the situation whenever she wasn't pressing her wild-flowers? You're so familiar with this group of people that you take a great deal for granted, but it's a curious picture you've painted. The triangle—or quadrangle, if one includes your aunt—may have been harmless but it could well have been most unwholesome. I think you should find out more about it. The more you find out, the more chance there is that you'll cease to regard these people as cardboard figures in a melodrama and see them as flesh-and-blood people with whom you can sympathise."

"I can't imagine—"

"That's because you don't want to imagine. Seeing them as cardboard figures in a melodrama is your way of neutralising the harm they've done you; if you can make them unreal and set them on a stage they can't hurt you as flesh-and-blood people would, and you can always ring down the curtain to keep them at bay. But Neville, this is where the curtain must go up and stay up. This is where the characters must be allowed to come down into the auditorium, because only when you meet them face to face will you be able to move past the warring dialectic and grasp the truth which lies beyond, the truth which will set you free. It's a question of facing the pain, you see. It's a question of facing the pain."

After a pause I said: "How do I do all this? Where do I begin?"

"I assume your uncle and aunt are dead. That means you must start with your brother and sister. Go to see them and find out how *they* see the past. You'll hear much that's familiar, but there's always the chance you'll hear something new which will put your memories in a different light. If you bear in mind that the truth is multi-faceted and your own knowledge is just one facet of that truth, you'll see that the facets provided by other people are of the greatest importance."

"You're saying I must play the detective."

"Yes, and the most successful detectives work in pairs. You'll need someone with whom you can discuss your investigations, someone who'll help you sift the wheat from the chaff, and this is where I make my next suggestion: Enlist Jon Darrow's help. I think his intuitive powers could be invaluable to you here."

At once I said: "I'm sorry, but I could never work with Darrow. We're so incompatible that he's incapable of helping me."

"Who sent you here to see me?"

I was silenced.

"Let me give you a little tip on how to handle Jon," said Lucas cosily, smoothing my ruffled feathers with effortless skill. "After all, I was his abbot for years; I should know what I'm talking about. The trick is to avoid any stance which he can regard as intolerably authoritarian—and Jon finds most authority other than his own intolerable. Did you ever clash with him in a situation where you, as the Archdeacon, represented authority?"

"Well, as a matter of fact—"

"I thought so. Then you would have seen him at his worst. But once the authority passes to *him,* the whole range of his remarkable gifts comes into play and he's capable of the most exceptional work. All you have to do now is say to him: 'Look here, let's forget the past—and let's forget I'm the Archdeacon. I'm sailing in uncharted seas and I need a navigator. Can you help?' (Jon always likes nautical metaphors—they remind him of his happy days as a Naval chaplain.) If you take that approach, then I think you'll find that the fierce dog will stop baring his teeth and start wagging his tail."

I was unable to resist exclaiming amused: "Don't think I'm so obtuse that I can't hear the real message you're sending me behind all this cosy advice of yours! You're saying urgently: 'Don't be too proud to seek help from a man you've never liked!' "

The old man laughed, much as a father might laugh when his infant offspring shows signs of promise, but all he said was: "And now, having suggested how you might approach the task of sorting out your past, let's examine the problem of your future. The first thing you must accept is that no fairy godmother is going to appear with a magic wand and transform it into a paradise. But nevertheless there are certain steps you can take to help yourself survive . . ."

6

"YOU'LL need crutches while you're so disabled," said Lucas, "but you must take care they're the right ones. Do you drink?"

"Yes."

"Then don't. Consider yourself a temporary abstainer. Drink's a luxury you can afford when you're strong but it must never be a crutch to help you along when you're weak. That way disaster lies . . . Is there someone, male or female, who normally acts as your confidant?"

"No."

"That's a pity. A sympathetic and trustworthy confidant can be an invaluable crutch. Have you never had an older clergyman in whom you could freely confide?"

"He died last year. But we were estranged for some time before his death."

"Ah. It had in fact occurred to me that you'd apparently been drifting along without effective guidance. I assume from your previous remarks that you're entirely opposed to the practice of auricular confession?"

"I'm sorry, I hate to sound like a bigot again, but—"

"You're perfectly entitled to your views. In the Church of England no one is obliged to make confession. There's no need whatsoever for you to apologise."

"But I'm sure you must think—"

"What I think is that I must deal with you as you are and not try to squeeze you into a mould which would only aggravate your distress. I do think you need spiritual direction, but what I mustn't do is impose a Catholic director on you. That wouldn't work at all."

"I'm sure you can rely on Darrow to have a go at imposing himself!"

"No, no, you underestimate him," said Lucas, effortlessly stroking my ruffled feathers again. "If he'd thought he could direct you, he wouldn't have referred you to me."

"But if—when—I ask him for help, surely he'll jump to the conclusion—"

"Just tell him you need a confidant, not a confessor—or perhaps you might even say a fellow-detective, not a spiritual director—and he'll know exactly what's required of him."

"But if Darrow's out of the running for giving me spiritual advice, how do I find a—no, I'm sorry, I hate that word 'director.' It conjures up all sorts of authoritarian Romish images which make my hackles rise. I know they shouldn't rise, I know I'm in the wrong, I know intellectually that I'm being a bigot, but emotionally—"

"Ah, those vital first seven years of our lives!" said Lucas, smiling at me. "What a very strict chapel it must have been in Maltby!" Then as I smiled too, grateful for his understanding, he added: "Why don't we use the milder word 'adviser' and agree to leave the phrase 'spiritual director' to those who didn't spend their early years among anti-Catholic Non-Conformists? I think later when you're stronger you'll have no trouble discovering a wise and devout Protestant with whom you can discuss your spiritual life, but meanwhile emergency measures seem to be called for. Could you bear it if I made some very general suggestions about how you might shore up your spiritual life in this crisis, or will you only feel driven to declare that all monks should go over to Rome?"

"I'm beginning to be very relieved that all monks haven't gone over to Rome. Tell me what I must do."

"No, I shan't dictate. That's not the way of our Church, is it? I shall only advise—or (milder still) suggest. I presume that most of your private prayers are *ex tempore*? Well, there's nothing wrong with *ex tempore* prayers, of course, but at present you want to be very careful that your prayers aren't merely a flurry of words which will mar the inner stillness you must cultivate in order not only to maintain your equilibrium but to receive the word from God which will undoubtedly come."

"But what makes you so sure there'll be a communication?"

"When a man stands at the crossroads," said Lucas, "there are invariably signs guiding him forward. What usually happens in such cases is this: either he'll be beckoned forward along the same road but given the grace to proceed in a much more effective way; or else he'll be directed on to a different road altogether. Now, I concede that perception might not be easy. You'll almost certainly be required to exercise the charism of discernment, and here again Jon can be of use to you. He's had considerable experience of helping people to distinguish the correct path from the incorrect path as they attempt to move forward from the crossroads."

"But how can I be sure I'll even hear any word from God, let alone discern the meaning of any message which comes my way? I feel so deaf—so muddled and confused—"

"That's exactly why your life of prayer and devotion is now so crucial. You must do all you can to cultivate your receptivity. Try cutting down the *ex tempore* prayers to the essential intercessions and concentrate on one or two formal prayers which you can say very slowly, thinking hard on each phrase. The Collects are always helpful and no doubt you have your own favourite prayers which you can use . . . Then try to allocate at least an hour a day to your reading; when one reads one has to be very still and very quiet. Try to take an hour early in the morning when there's nothing to distract you. Your concentration won't be good at the moment, so you must do everything you can to cut distraction to a minimum."

"What do I read?"

"For the first half hour you can stick to the Bible—reverent biblical study is such a strong feature of the Protestant tradition, isn't it? Doing familiar work will help by making you feel more secure, more relaxed, less at the mercy of your anxieties. Then for the second half hour you should read something less familiar—and something which takes you right out of the present century. Gaining a perspective on the present by examining the past can be very soothing to someone burdened with troubles. Try reading . . . No, I won't suggest the Fathers; they're too closely associated with the Oxford Movement in many Protestant minds. But what about the Cambridge Platonists? 'Spiritual is most rational,' as Whichcote says—very appealing to the Modernist, as Dean Inge would be the first to agree! But be warned: at the end of your hour's reading, when you should be calm and still, don't just read the office and switch off. Keep thinking and praying all through the day whenever you can and wherever you are—be on constant alert for that word from God which I'm sure will eventually arrive."

"I'm sorry, I know you must think me spiritually stupid, but *how* do you think God will communicate with me? What must I look out for?"

"Well, I think we can discount the prospect of a vision complete with heavenly choirs and a message written in fire in the sky," said Lucas, exercising his dry humour again. "And I think we can probably discount an experience as startling and clear-cut as your call in Christ Church Cathedral. However, there may well be resemblances to that exceptionally dramatic early call of yours. Watch out for the phrase which keeps recurring on the lips of different people; watch for the incident which strikes the chord of memory, just as Raven's sermon did; examine every event which occurs in your life and ask yourself if there's something to be learnt even from the most apparently irrelevant occurrence. I'm convinced that even if there's no one single revelation, there'll be a succession of signs which will add up to an enlightenment."

"That's fine," I said, "and I have confidence in what you're telling me, but how does all this solve my most urgent problem? How am I going to live with my wife?"

"Ah yes!" said Lucas. "I thought earlier that you might be having difficulty in identifying your most urgent problem. My dear Neville, your most urgent problem is to find out what God now requires of you, and when I say *you,* I mean your unified personality; I wasn't exaggerating earlier when I said that you'll never be master of your future unless you're master of your past. But once you've mastered your past and are set free to respond to the will of God, then I think all your present problems will prove to be surmountable. I'm not saying you'll fall passionately in love with your wife, but I suspect you'll be granted the grace to achieve a tolerable partnership. It's the only rational assumption to make, isn't it? God would hardly renew your call to serve Him as a churchman and then make no provision to ease your marital dilemma."

There was a silence.

"And now, of course," said Lucas wryly, "you're thinking I'm just a tiresome old celibate who knows nothing about the hell of being stuck with an unwanted woman."

Much to my surprise I heard myself say: "No, I wasn't thinking that." I had to pause to find the right words. "What you say makes sense," I said at last, "and I was thinking how clever you were to dredge up some hope for me from such a hopeless situation. I can stand almost anything so long as there's hope. It was the thought of a hopeless marriage, stretching ahead for the next thirty years, that was reducing me to despair." I thought for a moment longer before adding: "By turning my crisis into a quest capable of resolution, you've performed the miracle of making the future attractive—difficult and challenging, of course, but absorbing and exciting as well."

"Let me quote Professor Raven to you. I always remember that passage in his autobiography when he wrote: 'Of all the fascinating pursuits in the world is there any more absorbing than the quest of the knowledge of God?' "

The Anglo-Catholic was quoting the voice of Liberal Protestantism. I stared at him, and for a brief moment the divisions within the Church dissolved so that I could look past the warring dialectic at last to the essential unity beyond. I could only say: "Now for the first time I see what ecumenism could mean."

"Ecumenism!" Lucas heaved the sigh of a man who contemplates a future he will never live to see. "One of the founders of the Oxford Movement made several great prophetic speeches about that. He spoke of union not only within the Church of England but between the Anglican, Roman and Orthodox Churches as well."

"Was that Newman?"

"No, Pusey. When I was a young man I thought the prophecy absurd, but now I firmly believe that beyond the divisions there's unity—as I'm certain you'll discover in your own life in time." Abruptly he leant forward again on the table and I sensed he was preparing to conclude our interview.

"I can't end this discussion of your quest for unity without saying a word to you on the subject of guilt," he said. "I believe you feel guilty about many things, so guilty that you couldn't at present put your guilt into words even if you were a Catholic trying desperately to make an adequate confession. You'll have to confront this guilt in future; it'll be part of facing the pain, but let me at least try to ease the burden for you even though I'm still ignorant of those hidden sores which you feel forced to keep to yourself. I believe that during our conversations you've turned around and embarked on your road to repentance. You've got a long way to go because your repentance can only be achieved when you've faced your guilt squarely, but I do believe you earnestly wish to re-examine your past and begin a new life in God's service. That's a very big step forward, and whenever your guilt seems unbearable in future, I suggest you remember Luther crying: 'Justification by Faith!' Strictly speaking, as you know, it's God's grace that 'justifies,' but in my opinion your desire to repent entitles you to have faith that you now stand right with God—and I think you'll continue to stand right with Him so long as you work hard to achieve your new life."

Machiavellian old masterpiece, handling me with kid gloves and quoting one of the Roman Church's severest critics! "What you're really trying to do," I said amused, "is to increase my chance of recovery by setting the right psychological mechanisms in motion. You want to lessen the guilt because you see it as a crippling handicap to my mental health, demolishing whatever spiritual perception I still possess and driving me remorselessly to drink."

"Oh, I know nothing about 'psychological mechanisms'!" said the old boy, greatly entertained. "What a quaint little scientific phrase! Is that part of the Modernist way of expressing ancient religious truths?"

As we laughed the bell in the chapel began to toll and I knew the meeting had to end. With difficulty I said: "How can I ever thank you?" but he waved the question aside. "It's all in a day's work," he said, "and you've done me a service by alleviating the boredom of convalescence. Now, let me give you my blessing before we part. I'll keep it simple, I promise. No Popery."

"I'm quite sure I need all the blessings I can get, Popish or otherwise."

As I knelt before him he laid his hands on my head and said his few words in a brisk sensible voice. I noticed that his Yorkshire accent was now fading away again into the inflections of the BBC.

"Will you come to Mass?" he said afterwards. "Or would you find the Catholic touches too distracting?"

He was signalling that as I had repented sufficiently to consider myself "justified," I could now regard myself as fit to receive the sacrament. This touched me. I felt the invitation was an act of trust as I embarked on my very uncertain future, and I found I had no choice but to say: "Thank you, Aidan. I'd like to attend."

"Good. But you needn't come down to the chapel just yet. That bell's ringing for Prime. They'll ring the bell again when it's time for Mass."

I thought of him quoting Raven. "I've never been to a service called Prime before," I said. "I'd like to go. It would be interesting."

That pleased him even more than my belated success in calling him by his Christian name. We left the room, he walking ahead to lead the way, and descended the stairs to the corridor which led out of the guest-wing. It was as we entered the hall that I stopped dead. Two men were standing by the main staircase. One of them was Ingram, the Abbot-General, but it was not he who had brought me to a halt. I had been transfixed by the sight of his companion, a tall gaunt man with haunted dark eyes and black hair streaked with grey.

I recognised Charles Ashworth, the husband of the woman with whom I had so disgracefully misbehaved myself twelve months before.

XIII

"There is little prospect of getting rid of error except by the discovery of new truth . . ."

CHARLES E. RAVEN
A WANDERER'S WAY

I

I WAS so shocked by the change in Ashworth, whom I remembered as a smooth sleek customer, well marinated in the juices of ecclesiastical privilege, that I was not at first aware that he had failed to recognise me. Meanwhile Ingram, mindful of my anonymity, ignored me altogether and said to Aidan: "Here's someone who's dropped in specially to meet you—Jon Darrow's friend Canon Ashworth from Cambridge."

"I hear you're about to return home, Father," said Ashworth, "but if you have a moment to spare after Mass—"

"Yes, we must talk." The old boy was pleased. "Jon's often mentioned you."

In the chapel the bell ceased tolling. Ingram murmured abruptly: "Shall we . . ." and we all moved forward, but on the far side of the hall we were obliged to separate, the two monks passing into the enclosed section of the house while Ashworth and I embarked on a signposted route to the visitors' section of the chapel. I was just daring to hope that my anonymity had been preserved, when Ashworth stopped, snapped his fingers and exclaimed: "I've got it now—you're Neville Aysgarth, the Archdeacon of Starbridge. Don't you remember me? I was the clergyman who officiated at the Darrows' wedding."

Ten feet away stood the door which led into the chapel. I had to fight the impulse to mutter some banality and dive into the protective silence beyond.

"I remember you very well," I said, trying hard to sound untroubled.

"Forgive me for keeping quiet but to be honest I wasn't sure what to say. I thought you might be fed up with people asking how you are and exclaiming 'Welcome home!' with wide smiles."

This was evidently the right approach. Ashworth looked both amused and grateful. "I'm in London for one of my medical check-ups," he said, "but in fact I'm much better now and by coincidence I'm heading for your diocese. Lyle's joining me today at the Darrows' house for a couple of nights and then we're off to Devon for a holiday."

"Please give her my best wishes," I said, acutely conscious that he would think it odd if I didn't. I made another huge effort to be casual and in my guilt I overreached myself. "I was so glad for her sake when I heard you were safe," I added. "When I met her a year ago at Stoneyford she was convinced you weren't coming home."

"Met her where?"

"At Stoneyford. In Oxfordshire. At Bishop Jardine's funeral."

The silence which followed was broken with unexpected force by the monks as they began to sing the office. We both jumped. Then Ashworth said smoothly: "Ah yes, of course! I remember her telling me about the funeral," and that was the moment when I realised Lyle had told him nothing.

I was much alarmed. I had hardly imagined that Lyle would feel so guilty about her behaviour with me that she would decide to keep quiet about her entire visit to Stoneyford, but then I remembered that at the time of Ashworth's departure overseas they had both been estranged from the Jardines. Possibly she had remained silent not merely because she felt guilty about me but because she felt it was more convenient to gloss over the subject of that awkward and complex relationship.

Overpowered by the desire to terminate the conversation I said rapidly: "We're missing the service—shall we go in?" And I thrust open the door into the visitors' transept.

Ashworth made no attempt to detain me.

I was so disturbed, as I imagined the various marital dialogues which could flow from my disclosure, that I was unable to concentrate on the service. It was only in the brief interval between Prime and the celebration of Holy Communion that I managed to reflect calmly that even if Ashworth did cross-examine his wife about the funeral she would hardly reveal details of our idiotic behaviour.

Making a new effort to focus my thoughts I struggled to attend to the Communion service. It seemed intolerably alien but I beat down my raised Protestant hackles and tried to approach the sacrament in a humble, reverent frame of mind—no easy task when the stench of incense was assaulting my nostrils and an unfamiliar caterwauling was pounding on my ears. Nevertheless, remembering Aidan, I somehow managed to stifle the urge to bawl: "No Popery!" and walk out.

I also remembered Aidan's advice that I should be on the watch for any veiled communication from God, and as Ashworth knelt beside me to receive the sacrament I wondered if our meeting had some hidden significance. As far as I could see I had only been unpleasantly reminded of my disgusting lapse of twelve months before. Automatically I tried to blot out the memory by sinking myself in the act of worship, but to my distress the wine and wafer evoked no comforting response. I could only remember Aidan saying in his sternest mood that we were all sinners, all under judgement, and then I knew that although I had been led to the signpost marked SALVATION, my journey had barely begun out of that wasteland where once more I stood alone.

After the service Ashworth said to me: "Are you by any chance returning to Starbridge on the ten-fifteen?"

This was indeed the train I had intended to catch but by this time I wanted only to escape from his company. "No, I'm calling on my sister in South London," I said, seizing the first excuse to enter my head, and it was not until the words had been spoken that I remembered Aidan urging me to talk to my siblings.

"Never mind, I daresay we'll meet again before long. Certain people tend to recur in one's life, don't they?" remarked Ashworth pleasantly. "It's as if we were all dancing some vast metaphysical version of the eightsome reel."

"In that case I wish you well in the next phase of the dance!" I said with as much charm as I could muster, and finally succeeded in escaping from him.

Having packed my bag I left my room, handed the doorkeeper a donation to cover the cost of my visit and plunged headlong from the peace of the cloister into the roaring chaos around Marble Arch.

2

AT the tube station I incarcerated myself in a telephone kiosk and rang Starbridge Hospital to say I would be unable to visit Dido until the evening. Then I rang Emily to make sure she was at home. A moment later I was on my way.

I was able to travel entirely on the underground to the southern suburb of Balham, where Emily lived no more than five minutes' walk from the station. Her oppressively prim Victorian street was lined with close-cropped plane trees; lace curtains festooned the windows of the terraced houses, and even the flowers in the minute front gardens appeared to be stiff with respectability. My mother had once said the neighbourhood possessed "a very seemly air of refinement," but I had travelled far enough to know that this remark classified my mother even more damningly than the neighbourhood. Having absorbed southern social values I had no trouble in judging the street a monument to genteel bad taste.

My sister opened the door as I unlatched the front gate. It was always a great source of annoyance to Willy and me that Emily, taking after our father, was taller than either of us. She was five feet ten. I call myself five feet ten, but I'm closer to five feet eight. Willy had the misfortune to be only five feet two, but we always suspected that the long debilitating illness he had suffered in adolescence had somehow interfered with his growth.

Emily's best feature was her dark eyes, also inherited from our father, but unfortunately they were set in a plump nondescript face which Willy, in one of his misogynist's moods, had likened to a currant bun. She had heavy breasts, which gave her a prematurely elderly appearance, large hips and excellent legs. Her clothes were appalling. She was wearing a faded floral apron over a beige blouse and a sludge-brown skirt. The amazing legs were desecrated by thick stockings.

"Hullo, Nev," she said. "You look awful, about ninety. Come and have a cup of tea."

I derived a surprising degree of comfort from this laconic but not unaffectionate greeting. Feeling grateful, I followed her down the long narrow hall, past the pristine front parlour, which was reserved for formal occasions, and into the kitchen at the rear of the house.

"How's Reg?" I said, dutifully observing the convention of inquiring after my brother-in-law.

"Could be worse. How's that smart wife of yours?"

"In hospital. The baby was born dead."

"Nev!" I had jolted her. "Why didn't you ring me earlier?"

"Couldn't. Too difficult. Didn't want to talk about it." I slumped into a chair at the kitchen table before adding: "I called him Arthur."

"That's nice," said Emily politely, embarking on the ritual of tea-making. The gas was lit. The kettle was put on the ring. Out came the china teapot, the tea-caddy, the tea-cosy, the cups, the saucers, the milk-jug, the sugar-bowl, the spoons and the strainer.

"Dido had decided that a boy should be called Philip," I said, "but I felt she wouldn't want to waste that favourite name of hers on a baby that was born dead. Then I saw him and knew he had to be Arthur."

"I always wondered why you never chose that name before," said Emily, sniffing the milk to make sure it was fresh. "Four sons and not one called after Father."

"I've been in a muddle about Father for a long time."

"You? In a muddle? Never!"

"You'd be surprised. Em—"

"One lump of sugar or two?"

"One. Em, I must talk to you. It's urgent."

"It must be, if you've turned up on my doorstep. Nowadays Balham's not grand enough for you, it seems."

"Oh, good heavens . . . Emily, please don't feel slighted that I haven't visited you lately—it's just that I've been having a terrible time for some months now, and—"

"You? Having a terrible time? Never! You're always gliding through life on the crest of a wave!"

"Some wave," I said, aping Mr. Churchill. "Some life. Look, Em, I'm trying to sort myself out and there are things I need to know about Mother, Father and Uncle Willoughby. First of all I'd like you to tell me—"

"But you hate talking about Mother, Father and Uncle Willoughby! I remember so well after Grace's funeral—"

"Can we please just stick to one upsetting subject at a time? And can you make that blank-blank tea before your fidgeting drives me completely round the bend?"

She made the tea in silence, her lips pressed into a thin tight line of disapproval. When we were finally facing our steaming cups I made a supreme effort and managed to say: "Sorry. Not quite myself at the moment. Going through a bit of a crisis."

Emily made no comment but merely said crisply: "What do you want to know about Mother, Father and Uncle Will?"

"I want to know how you see them as you look back on the past. For instance, if they were characters in a play, how would you describe them?"

"What an extraordinary question! Let me think." As she allowed my challenge to interest her, she forgot to sulk. "Well," she said after a moment, "Uncle Will was the hero, of course, saving us all and taking me and Mother into his home for that year before we went to St. Leonards. I know what you and Willy thought of him but in my eyes he was always rather a pet."

"Rather a pet?"

"Yes, he was always giving me the odd penny to buy liquorice. I never told you and Willy that, of course, because I knew you'd be jealous."

"Well, I'll be . . ." Words temporarily failed me. Then I pulled myself together and demanded: "But if you see Uncle Will as the lovable hero, how do you see Father?"

"Oh, as the villain, naturally. Silly, insensitive brute."

"Insensitive brute? *Father?*"

"Well, he nearly killed Mother, didn't he? All those pregnancies! I think it was cruel, especially as she didn't even like that side of marriage."

"What side?"

"Well, you know."

"No, I don't. Are you referring to childbirth or sex—or both?"

"Honestly, Nev! Must you be quite so crude?"

"I suppose that means you're referring to sex. But how do you know she didn't like it?"

"She told me."

"Mother talked to you about sex?"

"Only when I wanted to get married!" said Emily hastily, as if she feared she had cast an aspersion on our mother's character. "She tried to put me off the idea by saying how awful it all was. I think she believed I had no idea what went on, although how she thought I'd reached the age of thirty-five in such a state of Victorian ignorance I can't imagine. As a matter of fact Willy told me on the beach at St. Leonards when I was sixteen. You were off somewhere, holding hands with Grace as usual, and that had put Willy in a bad mood. He didn't like sharing you with anyone, least of all with a girl—"

"But Em, this is quite extraordinary—are you saying Mother and Father were unhappily married?"

"Well, what else can one think? How would you feel if you didn't like s-e-x and your husband forced himself on you to such an extent that you had a baby every year?"

"But they were so happy—I can remember them laughing and joking together! And if Mother didn't want to be annually pregnant why didn't Father practise contraception?"

"Honestly, Nev! And you a clergyman! I'm shocked!"

"Oh, stop being so idiotic! Now look here, none of this makes sense—"

"Of course it does! Father didn't practise you-know-what because no one did in those days, but why he couldn't at least have exercised a decent self-control from time to time I just can't imagine."

"Emily, I don't know what you get up to down here in Balham, but I don't think you know anything about anything! There are two methods of birth control which have been practised from time immemorial, and although one would expect Father to refrain from sodomy, one would certainly hope he didn't fight shy of—"

"I'm sorry, Nev, but I think this is appalling talk for a clergyman, and if you continue to speak of such disgusting matters I shall leave the room. You're as bad as Willy on the beach at St. Leonards. Men are revolting sometimes, utterly revolting—as of course Mother knew all too well—"

"But if you see Father as a revolting villain, how on earth do you see Mother?"

"Oh, that's easy. Mother was the tragic victim of male cruelty and domination."

"Emily, I—" Words again failed me. All I could say in the end was a lame: "I had no idea you were such a feminist!"

"A feminist! I'm no such thing—no woman in her right mind would be a feminist: feminism just encourages men to kick you in the teeth and trample on you. No man likes a feminist, just as no man likes a woman who's too clever. Think of Mother—kicked in the teeth by three men and left to die in misery!"

After I had finished gasping I exclaimed: "I'm beginning to feel as a conventional historian feels when he reads history rewritten by a Marxist! Of course Mother didn't die in misery! She died loved and cared for in this very house by her devoted daughter!"

"I wasn't devoted. I just felt sorry for her. I only married to get away from her after being stuck as her unpaid slave for all those years. It's funny you should accuse *me* of not knowing anything about anything! I'm beginning to think *you're* the one who doesn't have a clue about what goes on!"

"Of course I have a clue but I deal with facts, not feminist fables. Who were these three men who kicked Mother in the teeth?"

"Father, Uncle Willoughby and you. Who else?"

"I absolutely, utterly and entirely deny—"

"All right, we'll leave you out of it. I don't want to quarrel. More tea?"

"Mother was behaving unspeakably to Grace. I had to put my wife first. I know it was all very awkward and difficult, but—"

"If that's the way you choose to remember the past, Nev, I'm not going to stop you, but if you think Mother didn't tell me exactly what happened—"

"She probably invented some fantasy to preserve her pride. But Em, I never knew Uncle Willoughby kicked Mother in the teeth! When on earth did that happen?"

"It was just before we left Maltby and went to live in St. Leonards.

I don't know exactly what happened, but they had some sort of row—anyway, whatever it was, Mother never forgave him. She pretended to; they had their reconciliation, but it was forever being spoilt by quarrels. Their worst quarrel was when you rejected him—that was when you decided to go into the Church, wasn't it?—and Mother elbowed her way past him to kidnap you. Uncle Will hated that. They didn't speak for months. Sometimes I think Mother kidnapped you just to pay Uncle Will back for whatever happened between them in Maltby."

I stared at her. "But are you saying Mother didn't really care for me at all? Are you saying she just started to take a keen interest in me because—"

"No, no, of course she adored you. All I'm saying is that I think she was pleased when her adoration gave her the chance to pay Uncle Will back. It often seemed to me that she secretly hated him."

"But she couldn't have done! She adored him, just as she adored me—and just as she adored Father! Good heavens, just remember what she was like after Father died—she wore black for years and put his picture everywhere and couldn't even mention his name without a sob—"

"Oh yes, I got so tired of it all! For some peculiar reason it suited her to live like a character in a Victorian melodrama. When I read the love-letters she wrote to Father during their engagement I was very struck by their unreality—and his letters to her were just as bad. God knows how they coped with the reality of marriage—if indeed they ever did . . . Nev, you never said whether you wanted more tea."

I pushed my cup across the table for a refill. "Do you still have those letters? I remember you offering them to me after Mother died, but I was too upset to read them."

"Well, that turned out to be your last chance. They all went during the war when there were those appeals for scrap paper. Like a lot of other people I patriotically turned out my attic and lived to regret it." She poured the tea before adding reflectively: "In many ways the letters told a lovely story, so romantic. The short plain dumpy heroine, much too clever for her own good, declared 'on the shelf' by everyone in Maltby and despised by man after man, chances to make a witty remark while organising tea down at the cricket club and immediately makes the tall dark handsome hero of the first eleven look at her with new eyes . . . What a wonderful catch Father was! It must have seemed to her like a dream come true. Never mind if things went wrong later. At least she had that perfect courtship—which is more than I ever had. Still, I can't complain. As a plain clever woman I was lucky to get off the shelf at all, and of course a woman's nothing unless she's married. I found that out during the years I spent playing the role of 'spinster daughter.' I suppose if I'd had an education my life would have been very different, but—"

"You wouldn't have liked being a blue-stocking, Em."

"How do you know? How do *I* know? I never had the chance to go to Oxford, did I? My sex alone classified me as inferior to you and Willy! Of course you think, in your bigoted narrow-minded masculine way, that all women should be wives and mothers, but all I can say is that I hope you won't deprive poor little Primrose of a decent education. I know you detest unusual women who don't fit into the conventional feminine mould, but—"

"Nonsense, I'm crazy about them!"

"I don't think you are, Nev; not really. In fact once or twice in the past I've wondered if you really like women at all. Oh, I know you like them in one sense, the obvious sense, and can't do without them, but I think that secretly makes you cross and then you hate yourself for needing them so much."

"Em, has it ever occurred to you that all this tea you drink might be softening your brain?"

"You wanted me to talk—how dare you complain now that I'm taking you at your word! It's such a novelty to have a man choosing to ask my opinion on anything that it's hardly surprising if I get carried away and start tossing out a few home truths! No man's ever wanted to talk to me intelligently—certainly you and Willy have always treated me as if I couldn't possibly have anything of interest to say, but then I suppose you took your cue from Father who always left me at home with Tabitha when he took his beloved boys out for walks—"

"The only reason he didn't take you was because you couldn't have kept up with us! You were too little!"

"Oh, was that the excuse he gave?"

"Good heavens, Em, what a chip you have on your shoulder!"

"Well, why *should* I gloss over Father's faults, as you and Willy always do? He ruined Mother's health, he ruined his business and he ruined his family!"

I stood up and headed for the door.

"Are you off? You haven't stayed long. I'll stop being clever now, if you like, and start talking about the bread queues and how I'm saving up for an Electrolux."

I reached the door but went no farther. I had somehow managed to control my emotion, and at last I moved awkwardly back to the table.

"Em . . ." We were not a demonstrative family, but I forced myself to take her hands in mine. "I'm very sorry. I really am. I know you've had a raw deal."

"It could be worse. I could be living in genteel poverty as a spinster in St. Leonards-on-Sea."

"Please don't think I don't care that you're unhappy—"

"Unhappy? Who said I was unhappy? I've got a home of my own and some privacy and a little dignity and self-respect at last. When one's had nothing for years and years, it doesn't take much to make one happy—and in fact I'm beginning to suspect I'm a great deal happier than you are: you with your wife you won't mention and your crisis you won't discuss! So don't pity me, Neville, and don't patronise me. Look to your own life and leave me to look after mine."

After that speech little remained to be said. At the front door I thanked her for the tea, muttered the clergyman's conventional "God bless you" and set off, deeply confused, on the next stage of my journey through the wasteland.

3

I MIGHT have postponed my visit to Willy, but after the interview with Emily I now had an overwhelming desire to discover if he too secretly harboured extraordinary opinions about the past. I reminded myself that the past had remained undiscussed by us in depth because I had never wanted to speak of it. Moreover, by an agreement which was all the more powerful for being unspoken, Willy and I had never, even in our closest years as children, discussed the circumstances surrounding our father's death. At first we had been numbed by our bereavement. Then later, when we found we could not mention him without crying, the other boys at our brutal Yorkshire boarding school had thought us soft and bullied us. This experience had made us realise dry eyes were essential for survival and in consequence our father had become a forbidden topic of conversation.

At the tube station I found another telephone kiosk and phoned Willy at his school, forty miles south of London, but the telephone rang unanswered in his rooms. Obviously he was busy teaching, and for a moment I pictured him planting his diminutive frame in front of the blackboard as he glowered at his pupils. Willy always boasted that despite his size he never had trouble keeping order in the classroom.

Backtracking on the tube to Clapham I caught an ordinary train heading south to Leatherhead, where I switched to the Horsham line, and as the train sped through the Mole Valley between Leatherhead and Dorking I looked up at the Starmouths' mansion, remote on its wooded hillside, symbol of another life in another world in another age, long ago. I thought of Aidan talking of the unbalanced Neville Three, and the memory reminded me of my duty to reflect on every event carefully to discern a possible hidden meaning. I soon gave up trying to make sense of the conversation with Emily; at present I felt incapable of regarding it as anything except a bizarre conundrum which defied interpretation. But I began to think again about my meeting with Charles Ashworth.

It seemed I was being prompted not only to recall the incident with Lyle but to re-examine it; although I had shied away from a re-examination earlier that morning in the chapel, I knew the disaster was still gnawing at the edge of my memory. On the other hand, surely it would be unconstructive to wallow masochistically in guilty memories? I regretted the incident profoundly, I had vowed it would never happen again. What was the point of a re-examination? What new truth was I supposed to extract if I now "faced the pain" and remembered that a year ago I had almost committed adultery? I could think of nothing which demanded to be re-examined . . . but it was strange how that insipid little word "almost" now had such an unmistakably sinister ring. A year ago I had almost committed adultery . . . I could imagine myself saying that to Aidan, and all too easily I could imagine Aidan replying: "Almost? No, that's not quite right, Neville, is it . . ."

I shuddered. Then I told myself that now was hardly the moment to remember that the legal and spiritual definitions of adultery didn't entirely coincide. I had to survive, not drive myself round the bend with unbearable thoughts. Surely it was enough that events themselves were crucifying me—why should I want to crucify myself all over again by telling myself I deserved to be defrocked? I had to think of something else. In panic my mind raced raggedly back to Ashworth again, Ashworth the POW, and as I tried to imagine the quality of the experiences which had so visibly changed him, I found myself remembering those other POWs, my Germans. They were reasonably treated; they did not suffer as I was sure Ashworth had suffered, yet I knew very well there was much suffering present at the camp.

"To be locked up indefinitely," said Hoffenberg, my favourite prisoner, when I had met him on my first harrowing visit to the camp in 1944, "to be cut off from one's loved ones, to be hated and despised by one's jailers—how does one go on believing in God in a world where God is absent?" I had been so embarrassed, so ashamed of my limited pastoral gifts, because I had not known how to reply. My Liberal optimism had nothing to say in the face of such dereliction; any facile message of hope would have fallen on ground too stony to receive it. Groping in despair for a reply I could only say hesitantly: "This is your Good Friday." I had to struggle to find each word. I, the Balliol scholar and the accomplished Archdeacon, had never felt more intellectually stupid or more spiritually inept than I felt at that moment. "But at the foot of your cross," I managed to add, still speaking with great difficulty, "stands an Englishman who shares the pain of all the innocent Germans caught up in the war." And I told him about Bishop Bell.

"He sounds a good man," Hoffenberg said drearily, "but he won't come here so he has no meaning for me."

It was then that the miracle happened. I no longer had to struggle for words. The right reply arrived fully formed on my tongue. "Bell himself may never come here," I said, "but *I've* come to tell you about him."

At once Hoffenberg said: "Will you come back?" and as I saw his despair replaced by a slender thread of hope, I knew there was only one answer I could give him.

The most agonising moment of his long Good Friday came when his family was obliterated by the fire-bombing of Dresden in 1945. I had no words of my own to offer; I felt the conventional words of sympathy could only be an impertinence, but I drove to the camp, and when Hoffenberg said: "You've come to stand in silence at the foot of the cross, haven't you?" I handed him a cutting which I had kept from a *Fortnightly Review* of 1939.

"The Church then ought to declare both in peace-time and war-time, that there are certain basic principles which can and should be the standards of both international social order and conduct," Bell had written. "It must not hesitate, if occasion arises, to condemn the infliction of reprisals, or the bombing of civilian populations, by the military forces of its own nation. It should set itself against the propaganda of lies and hatred. It should be ready to encourage a resumption of friendly relations with the enemy nation. It should set its face against any war of extermination or enslavement, and any measures directly aimed to destroy the morale of a population."

Hoffenberg read the cutting. Then he said: "Tell me more about him. Much more," and I described Bell's friendship with Dietrich Bonhoeffer, the young theologian of the German Confessing Church. Bonhoeffer had plotted against Hitler and been imprisoned. "A prisoner, just like me!" said Hoffenberg. "One day when the war's over I shall go home and meet him." But unfortunately this simple wish was never to be granted; just before the war's end, Bonhoeffer was hanged by the Nazis. His last message was for George Bell.

"He said very clearly, twice, to the English officer who was imprisoned with him: 'Tell him from me this is the end but also the beginning—with him I believe in the principle of our Universal Christian brotherhood above all national interests, and that our victory is certain.' "

"So he won!" Hoffenberg exclaimed. "He lost but he won—Hitler never defeated him!" Then he added confused: "No, that makes no sense. My English breaks down—and my German too."

I had at that time in 1945 given little thought to Aidan's "land of paradox," but I recognised that Hoffenberg was groping to express a profound truth. "Perhaps you feel," I said, "that Bonhoeffer's friendship with Bell, which endured even to the scaffold, symbolises the unity of all men in Christ and the indestructibility of the Holy Spirit even in a world crucified by war."

Hoffenberg thought for a long time but eventually said: "If God can be with Bonhoeffer on the scaffold, he'll be in Dresden among the ruins." He had to pause again to search for the right English words but at last he declared: "He's a *crucified* God, sharing our Good Friday."

Again the miracle happened and the reply arrived fully formed on my tongue. "Yes," I said, "but never forget that Christians always look back at Good Friday from the perspective of Easter Day."

I thought of that remark as the train drew into Horsham, and at once I found myself wondering how my own Good Friday would look to me when I could finally view it from the perspective of my new life. Easter Day was as yet unimaginable—but perhaps it always was unimaginable, to the man on the cross enduring Good Friday.

Hauling myself back from the inconceivable future to the intimidating present, I began to plan my approaching interview with Willy.

4

WILLY'S school was housed in a mansion two miles south of Horsham in the tranquil Sussex countryside, and as the taxi rattled up the drive towards the front door I could see the humps of the South Downs shimmering in a bluish haze on the horizon. It was a long time since I had visited Willy in his lair and it was a long time since he had visited me in Starbridge. When Grace had been alive he had joined us every year for Christmas, but this tradition had now lapsed. I was well aware that Willy detested Dido and thought I was a fool to have married her.

I saw no need to announce my presence formally at the front entrance, so as the taxi drove away I padded around the dark Victorian walls to the section of the building known as "Kitchener." This was Willy's House, not a house in the conventional sense but a self-contained wing which fifty of the school's two hundred boys could regard as home once the day's lessons and games had been concluded. Willy occupied some grand gloomy rooms on the ground floor. All the walls, even the walls of the lavatory, were lined with books. Every mantelshelf was crammed with photographs, some of past pupils, some of my four sons; Willy took a great interest in his nephews and wrote regularly to Christian. A photograph of our father was also on constant display. Willy kept the picture on his desk. The silver frame was always highly polished.

Knocking on the door of his study I called: "Willy?" but when there was no reply I walked in, dropped my bag and sank down in the swivel-chair behind the desk. Then I remembered that Willy kept excellent sherry. I thought of Aidan, advising me not to drink, but I was still wrestling with the most powerful temptation to ignore his advice when a bell rang somewhere to herald the end of the morning's lessons. A minute later Willy was walking into the room.

"Good God!" he exclaimed. "What on earth are you doing parked in my chair? And why are you looking as Brutus must have looked before Philippi? Has someone died?"

"Yes."

"Dido?"

"No. The baby."

"Oh." Willy opened the door of the sideboard and revealed not one but three decanters in addition to a full bottle of whisky. "Have a drink."

"No, thanks. Temporarily abstaining."

"How sordid! Obviously you're in some sort of demented state, but I can't quite see why. Of course it's a great pity about the infant, that goes without saying, but it didn't live long enough for you to get fond of it, did it, and no doubt Dido'll soon produce another to put matters right."

"I got very fond of him. And since he was unique he'll be irreplaceable, no matter how many children Dido has in future."

"Oh God, I've said the wrong thing. Look, change your mind and have some of this first-class claret! I usually only offer it to the headmaster—"

"I called the baby Arthur because I looked at him and remembered Father. That never happened with the others."

"You mean he looked like Father?"

"Newborn babies never look like anyone."

"That's what I thought. Emily looked like nothing on earth."

"I've just visited Emily—I had tea with her."

"My God, when that woman dies I swear they'll find the word TEA engraved on her heart! Why are you suddenly rushing around Balham and Horsham in order to call on your neglected siblings?"

"That sounds as if you've taken offence, just like Emily, because I haven't been in touch lately! Willy, I've had the most terrible year and I just haven't had the time to—"

"Oh, stop being so stupid! I'm not about to flounce around pouting just because you haven't had time for the social niceties recently! Now sit down, take this glass of claret and tell me exactly what's going on—no, wait a minute. Let me first deal with the dining-room. They'll be expecting me to say grace."

He made an abrupt exit and returned five minutes later with two plates of cottage pie on a tray.

"I'm not hungry, Willy."

"Well, you ought to be, especially after drinking tea with Emily. Let me pour you another glass of claret."

"No, I won't have any more."

"I'm beginning to be seriously worried about you! If you can no longer drink more than one glass of my best claret—"

"Willy, I want to talk about Father, Mother and Uncle Willoughby."

"That confirms it. You're off your head. Now, don't worry, Neville—being mad isn't *necessarily* a handicap in the Church of England—"

"Shut up. Listen, Will, this is very important. If those three people were characters in a play, how would you describe them?"

"Am I allowed to ask why you're posing this bizarre and apparently mindless question?"

"No. Just answer it."

"Very well, I see Father as Hamlet, Uncle Willoughby as Falstaff and Mother as—who else?—Lady Macbeth."

"Uncle Willoughby as Falstaff?"

"Of course. When I look back now at the nightmare years I can see he was just a pathetic buffoon with a witty streak. All that vulgar social-climbing! And all that ridiculous talk of winning the prizes! How you fell for it all I'll never know, but there you were, throwing yourself heart and soul into the role of Prince Hal—"

"There's no need to resort to mockery just because you chose not to compete with me!"

"Of course I chose not to compete—I came to see what bloody rubbish it all was! Why, any schoolmaster can tell you that prize-giving's quite the most boring day of the year. Life's not about the day when you win the prizes—it's about all the days in between."

"All right, let's not fight. I still don't understand how you can see Uncle Willoughby as Falstaff when you've always agreed with me that he was a villain, but—"

"I still agree with you. Falstaff was an old rogue. But on the other hand he hardly stood in the same category of villainy as Iago or—"

"Talking of Iago and remembering Desdemona and Othello, do you feel in retrospect that Mother, Father and Uncle Willoughby formed some sort of peculiar triangle?"

Willy looked intrigued but doubtful. "I don't think so. Isn't incest rather a daring theory for a clergyman?"

"Good heavens, I'm not talking about incest! I'm talking about . . . well, I'm not exactly sure what I'm talking about, but how did Mother keep the peace between those two men who must have been so incompatible?"

"That's easy. She had Father under her thumb and Uncle Willoughby in her pocket. She was Lady Macbeth before the sleep-walking phase."

"Let's forget Lady Macbeth for the moment. Why do you see Father as Hamlet?"

"How else would you describe a doomed romantic intellectual who got mixed up with the wrong woman, made a balls-up of his business and wound up a corpse in the final act?"

"Oh, I see. I wondered if you were putting forward the theory that Father, like Hamlet, toyed with the idea of suicide."

"Don't be ridiculous!"

"Why should you think I'm being ridiculous? If Father knew he was bankrupt—"

"I think he would have welcomed the bankruptcy as a chance to abandon his life in Yorkshire and go off to Africa to be a missionary. Can't you just see him preaching pantheism to the natives? And Mother would have adored it—endless opportunities to be bossy, plenty of servants to wait on her, a constant supply of black nurses for the children—"

"I'm sorry," I said, "but I'm not convinced. Willy, I've never been able to bring myself to speak about this to you before—in fact I've never been able to speak about this to anyone—but I've secretly thought for years and years and years that—"

"—that Mother had murdered him. Funny you should say that. I could never bring myself to speak of it either while we were little, and then of course as soon as I was grown up I saw the idea was too absurd to mention. I thought she'd killed him because she didn't want any more pregnancies! I concede murder's a rather extreme form of contraception, but when I was a child and had no idea other remedies were available—"

"Willy, I think Father committed suicide."

"Yes, well, of course children often retreat into fantasy when they're intolerably distressed, but . . . Wait a minute. Did you say 'think'? Did you use the present tense? Are you seriously trying to tell me—"

"Yes."

"But my dear Neville, what possible grounds could you have for thinking such a thing?"

"After Father died I heard Mother whispering to Uncle Willoughby: 'No one must ever know he took the laudanum.' "

Willy stared at me.

"Don't you remember Tabitha warning us about Mother's sleeping draught?" I said. "Don't you remember her telling us we must never take any for a prank because if we took too much we'd never wake up?"

Willy continued to stare.

"Well, naturally," I said, "after Father died and I heard Mother say in horror: 'No one must ever know he took the laudanum,' I realised there was only one conclusion to be drawn."

Willy finally regained the use of his tongue. "Rubbish!" he said angrily. "Father would never have deliberately abandoned us like that—but how typical that you, with your melodramatic Victorian streak, should have come to such a preposterous conclusion!"

"Then how would *you* explain those words of Mother's?"

"Very easily, with rational down-to-earth common sense! The obvious explanation is that Mother didn't want everyone in Maltby to know Father drugged as well as drank."

"But he didn't!"

"No, but the point is that people would think he did if they found out he'd died after taking laudanum that hadn't been prescribed for him."

"But why should he have taken the laudanum in the first place?"

"Oh, I daresay he purloined Mother's supply every now and then when he wanted to get a good night's sleep. Why not? God knows, if I'd been married to Mother I'd have grabbed every drink and drug in sight!"

"But Willy—"

"What beats me is not that you're flirting with this idiotic theory—after all, the history of philosophy is littered with clever men who flirted with idiotic ideas—but that you're trotting it out now, of all times. What on earth's this got to do with poor little Arthur?"

"I can't explain fully, but I'm in a big muddle at the moment and I've reached the stage where in order to make sense of the present I have to sort out the past."

There was a pause while we both gave up pretending to eat cottage pie and Willy drank deeply from his glass of claret. Finally he said: "I'm exceedingly sorry—though not, I confess, entirely surprised—to hear you're in a muddle. Since you volunteer no information I certainly don't intend to pry, but I can't help thinking you're talking like an addled romantic who's convinced the past is riddled with deep dark secrets of an enthralling and complex nature. But it isn't. There's no mystery about the past, and no complexity either. The past is merely prosaic—and that's the truth, pure and simple."

"Ah!" I said. "But as Oscar Wilde wrote in *The Importance of Being Earnest*—"

"Poor Oscar simply wanted to be amusing. I tell you, there's no mystery about the past, Neville. None at all."

"Then could you be very kind and explain to me what on earth was going on?"

"Why not?" said Willy affably, reaching for the decanter, and this time, no longer able to resist the temptation, I held out my glass for a refill.

5

"THE truth, pure and simple," said Willy, "is that Father died of liver failure, just as the coroner said. Of course that old rogue Uncle Willoughby talked to us about cirrhosis and tried to make out that Father was a drunkard, but quite obviously he was motivated by malice. The most likely explanation of the tragedy is that Father had a weakness in the liver which drinking—any drinking—aggravated."

"I can remember him drinking quite a bit—"

"So can I, but can you remember him roaring drunk? I certainly can't, and I refuse to believe he was an alcoholic even though he was trapped in that appalling marriage which would have driven even the most devout abstainer to hit the bottle—"

"You honestly see the marriage as appalling?"

"Well, of course it was appalling! I'd have thought that was obvious in retrospect. What could it have been like for a sunny-natured sensitive man like Father to be obliged to live with a female who spent all her time exuding a noxious miasma from a chaise-longue?"

"Emily takes a very different view. She sees Mother as a tragedy queen victimised by men."

"What complete and utter balls! The truth about Mother is that she was absolutely frightful. A lot of mothers are; it's not unusual—you should see some of the horrors my boys have to put up with! It's only romantics like you who think that all women are instinctively brimming over with mother-love—and how you've preserved *that* illusion after years of maternal neglect in the nursery, I can't imagine!"

"Mother wasn't good with small children, I agree, but she was willing enough to brim over with mother-love later on."

"God alone knows what she was brimming over with," said Willy, "but in my opinion it certainly wasn't mother-love. She washed her hands of me, gave Emily hell and had that peculiar flirtation with you that all ended in tears—"

"But Willy, if Mother was really so frightful, why did Father marry her?"

"My dear Neville, good men regularly marry frightful women; it's one of the great mysteries of life. Of course I'm well aware that you think I'm an ignoramus about such matters because my sexual experience has been limited to onanism ever since that ghastly encounter you egged me into up at Oxford—"

"I didn't egg you into anything!"

"Oh yes, you did! You bragged about how you'd lost your virginity to a Woolworth's shopgirl, so naturally I felt I had to lose mine too—except that I couldn't—"

"Well, you can't blame me for that!"

"God knows who I blame, sometimes I wish I'd been born bloody queer, at least I'd know then where I stood—in the cupboard alongside all the other social outcasts—oh God, what a bloody bore sex is, how we all stand it I'll never know. Anyway as I was saying, I'm well aware that you think I know nothing about women, but I'm neither wholly blind nor wholly stupid and I can recognise the women like Mother who make a profession of giving men hell."

"She never gave Uncle Willoughby hell."

"That was because she knew he'd biff her on the nose if she tried. My God, what a thug that man was! But I'm beginning to see why you played Prince Hal to his Falstaff. You were so angry with Father for (so you thought) abandoning us, that you adopted Uncle Willoughby in revenge—and that's why you remained dedicated to chasing the prizes even when you were grown up and old enough to know better."

"Willy—"

"All right, I know you think I'm just a case of sour grapes, but when I had glandular fever and spent that year feeling rotten, I had the chance—given by God, as a clergyman might say!—to work out what life was really all about. At first I was panic-stricken because I was falling behind at school and failing, as Uncle Willoughby would have put it, to Get On As I Should. And of course I hated the thought that you, my younger brother, would be overtaking me—I was eaten up with jealousy and despair because I thought you'd carry off all Uncle Willoughby's so-called Prizes of Life while I remained an invalid with nothing. But after a few months of feeling enervated I realised that contrary to all my expectations I was happy. In some mysterious way I'd been set free from our perpetual rivalry and set free from that awful chase for the prizes. Then I saw that all I really wanted was a room of my own lined with books, congenial work in pleasant surroundings, and a reasonable amount of civilised conversation with intelligent people. I didn't want to read for the bar! I didn't want to be Prime Minister! And I certainly didn't want to give Uncle Willoughby the pleasure of living his life over again for him on a grander scale, because when all was said and done my life didn't belong to Uncle Willoughby. My life belonged to *me.*"

"I understand all that, Willy—don't forget I rebelled against Uncle Willoughby myself!—and of course I've always respected your decision to be a schoolmaster—"

"No, you haven't! You've privately written me off as a failure, just as *he* did—a sad sort of person, perpetually consigned to the margin of life. Poor Willy, you think, stuck in that dreary school, no ambition to be headmaster, no wife, no children, no prizes, nothing. But now just you think again! I have my room lined with books. I have my congenial work in beautiful surroundings. I even have my civilised conversations with intelligent people now and then. I'm content, I'm at peace with myself—and that's the real prize, Neville, the prize you'll never win, because no matter how many prizes you tuck under your belt you'll always feel there's a better prize ahead which has to be chased. You're in a muddle, you say? Then forget that old rogue, stop putting on the act which was guaranteed to please him, and be yourself at last!"

All I could say after I had drained my glass was: "I don't put on an act. If you think my call to be a clergyman isn't genuine—"

"Of course it's genuine! That's why you disturb me so much—I see a deeply religious man who behaves like a power-mad *arriviste.* You've married a society girl, you hobnob with the aristocracy, you devote yourself to stroking that nice old pussy-cat of a Bishop—and you're probably already designing your future study at Lambeth Palace. But all that has nothing to do with *you* at all. The real you is the little boy with the Yorkshire accent who told Tabitha that when he grew up he wanted to be an engine-driver and give free rides to the poor. The poor! My God! When was the last time *you* went visiting the slums of Starbridge? Oh no, I forgot! Starbridge has no slums worth mentioning, does it?

Beautiful picture-book Starbridge, the idyllic cathedral city ringed by wealthy landowners—just the place for a smart young archdeacon with ambition!"

"My dear Willy, if you could somehow bring yourself to stop being so bloody-minded for a moment you'd have the justice to concede that not all clergymen are called to specialise in difficult pastoral work! My talent is to be a church executive. I know that sounds very secular and not at all spiritually exciting, but—"

"Your talent's for winning the prizes. But that's not a call from God. That's a call from Uncle Willoughby."

"Oh, drop it, Will, for heaven's sake—"

"But don't you think Father would agree with me if he were alive?"

"Don't you dare fling Father's name in my face like that! If it hadn't been for Father, deliberately abandoning us to a hell of deprivation, I'd never have been forced to model myself on that villain in order to survive!"

Willy's mood instantly switched from truculent hostility to appalled concern. "But Neville, you can't *seriously* believe in the suicide theory!"

"He killed himself. This is all his fault. He was the villain and Uncle Willoughby was the hero. But I can't bear that, so Uncle Willoughby has to be the villain and Father has to be the hero—which is impossible. So it seems I love Father although I hate him—and hate Uncle Willoughby although I love him—and that's impossible too, two conflicting truths perpetually grinding me towards dementia, a hideous dialectic which I've somehow got to surmount—oh, if only Father had lived! Then I wouldn't be in this mess, wouldn't be in hell, wouldn't be—wouldn't be—"

"However Father died it was a tragedy," said Willy, swiftly welding me together as I threatened to come apart at the seams. "But at least we have our happy memories of him; we can remember him as the hero he was to us. Perhaps if he'd lived our memories would be neither so happy nor so heroic. Maybe God was being merciful—even outstandingly generous—by giving us a few perfect years of paternal care rather than decades of increasingly tarnished paternal imperfection."

"So that was how you came to terms with it all." My voice was steady again. Grasping the decanter I poured myself a little extra claret, hardly more than a mouthful, just the merest drop of comfort to sustain me as I struggled to keep facing the pain. Then I said flatly: "Convince me he didn't commit suicide."

"He loved life. He loved nature. He loved us. And he was the perfect example of a nineteenth-century optimist—something unbelievably wonderful was always just about to evolve."

"That's all very well, but if you'd heard the fear in Mother's voice when she whispered about the laudanum—"

"You were in an emotional state at the time and your child's imagination concocted a fantasy."

"How I wish I could believe you!"

"But you don't." Willy sighed. "Have some more claret."

"No, I must be on my way."

"What, no Church gossip?" Willy made a vain attempt to lighten the atmosphere. "Stay a little longer! We haven't pulled the Church to pieces since Churchill finally got off his bottom, trampled Bell underfoot and sent Fisher to Canterbury!"

"Bell will be remembered when Fisher's forgotten." Rising to my feet I began to head for the lavatory.

"What's this? Don't tell me you've become one of Bell's supporters! I remember you saying he was a dangerous idealist whom any sane churchman would avoid like the plague!"

"Smart young archdeacons really can't afford to say anything else about Dr. Bell," I said. "Smart young archdeacons aren't soft on Germans. Smart young archdeacons approve the bombing of Dresden and support Churchill and cheer the translation of Fisher to Canterbury. If they did anything else they wouldn't be smart young archdeacons, would they?"

I reached the sanctuary of the lavatory just as the tears began to stream down my face. Disgusting. It was all the talk about my father. Dreadful. Time to calm myself by thinking of Aidan again as he mixed compassion and cunning into a knock-out cocktail, clever perspicacious old masterpiece, far away now, travelling home, back to that land I could never revisit, back to Yorkshire, horrifying Yorkshire, where long ago my mother had imprinted on my mind that the father I loved had deserted me.

I somehow succeeded in regaining my self-control. Then after using the lavatory I went next door to the bathroom and sluiced some cold water over my face. To my dismay I saw my eyes had a faint pink rim.

When I finally summoned the strength to return to the study, Willy said: "Look, I'm sorry I lambasted you like that. If you want to stand up for that pig-headed white knight George Bell, that's fine. It would remind me of the little boy who wanted to give free train-rides to the poor."

"I don't give a fig about Bell," I said. "He's nothing to me. What do I care if he messes up his career by being soft on the stupid Huns?"

"Nevertheless I shouldn't have said—"

"Perhaps it needed to be said." I bolted for the door.

He caught up with me as I stepped outside. "Neville, if there's anything I can do—"

"You've done it. You've told me what you thought. That was what I wanted." I offered him my hand and when he had shaken it anxiously I said: "I'm glad you're happy, Will. I can see now you've made a great success of your life. Father would have been very proud."

I said no more, but then no more was required to be said. Releasing his hand before I could make another disgusting exhibition of myself, I turned my back on him and walked rapidly down the drive to the road.

XIV

"What is needed and given is always the same—a new manifestation of the divine, a new vision of life as God wills it and we desire it—a new contact with the Spirit to set the man's career against a wider background . . ."

CHARLES E. RAVEN
THE CREATOR SPIRIT

I

HAVING thumbed a lift to the station, I was lucky enough to catch an express train back into London. I wound up at Victoria, took another extravagant taxi across the river to Waterloo and just managed to haul myself aboard the Starbridge train before it drew away from the platform. When one considered the post-war facts of life, which included an erratic railway service, this was successful travelling. Collapsing against the filthy upholstery (another post-war fact of life), I put a handkerchief over the back of my head to protect myself from lice and sank into a brief coma of exhaustion.

I arrived home at five o'clock. After a joyous reunion with Sandy and Primrose in the hall, I straightened my back to find my sister-in-law hovering disapprovingly in the drawing-room doorway.

"Dido was very upset when you didn't turn up this morning, Stephen."

"I did ring the hospital and leave a message."

"Yes, and very unsatisfactory it was too! Where on earth have you been? That rather stunning clergyman, the tall one with the matching grey hair and eyes, rang up just now and wanted to know where you were. I said: 'I thought *you* were looking after him!' and he said he'd loaned you to someone else for a few hours but I wasn't to worry. Stephen, would it be too much to ask you frankly what the hell's going on?"

"Yes." I bolted into the study to phone the Theological College.

"Are you all right?" said Darrow as soon as the call was connected to his room.

"Yes. Sorry I didn't ring earlier. On Aidan's advice I've been visiting my brother and sister."

"Shall I come and see you?"

"No, I'm off to the hospital to see Dido, and as soon as I get back I'm going to bed. I'm exhausted."

"Very well, but before you ring off there's one matter I must discuss with you. I've arranged the funeral for tomorrow morning at nine-thirty in the cemetery, and your senior curate will be taking the service. However, if you don't feel up to attending a funeral yet—"

"No, that's fine. Thanks."

"I'm still not sure if it should go ahead. I thought your wife had seen the baby, but your sister-in-law tells me—"

"Dido will never see that baby."

"It would be much better for her if she did. My wife's offered to visit the hospital and talk to her about it."

"That's very good of Anne, but she'd be wasting her time. Keep the funeral arrangements as they are."

"Very well, if you insist . . . How was Aidan?"

"Why bother to ask?" I said. "You're the famous clairvoyant. I'm sure you saw the entire interview in Technicolor on your very own private screen." I hung up, instantly regretted my burst of aggression and rang him back. Darrow would hardly be anxious to help me in the manner Aidan had suggested unless I made an effort to behave myself.

"Sorry," I said when the call was reconnected. "No offence meant. Thanks again for arranging the funeral."

"Aysgarth, have you eaten today?"

I tried to remember. "I had a bit of cottage pie."

"*You must eat.* Have something before you go to the hospital, and *drink tea.* Do I make myself entirely clear?"

"Yes, Nanny." I hung up, decided Aidan had been mad to imagine I could ever get on with Darrow, and wandered into the kitchen in search of something edible. My housekeeper offered me a quick snack of baked beans on toast with a poached egg. While she was cooking I started to trudge back to my study but I changed my mind. I was too afraid I might remember the whisky bottle behind the Oxford Dictionary.

Sandy joined me as I sat down at the dining-room table.

"Daddy, is it really true that before the war biscuits used to be covered with pale chocolate on both sides?"

"Milk chocolate, yes."

"Well, now the war's over how much longer will we have to wait for them to come back? I want a biscuit with pale chocolate on both sides!"

"So do I. I like chocolate too."

"Did Mummy like chocolate?" said Sandy, hauling himself purposefully onto my knees to ensure he retained my full attention.

"Be quiet, Sandy," said Primrose, entering the room. "We don't talk to him about Mummy. Daddy, Aunt Merry says the baby's funeral's tomorrow, but Sandy and I don't have to go, do we?"

"Maybe you'd like to go."

Primrose shuddered. "No, thanks. Christian says funerals are revolting and should be banned by law."

I was jolted out of my exhausted apathy. "When did he say that?"

"After Mummy's funeral."

"You said not to mention Mummy to him!" protested Sandy, but Primrose took no notice.

"I said to Christian: 'I wish I'd been old enough to go to Mummy's funeral,' and he said: 'No, you don't. Funerals are revolting and I never want to go to another as long as I live. They should be banned by law.' "

The housekeeper arrived with my snack but as soon as she had gone I said: "It's obvious Christian was very upset when he said that, Primrose, and he may well feel quite differently now. Funerals are important. Going through a formal ritual helps people to come to terms with the death by providing an opportunity to grieve."

"But Christian didn't want to grieve," said Primrose, "and neither did Norman and James. James told me they were all so afraid of crying and letting you down."

"I tasted pale chocolate once," said Sandy. "It was in the food parcel Dido got from America." Casually he ate one of my baked beans. "Dark chocolate's very nice but pale chocolate's better."

I suddenly realised I was unable to eat. "I must talk to the boys," I said to Primrose. "It sounds as if there's been a slight misunderstanding."

"Oh Daddy, don't let them know it was me who told you they were afraid of crying! Christian said you were never to know because you get so upset when anything's not quite perfect."

There was a long silence. Sandy ate another baked bean. Finally I pushed away my plate, swung him down from my knees and stood up. "I've just remembered another important telephone call I have to make," I said. "I'll be back in a minute."

I bolted to my study. Breathing quickly, I took a look behind the

Oxford Dictionary. The bottle was still there but, as I already knew, it was almost empty. If I finished it I would be doing myself a favour because then there would be no whisky left in the house.

I finished the bottle. Then I returned to the dining-room, said goodbye to the children and set off resolutely, with the aid of my triple whisky, for my next dreadful meeting with Dido.

2

I ARRIVED at the hospital to find Dido unconscious, heavily sedated after another bout of hysterics. Apparently someone had again tried to persuade her to see the baby. Feeling unutterably relieved that I had been spared another of our unreal conversations—and unutterably ashamed that I had disregarded Aidan's warning not to use alcohol as a crutch when I was desperate—I scribbled her a note to say I adored her, and fled back to the Close.

I felt much too exhausted to think clearly but now I was afraid to go to bed; I was sure sleep would elude me and I would be tormented by the most unbearable anxieties. I told myself I had to avoid worrying about my children while I was enduring my crisis, but I found I was haunted by the image of Christian struggling to ring down the curtain on his pain as he lectured his siblings on the need to appear perfect. The vignette presented by Primrose had devastated me. I saw now that something had gone very wrong with my entire family life, but in my weakened state that was a truth I found much too terrible to face and I could only push it in panic from my mind.

However my panic only increased as I contemplated the inevitable deterioration in my health which would result from a sleepless night. If I was to keep breakdown at bay in my already fragile mental state, I knew I had to have some respite, no matter how brief, from the wasteland which had suddenly acquired such a hideous new dimension.

I prayed for the courage to go to bed and face the possibility of being tormented throughout the night, but when I parked the car I could not even bring myself to enter the house. I sat rigid with despair in the driving-seat, and then gradually, very gradually, I became aware that I was staring at the Cathedral, that beating heart of Starbridge, that vast pale intricate concoction of stone and glass exuding its subtle message of human hope, that monster of architectural perfection, faultless, matchless but faintly sinister in its eerie power to ravish the eye and seduce the soul. It was one of those times when the Cathedral seemed to be no mere inanimate building but a living presence. I saw the windows of the west front suddenly glow gold in reflection of the shifting sunset, and as I held my breath, momentarily overwhelmed by the extraordinary glitter of the glass, the Cathedral seemed to hold its breath too, its stones honey-coloured in the evening light, its great spire radiant against the sky. I began to breathe again—and so did the Cathedral, invisibly but powerfully, and its breath was the breath of life to me as I toiled in the coils of my sickness. As if drawn by a magnet I left my car, I crossed the sward, I stretched out my hand to touch the walls—and at that moment in the depths of the building the organist began his evening practice with one of Bach's mysterious, unearthly fugues.

Trailing my hand against the stones I moved towards the north porch, and the fugue glided on and on, unravelling mystery after mystery, running backwards and forwards, up and down, weaving pattern after pattern of complex music until at the end, as I stood in the porch, all the threads were both united and transcended in a single final chord.

The enigma had proved capable of being solved. The message was clear. Hope was renewed. For a long moment I remained where I was, listening to the silence, the silence of the Cathedral, the silence of God. Then, knowing that I would now be able to sleep and escape for a few life-giving hours from my torment, I struggled home once more across the sward.

3

THE next morning I arose early, just as Aidan had suggested, and tried to follow his advice on prayer and reading, but I was soon so appalled by my poor concentration that I stopped. I then tried to reflect carefully on the interviews with Willy and Emily, but when my confusion continued unabated I was forced to realise how spiritually disabled I was. I tried to read again; I thought Aidan would want me to keep trying, and as I thought of him I wished he were with me to watch and listen on my behalf for the word from God which he had felt so sure would come. It seemed obvious now that I was spiritually far too blind and deaf to be capable of receiving the word myself.

This was such a depressing conclusion that I felt I could only stare out of the window in the hope of drawing strength once more from the Cathedral. The sun was now rising higher behind the spire and the building was again a living presence, constantly reflecting the changing angle of the light. As I watched, the sun moved a fraction to the south. Instantly the transept windows were ablaze and the north gargoyles were black demons rampant against an orange and azure sky. The room remained silent, but in my mind I could hear the Bach fugue.

I suddenly realised with great clarity that Aidan had been right to push me towards Darrow and that I had been wrong to resist him. I still wanted to resist, but I knew now that digging in my toes and playing the pig-headed Yorkshireman represented a luxury I could no longer afford. I somehow had to conquer my pride. I had to accept that a man who was blind and deaf needed a guide-dog. And I had to accept that in this emergency the best guide-dog within reach was Darrow.

Having read the office I prayed for the strength to survive the day ahead, but I found it hard not to feel I was asking for the moon.

4

I ATTENDED Holy Communion at eight in the hope of giving my spiritual strength a boost. There was no service that morning in my own church, since I did not subscribe to the opinion that Communion should be celebrated daily, but the Cathedral, providing as always a full range of services, offered a very tolerable celebration every morning.

On my arrival I found that the Dean was absent, but the Bishop was there and after the service he immediately buttonholed me in the vestry.

"My dear Neville, how are you? You've been so much in my thoughts and prayers ever since I heard the tragic news . . ." As he talked I was touched that his concern was so obviously genuine.

I gave him a censored account of my activities because I was determined that he should never know I had been to the Fordites; such a disclosure would be tantamount to admitting, as Darrow had put it so graphically, that I had hit rock-bottom hard enough to crack cement, and I did not want my superior to know I was now existing in a cement-crack. With immense care I said neutrally: "Darrow's been unexpectedly helpful. I spent a few hours at Starrington Manor yesterday, as I think he told you, and I feel better now."

"I'm very glad, but of course you musn't dream of returning to work just yet. Perhaps in a day or two—"

"No, I'd prefer to get back to work, Bishop. I really would. I'll call on you later this morning, after the funeral."

The Bishop almost but not quite masked his relief by asking tenderly after Dido and offering to accompany me to the cemetery. He was a good, kind old man and I was very fond of him, but when I remembered Aidan I was struck by the difference between the Bishop and the Abbot, the one able to offer a constructive help, the other able to provide only an ineffectual sympathy. It was like comparing a butter-knife with a meat-cleaver.

I thanked Dr. Ottershaw but told him I wanted the funeral to be private. Then escaping from the various clerical well-wishers who were hovering nearby in the hope of hearing the latest gossip, I went home and forced myself to eat breakfast.

5

THE first person I saw as I entered the cemetery was Darrow. He was standing outside the little chapel and talking to the sexton, but as I approached he came to meet me. He looked as if he were calculating my sobriety. Despite the obvious fact that it was now in my best interests to be charming and friendly to my guide-dog, I at once found myself seething with rage.

"Relax!" I said with an iron smile. "No brandy for breakfast!"

"I thought there might have been whisky for supper."

I could have hit him. "Do you have anything special to say to me or did you merely turn up to make sure I could walk?"

"I thought I might attend the funeral, but perhaps you'd rather be on your own. Shall I go or stay?"

"Go."

"Very well." He disappeared among the tombstones.

Time passed. My senior curate arrived on his bicycle. The undertakers drove up in a very large hearse with their very small coffin.

Crawshaw read the service well, with clarity and dignity, and avoided the pitfall of a lugubrious manner. Having trained him I felt proud of his professional competence. As I myself carried the little coffin to the waiting grave I tried to focus my mind on my memory of the child, but after a while I found I was thinking not of little Arthur, now being buried with such faultless simplicity, but of Christian, brilliant shining Christian, separated from me by a complex emotional abyss which neither of us could apparently bridge. Grace lay at the bottom of that abyss, I could see she did, just as I could see as the result of my meeting with Aidan that the name of the abyss was guilt, and suddenly I realised that my guilt was not only crippling my own existence but fouling my children, poisoning their lives.

Crawshaw concluded the service at the exact moment when Aidan said in my memory: "It's a question of facing the pain."

Somehow I managed to thank Crawshaw, and somehow, as we walked back down the path to the chapel, I managed to say to him: "I have to see the Bishop this morning, but I should be at St. Martin's by noon. Make sure Wilson and Cartwright are there, please, because I want a full report on everything that's been going on."

"Yes, sir," said Crawshaw crisply, obedient as a private in the presence of his sergeant-major.

Wilson and Cartwright were the other curates. I should perhaps explain here that I despise the namby-pamby modern habit of vicars and curates calling each other by their Christian names. When I had been Getting On up at Oxford I had quickly learnt that no man who considers himself acceptable in the higher levels of society dreams of calling another man by his Christian name unless the two of them are connected by either blood or marriage or a friendship of at least ten years' standing. I can still recall my amazement when my mentor had asked me to call him Alex. He had retired from the bishopric by then, of course, but his request had come only six years after we had first met. (I write "of course" because I could never under any circumstances have called my superior by his Christian name, even though he himself, as my Father in God, was entitled to address me as Neville.) I had admitted afterwards to Grace that although I had been flattered by Alex's invitation, I had also been shocked by it. It made me see why the people who mattered thought that Alex had never quite managed to become a gentleman.

Meanwhile I was realising that I ought to present some semblance of normality to Crawshaw by mentioning the parish, and hastily I delved into my memory of current parochial dramas.

"By the way," I said, feigning a benign curiosity, "what happened in that row over the Mothers' Union's homemade jam? Are they going to distribute it to the families on the dole in Langley Bottom as usual or are they going to—" I broke off. I had just seen Darrow sunning himself on a bench near my car. What was he doing? Spying on me in case I produced a hip-flask? Standing by to act as a nanny in case I broke down and howled like a woman? Loafing around to glean information about my visit to the Fordites? Dismissing Crawshaw abruptly I strode to the bench and planted myself in front of it.

"Why are you still here?"

"I was hoping for a lift back to the Close. Would you mind?"

After a pause I said tersely: "Get in," and opened the door of my car. Crawshaw was already riding away on his bicycle.

"I apologise for the ill-temper," I said at last to Darrow when he was sitting in the passenger seat and I had started the engine, "but I thought you were spying on me."

"I was. May I congratulate you not only on your sobriety but on your ability to function in a normal manner? In the circumstances that's a considerable achievement."

"There's no achievement." Reluctantly, knowing we had to talk, I switched off the engine. "The normal functioning's an act. It diverts me from facing the pain."

"Aidan's phrase?"

"Aidan's phrase." I made a superhuman effort to be well-behaved and friendly. "That's quite a technique he employs!" I commented jovially. "He broke rules, took risks—he even talked at length about himself in order to hit me over the head with the right parable. He rubbed my nose in the pain when I wanted to avoid it. He presented insights which made me howl with rage and walk out. In retrospect I find myself wondering what on earth a psychiatrist would have made of the interview."

"But all the chances he took came off, didn't they? The late Abbot-General Father Darcy used to say," said Darrow, "that it was only when one had had many years of experience of working obediently within the rules that one learnt how to recognise those moments when it was safe to step outside them."

"Aidan talked of Darcy." I suddenly found I had exhausted my supply of friendliness; the effort of being well-behaved and sociable towards Darrow was too great to be sustained for long in my weakened state, and in despair, knowing that he was necessary to me yet feeling quite unable to ask for his help, I said abruptly: "Look, I'm sorry, but I can't talk to you now. I've got to go and see the Bishop."

"I didn't come here to talk. Nor, in fact, did I come here to play the ecclesiastical nanny. My presence is more in the nature of a symbolic act."

I had been about to switch on the engine again but now I let my fingers slip from the key. I stared through the windscreen at the tombstones, I stared down at my left hand as it clutched the steering wheel and finally I stared at my passenger. My voice said: "You've come to stand at the foot of the cross."

"That's it. Sometimes mere words are no good. Sometimes in the presence of suffering only symbols have meaning."

I thought of Hoffenberg saying: "He's a *crucified* God," and again I was reminded of a law of science working automatically as soon as the right mechanisms were set in motion. When Darrow spoke, symbolically offering his hand to me as if impelled by an irresistible force, I saw the principle of atonement streaming into action. Once more God had entered into the wasteland and made himself at one with it so that all might be raised up, restored and renewed. Once more the ancient wheel of birth, death and resurrection had begun to revolve in my life after an agonising hiatus in time.

The next moment I found I had the strength to say to Darrow: "If you're at the foot of the cross you'll see that I'm past the 'My God, my God, why hast thou forsaken me?' phase but I'm still up there, waiting to be cut down. Just realised I can't do it myself. Need help. Bit of a problem." I was looking at the tombstones as I spoke, but I was aware of Darrow nodding as if he had often encountered this little difficulty and knew very well how tiresome it could be.

Then I knew I could no longer avoid the crucial struggle with my pride. It was a long, hard, bitter struggle and it left me limp, battered and bruised, but when my pride had finally collapsed in a vanquished heap, I was able to say in the casual voice I used for discussing minor diocesan problems: "Could we forget for a while that I'm the Archdeacon? Rank's no life-belt when one falls overboard, as an ex–Naval man like you might say."

"No life-belt at all, I agree."

"Being an archdeacon won't cut me down from the cross," I said. "Exercising a first-class brain won't cut me down from the cross. Flaunting a pugnacious nature won't cut me down from the cross. But if we could agree that I'm a limited and somewhat obtuse clergyman, while you're the expert at rescuing the crucified, maybe we'd get somewhere."

"Maybe we would. But of course I too have my limited, obtuse side—as no doubt you remember all too well."

It was the olive branch of peace. Switching on the engine again I realised with astonishment that my fingers were trembling. I could only suppose I was suffering from shock after slaying the dragon of my pride with a nautical metaphor and the grace of God.

"Aidan made it plain I'm in a situation that will require the exercise of the charism of discernment," I heard myself say, "but unfortunately I'm at present a little blind and deaf. Spiritually, I mean."

"Very tricky."

"If you could provide an extra pair of eyes and ears—"

"Delighted."

"I don't want spiritual direction, you understand. I don't want you giving me orders about how to pray or anything like that."

"Wouldn't dream of it."

"I just want a little help with the inevitable detective work. Of course I expect we'll still fight."

"Oh yes, I expect so."

"It may all be a complete failure."

"Possibly."

"But acting on the principle of nothing ventured, nothing gained—"

"Very sensible. Why don't you phone me after your interview with the Bishop and then perhaps we can arrange to meet later?"

"Fine." I drove somewhat erratically out of the cemetery and began to head through the suburbs to the centre of Starbridge. We did not speak during the journey to the Close, but as I drew up outside the Theological College Darrow said: "That was a brave thing to do, Aysgarth. You think, don't you, that I'm seeing you at your weakest, but in fact I'm now seeing just how strong you really are." He did not wait for a reply but got out of the car and vanished into the building without looking back.

Tears stung my eyes to remind me that despite my large step forward along Salvation's road I was still in the same disgusting emotional state. Slamming the car furiously into gear I drove on to the episcopal palace and prayed for a cascade of urgent diocesan problems which would temporarily divert me from my pain.

6

THE Bishop's palace at Starbridge was in fact not a palace at all; the original residence, destroyed by fire in the nineteenth century, had been replaced by a country house which now wore a dark bedraggled look as it lay limply among its untended lawns. Since post-war austerity seemed destined to stretch into the remote future, Dr. Ottershaw was now talking sensibly of ceding the palace to the choir school and moving to the South Canonry, a smaller house on the other side of the Close. Mrs. Ottershaw, exhausted by dilapidated premises and interminable servant problems, could hardly wait to leave.

I parked my car beside an unfamiliar Sunbeam Talbot and walked around the house to the side door, which in day-time was left unlocked for authorised visitors. Looking in at the former flower-room, now the secretary's office, I saw the old battle-axe who dealt with the flurry of paperwork generated by the post-war society. In the old days the secretary had been employed only on an occasional basis and the chaplain had been in charge of the correspondence, but now the chaplain had risen to loftier administrative heights as he helped his master deal with what Aidan would no doubt have called "The World." Since Dr. Ottershaw was of an unworldly disposition, the current chaplain had far more power than Alex's chaplains had enjoyed in the halcyon days of the Jardine episcopate before the war.

"Good morning, Miss Todd. Any news?"

The old battle-axe gave me a benign glare and retorted dryly: "That's the question I should be asking *you,* Archdeacon. I was extremely sorry to hear about your misfortune." The phone rang. She pounced on it, listened, said: "Mrs. Ottershaw already supports a charity for displaced persons. Good-day," and hung up the receiver with a thud.

Before she could embark on a discussion of my misfortune I said: "Is the Bishop free?"

"He does have a visitor, but he said you were to go straight in."

Crossing the hall I knocked on the door and heard the Bishop call: "Yes?" hopefully in his gentle tenor.

I walked in and stopped dead. Not even a thunderbolt could have halted me more efficiently in my tracks.

"Ah, there you are, Neville—just the man we wanted to see!" exclaimed Dr. Ottershaw pleased, but I barely heard him because I was so stunned by the identity of his visitor.

It was the greatest man in the Church of England, the Bishop of Chichester, Dr. George Bell.

7

IT is very hard, perhaps even impossible, to describe someone of spiritual power in terms which point beyond the outward appearance to the invisible reality within. Bell was not a tall man; his build was stocky—chunky, perhaps, would be a more evocative word—and his physique suggested he was someone who knew how to endure adversity. His hair, neatly cut, neatly parted, neatly brushed, was thin, fine and pale. He had a square face, a large nose, a cleft chin, a wide, slim, sensitive mouth and—his most famous feature—enormous blue eyes which instantly conveyed an impression of immense warmth and intelligence. I looked into those eyes, as so many troubled people had looked before me, and felt not only soothed but relieved, as if I had suddenly encountered a close relative after an agonising time among strangers, and then I remembered that among the persecuted and martyred Christians of Nazi Europe, Bell's sobriquet had been "Uncle George."

"You recognise Bishop Bell, of course," Dr. Ottershaw was saying quickly. "He's on his way to Salisbury, but he's just dropped in for . . . Dear me, if I say 'elevenses' will I sound like Winnie-the-Pooh?"

"But I didn't come to eat elevenses!" said Dr. Bell amused. "I came to meet Mr. Aysgarth." He held out his hand to me. "How do you do, Archdeacon—I've been hearing great things about you."

I was so astounded by this amazing piece of information that I could only say blankly: *"Me?"* Automatically I struggled to work out the nature of the colossal mistake which had obviously been made.

Dr. Bell said to his host: "Show him the letter," and Dr. Ottershaw, who had been holding some sheets of notepaper in his hand, at once proffered them to me.

I recognised the regulation paper of the prison camp. I read the opening words: "My Lord Bishop," and recognised Hoffenberg's clear script. Illumination dawned, and gradually, as my stupefied gaze travelled down the pages, I realised that my prisoners—not just Hoffenberg but all the men who had responded to my presence among them—had laboured to construct a testimonial. The final paragraph read: "Mr. Aysgarth brought hope where there was despair, faith where there was distrust and charity where there was only hatred and bitterness. He brought Christ to us and helped us to see the crucified God. He listened, he endured with us, he understood our sufferings, and we wanted the best bishop in England to know this, the bishop who knows that not all Germans are Nazis. Thank you for all you did for Dietrich Bonhoeffer and the German Confessing Church. Yours respectfully, sincerely, gratefully . . ." And then the long list of signatures began.

The letter slipped through my fingers and dropped upon the desk. Dr. Ottershaw was saying happily: "Now, *isn't* that a splendid letter! But I feel so guilty that it came as such a surprise to me—Colonel Laker did tell me, of course, that he was pleased with you, but I had no idea, Neville, *no idea* that you were giving those men such very exceptional pastoral care!"

"I wasn't. I'm not. The letter's quite undeserved." In my embarrassment I was at my worst: shy, wooden and awkward. "No good at difficult pastoral work," I said. "Not in the least accomplished. In fact really rather a failure."

"Could failure have inspired this letter?" said Bell before Dr. Ottershaw could attempt a well-meaning protest. "I think not. The gifts of the Spirit can be recognised by their fruits."

I at last managed to overcome my extreme shyness and look directly at him. His extraordinary eyes were brilliant with an unmistakably genuine interest, and it was then I realised he possessed that rare and fabled gift for making a stranger feel special, cared for, even cherished—and all within the space of a few minutes.

"I wonder if you have the time," he said, "to sit down for a moment and tell me how you became involved in this work and how you approached such a very demanding task. Would you mind talking about such matters to me?"

There could be only one answer to that. We all sat down, Dr. Ottershaw behind his desk, Dr. Bell and I in high-backed chairs opposite him, and driven by an irresistible compulsion to confide at last in someone who I knew would understand, I prepared to "deliver my soul," as the Victorian preachers used to say, to my Uncle George.

8

"I DIDN'T seek the work," I said, "but the work seemed to seek me. There were all kinds of obstacles in the way, ranging from the usual regulations against fraternisation to the fact that the camp wasn't even in my archdeaconry, but the more I hoped the work would pass me by the more the obstacles which separated me from it seemed to melt away. The other Archdeacon—" I hesitated, not wanting to tell tales about my rabidly anti-German colleague, but Dr. Ottershaw said firmly: "Quite unsuitable," and Dr. Bell, effortlessly hearing all that remained unsaid, murmured: "I understand."

"Then various unforeseen events occurred," I said. "There was a riot and a lynching. The few German pastors for one reason or another all fell by the wayside, but the new Commandant appointed after the riot was an active Christian and he felt strongly that in the absence of German pastors an English clergyman should be permitted to call regularly at the camp. War Office permission was eventually obtained and the Bishop asked me to deal with the matter as I thought fit.

"Immediately I made up my mind to delegate the work. I knew I had to go to the camp for a reconnaissance—there was no way out of that—but I thought I'd be able to push the work off onto a volunteer from the ranks of the retired diocesan clergy, someone who had considerable experience of a tough chaplaincy in the prison service or the Army. I thought that as Archdeacon all I was obliged to do was spy out the land: estimate the number of men likely to be interested, decide what kind of services would be possible and how often they should be held, get some idea how far an Englishman would be allowed to talk to the prisoners in distress. I thought it likely that there would be considerable antagonism to the idea of services and absolute antagonism to the idea of individual counselling—in fact I thought that the prisoners who talked to me might later be the victims of reprisals.

"However, the camp had been radically reorganised since the lynching—the camp hierarchy had been broken up when the super-Nazis were kicked north to Caithness, and with far fewer Grade C prisoners still around, Colonel Laker was determined that the Grade A's shouldn't be intimidated. He told me on my first visit that he was prepared to back me all the way in whatever I decided to do.

"Of course I didn't tell him I had no intention of coming back. I managed to get all the information I needed by talking to him about the men and inspecting the room which could be used as a chapel, and then just as I was deciding with relief that I could escape, he said: 'I expect you'd like to meet some of the men, wouldn't you?' And I couldn't quite work out how to say no. I didn't want him thinking I was flunking my Christian duty. So off we went to meet the men.

"He took me into the long Nissen hut where the Grade A's were quartered, and immediately I was reminded of a terrible boarding school where I spent a year at the age of seven. There was the same smell of mildew and sweat, the same atmosphere of apathetic misery, and in that instant the men ceased to be merely German prisoners. They became just prisoners who happened to be German, prisoners not so very different from the prisoner I myself had been long ago in my childhood up in Yorkshire.

"I thought: Poor bastards. And I was surprised because I hadn't expected to feel genuinely sorry for them. I suppose I had anticipated a stern aloof Christian compassion laced with fury whenever I remembered the Baedeker raids. To be honest, I've never had much time for any foreigners. I've had a hard enough time dealing with the foreigners who live directly beyond the boundaries of my native Yorkshire; dealing with the foreigners who live beyond the White Cliffs of Dover has always been a challenge I've never felt in the least inclined to meet.

"Anyway, no sooner had I stepped into the Nissen hut than I realised I had nothing to say. The whole scene was appalling, a clerical nightmare. I'd never felt cut out for pastoral work—and certainly not pastoral work on the heroic scale—yet there I was, dumped among a horde of hostile foreigners and apparently required to communicate with them. Dreadful. I felt so humiliated by my complete and utter incompetence. I could only think: I'll never come back, never, never, never. I'll make sure the poor devils get the very best chaplain I can lay my hands on, but I'll never set foot in this place again. And then . . .

"Then Colonel Laker said to me: 'Some of these fellows speak quite good English,' and he called out to the men: 'Can someone volunteer to tell Mr. Aysgarth a little about himself?'

"It was Hoffenberg who stepped forward first—the pen behind that letter. He wasn't at all an appealing young man. He was large and plain and ungainly. But he spoke excellent English, and as he told me how terrible it was to be locked up indefinitely, cut off from his home and family, I found myself back in Yorkshire again at that terrible boarding school. So when he said at the end: 'Will you come back?' I . . . well, I had to say yes, didn't I? I couldn't have said anything else. I knew how he felt, you see. I'd been there and I knew.

"Well, when I realised that I had to take on the work myself I tried to plan it like a military operation—being very thorough and paying great attention to detail. I thought that might make up for my pastoral deficiencies. I didn't actually have much time to set aside for the camp, but I made time, juggling my appointments during the day and staying up late at night to plan my campaign. I suppose I could have got away with one service a month and a bit of chat afterwards—just a gesture which would have ensured that the Church maintained a benign presence in the camp—but I thought: No, that's not good enough. If I'm going to be a failure, let me at least ensure that the failure isn't the result of sloppy work and lack of effort.

"I spent some time researching and planning a service which would be acceptable to anyone who wasn't a Roman Catholic. (No good trying to woo the R.C.s, of course—I knew it was a priest or nothing for them.) Once that was done I realised I had to surmount the language barrier, so I got hold of the master who teaches German at Starbridge Grammar and together we hammered out a short sermon. My schoolboy's German was very poor—although I'm fluent now after all the practice—but at least I knew the rudiments of the language and at least I was capable of achieving a passable accent.

"Finally I held my first service. A few listless spectators turned up but when I started speaking German they were electrified. Afterwards they said: 'We never thought you'd care enough to do that. When will you do it again?' They were almost friendly—and Hoffenberg was so pleased by my success. If he'd been a puppy he'd have wagged his tail.

"After a time I had to seek permission to use a larger room. Naturally a lot of prisoners never came near me, but it was surprising who did. Even the Catholics turned up to hear the sermons in the end! They would never receive the sacrament from me, of course, but at least there was some sort of participation. I slogged on. Sometimes I wondered if I was really getting anywhere at all—the apathy was so great that I often felt as if I was wrestling with a series of inert punch-bags—but sometimes on the better days I was able to think: Maybe there *is* some point in my presence here. I certainly enjoyed talking to Hoffenberg and I was pleased when after a while a sizeable number of other people wanted to talk to me as well—even the Grade B's, the neutrals who had been very stand-offish, began to drift into the chapel out of curiosity. That was a victory of sorts—nothing dramatic, just a small step forward—but so often it seemed that for every step forward I'd slide two steps back. I used to get particularly discouraged when new people turned up at the services, only to yawn and walk out.

"Then in May 1945 morale broke among the Nazis and suddenly there *was* drama, a lot of it, and I wound up trying to minister to the Grade C men as they went mad or tried to commit suicide or both . . . But don't think I was a wonder-worker. I wasn't. In fact I think I was probably absolutely useless. But perhaps all that mattered was that I was there, a symbolic presence in their macabre psychiatric hell—oh, what gruelling work it was, terrible, so harrowing, and all the time I was more conscious than ever of my painful shortcomings as a clergyman.

"Fortunately time's always moving on. Some of the Grade A's have already been repatriated—Hoffenberg himself is leaving soon—and perhaps by this time next year the camp may be closed. It's not so bad there now. Colonel Laker made a success of the place and at present there are plenty of activities and entertainments and opportunities for study. Life there became better too when the fraternisation regulations were relaxed and the prisoners could get out and about a bit. I organised regular Sunday outings to the Cathedral for Evensong—and arranged for the parishioners of St. Martin's, my church, to offer hospitality . . . There's a lot that can be done for the men nowadays. But I often wonder what will happen to them all when they get back to Germany—if indeed there's anything left for them to get back to. Hoffenberg lost his home and all his family when Dresden went up in flames.

"Perhaps I would have found my work at the camp easier if I'd been able to talk over the experience with someone, but it's always been my hidden ministry, the ministry I could never discuss. I couldn't speak about it because . . . to be absolutely honest . . . well, the real truth is that I couldn't bear the thought of anyone knowing how much I'd come to sympathise with the men—I couldn't bear the thought of people pointing a finger at me and saying: 'He's soft on Germans!' I've been such a moral coward. I thought if people believed I was soft on Germans my career would be adversely affected—but oh, how I despised myself for my cowardice! And every time you rose to your feet in the House of Lords to show me the right way forward—the way I hadn't the guts to take—I felt so weak, so unworthy, so utterly unfit to be a clergyman."

I stopped. My narrative had ended, and all I could add as a postscript was: "Crippling shortcomings. Contemptible behavior. Quite undeserving of that letter, as I'm sure you must now agree."

But Bell leant forward. I could not look at him, but I was aware of the warmth of his personality enfolding me as he exerted his fabled gift for making a stranger feel cherished. "But surely," he said in the famous mild reasonable voice which masked his stubborn determination to present the truth as he saw it, "actions speak louder than words? Many people support my beliefs publicly with fine speeches, but do nothing more. You said nothing in public yet in private you did everything which was required of you—and the result was that something very important happened—important for those men and important for you too . . . Forgive me for being inquisitive, but may I ask if you're a pacifist?"

"I was. But not since Munich."

"I was just wondering if you had some pressing reason for not volunteering to be an Army chaplain. You must have been within the age limit when war broke out."

"Neville thought of volunteering," said Dr. Ottershaw quickly, "but I talked him out of it. Pure selfishness on my part, I'm afraid. He's such a very able archdeacon."

But I looked at Dr. Bell and said: "The Bishop talked me out of nothing. I hated the thought of doing that type of pastoral work—but as the years passed I began to feel guilty that I was safe and snug on the Home Front while other clergymen of my generation were being so very much more heroic. And I've often suspected that it was this guilt which provided the psychological compulsion to keep visiting the Germans when all I really wanted to do was stay away."

"Neville's a Modernist," said Dr. Ottershaw hastily, as if this eccentric reference to psychology demanded an explanation.

"Far be it from me to cast aspersions on Modernism," said Dr. Bell amused, "but can the wonders of psychoanalytical theory really explain the whole of this remarkable success of yours, Archdeacon? I think not." He rose to his feet before adding: "Now that you've so triumphantly overcome your reluctance to deal with anyone born beyond the White Cliffs of Dover, have you ever thought of working in a European context?"

I could only stare at him.

"This era of post-war reconstruction is a very exciting and challenging time for the churches," said Bell, "and there's much work to be done, not only in the occupied zones but in Geneva at the secretariat of the World Council of Churches. A German-speaking clergyman with a first-class record as a pastor of POWs would have a lot to offer." Before I could attempt a reply he added with a laugh to Dr. Ottershaw: "Forgive me for behaving like a poacher, but I think your Archdeacon's admirable modesty is leading him to undervalue his achievements and narrow his perspective on the future."

Dr. Ottershaw at once became fluttery. "Well, of course Neville knows I'd never stand in his way—and if he should ever feel that God's calling him into a different field—"

"God may have quite other plans for Mr. Aysgarth." He held out his hand to me again. "Goodbye, Archdeacon, and when you're next passing through Chichester, do stop and call upon me. Remember three things: my wife and I keep open house, I shan't forget you, and I sincerely hope we shall meet again."

To my fury I felt myself blushing. I did manage to say: "Thank you, Bishop. You've been very kind," but this colourless understatement made me despair of myself. Having "delivered my soul" in such an uncharacteristic fashion, I had now apparently reverted to the role of the dour inarticulate Yorkshireman.

"Oh, and one thing more," said Bell, pausing to look back at me as he reached the door. "It's inevitable that you should have suffered from the non-combatant's guilt, but in fact all that matters is that you've managed to use that guilt constructively. And we're not talking now of mere psychological drives. We're talking of how all suffering can be redeemed and transformed by the creative power of the Holy Spirit."

As he spoke I remembered that during the First War he had been the Archbishop of Canterbury's chaplain, confined to the Home Front while two of his brothers had been killed in action. I said: "Thank you, Bishop," and heard my voice, no longer colourless, ring with gratitude. I felt as if I had received a very special absolution.

He departed.

Dr. Ottershaw also left the room in order to escort his guest to the front door.

Without more ado I collapsed stupefied into the nearest chair.

9

GLITTERING thoughts streamed through my head as I gazed out of the window and abandoned myself to fantasy. The World Council of Churches had been founded but it had not yet met. I could be involved in the organisation's work from the beginning, perhaps as some sort of liaison officer with the German churches—perhaps even as a personal assistant to Bell, who was certain to dominate the first meeting. The great irony about Bell, with his long history of support for German Christians and Jews, was that he spoke no German. Perhaps I could accompany him everywhere as an interpreter; perhaps—but my imagination had scaled such heights that I began to feel dizzy.

I told myself severely that I should deal in certainties, and at once I thought how working for the brotherhood of man, in the form of the World Council of Churches, would offer me endless scope for putting my Liberal Protestant ideals into practice. On a less rarefied level I also reflected that working abroad would give me the chance to escape from the English class system. What a liberation! Intoxicated with the thought of such a heady freedom, I abandoned myself to fantasy again and began to picture an idyllic version of Switzerland. Within seconds I was seeing it all in glorious Technicolor: mountains, valleys, lakes, summer sunshine, pristine snow, alpine flowers, picturesque towns—and shop-windows full of chocolate, bushels of chocolate, dark chocolate, pale chocolate, *even white chocolate,* that dim but treasured memory from the lost world before the war . . .

In the distance Dr. Ottershaw closed the front door. My fantasy ended. I was left remembering that since I had five children, no private income, and an expensive wife, probably no man in the Church of England needed an archidiaconal salary more than I did. But on the other hand, if God wanted me to work for the World Council of Churches, He would surely help me surmount the financial stumbling-blocks in my path. Or was the existence of the financial stumbling-blocks an indication that I wasn't being called to chase my dreams on the Continent after all?

I had no idea.

Confusion descended on me again, and I was still toiling futilely to perceive what the extraordinary interview with Bell had really meant, when Dr. Ottershaw returned to the room.

10

"WELL, wasn't that typical!" he exclaimed, closing the door behind him and returning to his desk. "George Bell has only to hold out his hand and within five minutes even the most reserved of men is pouring his heart out to him!"

"I'm afraid I talked far too much."

"Nonsense! He was wholly absorbed—and so, of course, was I." The Bishop hesitated, and as he did so I was aware of the depth of his personality, the seriousness which his detractors, who wrote him off as a light-weight, consistently underestimated. He said simply: "I hope you weren't embarrassed that I was present," and at once I answered: "I was glad. I'm only sorry I'd never confided in you before."

"I hardly encouraged you, did I?"

"Bishop, you really can't blame yourself for my tiresome reticence!"

"But I do. I'm supposed to be your Father in God, but George Bell learns more about you in ten minutes than I've learnt in nine years. I feel very strongly now that I've failed you in some profound way not easy to define."

"But you've been the best boss I could ever have wished for!"

"Ah, but that's all part of the problem, isn't it? The roles of confessor and superior aren't really compatible, as the religious orders discovered long ago, and the inevitable gulf between us has been exacerbated by your natural reserve and my horror of being a prying spiritual busybody. But that doesn't excuse my failure. The truth is I've consistently exploited you; you take such a load off my shoulders that I've succumbed to the temptation to sit back and let our relationship remain at a secular level, but of course that's unforgivable behaviour for a bishop entrusted with the care of souls. I've sensed you've been through difficult times since your first wife's death. I suspect you're very troubled now, but what have I done to try to help you? Nothing! I've feebly allowed our conversations to be restricted to diocesan matters—and by doing so I've connived at a situation in which we continue to take refuge from each other in our formal, familiar roles."

After a pause I said: "There's comfort in familiarity. And if you've connived at the situation, then so have I."

"A willing victim of my pastoral neglect? I can hardly believe that excuses me. Neville, if there's anything I can do for you at this troubled time, anything at all, I do most earnestly hope that you'll overcome your reserve and let me know."

I was more conscious than ever of his essential goodness, and realising that he deserved to have his mind set at rest, I disclosed the information which I had earlier vowed he would never know. "I've been to the Fordites," I said. "I'm very grateful to you for your concern, Bishop, but you mustn't worry. I'm not without guidance at present."

Dr. Ottershaw made no attempt to conceal his relief. "You went to Starwater?"

"No, to London. Darrow organised it. I saw the Abbot of Ruydale who was staying there for a few days."

"I've never met him, but I know those senior Fordites are all exceptional men . . . What did he advise you to do about your work? It's very important that you don't overstrain yourself during this distressing time."

"I'm sure if Lucas had thought I was unfit for work he'd have suggested a prolonged retreat. But he didn't, and as I told you earlier at the Cathedral, I want to keep working. I feel I must try to lead as normal a life as possible while Darrow helps me sort out my difficulties."

"Darrow! But can you work with him?"

"Lucas thought it was worth a try."

"Well, of course Darrow's exceptionally gifted in his own way," said Dr. Ottershaw troubled, "but bearing in mind your past difficulties with him—"

There was a knock on the door, and the lean, lynx-eyed chaplain poked his long nose into the room. "Excuse me, Bishop, but I just wanted to make sure that in all the excitement of Dr. Bell's visit you hadn't forgotten to tell the Archdeacon about our latest crisis."

"Bless my soul, it had entirely slipped my mind—I must be going senile!" exclaimed Dr. Ottershaw, and I knew, just as he did, that we were being offered the chance to slink thankfully back into our familiar roles after our awkward performance in a far less comfortable play. "Come in, Freddy. Neville, I really do hate to bother you about this, but—"

"No need to apologise, Bishop. I can hardly wait to be diverted by a lurid diocesan crisis, the more lurid the better."

"You may live to regret those words, Archdeacon," said the chaplain, sitting down beside me, "but I confess I'm eternally grateful you've uttered them. Bishop, would you like me to summarise the gory details for Mr. Aysgarth?"

Barely able to suppress a sigh of relief, I thanked God for yet another respite from my troubles and prepared to glide smoothly back into my role of Archdeacon.

XV

"It has been urged that man's spiritual life is the emergence in him of a new level of experience, a new integration of the aesthetic, intellectual and moral elements in his nature . . . In it the whole personality is involved, in both its inward completeness and its outward relationships . . ."

CHARLES E. RAVEN
THE CREATOR SPIRIT

I

"BEFORE I begin, Archdeacon," said the chaplain, "may I say on behalf of all the staff at the palace how sorry we were to hear about the tragedy. We wish to extend our deepest sympathy to you and your wife."

"Thank you." Freddy Hampton's well-meaning platitudes sounded a shade too slick, but then the conversation of Old Etonians always did seem a shade too slick to me. I usually managed not to hold his privileged background against him.

"And now for the crisis." Hampton fortified himself by taking a deep breath. "It's about Mellors."

It says much for my disordered state of mind that I immediately thought of the gamekeeper in *Lady Chatterley's Lover.*

"The Vicar of Flaxton Pauncefoot," said Hampton, seeing my glazed expression.

The village which possessed this ridiculous but not untypical name lay in my colleague's archdeaconry, but I had heard of the incumbent. Flexing my memory I recalled that after his wife's death during the war he had taken to drink, with the result that Archdeacon Babbington-French had hauled him before the Bishop for a stern reproof. Fortunately for Mellors Dr. Ottershaw had instead offered kindness and sympathy, a far more effective cure for that type of behaviour, and Mellors had been sufficiently encouraged to pull himself together.

Tentatively I ventured: "He's been drinking again?"

"Oh, much worse than that!" said Hampton, looking severe. "He's been giving peculiar sermons."

"Who says so? Babbington-French?"

"As a matter of fact the Archdeacon doesn't know anything about this yet." Hampton contrived to signal to me by the conspiratorial tone of his voice that this was a matter of the very greatest good fortune for us all. "Let me tell you exactly what happened. At nine o'clock this morning Lord Flaxton phoned, and— Do you know Lord Flaxton, Archdeacon?"

"Only by reputation." Flaxton, a moody peer noted for his eccentric intelligence and his devotion to the parliamentary Liberal party, spoke regularly in the House of Lords. In addition to his townhouse in London he owned a country estate which included the entire village of Flaxton Pauncefoot.

"Well, you can imagine how the conversation went," Hampton was saying. "He demanded to speak to the Bishop. Then he announced that Mellors was preaching heresy and had to be immediately defrocked. Of course the Bishop expressed the necessary shock, horror and regret—"

"So embarrassing," murmured Dr. Ottershaw, "because you see, it was I who appointed Mellors. You'd think Lord Flaxton would have the right to appoint the vicar, but the Flaxtons sold the advowson to the Bishop in the eighteenth century."

Ignoring this historical aside Hampton continued: "Dr. Ottershaw then explained to Lord Flaxton that his custom was always to send an archdeacon to investigate parish trouble because once the Bishop himself became involved, there was a risk of publicity—and anyway most cases can be sorted out at the archidiaconal level. I honestly think Lord Flaxton expected the Bishop to drop everything, rush to Flaxton Pauncefoot and drag off Mellors by the scruff of the neck! However when he realised that the Church of England was no longer in the Middle Ages he said: 'Well, don't sent that blank-blank ass Babbington-French'—sorry, Bishop, but I do think Mr. Aysgarth should know Lord F. was absolutely *virulent* on the subject—'send that other Archdeacon, the one the Starmouths rate such a capital fellow. I'll see him at three o'clock this afternoon.' Then he rang off before the Bishop could say you weren't available."

"The aristocracy don't mean to be thoughtless," said Dr. Ottershaw, who could never bear to say an unkind word about anybody. "It's just that they're so accustomed to getting their own way. What shall I do, Neville? I can hardly believe you're in the mood to face a furious peer and a heretical vicar, but if I call in Hubert Babbington-French—"

"Don't do it, Bishop—don't do it!" begged his chaplain. "We'd have

Lord Flaxton storming the palace, Mellors shrieking that he's being persecuted and Jack Ryder of *The Church Gazette* roaring down from London to investigate heresy in Flaxton Pauncefoot!"

"He's right," I said to the Bishop. "Let's forget Babbington-French for the moment and concentrate on calming down Lord Flaxton. What's this heresy that Mellors is supposed to be promulgating?"

The Bishop said simply: "I didn't dare ask."

"It's always so awkward when clergymen go round the bend," mused Hampton. "Thank goodness it doesn't happen often."

We shuddered. "May heaven preserve us all from nervous breakdowns!" said the Bishop with feeling, and I hardly knew how to restrain myself from muttering a fervent amen.

2

WHEN I left the palace all I wanted was to reflect on my meeting with Bishop Bell, but there was no time. My curates were waiting for me at St. Martin's; I had to hear their reports, discuss parish business and delegate as much work as I could. Afterwards I telephoned Darrow. He was unavailable but I left a message to say I was engaged in urgent diocesan business and that he was on no account to delay his return home that evening in the hope of hearing from me. I had no idea how long it would take me to clean up the mess in Flaxton Pauncefoot, but a heretical mess was unlikely to be eliminated merely by the quick flick of an archidiaconal duster.

Having dealt with Darrow I realised with a sinking heart that it was once more time to face my wife. I dragged myself to the hospital, but again the meeting proved easier than I had anticipated. Dido talked incessantly about herself, and all I had to do, as I listened to the catalogue of her infirmities, was to exude sympathy. Occasionally I did wonder if this sympathy was ringing false, but I spent most of the time asking myself, with that apathetic detachment which so often accompanies despair, how I was going to live with her for the next thirty years. I did remember Aidan talking of the grace of God, but once I was in Dido's presence it was much harder to resist the temptation to write him off as an ancient celibate preaching a holy optimism which had no meaning in a marital hell.

At last after an apparently interminable interval the ward-sister arrived to conclude my visit. "But I haven't asked him yet if he has any news!" Dido protested.

"I've no news at all," I said, standing up. I knew better than to talk to her about the funeral. "Sandy and Primrose send their love. Merry will be visiting you this evening."

"But won't you be visiting too?"

"I may not be able to make it. There's a very urgent diocesan problem—"

"Aren't I more important than a diocesan problem?" Without warning she burst into tears.

"There, there!" said the ward-sister, bustling forward. "It's not your husband's fault, is it, that he's such an important man!"

"Oh, shut up, you old cow!" stormed Dido, tears streaming down her face.

As the ward-sister recoiled in rage I frantically tried to create a diversion. "Darling, I really do have urgent business to attend to—I've been summoned to see Lord Flaxton. Do you know him?"

"Flaxton!" The sobs halted as Dido gazed at me in surprise. "Oh, he's dreadfully serious-minded and peculiar, all Latin and Greek and pre-1914 Liberalism and acid speeches in the House of Lords, and *she* can't talk about anything except gardening, but the girls are quite fun, nothing dazzling but quite fun, and there are two sons in the F.O. or the Guards or something, and there's a little afterthought, another girl, I think, although it might be a boy, I can't quite remember, but anyway it's too young to be amusing. Why on earth are you going to see Lord Flaxton?"

The ward-sister said in a voice cold enough to chill molten lava: "You'll have to hear about that later, Mrs. Aysgarth. And now if you don't mind, Archdeacon . . ."

I didn't mind in the least. Retreating with haste to my car I found the dog-eared county road-map and began to work out the quickest route to Flaxton Pauncefoot.

3

FLAXTON PAUNCEFOOT was one of those villages which had been a picturesque rural slum in the nineteenth century and was now a picturesque rural landmark much favoured by holiday-makers in search of a mythical "Merrie Englande"; there was even a maypole on the village green. The previous baron had spent much money improving the lot of his tenants, and his son was apparently following his example by keeping the cottages in a good state of repair. The vast quantities of dark thatch looked spruce and crisp; many of the little latticed windows were neat enough to be modern replacements; the pale golden stone, so typical of the Starbridge area, conveyed the impression that it had recently been scrubbed. The pub, which was called the Flaxton Arms, inevitably had roses growing around the door.

Flaxton Hall, a starkly symmetrical hulk, was set on a hillside facing away from the village towards the distant port of Starmouth. I noticed that the lawns, though not immaculately manicured, were still trim, while the house appeared as well-kept as the village cottages. The Labour Government would almost certainly be making life less comfortable for the Flaxtons, but it seemed this difficulty could still be shrugged off as a minor inconvenience.

I was just waiting for some pre-war relic of a butler to respond to my arrival, when the front door was opened by a child of about nine years old, a bony angular child with a cloud of frizzy dark hair which was held in place by a headband. Beneath her heavy dark brows her eyes were an unusual shade of greenish gold which I thought might make her attractive later. She was wearing a blue frock, possibly part of a school uniform. Her fingers hinted that she had recently had an accident with an ink-bottle.

"Good afternoon," she said grandly. "But you shouldn't have come to the front door. All chauffeurs have to go round the back to the servants' entrance."

"I'm not a chauffeur."

"Then why are you wearing gaiters?"

"I'm an archdeacon. May I come in, Miss Flaxton? I have an appointment with your father."

"How did you know who I was?"

"I made an inspired guess. Has school closed early today?"

"I never go to school. I don't believe in it."

"How sensible," I said, realising she was bending the truth in the hope of shocking me, and stepped past her into an oval-shaped hall. White marble statues gleamed in pale blue recesses; a blue and white frieze decorated the rim of the lofty ceiling far above the white marble floor. As I gazed at these austere examples of eighteenth-century classicism, I began to feel as if I had shrunk, like Alice in Wonderland, and was now trapped in an inverted Wedgwood bowl. The child's bold, somewhat bizarre manner only strengthened the resemblance to Carroll's fantasy.

"I've got a daughter of your age," I said, trying to inject a little normality into the scene in order to ease my nervousness. "What's your name?"

Without a second's hesitation the child said: "Vanilla."

It seemed we were still in Wonderland. Not to be outdone I immediately said: "How very charming and original. Congratulations!"

She smiled but looked suspicious. "You don't believe me, do you?"

"No, but never mind, I'm greatly entertained. You remind me of *Alice in Wonderland.*" Out of the corner of my eye I saw the butler belatedly gliding to my rescue.

"If I'm Alice," said the child, "who are you?"

"If you're Alice I think I'd like to be Lewis Carroll."

The butler, a large individual with an asthmatic wheeze and hands the colour of lard, assumed an appropriately deferential expression at the sight of my uniform. "Good afternoon, Mr. Archdeacon. Lord Flaxton is expecting you."

"What exactly is an archdeacon?" said the child to him abruptly.

"A very important clergyman, Miss Venetia."

"A *clergyman?* Oh, we don't have any of those here!" she exclaimed, and added severely to me: "We're all agnostics in this family. Papa eats clergymen on toast for breakfast."

"Grilled, fried or scrambled?"

She burst out laughing. The butler looked scandalised but recovered himself sufficiently to lead the way across the hall to an enormous pair of doors. In the niches nearby, muscular marble males toyed coyly with their fig-leaves.

Opening the doors, the butler announced grandly: "The Archdeacon of Starbridge, my lord," and feeling like a Christian entering the Roman amphitheatre to meet his very own hungry lion, I stepped forward across the threshold to meet my fate.

4

THE room was about sixty feet long and littered with an eclectic collection of furniture; eighteenth-century masterpieces of design stood cheek-by-jowl with overstuffed Victorian monstrosities. There were two magnificent fireplaces—more white marble—and a painted ceiling reminiscent of the dining-room of the Ritz where Dido and I had been invited to dine with Merry and her husband after our engagement had been announced.

At the far end of the room stood Lord Flaxton. As the doors closed quietly behind me he remained motionless and watched in silence as I embarked on my lengthy journey towards him.

It was a clever trick. I guessed he adopted it not merely to stress that he was the king of this particular castle but to gauge the staying-power of his callers. Exerting an iron will not to appear disconcerted, I ploughed steadily across a succession of vast carpets and only halted when I was six feet away from him. Then I looked him straight in the eyes and said in a firm polite voice from which all hint of nervous sycophancy had been ruthlessly excluded: "Good afternoon, Lord Flaxton. It's kind of you to receive me at such short notice. I sincerely hope I may be of help to you in resolving your parish difficulty."

Hooded dark eyes looked me up and down. A narrow mouth tightened for a second before relaxing into a subtle, charming smile. To my relief I realised I had made a favourable first impression.

"How do you do, Archdeacon." He offered me a muscular handshake intended, perhaps, to repel any notion that he might be one of the effete members of the aristocracy, but by that time I needed no extra hint to convince me I was dealing with a tough customer. He was of medium height, but because he was so slim and held himself like a soldier he seemed taller than he was. I judged him to be about ten years my senior. In typical aristocratic fashion he was wearing shabby country clothes and looked like a rather cunning poacher.

"I've heard about you from the Starmouths," he said. "I understand you were Bishop Jardine's protégé. Now, *there* was a great man! Bold, brilliant, blindingly honest—what a fighter for truth! We need more men like that in the Church today and maybe now Fisher's Archbishop of Canterbury we'll get them. Do you know Fisher?"

"No, but I hear—"

"A very sound fellow, sensible and down-to-earth, not like that lunatic Bell who regularly drives us all mad in the House of Lords with his idiotic idealistic drivel. And Fisher's fathered six sons—six! Anyone who can father six sons, wind up Archbishop of Canterbury and survive to tell the tale deserves a prize for indestructibility. How many sons have you fathered, Archdeacon?"

"Five."

"Splendid! That's what we need in the Church today—clergymen with balls. No limp handshakes, no idealistic bleatings, no damn Papist mumbo-jumbo—and I trust, Archdeacon, you're not a High Churchman who's sentimental about the Pope?"

"Certainly not, my lord."

"Quite right too. England for the English, that's what I say, and no kow-towing to a bunch of foreigners. Can't understand these people who are soft on Germans and Italians—although that doesn't mean I can't appreciate the masterpieces of German literature or the grandeur of ancient Rome. How amazed those early Christian martyrs would be if they came to life today and discovered an age in which the Roman Empire was just a collection of ancient monuments and Christ was worshipped by millions! *Sic transit gloria mundi.*"

"With respect, Lord Flaxton," I said, "I suggest the martyrs wouldn't be in the least amazed. They believed in the ultimate triumph of eternal truth over worldly values. *Veritas filia temporis est.*"

Flaxton gave a delighted smile. "So you're not a yes-man!" he said satisfied. "You've got the guts to stand up to a bigoted, bad-mannered agnostic who always likes to have his own way! Sit down, Archdeacon, and pray forgive me for keeping you standing while I put you through your paces. I have a feeling you and I are going to get on very well together."

5

"AS you probably know," said the Baron when we had arranged ourselves in the upholstered tubs which masqueraded as armchairs, "I own this village but I don't have the right to appoint the incumbent. Until now this hardly seemed to matter, since I take care never to set foot in a church unless my social obligations require me to attend christenings, weddings and funerals. However, although I'm not a religious man, I'm an exceedingly moral one. Let no man say," said Lord Flaxton, eyeing me sternly, "that I'm not exceedingly moral."

I assumed an interested expression but made no comment.

"In my opinion," pursued Lord Flaxton, "a parson in a parish such as this has an absolute moral duty to offer his flock comfort, reassurance and stability—and particularly now in this post-war world where so many of the pre-war certainties have been swept away. We live in a world of constant change, Archdeacon. As Heraclitus said—"

"Πάντα ῥεῖ, σὐδὲν μένει."

"Exactly. Can I conceivably be talking to a man who like myself attained a first in Greats?"

"You can, my lord. I'm a Balliol man."

"I knew it! It takes a Balliol man to have the nerve to steal my Greek quotations and wave them in my face . . . Where was I?"

"A parson should represent stability in a world of change—"

"Ah yes. Well, I'm sorry to say this particular parson has no interest in offering his flock—my tenants, for whom I'm morally responsible—any comfort in religion. He's been preaching heresy. And I don't just mean he's been cocking a snook at the Virgin Birth. I believe even bishops do that occasionally, and quite right too. No educated man could swallow such a fable."

"Faith isn't dependent on education, Lord Flaxton, although the intellect may well be expanded through faith. As St. Anselm said: *'Credo ut intelligam.'* "

"Those saints would say anything. Am I to understand you believe in the Virgin Birth, Archdeacon? What can Balliol be coming to!"

"My years at Balliol taught me to appreciate the finer points of scholarly criticism. For instance, the phrase 'Virgin Birth' can be capable of more than one interpretation. To the Jewish people two thousand years ago it might have meant no more than a first birth, a birth by a woman who'd never had a baby before. Alternatively a 'virgin' in this context may merely mean a young girl, and a sexual inference needn't be drawn at all. So with all due respect I submit to you that you're asking the wrong question. It should be not: 'How can you believe in the Virgin Birth?' but: 'What does the term "Virgin Birth" mean in this particular historical context?' "

"But once you start splitting hairs like that, where are you going to stop? The ordinary parishioner in the pew doesn't want split hairs! He wants certainty. He wants his parson to roar out from the pulpit: 'Jesus Christ was begotten by God on the Virgin Mary, a girl with no sexual experience!' "

"With the very greatest respect, Lord Flaxton, may I ask how you know what the ordinary parishioner wants if you never enter a church except for the rites of passage?"

"My God!" said Lord Flaxton. "That's cut me down to size!"

"I'm most extremely sorry if I've given offence—"

"You haven't. Just food for thought. Very well, we'll pass over the Virgin Birth—that's not actually relevant at present anyway; damned Mellors hasn't attacked the Virgin Birth. He's saying Christ was just one of many long-haired prophets who ranted on and on about the imminent end of the world—like those modern lunatics who jump up and down on soap-boxes at Speakers' Corner. He's saying Christ got it all wrong, the world didn't end and there was no resurrection. He's saying that the disciples conspired together to invent the resurrection in order to give their rebel movement a new lease of life."

"This sounds like a garbled version of Schweitzer's *The Quest of the Historical Jesus.* It's a powerful book but it was published many years ago and the general opinion now among scholars is that Schweitzer over-emphasised the eschatological side of Christ's preaching. In other words, Christ wasn't 'just another long-haired prophet' after all."

"But what about the resurrection?"

"The theory that the disciples got together and manufactured a fiction doesn't actually correspond with the evidence—which must include, of course, their transformed lives. Is Mellors disputing the empty tomb?"

"Disputing it? He's bloody well abolished it! His last sermon concluded with the words: 'So what does it really matter what happened two thousand years ago?'—at which point the congregation walked out and the churchwardens decided to seek my help. And quite right too! You can't have a clergyman saying it doesn't matter what happened two thousand years ago! That's not playing the game at all! The man must be instantly removed and defrocked!"

"Excuse me, Lord Flaxton, but I assume I'm right in thinking you've heard none of these sermons yourself? It's just possible that Mellors has been quoted out of context and misinterpreted."

"Now look here, Aysgarth. A good decent sensible clergyman who plays the game shouldn't lay himself open to misinterpretation. We've had trouble with that man before, you know. Took to drink after his wife died. In my opinion he should have been sacked then, but that old Bishop's as soft as butter; all he did was forgive him—and what sort of episcopal behaviour is that, I'd like to know?"

"I believe they call it Christian, my lord."

There was a moment of absolute silence. Then Flaxton gave a short bark of laughter and exclaimed: "Floored again! You're a formidable man, Archdeacon. Where do you come from?"

"Yorkshire."

"And what did your father do?"

"He ran a draper's shop."

"A draper's shop!" Flaxton was entranced. "You've come a long way, haven't you? And when did you first realise you were called to minister to the rich?"

"Minister to the—"

"No, don't pretend you don't know what I'm talking about! It's quite obvious that with your first-class education and iron nerves you're uniquely qualified to be a missionary to the upper classes. Why aren't you hammering on the pagan doors of Mayfair and Belgravia?"

"Well, I—"

"And don't you dare give me a sermon about how all clergymen are obliged to serve the bloody poor! My dear Aysgarth, never mind the unfortunate inhabitants of the East End slums—they'll always have a stream of masochists fighting to minister to them, but who ministers to the ghastly crowd of bone-idle, self-centred, hard-drinking adulterers who languish in the spiritual desert of the West End? Time-servers who know how to simper over a tea-cup! Yes-men who tell their pampered parishioners exactly what they want to hear! Fund-raisers who know how to ingratiate themselves with those who hold the purse-strings! It's enough to make a decent agnostic puke. The able men slip away into the bishoprics and deaneries, the saints get siphoned off into the slums, and we're left with the damned dregs! Now, if *you* were Vicar of St. Mary's

Mayfair . . . but of course you wouldn't want to be a mere vicar after your years as an archdeacon. Maybe a canonry at St. Paul's . . . or Westminster . . . I'll have a word with the Prime Minister. I get on well with Attlee even though I'm no socialist. He's an old Haileyburian. Civilised. Not like some of the horrors you find nowadays on the Government front bench . . . Now, where were we? Every time you trounce me in debate I go off at a tangent—"

"Mellors' drinking after his wife's death." I hardly knew what I was saying. The words "St. Paul's" and "Westminster" were still ringing in my ears, and for a moment, as I remembered Sydney Smith's famous reference to heaven, I felt as if I were eating pâté de foie gras to the sound of trumpets.

". . . and I wouldn't be surprised if he's taken to drink again," Lord Flaxton was saying. "Nor would I be surprised to hear that there was woman-trouble in the offing. If a clergyman's hitting the bottle and preaching heresy, can fornication be far behind?"

"Possibly not, although I believe hitting the bottle tends to depress the sexual appetite. But do we know for certain that he's hitting the bottle again?"

"To be strictly truthful, no, we don't. But like Hobbes I take a pessimistic view of mankind."

"I'm sorry to hear your agnosticism doesn't have a more uplifting effect on you, my lord. Very well, I'll call now at the vicarage and report to you in due course. I regret that you've been troubled, but on behalf of the Bishop I'd like to thank you for drawing the matter to his attention."

"Neatly put," said Lord Flaxton with a thin smile. "I particularly enjoyed the swipe at agnosticism."

"I—"

"No, don't start apologising again, Archdeacon, or I shall get cross. I invited you to stand up to me, didn't I? Have you forgotten that at the start of this conversation I expressed approval of clergymen who had balls?"

"I assure you, my lord, I've forgotten nothing that you've said." I paused, and as I did so I saw clearly that my next move could prove fatal. For a moment I hesitated, paralysed by my old familiar cowardice, but then I thought of George Bell rising to his feet time after time in the House of Lords to make the courageous speeches which would cost him Canterbury.

"Lord Flaxton," I said evenly at last, "you've been very kind and paid me far more compliments than I deserve, but I'm afraid that if you knew me better you wouldn't approve of me at all. You'd think me soft on Germans. I'm a supporter of Bishop Bell."

The hooded dark eyes widened. We stood there, both of us quite motionless in that vast room, and the silence was broken only by the ticking of clocks. Then Flaxton said: "Now I *know* you've got the guts to take on the rich. May I congratulate you, Archdeacon, on your outstanding integrity and moral courage? I'd like to see a man like you go all the way to the House of Lords."

6

DOWN the long room with me he walked, and across the oval hall to the front door. He was talking about the Church but I was in such a state of stupefaction that I was unable to concentrate on his words. It was only when he opened the front door that I found I could reconnect my ears with my brain.

". . . and the Church never seems to consider how its appointments look to those outside it," he was remarking. "I suppose the senior churchmen don't care, but the Church belongs to all of us, doesn't it, to anyone who can call himself an Englishman—it's our great legacy from the past, a legacy which should be cherished even by incorrigible agnostics, and personally, as a man who has the intelligence to see the vital importance of history, I consider it my moral duty to assist such a unique institution to survive and flourish. There should be more favour shown to self-made men and more emphasis on brains and guts. We want a return to Muscular Christianity—a return to the glorious days of the nineteenth century!"

I forebore to remind him of the raging controversies over Darwin, the internecine feuds between the Broad Church Liberals and the Evangelicals, and the violent disruption caused by the Oxford Movement. All I could say was a meek: "I congratulate you on your robust views, my lord." I was sounding like a sycophant. Without doubt it was time to go.

All the way down the steps of the porch he walked with me, and all the way across the forecourt to my car.

"Well," he said as I at last succeeded in taking my leave of him, "rest assured that I shall never see the Virgin Birth in quite the same light again! I wish you luck, Archdeacon—or as Virgil put it: *'Macte nova virtute, puer, sic itur ad astra'*!"

This meant something like: "Good luck, young chap—keep going and you'll scale the stars!" With a mighty effort my trusty memory produced the tag about Fortune favouring the brave. "And as Virgil also said," I responded valiantly, " *'Audentes Fortuna iuvat'* !"

Lord Flaxton gave another bark of laughter and stood back to allow me to collapse into my car. I was no longer capable of rational thought, but like a robot I switched on the engine, and like a robot I guided my machine away down the drive.

As far as I could gather, God and the Devil were now both busy fighting for the possession of my soul. Could a good Modernist, who shunned all mention of the Devil, seriously resort to such old-fashioned symbolism? Apparently. But perhaps I was more deranged than I realised.

Abandoning all hope of exercising the charism of discernment, I stopped wondering what on earth God wanted me to do and drove down to the village to confront the unfortunate clergyman who, like me, was quite obviously on the brink of a breakdown.

7

THE church in Flaxton Pauncefoot had a youthful look; I judged it to be no more than three hundred years old and I wondered what had happened to the medieval church which must have stood on the site. Inside by the alms-box I found a pamphlet which gave the explanation: Cromwell's soldiers, judging the church to be a peculiarly revolting example of idolatry, had been unable to resist the urge to commit arson. Having been brought up to regard Cromwell as a hero who had rescued England from the Papist influence of a foreign queen, I never failed to be shocked by evidence of his followers' hooliganism.

In the vestry I checked the cupboards for empty bottles but found only Communion wine. The key to the wine cupboard was placed trustfully on top of the door-frame but this was not unusual; many country parishes were still living in blissful ignorance of the post-war crime wave.

Leaving the church I crossed the graveyard to the large dilapidated house which sprawled beyond an uncut hedge. Weeds were thriving in the drive. The garden was a wilderness. Faded lettering on the broken gate proclaimed that this run-down dwelling was the vicarage. Walking up to the shabby front door, I tried ringing the bell but it was broken. I resorted to the knocker. No one came but the door was on the latch and creaked inwards. Warily I stepped into a dark dirty hall.

"Hullo?" I called. "Anyone at home?" And to my surprise a man's surly voice replied reluctantly from a room nearby: "Just a minute."

I heard the clink of a glass knocking some metal object and then the click of a closing cupboard door as the evidence of the afternoon drink was concealed. A moment later a man emerged into the hall. I judged him to be about my age. He had some hair like steel wool growing in a fringe around his bald pate, pale eyes behind thick spectacles, and a damp unhealthy look. His lips were moist, hinting that he had just licked them nervously. When he saw my uniform he was appalled.

"Good afternoon, sir," I said, very civil. "My name's Aysgarth. If you're not too busy, I'd like to have a word with you."

"Delighted, I'm sure," he said, looking wretched, and led the way into a dishevelled study where the dust lay over the furniture like a pall of brown frost. "Do sit down," he added, removing a pile of junk from a worn chair.

"Thanks." I waited till he too was seated before I said: "I'm here on behalf of the Archdeacon of Starmouth, who's engaged elsewhere at present."

"That's welcome news. I can't stand that man Babbington-French." With an unexpected flash of humour he added: "And now I suppose you'll say he's a personal friend."

"My acquaintance with Mr. Babbington-French is purely professional."

"Heavens, that's cagey! I can see you're one of the Church's diplomatists, effortlessly gliding up the ladder of preferment to the palace at the end of the rainbow. I've heard of you, of course. You've got a house in the Close and a society wife. Well, good luck to you, I say—good luck! I'm glad there's at least one clergyman of my age who's not buried alive in a rural tomb on a salary which would make a dustman laugh—and you can tell that to the Bishop. And talking of the Bishop, why am I being visited by his henchman? Has someone been complaining about the drink again?"

"No, but if you regularly throw sobriety to the winds at four o'clock in the afternoon, it can only be a matter of time before someone does."

"I never drink before a service. *Never.*"

"Congratulations. What do you do with the bottles?"

"Bury 'em in the garden. If you think I'm too far gone to keep up appearances, I assure you—"

"Where do you buy them?"

"Starmouth. You don't think I have a standing order at the local off-license, do you?"

"Whisky, is it? Gin?"

"At twenty-two-and-six a bottle? How could I afford it?"

"It's amazing how many tight-fisted bank managers become sentimental at the sight of an impoverished parson."

"Ah. Yes. Well, as a matter of fact—"

"Name of the bank?" I said, taking out my notebook.

"The Westminster at Flaxfield. But the loan's only a hundred pounds!"

"That's too much for someone in your circumstances. It'll have to be mopped up." I wrote down: "Debt: £100 (£200?) WB @ Flax." and added aloud neutrally: "Once a loan gets into three figures it's best if the diocese pays off the bank in order to avoid the risk of scandal; three-figure loans have a fatal habit of rapid expansion. Then once the bank's out of the way we work out how the incumbent can pay back the diocese and still live within his income. Have you been borrowing from church funds?"

"Are you accusing me of embezzlement?"

"No, I'd assume there was no criminal intent to defraud."

"Well, actually I do borrow the odd fiver from the organ fund every now and then, but I *always pay it back in the end*—"

"How much is currently outstanding?"

"Twelve pounds five-and-six."

"You're quite sure of that figure?"

"Are you accusing me of—"

"I'm not making accusations, I'm ascertaining facts. All right, let's get down to the fundamental cause of this situation; so far we've only been discussing symptoms. What do you see as your real problem, the problem that's driving you to drink, debt and despair? Bereavement? Loneliness? Intellectual isolation? The depressing atmosphere of this obsolete hulk of a house? Middle age? Women? Choirboys?"

"My God!" To my relief I realised his horror was genuine. No clergyman normally uses God's name as an expletive, least of all a clergyman in the midst of an awkward interview with an archdeacon.

"Lost your faith?" I persisted, determined to ram my advantage home while he was in shock.

However shock was now giving way to anger. "Lost my faith? Certainly not! And will you kindly stop bullying me this instant? I feel as if I'm being repeatedly hit over the head with a hammer!"

It was time to explain my technique and soften him up. "I'm sorry," I said sympathetically, "but I find that these very difficult interviews usually run more easily if all the unspeakable possibilities are dragged out into the open right at the beginning. Otherwise one can tiptoe tastefully around for hours—with the result that by the time the truth's exposed, the poor victim, who's probably already under strain, is only fit for a lunatic asylum. You may scoff but I honestly feel I'm being cruel only to be kind."

He plainly saw the logic of this argument; he looked first mollified and then relieved as it occurred to him his plight could be worse. At least there was no trouble with choirboys. "Well," he said, spurred to honesty by the desire to convince me that he wasn't such a bad fellow after all, "I suppose my main problem is that I'm bored."

I kept my face expressionless. "Could you elaborate on that statement, please?" I said politely while I asked myself how a bored believer could transform himself into a raging heretic. The true raging heretic is usually the product of passionate emotions, not of an impoverished middle-class ennui.

"I'm bored with being poor," said Mellors, "bored with having no wife and being unable to afford another, bored with all the bovine parishioners, bored with rural life, bored with knowing I've smashed up all hope of preferment by hitting the bottle after my wife died, bored with having no future, bored, *bored,* BORED. So you see, all I'm suffering from is sloth. Trust me to choose the most boring of the seven deadly sins. Boring of me, isn't it?"

"Speaking from a practical point of view, I'd rather you were indulging in sloth than in illicit sexual activity," I said good-humouredly, beavering away at the task of appearing friendly and sympathetic. "Sex is always so much harder to cover up. But let's put worldly considerations aside and spare a passing thought for God. I assume you're bored with Him too."

"Not in the least, although I'm sure He's very bored with me. I repeat: I haven't lost my faith. I still believe God exists, but the trouble is I seem to be in some sort of a—how can I put it—"

"Wasteland."

"—wasteland—thank you—which is so boring that He can't be bothered to enter it."

"Must make sermonising a bit tricky."

"Well, it did for a while," said Mellors as I fought a losing battle to preserve my detachment, "but then I found the cure. I had to go to Starbridge not long ago to see my dentist about a tooth which was making a nuisance of itself, and afterwards I visited the library of the Theological College. I suppose I felt guilty enough about my sloth to want to ginger up my sermons with a dash of current religious thought. Anyway, I was just browsing through an issue of *The Modern Churchman* when I discovered the most amazing article by Bishop Barnes of Birmingham."

"Ah! Light begins to dawn on the horizon!"

"Exactly what I thought. An end to boredom, courtesy of Bishop Barnes! But really, that man's a disgrace. If that's what Modernism is all about—"

"It's true Barnes is a trifle eccentric and often lays himself open to being misunderstood, but essentially he's a good man."

"Possibly, but all I can say is he makes me want to shout HERETIC! at every Modernist in sight. However at least he gave me the inspiration to do a bit of quick research into current Modernist thinking, and for the next three Sundays I sailed into the pulpit and lit a fire under all the bovine members of the congregation by preaching a lot of Modernist rot—you know the sort of thing: all a myth, no resurrection, no incarnation—"

"I hate to disillusion you, Mellors, particularly when you were obviously enjoying yourself for the first time in months, but that's not true Modernism. True Modernism holds fast to the divinity of Christ."

"What about the resurrection?"

"Modernists believe in that too, although of course they think the actual mode of the resurrection is open to—"

"But how can Modernists believe in the resurrection when they don't believe in miracles?"

"They don't class the resurrection as a straightforward old-fashioned miracle which is clearly either a fable or a metaphor. They see the resurrection as a unique event which can't be explained by our current knowledge of the laws of physics."

"But how can the Modernists possibly know for certain what's a fable, what's a metaphor and what's scientific ignorance? Personally I think the whole Modernist attitude shows the most revolting spiritual arrogance—this worship of science is nothing but a perverted form of idolatry! Science doesn't know all the answers! How can it? And if one believes in an utterly transcendent God—"

"Ah well," I said, having long since forgotten that I was supposed to be an archdeacon on the warpath, "if you make the mistake of seeing God as utterly transcendent, a remote force which shoots off the occasional impossibility whenever it chooses to do so, then of course you'll wind up by deciding He's above the laws of science and you'll be seeing miracles everywhere. But the Modernists prefer to think of God as immanent in the world, working through the laws of science and nature. They believe that if only one can dispose of this archaic and unhelpful model of the transcendent God, one can form a theology which is far more pertinent to the mid-twentieth century."

"What utter rubbish! If we've got to be alive in the middle of this abominable century, the last thing we need is an immanent God who's wallowing around in this disgusting pig-sty with us—we want a God up above the mess who can lean down and haul us out of it! It's *your* model of God which is unhelpful and archaic!"

"But it seems to me that people who harp on a transcendent God always end up by undervaluing the importance of Christ. If one keeps in mind that the Incarnation symbolises God's immanence among humanity—"

"Oh, I've no patience with this cosy, benign God whom you Liberals dress up in Christ's clothes and reduce to your own mundane human level! God's no soft-hearted Liberal! He's harsh, firm—even brutal if necessary—"

"But if God is love—"

"Sometimes love requires harshness and firmness—and yes, even brutality too. What use is a parent who doesn't care enough to discipline a child who goes wrong? Of course the Modernists say no one ever goes wrong, they deny the existence of sin, but in my opinion—"

"They don't deny the existence of sin, Mellors! They simply say we should consider wrong-doing in the light of modern psychology and sociology—"

"They can consider evil in whatever light they please, but they'll never alter the basic fact that we're all sinners—and we're all under judgement! We all need to be redeemed, and contrary to what you Modernists think, redemption isn't to be had by sidling up to God with a winsome smile and lisping: 'Excuse me, Lord, I think I'll repent now—can I have my ration of sweetness and light, please?' The road to redemption is decked in blood, sweat and tears, not in moonlight, red roses and a bunch of angels twanging harps!"

"My dear Mellors," I said, "why aren't you preaching this stuff in the pulpit instead of flagellating your congregation with pseudo-Modernist claptrap? There's nothing wrong with a fashionable neo-orthodoxy!"

Mellors said flatly: "I was bored." Then he said: "My own struggle for redemption's been too difficult. One day I woke up and found I'd run out of strength." And finally he whispered: "I've ruined myself. I had such high hopes and now they're all dead. I've no hope left any more."

"You say that because you're standing in your wasteland, but—"

"What do *you* know about my wasteland?" shouted Mellors in a paroxysm of rage and despair. "What do *you* know about grinding poverty and drinking too much and feeling utterly cut off from God?"

"More than you think." I stood up abruptly. "I'll talk to the Bishop and try to ease this situation as soon as possible."

"You mean you'll recommend that I should be kicked out of the Church!" He was trying to sustain his anger but his voice broke. Taking off his spectacles he began to polish them furiously with a filthy handkerchief.

I sat down again. "Mellors," I said, "you completely misunderstand the nature of my mission. My task is to enter your wasteland and work out how you can best be cut down from your cross, not to crucify you all over again."

There was a silence, and when I realised he was incapable of replying I added: "My first recommendation to the Bishop will be that you should have a holiday. You've been worn out by all your unhappiness. Then I shall recommend that you have regular talks with a sympathetic older clergyman who's good at sorting out clerical problems. And finally I shall recommend that after you've had sufficient rest and help, you should resume your work—though whether here or elsewhere in the diocese is a question which only the Bishop can decide."

His pathetic attempt to maintain a stiff upper lip failed. I sighed, reminded of the more harrowing aspects of my work among the Germans. I never knew what to do when men wept. It was all so deeply embarrassing and reminded me what a ham-fisted pastor I was. Yet my Germans had written—and Dr. Bell had said—

"Sorry," said the wretched Mellors, mopping himself up with his filthy handkerchief.

"That's all right. I've shed a tear or two myself recently, as a matter of fact. Sort of thing that could happen to anyone."

To my surprise Mellors seemed to find this idiotic remark comforting. As he accompanied me to the front door he even said: "I'm glad it was you who came and not that pompous prig Babbington-French."

Not for the first time I wondered how Dr. Ottershaw and I were going to appease Babbington-French after my pastoral sortie into his archdeaconry. Babbington-French was jealous of me and resented my influence over the Bishop. I foresaw trouble ahead, and suddenly for the first time in my career as an archdeacon I experienced a powerful urge to plunge into fresh woods and pastures new.

Having shaken hands with Mellors I remembered to give him my telephone number in case his frail new hope lapsed into a suicidal despair which required a prompt verbal antidote. Then with my mind beginning to seethe with chaotic thoughts about the future, I embarked on my journey to Starbridge.

8

WHEN I arrived back at the palace the chaplain greeted me with the news that Dr. Ottershaw was in a dither; Darrow had finally deigned to reveal his plans for the extension of the Theological College.

"This is my fault," I said. "Amidst all my domestic troubles I quite forgot to warn the Bishop that Darrow was planning to go on the rampage again."

"It's noble of you to take the blame, Archdeacon, but you can hardly be held responsible for Darrow waltzing in, cool as a cucumber, and demanding thousands of pounds in the name of the Holy Spirit. Honestly!" said Hampton scandalised. "You'd think, wouldn't you, that a famous spiritual director would know better than to behave like a gangster extorting money at gunpoint—oh, and talking of high-handed gangsters, how was Lord Flaxton?"

"Breathing fire but I managed to apply water."

"And the heretic?"

"He's no heretic. He's just been having fun and games with Modernism." Abandoning Hampton in the hall I entered Dr. Ottershaw's study and found him poring over one of the large blue diocesan finance files. There was a worried expression on his face and an untouched cup of tea at his elbow. "My dear Bishop," I said firmly, recognising my duty to cut him free from this worldly thicket into which he had been so brutally dumped, "if you're trying to work out how to pay for Darrow's pipe-dream, stop worrying this instant. All calculations can be left to the Board of Finance. It's quite unnecessary for you to bother yourself with complex arithmetic when you have better things to do."

"Well, I don't know that I do have better things to do," said the Bishop harassed. "What can be more vital than to solve the problem of how we can temporarily expand the Theological College with the minimum of expense? And I really do feel that we can't ignore the call of the Holy Spirit in these circumstances—"

"Darrow's not the Holy Spirit. He's Darrow."

"Yes, but it's an inspired idea, isn't it? It would mean free premises in beautiful and appropriate surroundings for just so long as this huge influx of ordinands lasts—"

"I agree it's a bold scheme, but it'll still cost a lot of money and it might well be more practical to lease premises here in the city. An extension in Starrington would cause administrative problems. Darrow won't like sharing the power."

"But Darrow says—"

"I know exactly what Darrow says! He thinks he can play the miracle-man and be in two places at once, even though they're twelve miles apart, but that's nonsense and you must tell him so."

"Dear me," said the poor Bishop, looking more harassed than ever at the prospect of having to be firm with Darrow, "how worrying it all is!"

"Not at all—the situation's really very simple. Leave the necessary inquiries to me. Then when I present the relevant facts together with my recommendations, all you'll have to do is pray for guidance and make up your mind."

The Bishop was just brightening at the thought of prayer when the chaplain looked in. "Excuse me, Bishop, but I've got Lord Flaxton on the phone demanding to know what the Archdeacon thought of Mellors."

The Bishop groaned.

"I'm not back yet," I said to Hampton, "and the Bishop's attending a meeting."

Hampton gave a mock salute and vanished.

"What with Darrow on the one hand," said the Bishop, "and Lord Flaxton on the other, I'm beginning to wish I were an obscure country curate. Neville, what on earth happened at Flaxton Pauncefoot?"

I delivered a succinct account of Mellors' plight.

"Poor fellow!" sighed Dr. Ottershaw predictably when I had finished. "Poor, *poor* fellow! It would seem, wouldn't it, that he hasn't recovered properly from his wife's death two years ago . . . Can we risk Allington Court or should we play safe and send him to the Fordites?"

"I think his most urgent need is to have a complete rest in comfortable surroundings—which means Allington Court, with the Warden tipped off about the need for counselling. I agree it's a risk because of the drink, but I think it's a risk worth taking. After all, he's not a genuine heretic—the sermons were just his way of signalling that he was in acute distress."

"I'll ring the Warden tomorrow," said the Bishop, making a note on his calendar, "and I'll ring poor Mellors tonight and find out when he can come to see me. But Neville, what do I say to Flaxton when he starts fulminating again that Mellors should be defrocked?"

"All Flaxton's concerned about is that his tenants should be protected from heresy. If you transfer Mellors—and I really think that for Mellors' sake a fresh start is essential—then I'm sure Flaxton will stop bawling about defrocking. The real problem here, as I see it, isn't Flaxton but Hubert Babbington-French."

The Bishop winced. "I'd already thought of that. I'm afraid there'll be a terrible tantrum."

"There's only one line to take, Bishop, and that's to put the blame squarely on Flaxton: Tell Babbington-French that Flaxton demanded my presence and that because the situation was potentially scandalous you judged it essential—not merely politic but *essential*—that Flaxton should be humoured."

"But supposing Hubert wants to know why I didn't at least consult him?"

"Then you put the blame squarely on me. I advised you that there was no time to waste and I insisted on rushing immediately to Flaxton Pauncefoot."

"But surely I have a moral duty to take some of the responsibility for the decision!"

"No, Bishop. If you fall out with Babbington-French the worry's bound to affect your work, and that would be bad for the diocese. Your absolute moral duty here is to appear entirely innocent."

"And what do I say, in my innocence, when he demands to take over the case?"

"There'll be no case to take over. As soon as the arrangement's been made with Allington Court you can present the rescue operation as a *fait accompli,* announce that Mellors is being transferred to my archdeaconry and declare that all Babbington-French has to do is make arrangements for the essential services in Flaxton Pauncefoot until you can appoint a new man. Game, set and match to the Bishop."

Dr. Ottershaw's sense of humour finally came to his rescue. "One of the reasons I was so delighted to receive my call to enter the Church," he said, "was because I thought I'd escape the cut-and-thrust battles—not to mention the sheer Machiavellian skulduggery—of the more worldly professions. Those were the days, of course, when I was truly innocent." And when I smiled at him he said impulsively: "Whatever would I do without you, Neville? I have a feeling I may not be allowed to keep you much longer—and as I said this morning I'd never stand in your way—but I can't help wishing selfishly that you'll stay until my retirement next year."

The chaplain peeped in again before I could attempt a reply. "The Rector of Upper Starwood's just phoned to ask what the official policy is on curates who join the Communist Party. What shall I say?"

Dr. Ottershaw groaned again.

"Cheer up, Bishop," I said. "It's not so difficult. If Canterbury can have a red dean, why shouldn't Upper Starwood have a red curate?"

Hampton laughed, and I was relieved to see that Dr. Ottershaw stopped looking so harassed. Taking my leave of them both I abandoned the palace and drove away once more into the Close. It was time to seek help from Darrow.

9

I STOPPED at the Theological College, but when I discovered the lateness of the hour I was hardly surprised to be told that Darrow had gone home.

Nevertheless I was sufficiently disturbed by his absence to wish I had never left the message telling him not to wait for me. This craving to see Darrow was so unprecedented that I found myself pausing to marvel at it, and the moment I paused I found myself engulfed in a terrifying silence. For forty-eight hours, ever since I had left Starrington Manor on my journey to Aidan, I had been running around southern England in a whirlwind of activity. But now I was becalmed. Even my work for the day, that splendid diversion from my troubles, had ceased. I was face to face once more with my appalling problems, and I knew very well I was too debilitated to face them alone.

Arriving home I reluctantly opened the front door and was at once waylaid by Merry in the hall. "Stephen, you've got to go back to that hospital tonight, you've simply got to! Dido's in the most awful state—she's saying you don't love her any more, and to be quite frank I'm not surprised! How you can be so insensitive absolutely beats me—haven't you *any* idea of the extent of her suffering?"

My endurance finally snapped. My iron self-control exploded into fragments. My clerical mask was blasted apart by the force of my rage. "*Her* suffering?" I shouted. "Yes, all she can think about is herself, but what about me? What about *my* suffering? And what about that poor dead baby which she rejected as brutally as if it was mere rubbish fit for an incinerator? I buried that child this morning. I buried *her son.* Yet did she so much as ask about the funeral when I visited her today? No, she did not! It was all 'I—I—I—' as usual, but you can tell her from me that I think it's time she grew up and started thinking of other people instead of whining on and on and on about herself like some revolting spoilt child!"

I blazed into my study, slammed the door, wrenched the key around in the lock, shoved aside the Oxford Dictionary and reached for the whisky bottle—which was empty. I had forgotten I had finished the dregs to do myself a favour. Muttering an expletive which was an obscenity but not a blasphemy, I cuffed the dictionary back into place and headed for the sherry decanter in the dining-room, but the moment I left my study Merry waylaid me again in the hall.

"Honestly, I do think men are absolutely the frozen limit, I really do! Just because you have ten minutes' pleasure thirty-nine weeks ago, Dido has to go through months of hell and nearly dies giving birth to your child—and what do you do to make amends? Damn all! You pop in and see her for a couple of minutes when you've nothing better to do, and then you have the infernal nerve to complain about the funeral! I'd have thought that in the circumstances the least you could do was organise the funeral without bothering her with all the gruesome details, and in my opinion it's absolutely disgraceful that a clergyman of the Church of England should treat his poor sick wife with such an utterly *brutal* lack of feeling! In fact if you ask me—"

I drew back my arm to hit her. I actually swung back my arm and raised my hand. Her eyes widened. I heard her gasp of fear, and as the adrenaline blazed through me with a ferocious force I was overwhelmed by the vile black ecstasy of violence. But a second later from the top of the stairs Primrose called: "Daddy!" and the force died. Turning my back on Merry I wordlessly held out my arms to my daughter as she scampered down the stairs.

"Daddy, where have you been all afternoon?"

I had to hug her for ten silent seconds before I was capable of saying: "I went to a village called Flaxton Pauncefoot and met a little girl called Vanilla."

"Like the ice-cream?"

"Yes, but in fact her name turned out to be Venetia . . ." While I talked I was moving into the dining-room, escaping from Merry, extracting a glass from the sideboard, reaching blindly for the decanter.

"Daddy, your hand's shaking."

"So it is." I filled the tumbler to the brim. "Now I shan't be able to drink the sherry without spilling it."

"You could pretend you were a cat and try lapping."

"True." I stood looking at the sherry. I was trying to beat back my horror as I remembered that sinister surge of adrenaline. Of course I had to pretend it had never happened, I could see that clearly. Good clergymen never suffered from sinister surges of adrenaline, just as good Modernists never spoke of the Devil.

Aidan said in my memory: "It's a question of facing the pain."

I thought of my idealised world where sinners were just victims of circumstances who made little slips and guilt was a mere unprofitable reflex of the psyche. No need, of course, for a Liberal Protestant Modernist to soil his hands with the blood, sweat and tears which lay in wait for him on the neo-orthodox road to redemption. In his dream world everyone had a painless access to the forgiveness and compassion of Christ; everyone travelled a moonlit, rose-scented road which, as Mellors had put it with such crushing contempt, was perpetually flanked by a bunch of angels twanging harps.

I thought of Merry again, and as I thought of her I knew that I could not, either now or in the future, pretend the incident had never happened. That type of self-deception had been shattered for all time by the events of the past twenty-four hours. I had to use my Liberal Protestant idealism as a sword to slice away the lies, not as a shield to protect myself from the truths I was too terrified to face. There could be no more hiding among the red roses and the twanging harps as I distorted my faith to escape into a dream world. That road to repentance, that facile travesty of a highway, was no road to repentance at all.

"It's a question of facing the pain," said Aidan again. His voice rang out so clearly in my memory that for a second I thought he was standing beside me in the room. I even looked around, for fear I might be hallucinating, and as I did so I saw the window. It was open. Picking up the glass I carried it to the sill and flung the sherry into the garden.

"Gosh!" said Primrose. "Why did you do that?"

"Fancied it. Give the roses a boost." I tried to collect my fragmented thoughts. I knew I was on the brink again. Facing Merry for dinner was obviously impossible. Somehow I had to get myself to Starrington Magna and grab Darrow, the lifeline, before my triple personality finally disintegrated.

"Darling," I said to Primrose, "I've got to go and see Mr. Darrow, but I don't remember eating since breakfast, so I think it might be a good idea to have a snack before I leave. Can you please raid the larder for me?" I felt I dared not leave the dining-room in case Merry waylaid me a third time in the hall.

Primrose made a successful foraging expedition and returned with two slabs of bread liberally endowed with Marmite, an apple, four water-biscuits and a glass of orange squash. "But don't give the orangeade to the roses," she said, "because if you don't want it I'll have it."

We shared the squash. We also shared the picnic; although I wanted to eat in order to ward off the risk of suffering a dizzy spell at the wheel, I could manage no more than a few mouthfuls of bread. Finally after kissing Primrose, I scuttled through the empty hall, plunged outside into the cool still air of early evening and began, like a shipwrecked mariner, to swim for my life towards the shore.

XVI

"The issue presents itself as a choice between alternate lines of conduct. It is our business to wrestle with it, giving full weight, if we can, to the emotional, intellectual and moral arguments for and against each possible course, and striving to see the whole dispassionately."

CHARLES E. RAVEN
THE CREATOR SPIRIT

I

HALFWAY to Starrington I had to stop the car. I felt dizzy, just as I had anticipated, although whether this condition was caused by lack of food or by exhaustion I could not decide; having bounded around so busily for so long, perhaps it was inevitable that I should have run out of energy. I sat shivering behind the steering wheel and occasionally wiping the sweat from my forehead. By that time I would have given my eye-teeth for a triple whisky—or even better, a triple brandy. Could I stop at a pub? No, I was still wearing my archidiaconal uniform. I could only struggle on to Starrington—where Darrow would have measured the levels in the decanters. But at least there would be decanters. I pictured them longingly but still I remained shivering behind the wheel.

After a while I began to wonder if I had reached the moment of complete breakdown. My emotions seemed to be paralysed. I thought I must inevitably be terrified but I felt only a numbed tranquillity and I was reminded of Arctic explorers who died of hypothermia; there came a point, near death, when they no longer noticed the cold.

I tried to pull myself together. Was I or was I not a clergyman? This was surely the moment to attempt a quick prayer, but the only word that entered my consciousness was: HELP. How feeble! But even one word was better than nothing. Squeezing my eyes shut, I yelled HELP! at the top of my mental voice, but of course nothing changed. Opening my eyes I found that the cow in the nearby field was still chewing placidly on its cud. But on the other hand, what else had I expected? Surely not a phalanx of angels descending from the sky with a stretcher! Wiping the sweat from my forehead again I gazed at the cow and wondered what to do next.

After a while it occurred to me that my prayer had hardly been very reverent and that it had been the height of impudence to assume God would pay it any attention. I had to phrase a humble request for aid, but suddenly all I could think of was Aidan talking about prayer, Aidan telling me to remember Luther, Aidan easing the burden of my guilt and giving me the courage to fight on, and when, automatically reliving the memory of the most crucial point of our meeting, I stretched out my hand, I seemed to feel again the clasp of his fingers as he stepped into the wasteland beside me. The memory lit up my consciousness. Once more I sensed Christ moving through the closed door of the room to be at one with his disciples, and as Aidan's fingers closed on mine I was finally able to summon the strength to drive on down the lonely road to Starrington.

2

BEFORE I had even halted the car in the drive Darrow was opening the front door of the Manor and hurrying down the steps to meet me.

"Hullo," I said, hauling myself nonchalantly out of the driving-seat. "Sorry to drop in on you without warning like this. Should have phoned but I left home in rather a hurry."

"Are you all right?"

"Absolutely fine. A little tired, but . . . absolutely fine. Not drunk. Gave the sherry to the rose-bush. Probably grow into a tree. Sorry, not making much sense, feel a trifle disconnected . . ." I had to lean for support against the car.

"I was afraid you'd had an accident," said Darrow. "I phoned your house just after you'd left so I knew you were on your way, and when you didn't turn up—"

"Ran out of steam." I managed to abandon the car and take a few unsteady steps across the gravel. "But it didn't matter, not in the end, because I created some more steam *ex nihilo,* as Lord Flaxton would say. I did ask God for some extra steam, just a little puff or two, but I didn't ask properly and He didn't hear so I had to do it myself. But that's all right, doesn't matter, God helps those who help themselves—"

"I can't tell you how glad I am to see you," said Darrow, paying scant attention to my idiotic drivel in the vastness of his relief. "I was seriously worried. I kept praying you'd remember Aidan."

I slumped instantly against the first object I could find. It was the frame of the front door. When I could speak I said: "Could you repeat that last sentence, please?"

He repeated it and added: "Whenever I was exhausted at Ruydale, the memory of Aidan's kindness would always give me the strength to go on."

"Well, I'll be . . . Sorry. Extraordinary coincidence. Temporarily dumbfounded." I sagged a little harder against the door-frame.

Darrow, who seemed taller than ever, gently steered me across the threshold into the hall. I felt a little worried that he should be so quiet and earnest and concerned. Patients become nervous when confronted by such a sinister gravity; they begin to hanker for their healthier days, when their doctors bounced around being arrogant nuisances.

"You present me with an interesting problem, Aysgarth," Darrow was saying. "I'm very unwilling to offer you a drink but nevertheless I'm tempted to prescribe a stiff brandy."

"Yes, please. Just one. Very nice." I looked for something new to lean on and found the bannister. "No more moonlight," I said, "no more roses. No more angels twanging harps. But a little drop of brandy wouldn't go amiss at all."

Before Darrow could comment, a door opened nearby and his wife, Anne, who had always been so kind to Grace, bustled into the hall. She was a statuesque brunette of thirty-eight, with a determined jaw and the bossy air of a successful business-woman. Although reputed to run the Manor's estate with a most lucrative efficiency, she was clever enough to play down this masculine skill and cultivate a somewhat eccentric femininity. She wore plain, well-cut clothes, so plain and well-cut that they probably cost a fortune, and avoided heavy make-up in order to show off her excellent skin. At dinner-parties she was notorious for wearing at least one of her large collection of diamond trinkets; the juxtaposition of the lavish stones and the lush skin was curiously alluring. Naturally I had often wondered, just as one inevitably does when one considers one's female acquaintances, what she was like in bed, and I had long since formed the suspicion that she was probably very hot stuff indeed. After all, Darrow would hardly have bothered with a woman who was frigid. Having spent seventeen years in a monastery, he would have been certain to prefer a rocket to a damp squib.

"Neville!" she was exclaiming as she crossed the hall towards us. "Thank goodness you've arrived!" She turned to her husband. "So much for your premonitions, darling! Here he is, safe and sound, and looking remarkably well, considering all the ghastliness he's been through! Neville, I was so sorry to hear . . ." And she embarked on a few brisk but well-chosen words of sympathy about the baby.

I suddenly realised that she was wearing not only a diamond necklace but diamond earrings, and as the knowledge dawned on me that I was interrupting a dinner-party I became aware of the murmur of conversation beyond the open dining-room door.

". . . and anyway, it's lovely to see you!" Anne was saying warmly. "Come and have a drink. We've finished eating and the men are about to start on the port."

In confusion I said: "I'm sorry, I had no idea I was interrupting a dinner-party."

"Oh, I thought you knew! Charles said he met you yesterday. He and Lyle are staying with us for a few days before going off on holiday to Devon."

Before I could even gasp with horror Darrow said smoothly: "Aysgarth and I have business to discuss. We'll give the port a miss and go straight to the library."

"Oh no!" I said at once, driven by all manner of complex feelings. "Of course I must say hullo to the Ashworths—what on earth would they think if I didn't?"

"Aysgarth—" began Darrow, but I refused to let him finish.

"A glass of port would be delightful!" I said firmly to Anne. "Just what I need to cheer me up after a long hard day!" And turning my back on Darrow, who was shaking his head in a paroxysm of disapproval, I rushed forward, eager as a lemming, to the disaster which lay waiting ahead.

3

THE first person I saw as I entered the room was Lyle. She was wearing her hair longer; it cascaded around her shoulders in a series of subtle waves. Her sleek black dress was unadorned by jewellery so that she appeared to be saying silently to Anne: "You can dress yourself up like a Christmas tree, but I don't have to." As our glances met she gave me the kind of look one would normally reserve for dead cod on a fishmonger's slab.

"Good evening, Mrs. Ashworth," I said.

"Good evening, Archdeacon." Not even Garbo could have sounded more ravishingly aloof.

"Hullo, Aysgarth," her husband was saying casually as my feet carried me forward to the nearest chair. "I thought it wouldn't be long before we met again."

"Congratulations on your gift of prophecy!" As I sank down in a chair on his side of the table, I was aware that he had made no move to offer me his hand, but then why should he? After a good dinner he was probably feeling too relaxed to bother with the formalities.

"We were sorry to hear of your loss," said Lyle, immaculately polite. "We do hope your wife's now on the road to recovery."

"She is, yes. Thank you." Having mentally flailed around for another topic of conversation, I found myself saying rapidly to the man beside me: "How are your boys?"

"How nice of you to ask!" To my relief Ashworth was suddenly all charm. I was reminded of my first meeting with him long ago in 1940 when he had effortlessly exuded his privileged southern background, his public school education and his ecclesiastical success. I could still remember my instinctive pang of envy and resentment. I had had to fight hard for my success; Ashworth would merely have glided up the ladder. He was one of those people who quite obviously have no family problems, no career difficulties and certainly no personal crises. No matter how arduous his experience as a POW he would slough it off without difficulty and slide elegantly back into his role of the charming academic theologian marked out long since for high preferment. I could well imagine him being offered a bishopric before he turned fifty.

"Charley goes to prep school this autumn," he was saying in response to my enquiry, "and Michael's still at kindergarten."

"They must have grown since I last saw them." It was a banal comment but I could think of no other. I was too busy trying to avoid looking at Lyle.

"When in fact did you last see them?" said Ashworth with interest.

"Well . . ." I suddenly realised I was again on the brink of mentioning Alex.

"I don't remember when he last saw Michael," said Lyle, "but he saw Charley at the Jardines' house a few days before the funeral."

"Ah yes," said Ashworth, once again producing his most charming smile, and added to me: "My wife's now told me exactly what happened at that funeral."

I felt as if I had fallen off a cliff. No lemming could have experienced a longer drop.

"That must have been such a harrowing experience, Lyle!" Anne was exclaiming sympathetically. "Both the Jardines were so devoted to you, weren't they?"

"They were like parents. I suppose that's why I found it difficult to talk of the funeral afterwards, even to Charles."

"Well!" said Darrow, suddenly deciding to intervene. Having closed the door he now opened it again as a signal to the ladies. "Anne?"

"Yes, of course." She turned to Lyle. "Let's leave the men to their port and Church gossip. Coffee in the drawing-room in quarter of an hour, Jon, and no interminable ramblings tonight, please, about Reinhold Niebuhr, D. R. Davies, 'Uncle Tom Cobley and All.' "

"Very well, darling," said Darrow meekly. Anne was the only person on earth who could boss Darrow around and meet with no resistance. Usually I found this a fascinating spectacle, but at that moment I was in such a state of shock that I barely noticed it. I was acutely aware of Lyle ignoring me as she left the room.

"Help yourself to port, Charles," Darrow said, closing the door and moving to the sideboard. "Aysgarth, I think you'd prefer a brandy."

"I wouldn't mind a brandy myself," said Ashworth, effortlessly debonair.

By this time I was trying to crawl back up the cliff by telling myself it was inconceivable that Lyle had embarked on anything so insane as a full confession. I decided to risk a cautious probe. "Look, I'm sorry," I said to Ashworth. "I had no intention of bringing up the subject of the Jardines a second time when I know you can only find them an awkward topic of conversation. Before he died Alex told me all about the difficulties in 1937 when—"

"Oh, 1937's gone with the wind," said Ashworth carelessly. "None of that matters any more now."

"It doesn't? That would have pleased Alex! He came to regret the rift very much," I said, sure now that Lyle had kept our secret. It seemed plain that although she had been reticent about the funeral because of the old awkwardness with the Jardines, Ashworth, fresh from experiencing far greater horrors, had finally been able to write off the Jardines' pre-war hostilities as unimportant. "Alex actually told me how glad he was that it was you she married," I said, relaxing at last. "He liked you."

"Decent of him," said Ashworth dryly, but added good-naturedly enough: "*Requiescat in pace!* In his own eccentric way he was without doubt a most remarkable man . . . Jon, where's that brandy?"

"Charles, are you sure you wouldn't prefer port?"

"Very sure. Aysgarth and I are going to get drunk on brandy together, aren't we, Aysgarth?"

I found this suggestion a trifle surprising but assumed it was a joke. As Darrow put our drinks on the table before us I protested lightly: "Good clergymen don't get drunk!" but at once Ashworth exclaimed with a chilling irony: "Oh no, I forgot! Good clergymen don't get drunk—and good clergymen don't commit adultery either, do they?"

I fell over my second cliff. Downing my brandy in a single gulp, I headed to the sideboard for a refill.

"Aysgarth," said Darrow at once, "I really think we'd better retire to the library to discuss the Theological College."

"Oh, no hurry!" I said. "Why are you shifting from one foot to the other like a cat on hot bricks? We haven't had our Church gossip yet!" I reached for the decanter but Darrow grabbed it first.

"Well, as you're both drinking brandy," he said, "maybe I'll join you." And having poured himself a couple of drops into a liqueur glass barely larger than a thimble, he incarcerated the decanter in the cupboard.

In fury I turned my back on him. "What's the Church gossip up in Cambridge?" I said boldly to Ashworth as the brandy rapidly built up a Dutch courage. I noticed that the port decanter was still standing on the table. "How goes it at Cambridge Cathedral? Has your Bishop finally decided whether Ezra came before or after Nehemiah?"

"No idea. I'm having trouble settling down again in Cambridge—not that I'd expect you to understand that. You wouldn't know anything about POWs and their problems."

"That's just where you're wrong. I've been ministering to the German POWs on Starbury Plain." I was now determined to keep up appearances by pretending nothing was wrong. No one was going to catch *me* running away from a privileged southerner who oozed the ethos of a leading public school from every pore.

"German POWs?" said Ashworth amused. "And how does that flabby Liberal theology of yours go down with the Nazis?"

Darrow said quietly: "Charles," but Ashworth, ignoring him, followed my example and knocked back his brandy in a single gulp.

"What's so flabby about the Christian doctrine of hope?" I said truculently. "It was hope which kept us all alive as we endured Europe's darkest hour!"

"May I suggest to you that only a man who endured Europe's darkest hour tucked up in the Starbridge time-warp could preserve his nineteenth-century theology in such a peculiarly facile form?"

"Charles, that's offensive," said Darrow, never raising his voice but speaking with great firmness. "I'm afraid I can't let any guest of mine be subjected to that kind of remark."

"It's all right," I said, refilling my glass from the port decanter. "Ashworth's got a point. He's been through hell while I've been in the war-time equivalent of heaven. Where he's wrong is to assume that it's this fact alone which has allowed me to maintain an optimistic theology. Of course it's fashionable now to be pessimistic—and why not, after the concentration camps and Hiroshima?—but a valid theology should be beyond mere fashion, and in my opinion Liberal Protestantism at its best is—"

"You gloss over the horror of evil," said Ashworth. "Your theology, in 1946, is meaningless."

"The best Liberal theology doesn't gloss over anything! Obviously evil constitutes a problem but—"

"A *problem?* Did you say a *problem?*" Ashworth leant forward, swiped the port decanter and refilled his own glass with an unsteady hand. That was the moment when I realised that contrary to my expectations he too was standing in the wasteland, a very different wasteland from mine but one which still required Darrow's presence at the foot of the cross. "Millions of people have been tortured, starved and done to death in the most disgusting ways, whole cities have been incinerated, whole nations have been brutalised, and you write off all that as a *problem?*"

"You wholly misunderstand," I said as Darrow silently removed the port decanter. "I'm not denying the war was vile—"

"Why don't you use the word 'evil'?"

"Well, all right, if you insist—"

"I do insist! You can't face the reality of evil, can you? You Liberal Protestants never can!"

"That's grossly unfair!"

"Is it? Then how would you describe the nice ordinary family men, just like you and me, who spent their days conducting medical experiments on children? Do you call them evil? Oh no! You call them a problem, and at once the evil's obscenely reduced to an inconvenience!"

"Well, of course, the obvious truth is that these evil villains *weren't* nice ordinary family men just like you and me—"

"They were human beings. They were like us. And we could have been like them—"

"What absolute rubbish!"

"No, it isn't! Pontius Pilate was probably a nice ordinary family man. The people who nailed Christ to the cross were probably nice ordinary family men. I tell you, the capacity to commit evil is in every single one of us, and unless you face up to that fact—"

"The fact you should face up to, Ashworth, before you drown in your neo-orthodox sea of doom and gloom, is that every man has the spark of the Holy Spirit in him, and against Christ all evil is powerless!"

"Then how do you explain the situations where Christ is absent and evil rules the roost?"

"He's never absent. I agree that sometimes he appears to be absent, but—"

"I've been in situations where he *was* absent—absolutely, utterly and completely absent!"

"He couldn't have been absent if you, a man of God, were there. The fact that you thought he was absent was your nightmare, your cross, but it was a delusion. He's there in every private crucifixion because he's a crucified God. Why, the very fact of the Incarnation means—"

"Oh my God!" shouted Ashworth, suddenly slamming his fist on the table and leaping to his feet. "How can you be so blind! Can't you see? *We must face the evil in order to be redeemed!* We don't need a theology of the Incarnation, not now, not in 1946, not after all those years of global hell! We need a theology of redemption! We've got to repent in shame and live, not fester in guiltless optimism and die!" And seizing his empty glass, he smashed it in the fireplace before blundering blindly from the room.

4

DARROW said at once: "Forgive him. He's nowhere near recovered yet from his experiences." He was moving to the door as he spoke, but before I could attempt a reply he added over his shoulder: "Wait there—I must just make sure he's all right."

When I was alone I moved automatically to the sideboard but found Darrow had not only locked up the decanters but removed the key. I had just given a grunt of disgust when I noticed that his own glass was still standing untouched on the table. I hesitated, remembering Aidan—and at that moment Darrow returned to the room.

"Is he all right?" I said rapidly.

"Yes, he sends his apologies."

"I'd like to send mine to him. I'm very, very sorry I upset him like that. What a disaster!"

"Not at all," said Darrow astonishingly. "On the contrary, I suspect you both did each other a lot of good."

I stared at him. "How can you conceivably say that?"

"I believe you each needed to hear what the other had to say. Of course on the surface it merely sounded like a clash between rival theologies, but underneath I seemed to hear vital messages being exchanged . . . Sit down, Aysgarth, and help yourself to that jug of water."

I sank abruptly into the nearest chair. "Well, whatever was going on," I said, "the fact remains that I should have remembered his suffering and been more tolerant."

"Oh, that wouldn't have suited Charles at all! He deliberately provoked you into argument because he wanted—even longed—to hear you stand up for the idealism which he fears the war has destroyed. And you were willing to argue because for some reason what Charles was saying had a dreadful fascination for you. I was watching your face. You could, in fact, have terminated the argument right at the start, but you were riveted. You had to let him speak his mind."

I poured myself some water. I nerved myself to face the pain. And I said: "I'm afraid there was much more going on than that. What you say may be true, but that's only half the story. Ashworth wanted to lash out at me primarily because he knew I'd made a heavy pass at his wife after Alex Jardine's funeral."

There was a silence, and gradually the truth dawned on me. I looked at him. He looked back calmly. In no line of his face did I see the faintest glimmer of surprise.

"You knew," I whispered. *"You knew."*

"Is that so surprising? I'm Charles's spiritual director."

"No, I meant you knew all along. Right from the beginning. You knew."

"My dear Aysgarth, there's no need to behave as if I've exhibited some peculiarly diabolical form of clairvoyance! The truth was fairly obvious. As soon as I saw you that morning in the Crusader I realized something had gone very wrong, and when I heard later from Lyle (who I knew was severely disturbed by Charles's disappearance) that you and she had been alone in that house with only an exhausted widow for company—"

"Was it you who told Ashworth?"

"Don't be absurd! I'm a priest, not the village gossip!"

"But in that case how on earth did he find out?"

"How do you think? As soon as he heard from you yesterday that she'd attended Jardine's funeral, he asked her to tell him the whole story and she did."

"But she couldn't have done! She promised to treat the incident as if it had never happened—"

"Lyle came to the sensible decision that the best way out of the resulting mess was to be honest."

"But how disastrous!"

"Not at all. With the truth disclosed, not only about you but about the funeral, she and Charles were able to sort themselves out, smooth away that old problem about the Jardines and discover that their future now looks most encouraging. I concede that Charles is still disturbed enough to want to lash out at you, but he'll get over that; he knows now Lyle loves no one but him. *You're* the one, I'm afraid, who won't get over it so long as you pretend the adultery never happened."

"There was no adultery. Not in any legal sense."

"Aysgarth, you're a clergyman. Shouldn't you leave the legal definitions to the lawyers?"

"Oh yes," I said, "I should. But I daren't. Sheltering behind legal definitions is easier than facing up to what I did." I drank some water and groped for a cigarette. "Not a very good clergyman, I'm afraid. In fact very flawed. Psychological problems. Dark side of the ego." I somehow got the cigarette alight. "Must use modern terminology," I said. "I refuse—I absolutely refuse—to talk of demons and the Devil. Outmoded symbolism. Won't have it. *I won't talk of demons and the Devil.*"

"No, no," said Darrow mildly. "Quite unnecessary. Why should you?"

"Lots of people have psychological problems," I said. "Quite normal. Nothing to get excited about. So long as one's in control it's all right."

"Quite so."

"The only trouble is: what happens when one's not in control?"

"Very difficult. Almost frightening, perhaps."

"Very frightening. I'm frightened," I said, shivering from head to toe. "I'm so frightened."

Darrow said nothing but rose to his feet, poured me some more water and sat down in the chair next to mine.

"Something terrible happened tonight," I said. "I nearly hit my sister-in-law. I would have hit her if Primrose hadn't interrupted me."

"Punched her, you mean? Or just given her a slap?"

"Both. I'd have beaten her up. Wanted to. Longed to. Pleasure. Excitement. Disgusting." I covered my face with my shaking hands and said: "I keep him locked up but sometimes he gets out. I'm so afraid of him. So afraid."

"It's good that you can say so out loud. It means you're not trying to hide him behind the curtain, where he can build up his strength. It means you're facing up to his reality."

"It's a question of facing the pain, as Aidan said."

"I was going to ask you about Aidan—"

"Aidan—Ashworth—even Mellors, the poor clergyman I saw this afternoon . . . They all in their different ways spoke the same message, they all showed me the pattern of sin, judgement, repentance and redemption, and Ashworth said . . . Ashworth talked of nice ordinary family men who can do evil deeds—Ashworth insisted that we must face the evil in order to be redeemed . . . Yes, you were right—what he said did indeed have a dreadful fascination for me: his words were the sign telling me that I have to face my demon and exorcise him . . . Not that I believe in exorcism, of course. Or demons. Just speaking symbolically."

"I quite understand," said Darrow soothingly and added without even a pause to search for the right words: "You're saying that you feel it's time for your psychological disability to be explored by your conscious mind so that a satisfactory adjustment can be achieved."

"Exactly." I felt better, safer, once we were using modern terminology, but then before I could stop myself I was saying: "He'll destroy me if he's not exorcised. I saw that clearly tonight. So I've got to destroy him before he destroys me."

"It's very important that you've adopted this positive attitude towards overcoming your difficulties. Very well," said Darrow, still miraculously serene in the face of my disordered ravings, "let's get down to business. Is it possible, do you think, that you can give me a synopsis of your meeting with Aidan? I need hardly stress that you're under no obligation to reveal the secrets of the confessional, but—"

"I wasn't in the confessional. We just talked."

"I see. Nonetheless you may well have told Aidan things you'd prefer me not to know—"

"Since you already know what I did to Lyle when I was drunk and since I've just told you what I almost did to my sister-in-law when I was sober, why on earth should I suddenly become coy about my meeting with Aidan? I may be a spiritual wreck," I said crossly, "and I may be sufficiently disturbed to resort to outmoded symbolism, but there's still no need to conclude that I'm a certifiable lunatic!"

Darrow smiled and said: "Personally I think your use of that particular symbolism indicates the height of sanity. Why call a spade a gardening implement when you can call it a spade?"

"Darrow, you can't *seriously* believe in demons—"

"No, of course not. Tell me about Aidan."

Reassured I flexed my brain in the manner of a barrister about to sum up a complex case for the jury, and embarked on a description of my experiences in London.

5

I HAD just completed my account of the meetings with Aidan and was about to describe my encounters with my siblings, when Anne Darrow returned to the dining-room.

"Jon, you really are impossible! 'Coffee in quarter of an hour,' I said—"

"I'm sorry," I said hastily. "This is all my fault."

"No, it isn't, it's his. He takes on far too much and then throws the social niceties to the winds when he inevitably finds he doesn't have time for them—it happens constantly! He's very naughty." Stooping over him as he sat in his chair she kissed the top of his head. "Lyle's long since followed Charles up to bed," she said, "and I'm tired of sitting in solitary splendour in the drawing-room. I suppose I've no hope of seeing you before midnight?"

"Well, perhaps it would be better not to wait up for me—"

"Those words are beginning to seem just a little too familiar, Father Darrow!"

"Yes, darling, and every time I utter them I give thanks they're not grounds for divorce. I'm sorry I'm being so impossible."

"I give up!" said Anne, kissing him again, and added: "Good night, Neville," before withdrawing to the hall.

"Darrow, I feel guilty about imposing myself on you at such an inconvenient hour," I said as soon as the door closed. "If you'd prefer me to come back tomorrow—"

"Aysgarth, you're in crisis. Your need is desperate. You did absolutely the right thing to come here, and now you're here you must stay. Do you really think I'd be capable of sending you away just so that I could have the pleasure of being in bed with my wife before midnight? What kind of a priest do you think I am?"

This was my personal tank rolling to the rescue again, unstoppable, undeflectable, infinitely comforting. Relaxing in my chair I gave him a tentative smile in an attempt to signal my gratitude, and once more resumed my narrative.

6

HAVING recounted my meetings with my siblings, I told him about Bishop Bell, Lord Flaxton and Mellors. I even told him how I had calmed down Dr. Ottershaw by promising to make all the necessary enquiries into the proposed Theological College extension.

"I'm sure he was most grateful," said Darrow wryly.

"His exact words were: 'Whatever would I do without you, Neville?' "

"A very pertinent question!"

"Not half so pertinent as the question I must now ask you: Which direction am I supposed to take? I frankly confess I'm in such a muddle that I can't see the wood for the trees. What does God now require of me?"

"What indeed! The first point to grasp, Aysgarth, is that neither you nor I, on the present evidence, can answer that question at this moment. I think Aidan was right. The future's not going to fall into place until we've dealt with the past."

"But I want to deal with the future!" I said obstinately, anxious to postpone the ordeal of wrestling with my demon, but realising that I sounded like Sandy as he demanded a biscuit adorned with pale chocolate on both sides, I added in a milder tone: "Are you saying we can't talk about Bell and Flaxton at all?"

"Oh, we can talk about them," said Darrow agreeably, "but I don't think we'll get anywhere. We'll quickly become bogged down in a mass of speculation."

"How can you behave as if the meetings weren't important? I feel as if I've been walloped by two separate sandbags!"

"Of course you do—and of course the meetings were important. But their significance may not lie quite where you think it does. Very well," said Darrow, changing course as he decided the patient needed to be humoured, "let's see what happens when we look at the future. Now what would you say actually took place at these meetings with Bell and Flaxton?"

"Two very different careers in the Church were sketched for me by two very different men. As far as I can make out, Bell must represent God and Flaxton must represent the Devil—although of course when I say 'the Devil' I don't mean—"

"Don't worry, Aysgarth, not even I see the Devil as a charming little imp with horns. But why should you automatically assume that Flaxton represents the Devil? After all, someone's got to minister to the rich, and if, as it seems, you have some peculiar flair for getting on with the aristocracy, this may be just as important a gift as your ability to get on with German POWs."

"Yes, but I feel Bell would fulfill all the dreams of my Liberal idealism—"

"That might not be a good thing at all," said Darrow promptly. "If it can be argued that your idealism has impaired your ability to cope with the reality of sin and evil, it can also be argued that your idealism needs damping down, not stoking up. Stepping into Bell's world could be risky for you. You'd be like an alcoholic who decided to go to work in a pub."

"Surely you exaggerate! I admire Bell so much—and how could that be harmful? The truth is I feel I need a new hero in my life, an older clergyman who—"

"Excuse me, Aysgarth. I hate to sound as if I'm carping and sniping at every word you say, but I must be quite honest and tell you that in my opinion the very last thing you need to do at the moment is to escape from reality by adopting a hero. You may well need the friendship of an older clergyman of great spiritual wisdom, but in your case I think he should be retired and living quietly in obscurity. Otherwise you'll be tempted to regard him as a prize, and the relationship will soon cease to be either real or productive or wholesome."

"But aren't I allowed to admire Bell at all?"

"By all means admire him, but don't forget he's not a saint and he has his faults. For instance, it seems to me he's often much too stubborn—it's almost as if he takes a perverse pleasure in putting people's backs up. And then I feel he's not at ease at running in harness—he likes to be out on his own, preaching his special message. It makes one suspect he was lucky to be passed over for Canterbury. Being head of the Church would have shown up his limitations; being Bishop of Chichester gives him full scope to display his remarkable gifts . . . But we're digressing. To return to the subject of your future—"

"Darrow, I wouldn't have thought it possible that you could make me even more confused than I was before this conversation began, but I'm beginning to feel as if—"

"You're only confused because you haven't answered my original question correctly. My original question, which was intended to bring you out of the world of dreams and into the world of hard facts, was: What actually took place during these meetings with Bell and Flaxton? And the correct answer is: Not much. Bell's talked vaguely of European reconstruction and invited you to call on him, but as yet there's been no offer of work. Flaxton's bragged about his political connections and implied how much he'd enjoy being chums with a London churchman who could consistently cap his classical quotations, but in fact you're still a long way from Westminster or St. Paul's because Flaxton himself has no influence in the Church. We all know political influence can be crucial, but nowadays the politicians do at least try to work with the Church in a deferential manner. Mr. Attlee, I hear, is very scrupulous in the matter of Church appointments."

"Flaxton's obviously still romping along in the nineteenth century. But Darrow, if these meetings with Bell and Flaxton were inconclusive, does this mean—"

"Yes, let's think about what it means. In my opinion the real significance of the meetings lies not in the fact that they've opened up miraculous opportunities for you. They haven't. What they've actually done is to spell out to you your own particular gifts as a clergyman so that you have the chance to decide how you can use them with maximum effect in God's service. For example, it's now obvious that you're not such a pastoral disaster as you always thought you were. You've been liberated from your—shall we use modern terminology?—your inferiority complex, which I suspect arose not only from your innate shyness but also from the fact that you've travelled a long way socially. I think it's not without significance that this great pastoral success of yours took place among a group of people who stood right outside the English class system."

This truth had never before occurred to me. When I had finished boggling at him I said: "So what you're saying is—"

"I'm saying your horizons have been expanded. You no longer have to feel you can only serve God successfully as an administrator. But on the other hand—and this is a point which appears to have completely eluded you—it's also been emphasised what an effective administrator you are. 'Whatever would I do without you?' Dr. Ottershaw exclaims as you step forward for the umpteenth time to iron out his difficulties. You've been so busy considering Bell and Flaxton, Aysgarth, that you seem to find no significance in Dr. Ottershaw's heartfelt paean of praise."

"That's because paeans of praise from Dr. Ottershaw are nothing new."

"Yes, but their significance in this context is that it's neither Bell nor Flaxton but Ottershaw who actually has the greatest power to influence your future. Of course he must have been mentioning you for some time to the people who matter. I don't pretend to have a direct telephone line which enables me to eavesdrop on the counsels of these exalted gentlemen, but I'd assume they'd be saying something like: 'Let Aysgarth see the old man out and steer the new man in. By that time he'll be in his late forties and ripe for a plum preferment.' "

"But I'm not sure I want to go on as an archdeacon."

"The point is that you wouldn't be going on in the same way. Your liberation from the inferiority complex means you'd be much more effective in the pastoral work—and there's a fair amount of pastoral work attached to the office of archdeacon, isn't there? It's not all attending diocesan committees and inspecting churches and keeping Dr. Ottershaw organised."

"That's true." I thought of Mellors. Then I said: "I don't deny it would be nice to sit tight and wait for the plum preferment to drop into my lap. Certainly a little while ago I'd never have dreamed of doing anything else. But nevertheless—"

"You want to work for Bell. That's fine. It's always helpful to know what one really wants. But Aysgarth, what you want isn't necessarily going to be what God wants. You may at present not have the perspective to see—"

"You're telling me politely that I'm deluded."

"Certainly not!" Darrow was scandalised. "I'm telling you politely that since we have insufficient information at present to discern what God wants, all talk of what you want—although very interesting—really doesn't get us very far. And now, having proved to you, I hope, that at present the future can only be a clouded mass of speculative theories—"

"Another possible future is that I fail to survive my marriage and get kicked out of the Church for heavy drinking and adultery after a steamy session in the divorce court."

"That's yet another speculative theory, I agree, but personally I don't believe we should waste any more time ruminating on things which may never happen. Let's try to get to grips now with the things that *have* happened—let's talk about those meetings with your brother and sister. I'll start by posing the same question that I posed before: What do you think actually took place here?"

"What happened," I said gloomily in a fit of despair, "was that I felt like Alice adrift in a looking-glass world where all my preconceived ideas were turned inside out."

"Excellent!" said Darrow delighted. "Well done! Now we're really beginning to make progress . . ."

7

"WHAT happened," said Darrow, "was obviously what Aidan hoped would happen: You managed to uncover new facets of an exceedingly complex reality, with the result that you're now much closer to the truth."

"That's wonderful," I said dryly, "but I'm still completely at sea. All I can think is: Everything Emily and Willy said was true—and yet at the same time everything they said was false."

"But that's good—we're now in what Aidan calls the land of paradox, and that means we're very close to the truth. Now let's try and grope our way forward. Can the paradox be illustrated? Can you give me a specific example of this truth-falsehood—or was the impression of paradox much more general and diffuse?"

"No, I can think of specific instances. For example, Emily and Willy were convinced that my parents' marriage was a disaster, but I don't remember it as a disaster at all. I remember my parents being happy, joking and laughing together. So I'm sure the view of a disastrous marriage must be false. Yet at the same time I can understand why Willy and Emily take this view. All the childbearing affected my mother's health and she was capable of being a very demanding invalid. As for Father . . . well, he must have been a disappointment to her in some ways. She would have wanted a successful husband like Uncle Willoughby . . . So you have a situation where both partners of the marriage could have wound up unhappy—and maybe they did; maybe I've just blotted out what I don't want to remember."

"Not necessarily. Maybe both views of the marriage are correct."

"How can they be?"

"Even the happiest marriage can go through a miserable time. All right, can you give me another illustration of the paradox?"

"The most striking illustration of all lies in the way we see Mother. She seems to be the point at which all three of us peel off into radically different camps."

"What about your Uncle Willoughby?"

I shook my head. "No, I can reconcile our differing views of Uncle Will. I can understand why Emily sees him as a hero, and if I make a big effort I can even understand how Willy manages to see him as Falstaff, an old rogue instead of a complete villain. But as far as Mother's concerned . . ." I lapsed into silence.

"The views are irreconcilable."

"Completely. Here we have the triple paradox of the victim-villainess-heroine."

"Emily, I remember, sees her as the victim oppressed by men."

"Yes, and that's rubbish! Mother was no one's victim—she was tough as old boots!"

"So you're saying Willy was right and she was absolutely frightful."

"No, no, no—that was rubbish too! Mother was quite wonderful—very charming, very witty and a fascinating conversationalist. Where Emily and Willy go wrong is to see her as just a plain woman, too clever for her own good, who was only saved from a life of pitiable spinsterhood by a miracle. The truth about Mother—the real truth—is that for most of her life she had at least one of three men doting on her: Uncle Willoughby, my father and I myself. My mother," I said firmly, "was a *femme fatale.*"

"So was Lady Macbeth."

"Yes, but Willy's drawn quite the wrong parallel by equating her with a literary villainess! I'd equate her with a literary heroine."

"What sort of literary heroine?" said Darrow interested. "I realise we can rule out Little Nell, Dora Copperfield and Amelia Sedley, but what about Catherine Earnshaw—or Elizabeth Bennet?"

"No, no, no!" I said again impatiently. "You're in the wrong era altogether—and quite the wrong country. My mother was like Hedda Gabler."

"Ah yes, of course!" exclaimed Darrow as if cross with himself for being so slow. "Willy's female monster who was also Emily's tragic victim!"

"No, no, no!" I exclaimed for the third time. "The alluring *femme fatale* who had three men mesmerised!"

"Yes, but all those views are true, aren't they?" said Darrow. "Hedda Gabler was a monster *and* a victim *and* a *femme fatale* who had three men mesmerised."

I stared at him. "No," I said at last. "That's not right. Forget Hedda Gabler—she seems to have led us astray. My mother was not a victim. I insist that she was not a victim. And she was not a monster. I insist that she was not a monster. She was a *femme fatale* and I adored her and she adored me and we got on wonderfully well always—except when we had that little tiff in 1938, but that didn't count, that was nothing, and we both agreed to treat the incident afterwards as if it had never happened—"

"What did happen exactly?" said Darrow.

"We had the kind of row that I'm sure goes on all the time up and down the country whenever a husband and wife take in an aged parent who's capable of being very difficult. Anyway, never mind that now—forget it. My mother's not important at the moment."

"Isn't she?"

"No. She's not the one I'm in a muddle about—my relationship with her was perfectly straightforward. The person I'm in a muddle about is my father. Did he or did he not commit suicide?"

"That question, I agree, is a crucial one."

"You do agree? Thank heavens for that! For a moment I thought you were turning Freudian and preparing to go on and on and on about my mother."

"I hope," said Darrow urbanely, "I'd never go on and on and on about anybody's mother. No, I too think that the first person you have to deal with here is your father, and I'll tell you why: It's because I've got a hunch that it's the relationship with your father which is the straightforward one here."

"But how can you say that when I've tied myself up into such a knot over this suicide business?"

"It's because you're tied up in this particular knot that I think we're on promising ground. The knot can be easily cut by finding out how your father died."

"But surely—"

"If I thought you were in a deeper muddle about your father, Aysgarth, I'd agree that cutting you free wouldn't be so simple, but I suspect that this is the one place where you've got a solid grasp of reality. You've worked out, haven't you, that you felt angry with your father for leaving you deliberately, and that it was this anger which prompted you to mould yourself in your uncle's image; you know that if your father didn't commit suicide you'll not only be able to forgive him for leaving you in such desperate straits, but you'll finally be able to live in harmony with his memory."

"Is that the point where I start living happily ever after?"

"No, that's the point where the real hard work will begin. As Aidan pointed out, you have to bring each one of those three people into harmony with yourself. You can't just stop with your father. You'll have to put yourself at ease with your mother and uncle as well."

"All right, there's no difficulty about my mother, as I've already said, but if you think I could ever forgive Uncle Willoughby for sending me to that prison camp when I was seven years old and bullying me all through my adolescence—"

"Let's leave your uncle for the moment and concentrate on your father. Do you still have no doubt that he committed suicide, despite Willy's profound disbelief?"

"I'm very tempted to share that disbelief. But the trouble is that I'd always feel I never knew for certain, and unless I know for certain—"

"How can you set about knowing for certain? How can you finally establish the truth here?"

"No idea." I tried to be constructive. "I suppose I could send a private detective up to Maltby to dig up the report of the inquest."

"Why not go up to Maltby yourself?"

"Oh, I could never go back to Yorkshire."

"Yes," said Darrow. "You told me that once before. I wondered then why you were so adamant and now I'm wondering again. There's something up there that frightens you, isn't there? Something very large and very terrifying which has to be kept nailed down under a very thick rug behind the heaviest curtain you can find."

I felt as if all the blood had been instantly drained from my body. Breathing was difficult, speech quite impossible.

Darrow said idly: "He's still alive, isn't he? Yes, I thought he probably was. It occurred to me some time ago that he was the only one whose death you've never mentioned."

And as I stared at him in horrified fascination I realised I was face to face at last not with Darrow, that sinister magician who produced his terrible truths so effortlessly from his conjuror's hat, but with Uncle Willoughby, eighty-two years old but apparently indestructible, outliving my father, outliving my mother, outliving all his friends, but still famous as the richest man in Maltby, still enjoying, so he had boasted to Emily on his latest Christmas card, all the dazzling prizes he had won.

PART THREE

SALVATION

"The experience of the eternal with which this book is concerned . . . is unification by synthesis, the attainment of a new relationship by a fully integrated personality."

CHARLES E. RAVEN
THE CREATOR SPIRIT

XVII

"Yet there are times in every man's journey when he chooses his path in obedience less to the demands of his own nature than to a summons from without . . ."

CHARLES E. RAVEN
THE CROSS AND THE CRISIS

I

"IF you think for one moment," I said to Darrow, "that I'm ever going to go within fifty miles of that man, you're out of your mind."

"But didn't Aidan establish that although you fiercely resented your uncle for many good reasons you also had a sneaking affection for the old boy? How has Willy's Falstaff become your Count Dracula?"

Unable to reply I sat trembling in my chair.

"If you did see him again," said Darrow at last in his calmest voice, "what do you think he'd do?"

"Kill me."

"Oh yes? What a splendid story for the popular press! 'Archdeacon Slain by Old-Age Pensioner—Ex-Mayor Exacts Revenge!' "

"Darrow, this is a serious matter!"

"That's exactly why I'm trying to expose the absurdity of your statement. Of course the old boy's not going to kill you! How old is he? Seventy-five? Eighty? Old boys of that age are delighted when someone unexpected turns up to reminisce about the past!"

"Not this old boy. Not after what happened between us when I told him I was going into the Church."

"Maybe I misunderstood you, but I was under the impression he adjusted splendidly to the fact that you weren't going to be Prime Minister after all. Didn't he immediately picture you as Archbishop of York and start planning his first visit to Bishopthorpe?"

"Yes, it was intolerable. I couldn't bear the way he converted my call into just another race for the prizes. All I wanted to do was reject him and his whole way of life."

"But you'd slaved for years to win his love and approval—"

"Exactly. I'd at last worked myself into a position where I could pay him back for all the suffering he'd caused me."

"Ah yes," said Darrow, "of course. I think I understand now. The real prize was revenge, wasn't it?"

This statement, spoken in a manner which was devoid of criticism, came as an extraordinary relief. I felt the burden of explanation had been lifted from my shoulders; I felt I had been saved the horror of having to speak the unspeakable.

"So the moment finally arrived when you could tear up his love and approval and fling them in his face," mused Darrow. "And something tells me he wasn't the sort of man who'd meekly turn the other cheek when faced with that kind of behaviour."

"No, he wasn't. He hit me."

"I'm not surprised. I don't suppose you were surprised either, were you?"

"No. I'd deliberately provoked him into hitting me so that I could hit him back."

"It must have been quite a fight. And did you feel better afterwards?"

"Better!" I stopped staring down at my writhing hands and gazed at him incredulously. "I was a young man who'd decided to be a clergyman. I'd had too much to drink—but not just to steady my nerves. I'd wanted to rev myself up. But all I succeeded in doing was letting my demon burst out of his straitjacket and take control of me. I said cruel things, things no Christian should even think, let alone utter, and once I started hitting him—"

"You enjoyed it."

"My demon enjoyed it. But once I'd got him back in his straitjacket I was appalled by what had happened. It wasn't just that I felt sickened and polluted by the demon—I felt frightened of him, frightened of what he might do in the future. I did feel safer once I was able to wear a clerical uniform—it was like a suit of armour protecting me—but periodically I used to relive that fight with Uncle Willoughby in my dreams and then he'd be killing me or I'd be killing him—"

"No wonder you never dared go near him again."

"Oh, another meeting would have been quite impossible. I was so afraid that if we met again—"

"—the demon would burst out of his straitjacket and reclaim you. Yes, this demon will have to be exorcised, there's no doubt about that, and the way to exorcise him is not, I'm afraid, to continue saying: 'I can never go back to Yorkshire.' You've got to give yourself a chance to set down this massive burden of fear."

"But I can't see my uncle again, I can't! You don't understand—such a meeting's quite unimaginable!"

"Oh, I think one could imagine a safe little scene without too much trouble. Why not turn up on his doorstep and say something harmless, such as 'Hullo'?"

"But what would I say next? What makes you think my demon wouldn't take over?"

"What makes you think he would? It seems far more probable to me that the demonic force was in fact expended in that fight all those years ago. If it hadn't been expended I think that you'd have felt driven to seek him out and beat him up all over again."

After a pause I said: "I hadn't thought of that." There was another pause while I thought about it gingerly, doubtfully, fearfully, but was unable to reach any conclusion.

"It also seems probable to me," said Darrow at last, "that what you're most frightened of at present is actually not the demon of violence. I know he's currently giving you hell, but nevertheless you do have him under lock and key. I think what's really got you paralysed here is the demon of guilt."

I did not answer.

"Your uncle made bad mistakes," said Darrow, "but he also did a great deal for you."

Still I remained silent.

"Guilt can be a terrible demon," said Darrow. "It can cripple, crush and destroy. But no demon is beyond exorcism."

"This one is." I shivered again. "I can't see Uncle Willoughby, not now, not ever. Better to keep the curtain down and the rug in place and—"

"Aysgarth," said Darrow, "we all have our demons which have to be fought and vanquished. But the way to vanquish them is not to let them crowd you into such a tight corner that all you can do is crouch down and shudder with fear. You've got to straighten your back, beat your demons to pulp and march to freedom over their corpses."

I exclaimed startled: "That's a violent metaphor!"

"It's time to stoke up that fighting spirit of yours, which is going to save you."

I sat shuddering with cowardice in my chair, but Darrow refused to give up. Leaning forward he said urgently: "Think of the father who loved you, Aysgarth! Don't you owe it to him to find out exactly how he died? And think of Professor Raven talking of unity! Do you really want to spend the rest of your life as a collection of warring fragments?"

I slid my tongue around my lips and listened to my heart thumping. At last I heard myself say: "If I turn up on his doorstep he'll slam the door in my face."

"Why should he? Why shouldn't he too want to talk honestly about the past? He's an old man at the end of his life, and such people often have a powerful need to pass their past on to the next generation."

"I can't imagine him talking to me," I said, "and I can't imagine myself talking to him."

"Well, that's easily remedied. Let's ring him up."

"Ring him up?"

"Yes, why not? Once you've spoken a few words and arranged a meeting, you'll have brought him out of the Count Dracula myth and into reality—with the result that he'll be much easier to face. I'll talk to the operator and find out the number for you. What's his surname?"

"I can remember the number. But Darrow—"

"Let's adjourn to the telephone in the library." He stood up but when I remained seated he grasped the back of my chair and leant over me. "Come on, Aysgarth! Isn't Truth the ultimate prize here? And isn't it at this moment the prize you want to win more than any other prize on earth?"

Wordlessly I levered myself to my feet and staggered after him into the library.

2

"ALL the Maltby numbers now have four digits," said the operator drearily five minutes later. "Mr. Stoke's number has been changed to double-six-two-five."

"Thank you." Unable to stand any longer I sank down in the chair behind the library table and listened to the bell ringing at the other end of the line. I had just opened my mouth to say to Darrow: "He's probably in bed," when the receiver was removed from the hook and a woman's voice said peevishly: "Mr. Stoke's residence."

I thought this sounded more like a housekeeper than my cousin Mercy. "I'd like to speak to him, please."

"He's not here." The Yorkshire accent was heavy and dour. "He's gone with Miss Mercy on his holiday to Brighton."

"Brighton!"

"It's a seaside resort in the South."

I managed to say: "I need to see him urgently. Whereabouts in Brighton is he staying?"

"The Metropole Hotel."

"Thank you," I said, replacing the receiver, and sagged back, almost unconscious with emotion, in my chair.

"So once again you're saved a trip to Yorkshire!" said Darrow mildly, keeping the conversation at a calm, prosaic level. "And of course there's a good train service to Brighton from Starmouth via Southampton and Chichester. You can stay the night here and set off early tomorrow morning."

All I could say was: "I can't quite think how I'm going to tell my sister-in-law I won't be home tonight."

"Leave her to me," said Darrow.

I left her. I was unable to take in what he said. I was almost unconscious with emotion again.

After the call had been made, my clerical nanny led me to a small spare-room, drew the curtains and even produced a Bible and a Prayer Book to adorn the bedside table. While this was going on I stripped to my underclothes and slumped into bed.

"Have you read the evening office?"

"No."

"Very well, I'll read it to you," said Darrow, producing a pair of spectacles. It was part of Darrow's vanity that he always liked to pretend he had perfect sight, but of course at his age he had to wear glasses for reading. When he had finished he said: "I'll be celebrating Mass here tomorrow. If you'd like to attend—"

"No. Thank you, but no."

"I'll keep it simple, I promise. No Anglo-Catholic touches."

"It's not that. I'm sorry, I can't explain, but—"

"There's no need to explain. Or to apologise. I just wanted you to know the service will be held."

I said: "I'm not fit to communicate," and turned my face to the wall.

There was a long silence. At last he said: "Would you like me to sit with you for a while?" but I answered: "No, thanks. I'm fine."

He made no attempt to argue with this idiotic assertion. Accepting me as I was, pathetically entrenched in my pride, he said simply: "I'll pray for you," and left me, as I wanted, on my own.

3

I FELL asleep around three and was woken four hours later when Darrow arrived to loan me his shaving equipment. "I'll bring breakfast to you on a tray at eight," he said. "I'm not going to Starbridge till noon today because I'm taking the morning off in order to spend time with Charles. By the way, do you have enough petrol coupons to get yourself down to Starmouth and back?"

"Yes, I should be all right. I filled the tank yesterday when I went to Flaxton Pauncefoot."

"Good." He picked up the Bible and the Prayer Book and handed them to me. "I'll come back in an hour's time."

The door closed. I was left clutching the books as I sat on the edge of the bed.

When Darrow returned he said: "Did you read the office?"

"No."

"Did you pray at all?"

"No."

"Have you opened the Bible?"

"No."

"Then let's open it straight away," said Darrow, dumping the tray on my lap. "I'll read while you eat. We'll start with St. John, chapter eight, the part where Our Lord says—"

" 'The truth shall set you free.' " Shoving the tray aside I covered my face with my hands.

4

I WAS forced to eat breakfast. I had to consume a boiled egg, a slice of toast and two cups of tea. Then I had to promise to read the morning office on the train, and finally I was obliged to kneel while Darrow said prayers.

"Sorry to be such a mess," I said afterwards.

"It's a very brave mess."

"How can you say that when it must be patently obvious I'm scared out of my wits?"

"Scared out of your wits but struggling on. That's brave."

He accompanied me outside to my car. It was a cool morning, windless and serene. "As soon as you get back from Brighton," he said, "come straight to the College. I'll be waiting."

"One day," I said vaguely as I dumped myself into the driving-seat, "when all this is over, I suppose I'll find the words to thank you. If I survive, that is."

"You'll survive, Aysgarth. I foresee numerous stimulating debates over the College extension as we revert with relief to our roles of piratical principal and axe-swinging archdeacon."

"I must remind the Bishop to replenish his stock of indigestion tablets."

There seemed no more to say. Starting the engine I rammed the car into gear and began my drive south to the port of Starmouth.

5

THE train arrived at Brighton soon after noon and I took a taxi from the station to the Metropole Hotel on the Esplanade. A soft blue sea was simpering beyond the shingle beach. I was reminded of all my visits to St. Leonards. Entering the hotel abruptly before I could lose my nerve, I walked across the foyer to the reception desk.

"I think you'll find Mr. Stoke in one of the lounges, sir," said the receptionist in response to my request that a messenger-boy deliver a note to the bedroom to announce my presence. "I noticed him crossing the hall with Miss Stoke about half an hour ago."

My immediate reaction was one of relief that the meeting would take place in a public room; it would lessen the risk of a violent scene. On the other hand, if either of us succumbed to rage anything could happen. Rigid with dread, I opened the glass swing-doors and stepped into the nearest of the reception rooms.

I saw him straight away. He was sitting by the window which faced the sea, a stout old man with wispy white hair and a red face. I was surprised how small he was; he had always conveyed the impression—an illusion accentuated in my memory by the passing years—that he was at least six feet tall. He was wearing a grey suit, a Maltby cricket club tie and black-framed spectacles. His hands, gnarled and ugly, clasped the pink pages of the *Financial Times.*

Beside him sat my middle-aged cousin Mercy, knitting a long purple garment which defied identification. She had scraped her grey hair into a bun and was wearing a shapeless frock garnished by a cardigan. I was reminded unexpectedly of Emily.

I walked over to them. By this time my legs were moving as awkwardly as if I were wading knee-deep through mud, and every step seemed a considerable achievement. I approached unobserved. It was only when I halted by Mercy's chair that Uncle Willoughby glanced up from the newspaper. At once I said two words in my politest voice. They were: "Good morning."

The world continued to turn. I remained upright and, apparently, conscious. I could hear Mercy as she gave a little shriek and cried: "Heavens above!"

Uncle Willoughby opened his mouth, shut it again and slowly removed his spectacles. As he did so I realised for the first time that his blue eyes, a little faded now but still capable of exuding their hot bold glare, were a recognisable reflection of my own. Moreover his firm straight mouth, which I had always associated with his brutal ruthlessness, was the mirror-image of my own mouth, which I had always thought manifested my praiseworthy strength of will. When I was young and he was middle-aged, I had been blind to the family resemblance between us, but now that I myself was middle-aged I could clearly see the likeness we had once shared with my mother.

I was speechless. Meanwhile Mercy was gabbling indignantly: "I don't believe it, it can't be true, it's Neville—look, Father, it's Neville—did you ever—can you believe—after all these years—" And as Uncle Willoughby, as speechless as I was, remained motionless in his chair, she rose majestically to her feet to face me. "Well, you've got a nerve, I must say! Dead silence for over twenty years and then you turn up, bold as brass, without even so much as a by-your-leave—and all you can say is: 'Good morning'! The insolence of it! How dare you! You threw Father over, you broke his heart—*and* after all he did for you—oh, it's a scandal, that's what it is, a *disgrace,* and how a clergyman could ever behave in such a cruel, wicked way I just don't know! In fact in my opinion—" She broke off.

Uncle Willoughby had raised his hand to terminate the stream of abuse. In the silence that followed he carefully set aside his newspaper and levered himself to his feet. Age had removed an inch or so from his height. He was smaller than I was now, but I barely noticed. He was still capable of appearing six feet tall.

Looking me straight in the eyes he said: "So you've come back."

"Finally. Yes." No four syllables had ever cost me greater effort.

"Well!" said Uncle Willoughby in his most aggressive voice. "Don't you believe for one moment that *I* don't know what to do! If you think I'm just a senile old man who's forgotten his Bible, you've made a very big mistake!" He turned to his daughter. "Ring the bell for the waiter."

"The waiter? But Father—"

Again he held up his hand and again the whining voice ceased.

Then he said to her proudly: "My boy's come back at last—kill the fatted calf! Neville and I are going to drink champagne."

XVIII

"If I can find someone who forgives, that is, refuses to be embittered and estranged, someone who, bearing the effects of my sin, loves me still; then the power of that appeal is, I think, to all normal people—and I would venture to say in the last resort to all human beings—irresistible."

CHARLES E. RAVEN
THE CROSS AND THE CRISIS

I

HE ordered me to sit down, terrified the waiter, who tried to tell him that the hotel's pre-war stock of champagne had long since been exhausted, and dispatched Mercy by reminding her that she never drank at noon. "And I'm tired of that nasty purple piece of nonsense you're always mauling," he added. "Go away and knit it somewhere else." Mercy did try to protest but when he glared at her and growled: "Don't you be missish with me, my girl!" she sloped off with her mouth well turned down at the corners.

"Now!" He beamed at me. "So you're an archdeacon, wearing a fancy uniform so that everyone can see what a successful clergyman you are! I know all about archdeacons. When Emily wrote in her 1937 Christmas card that you'd been promoted I visited the library in Huddersfield to find out exactly what was going on. You're 'The Bishop's Eye.' You bring to his attention what needs correcting or praising. You hold visitations in your archdeaconry to keep all those vicars up to the mark and to see that the fabric and contents of each church are as they should be. You present the candidates at an Ordination Service. You launch a new vicar in his church once the Bishop's given his approval. You're entitled to be addressed as 'The Venerable' on all correspondence. And all this was going on when you were only thirty-five years old! I said to Ella—she was still alive back in '37—'Ella,' I said, 'that's champion, that is! My boy's Getting On and Going Far.' "

I was still far beyond speech. All I could do was listen.

"Of course," said Uncle Willoughby, ignoring me as he reflected on the memory, "Ella behaved as Mercy did just now." He adopted an astonishing falsetto as he aped his wife's voice. " 'Oh, how can you still speak of him when he's turned his back on you so wickedly!' Silly woman! I said to her: 'Why shouldn't he turn his back on me if he wants to? There's a price to pay for everything,' I said. 'Nothing's free. I set my heart on that boy Going Far, and the price I'm paying, now that he's travelled out of sight, is that he doesn't want to know me. But so what? It's a price I'm proud to pay—and if it was necessary I'd pay it all over again! I gave that boy the gift that was beyond price—the opportunity to be the man he had the ability to be—and my reward doesn't lie in him visiting me regularly with gritted teeth in order to be dutiful. My reward lies in knowing he's a success in his chosen profession, with the best of his career still to come!' But Ella still didn't understand, silly woman—she thought we should be slobbering over each other every Christmas and writing sentimental letters every week, but I'm not sentimental and I don't slobber. That's not my nature," said Uncle Willoughby as the champagne arrived, and added dourly to the waiter: "You took your time! Now show me that bottle. Don't think you can get away with some nasty imitation by hiding the label in that bucket! Did the manager produce the pre-war stuff or didn't he? Because if he didn't—"

"He did, sir," said the unfortunate waiter faintly. "It turned out there were one or two bottles left after all."

"There always are in a place like this—for those who can pay." He read the label, grunted and said: "That'll do." By this time the waiter was so unnerved that he could hardly untwist the wire around the cork.

I finally managed to speak. "Uncle Willoughby—"

"No need for you to put on that posh voice for me, lad. You can be yourself now."

"This *is* myself. I mean, nowadays—well, I always speak like this. I don't think twice about it."

"My God, that's bloody marvellous! Last time I saw you, you talked posh for Oxford and natural for me. What a long way you've travelled! You're a real gentleman now!"

The waiter succeeded in extracting the cork.

"Why isn't the champagne foaming out of the top?" demanded Uncle Willoughby. "It must be flat!"

"I assure you, sir—"

"Very well, get on with it, man—we don't have all day!"

The champagne, pale gold and perfectly preserved, effervesced in the delicate glass. Uncle Willoughby grabbed the stem, took a sip and pronounced: "Could be worse." Almost reeling with relief the waiter filled both glasses and fled.

"Well, what shall we drink to?" said Uncle Willoughby. "The past? The present? The future?"

"It's all a unity," I said. "It's all one." And once more I felt as if my father was moving silently to my side.

2

"LET'S drink to the future," said Uncle Willoughby. "Plenty of that still left. I'm going to live to be a hundred. Look at me—eighty-two years old and happy as a lark! But that's because you've come back, and I'll wager I know why you've come. You've been promoted to bishop and you couldn't resist the temptation to brag about it to me!"

"I'm a little young for that kind of preferment, Uncle Will, and anyway I'm surprised you think I'm worthy of a bishopric. Look, I must say this—it's got to be said—it's about that final row we had—"

"Oh, that! A lot of silly nonsense. What does all that matter now?"

"Well, I want to say I'm very, very sorry I hit you. I—"

"I hit you first, didn't I? If you hadn't hit me back I'd have wondered what was wrong with you!"

"But since I'd decided to be a clergyman it was utterly unforgivable of me to—"

"Well, you weren't a clergyman then—you were just a young lad in a muddle." He paused to toss off some champagne. "Now stop harping on things that don't matter any more and tell me what's brought you here."

"I was hoping you could help me."

"Help you?" He was baffled. For a moment his razor-sharp intelligence, unblunted by age, examined this mysterious statement warily. Then he exclaimed: "Well, speak up! No beating about the bush! Is it money?"

"No."

"Women?"

"No."

"Oh well, you're all right, then. You had me worried for a moment. I thought it was something serious."

"It is. I want to talk to you about the past."

"The past?" He looked indignant. "What sort of an old woman do you take me for? It's only sentimental old females who sit around mooning about the good old days and viewing the past through rose-tinted spectacles!"

"I'm not interested in rose-tinted spectacles, Uncle Will. I want you to tell me about the way things really were back in Maltby before my father died."

He boggled. "Why?"

I reached for the one explanation which I knew he would understand. "I'm in such a muddle about the past that it's affecting my work, and unless I sort myself out very quickly I'll be out of the running for the next prize. So if you could tell me the truth about my parents and their marriage—the truth, the whole truth and nothing but the truth—"

"Can't see what good raking over those old ashes will do you, but if your future's at stake—"

"Everything's at stake, Uncle Will. Everything."

"Sounds to me as if you're off your head. Sure you won't start hitting me again if I tell you things you don't want to hear?"

"I've got to hear everything."

"So be it. Pour me some more champagne."

I topped up his glass. "What I really want to know about my father," I said, "is—"

"Poor Arthur!" said Uncle Willoughby, ceasing to listen to me as he set out on his long journey back into the past. "So stupid, but such a nice nature. A good man in his own way. In fact," said Uncle Willoughby, very mellow as he sipped his champagne, "now that I can look back on the whole tragedy from a distance of nearly forty years, I can see I was really rather fond of poor Arthur . . ."

3

I EXCLAIMED: "But you despised him!"

"Yes—when he got in such a stupid mess. And before that I was jealous of him, of course, but nevertheless—"

"Jealous?"

"Yes, why not? I was short and ugly and had to make my own way in the world. He was tall and handsome and set to inherit his father's business. Gnashed my teeth, I did, whenever I saw him being a hero at the cricket club! And then to cap it all, he came between me and my sister, and I didn't like Adelaide doting on someone else. It took me some time to get used to that, but poor Arthur, he was so nice-natured that he put everything right. He was like a dog that walks up to you and stands there, wagging its tail. In the end you can't resist giving it a pat, and then the next moment it's offering you a paw and you're its friend for life. So it was with your father, although mark you, I always had my suspicions he was stupid. Stupid in life, stupid in death, stupid, stupid, stupid."

"Uncle Will, about my father's death—"

"No, you be quiet, my boy, and let me tell this story the way I want to tell it! I'm not having you barging in and interrupting me the whole time—you'll put me off my stride! Now where was I? Ah yes, Arthur's stupidity. Poor Arthur . . .

"Well, when I say 'stupid' I don't mean he was block-headed stupid. He was an intelligent man—all those books! All that poetry!—but he was what one might call worldly-wise stupid, so naive and innocent and trusting. The way he used to treat his servants! He nearly mollycoddled them to death, and as for his employees—ridiculous! I never met such a pampered, over-paid, idle bunch of workers in all my life! No wonder the business went to the wall . . . Poor Arthur. Very sad.

"Well, it was bad enough him being stupid about business matters, but the trouble was he was also stupid about Real Life. Now, you know what I mean by Real Life, don't you, Nev? I mean everything that doesn't happen in romantic fairy-tales. Your father wanted to live in a romantic fairy-tale—that was his trouble—and so, for a time, did your mother. Well, a woman can be excused for wandering around with her head in the clouds when a handsome young man pays court to her, but there's never any excuse for a man to keep his head anywhere except on his shoulders. Marriage, as we both know, has nothing to do with living in a romantic fairy-tale. Marriage is about facing up to Real Life, and what did poor Arthur know about that? Absolutely bloody nothing.

"Of course he should never have married her. Only a stupid man would ever imagine he could be happy with a wife like my sister. Adelaide was the most wonderful woman in the world, but she should have been a man. Maybe that was why she was so wonderful. No fluttering, no cooing, no sickly feminine chatter—just wit and charm and fascinating conversation about things which interest clever men—what a woman! But a man, if he knows what's good for him, wants a soft, mild, biddable woman to look after him, not a tough intellectual siren, and he wants someone who can bring up his children properly, not someone who . . . well, we won't go into your mother's shortcomings on that score. You'd have thought, wouldn't you, that God in His wisdom would have made her sterile, but no, there she was, fertile as a rabbit. What a mess! And all because poor Arthur hadn't the brains to see he was marrying a man in a woman's body.

"Mark you, it did occur to me years later that this might have been exactly what he wanted. He was shy with soft, mild, biddable women, and he was always much happier when he was down at the cricket club with the boys. Not that I'm implying anything nasty, mind. They were a very decent and wholesome bunch of lads down at the cricket club, and no one was more decent and wholesome than your father, but all the same . . . He was a strange boy in some ways, all that gentleness and innocence. Sometimes, now that I'm a wicked old man who's seen everything, I wonder if he was a woman in a man's body and that the pair of them, he and Adelaide, were better suited than I'd ever dreamed. Carnality's a funny thing, Nev, you mark my words. It's not half so simple as you think when you're young. Then you just think lads are lads and lasses are lasses and everything else in between is a disgusting aberration of nature, but later you realise that the most amazing thing about nature is its infinite variety—and who can say with any certainty where aberration begins and ends?

"Anyway, there was no doubt Adelaide was an aberration—but not a disgusting one, of course. She had the makings of a good mistress, I always thought, guaranteed to cheer a man up in no time by the sheer strength of her conversation, but unfortunately as a respectable girl that career wasn't open to her. But even if she hadn't been respectable, you can be sure Arthur would have married her anyway. Too romantic to do anything else. You may find this hard to believe—I certainly did—but it turned out he was a virgin when he married her; Adelaide said he swore there'd never been anyone else. Can you imagine anyone being quite so stupid? Selfish too, no consideration for his bride-to-be, and of course you won't be one bit surprised if I now tell you that their intimate life was a disaster.

"The really stupid part was that it needn't have stayed a disaster. My wife, being just as respectable as Adelaide, also hated all the goings-on at first, but in the end she didn't mind them in the least—and why was that? I'll tell you. Number one, because I had the brains and the experience to take trouble—I didn't go lumbering all over her like a hippopotamus taking a bath; number two, because I showed consideration—I didn't inflict her with annual pregnancies; number three, because when she finally felt, if I may borrow a cricketing term, that her innings at the marital wicket was over, I let her retire to the pavilion with good grace and no hard feelings. Of course I was never faithful to her, but that wasn't adultery, that was sheer Christian charity—and don't you go telling me God wouldn't have understood! God and I understand each other very well. I've always been on excellent terms with Him, paying my respects at chapel every week and leading a hard-working, law-abiding life. What more can He want, I'd like to know?

"Well, there was poor Arthur, too stupid to be a resourceful husband, and there was poor Adelaide, trying to work out how to make life endurable for herself. How much did she love him, you may ask (since love's supposed to conquer everything, even an aversion to copulation), and that's a good question. Of course she swore she was passionate about him, and perhaps she was in a way, but I think her primary emotion wasn't love at all but gratitude. She didn't marry because she wanted to be loved; she was already loved—by me. No, she married because she was terrified of winding up on the shelf, a failure as a woman, and Adelaide wanted to be a success. Like me, she wanted to go chasing the prizes, and as we both know, even today after all that female emancipation rubbish the suffragettes churned out, the greatest prizes for a successful woman are still marriage and motherhood—and if she can manage to catch a tall, dark, handsome hero and produce a string of fetching children, all bright as buttons, so much the better.

"She liked Arthur, there's no denying that, but love? If you ask me, *he* was the one who was genuinely in love, because he married her for herself. She had no money, no pretty face, no alluring figure, no exalted rank, yet he married her anyway. And I'll tell you this: I think if he'd lived she'd have come to love him in the end. They were good friends beneath all the romantic twaddle, and they could always make each other laugh. In fact I'll wager they'd have wound up a real Darby and Joan once all the passion had been spent. It was spending the passion that destroyed them. Your father wouldn't show consideration by taking a mistress, so in the end poor Adelaide got desperate and decided to have babies continually to get away from him.

"Mark you, they might well have ended up producing babies continuously anyway, Arthur being the man he was. I can't see him ever making a success of anti-conception, although to be fair to Arthur, I have to admit he did offer to withdraw; he had a nice nature. But poor Adelaide was so desperate she just said that was against her religious principles. Adelaide told me that. Adelaide told me everything. Adelaide and I . . .

"Well, I tried to keep out of their marriage, but it wasn't so easy, particularly when she tried to drag me in. After the last miscarriage she decided she was fed up with childbearing and she finally nerved herself to tell him straight that she didn't want any more marital intimacy. And what happens? Pathetic scenes. Misery. Disaster. Does he get off his backside and take a mistress? No, he gets off his backside and takes to drink. Stupid fellow! Adelaide wanted me to speak to him, and in fact when I saw how miserable she was I wouldn't have minded trying to drill some sense into him, but I knew I shouldn't interfere, so although I promised Adelaide I'd have a word with the silly fellow I kept putting it off. And then . . . he died. That was stupid too. Stupid, stupid, stupid . . . Drink up your champagne, lad, you look as if you're about to pass out. Maybe I've been too blunt. You did say I was to tell you the whole truth, but perhaps—"

"Yes, that's what I want. Uncle Willoughby, about my father's death—"

"My God, what a nightmare that was! How I survived it I'll never know, but then of course I'm a born survivor."

"Uncle Will—"

"I can remember it all as if it was yesterday, your mother weeping and wailing, that old besom Tabitha having hysterics—"

"Uncle Will, about my father's death—"

"There's no need to shout, lad! I may not hear as well as I used to, but I'm not deaf as a post! What is it you want to ask?"

"Did Father commit suicide?"

"Did he *what?*"

"Kill himself."

"*Your father?* Don't talk such piffle! That one was much too stupid to kill himself successfully—that one was the sort of man who'd play Russian roulette and forget to put any bullets in the gun!"

"But I can remember Mother whispering to you—"

"Whispering! She bloody nearly screamed the house down! And as for that illiterate interfering old besom Tabitha, she made a noise like a bloody foghorn. Disgusting. Of course if it hadn't been for her your father would be alive today."

"But good heavens, Uncle Will, what are you saying? Are you trying to tell me that *Tabitha*—"

"It was an accident, lad. It was all a bloody accident. The old besom went and poisoned him by mistake."

4

"ADELAIDE and I agreed never to tell you children because we knew how fond of the old besom you were," said Uncle Willoughby. "We also agreed that Dr. Buller would have to be muzzled, but luckily that presented no difficulty because I happened to know he was carrying on with one of his female patients, so—"

"But how on earth did such a catastrophe happen?"

"I'm telling you, aren't I? Dr. Buller had prescribed two bottles of medicine, a potion for your mother to help her sleep—we called it laudanum because we called all sleeping draughts laudanum in those days, but in fact it was called—no, I can't think of the name. Veronal? Don't remember. Damnation. Usually I remember everything, even though I'm eighty-two—"

"Never mind the name, Buller prescribed a sleeping draught for Mother—"

"—and a potion for your father to ease his innards after a stomach upset. Your father's innards were always troubling him; nerves and too much bloody gin. Anyway, there were the two bottles, standing side by side in the kitchen, and that old besom Tabitha—who should have been hung, drawn and quartered for lethal busybodying interference—takes it upon herself to play Florence Nightingale.

" 'Make sure we take our medicine tonight, Tabitha,' says Adelaide, meaning, of course, 'remind us,' and the old fool adds the medicine to their evening cups of cocoa. Being illiterate she couldn't read the labels, and the bottle she thought was Adelaide's was Arthur's and the bottle she thought was Arthur's was Adelaide's. So your father got a hefty dose of the sleeping draught, and on top of his usual ration of bloody gin it bloody killed him! Poor Arthur! But wasn't it typical that he should die as the result of stupidity?"

I leant forward, elbows on my knees, and put my head in my hands. All I could say was: "I should have been told."

"Rubbish! It's nearly killed you now, when you're a man of forty-four. What would a truth like that have done to a boy of seven? Besides, we wanted to avoid a scandal—the last thing we needed was the old besom on trial for manslaughter and all Maltby wallowing in the details of your father's gin-swilling—and how can one ever trust a child to keep its mouth shut? No, the less you knew the better, and anyway the old besom pleaded on her knees that you and Willy should be kept in ignorance for ever. She doted on you both so much that she couldn't bear to think of you hating her for what she'd done."

I let my hands fall. "But if it was only an accident, why couldn't you have provided for her properly? Why did you leave her to die in a workhouse?"

"That one never died in a workhouse!"

"But Mother said—"

"Adelaide just told you that because she was afraid you might go looking for her later. It was true the old besom had to go to the workhouse as a temporary measure as your mother couldn't bear to have her in the house, but later I arranged for her to go to her sister in York and she lived happily ever after on the pension I provided—which was more than she deserved, silly old woman."

All I could do was repeat: "I should have been told," and again Uncle

Willoughby retorted: "Rubbish! From a practical point of view the connection had to be severed—and about time too! That old woman spoilt you—little terrors you and Willy were! I could see at once, when I stepped in to clear up the mess, that you both had to be taken very firmly in hand, but the trouble was I was so overcome by the bloody awfulness of the mess your father left behind that I daresay I took you in hand too severely. You know what upset me most years later when we had our final quarrel? You, raking up that incident when I wouldn't lend you the money to buy back your toys from the bailiffs. Poor little lad! And you remembered, even after all those years! I was too harsh, I can see that now, but you've no idea what a state I was in. What with the bankruptcy and the manslaughter and the blackmailing of Buller—"

"Yes," I said. "Yes, I do understand." I tried to breathe very slowly and evenly. "So that's how it really was. That's the whole story."

"Whole story my arse!" said Uncle Willoughby. "Just you wait till I tell you what happened next . . ."

5

"IT wasn't just the bankruptcy, the manslaughter and the blackmail that turned my hair snow-white," said Uncle Willoughby. "It was your mother. She couldn't come to terms with your father's death, and she went into a decline. All guilt, of course. She kept wishing she'd been nicer to him in bed. 'For God's sake, Adelaide!' I'd say. 'What's done's done! Let it alone, let it be!' But she couldn't. She sobbed and sobbed and said what a failure she'd been as a wife and how much she despised herself. Poor Adelaide—and she was such a wonderful aberration! 'Never mind,' I said to cheer her up. 'I'll always love you just as you are.'

"Well, that was all very fine, but I'll tell you straight: it led to problems. She eventually assuaged her guilt about your father by canonising him, having his photograph everywhere and talking about him in reverent whispers, but at first she was in such a state that she had to be looked after—so naturally I took her into my home along with little Emily, who could be cared for by my daughters' nurse. You boys had to go to boarding school, no choice. The nurse couldn't have managed two noisy spoilt boys, your mother couldn't have managed anything, my wife felt a bereaved sister-in-law was as much as she could stand—and more. So off you went and of course you were soon whining that the school was too tough, but I knew it was a decent Christian place just as I knew you had to be toughened up. 'I'm letting my little boys be tortured!' Adelaide would sob. 'Rubbish!' said I. 'It'll be the making of them!'—but she couldn't accept that. She just went on and on about what a failure she was as a mother. 'I hate myself!' she'd weep. 'I'm not fit to live!' Poor Adelaide! Pathetic . . . I suppose nowadays they'd say she was having a nervous breakdown.

"Anyhow, I put up with all this because I loved her, and Ella put up with it because I told her to, but eventually Ella got fed up and who can blame her? She'd never liked her sister-in-law, and now here was Adelaide, taking up all my time, just like a demanding wife, whenever I was at home. In fact I began to feel I had two wives—and what was worse, I knew I loved the wrong one best. Carnal desire didn't come into it, I hasten to add—I had a very fetching mistress at the time and besides, neither woman appealed to me in that way. But we were in some sort of peculiar eternal triangle, no doubt about that, and eventually Ella told me she found the situation intolerable.

"Well, I knew my Christian duty. My wife had to come first, so I rented a little house for Adelaide and eased her out of my home.

"But in fact that solved nothing. I found myself calling on Adelaide every day, and as she recovered and became her old entertaining self again I used to spend an increasing amount of time with her. She was such fun and Ella was so dreary . . . But I was in the wrong, I knew I was, and finally Ella told me she'd had enough.

"Meanwhile Adelaide had decided she wanted Ella out of the way so that she could have me all to herself, and it was at this point that she made her fatal miscalculation. In an attempt to force my hand and push me into a marital separation, she said: 'I can see there's nothing else I can do but go and live a long way away!'—expecting that I'd reply: 'Oh no, no, no! I'll never let you leave Maltby!' But I didn't say that. For several seconds I didn't say anything. I just thought of my girls, their future prospects blighted by gossip. I thought how my hope of becoming mayor would come to naught if Ella and I separated. And I thought of Ella's money, tied up snugly in my investments. Then finally I said to my sister: 'Yes, I think it would indeed be best if you went to live somewhere a long way away.'

"She never forgave me. Never, never, never. Oh, she pretended she did. Once she was in St. Leonards she began to write me long witty letters—ah, no one could write letters like your mother! What a masterpiece of an aberration she was!—but she never forgave me. I found that out after you and I quarrelled and I went all the way to St. Leonards to beg her to act as a mediator. 'Of course!' she said, honey-sweet. 'Dearest, *dearest* Will and dearest, *dearest* Neville—what could give me greater happiness than to reconcile the two people I love best?' But she did nothing. That was when she paid me back. 'Hell hath no fury like a woman scorned . . .'

"In the end, when I realised she'd done nothing, I returned to St. Leonards to have it out with her. St. Leonards-on-Sea! I was there yesterday. I would have been there every year since she died, but the South Coast was closed to visitors during the war and afterwards the big hotels took time to reopen for business. I came to this particular hotel because it was recommended to me as well-mannered—you wouldn't credit how snobbish some of these places can be once they hear a Yorkshire accent. Couldn't stay in St. Leonards itself, of course. Too many memories. I've only been there to lay flowers on the grave.

"It was Dr. Buller who recommended St. Leonards to her as being not only genteel but cheap for an invalid in need of sea air. We had to pretend she was still an invalid; she had to have a good excuse for leaving Maltby, and it seemed easiest to say she was leaving on medical advice to live in a warmer climate, but in fact there was nothing much wrong with her by that time. If she played the role of invalid it was because she liked it—it gave her plenty of time to lie around reading books—and as things turned out, she liked St. Leonards too. 'No one here knows what a failure I am,' she wrote to me once. 'Everyone thinks I was a successful wife and mother.' That meant everything to her. Poor Adelaide, she did so long to be a success in life . . . I suppose if she'd been young today—and born into another class, a class in the South—she'd have wound up a member of Parliament or a tutor in one of those women's colleges at Oxford. But she wasn't young today and she wasn't born into the right home, so all those brains went to waste.

"Well, there I was in 1923, charging down to St. Leonards as soon as I realised how she'd paid me back by never mediating as she'd promised, and we had a big row, the biggest row we'd ever had; it was over a year before we started writing to each other again. The row was all about you, of course. She told me I'd monopolised you for quite long enough. 'You keep out of his life in future!' she said. 'He's mine now!' We might have been back in the nursery and squabbling over a favourite toy. 'Neville's my success!' she said, eyes shining. 'Neville's redeemed the past and made sense of all the suffering. Even if I've done nothing else in my life,' she said, 'I've produced Neville—so clever, so charming, so attentive, so absolutely *devoted* to me!' That was when I realised she'd transferred all her most intense love from me to you, and I couldn't help it, I just had to give her a word of warning.

" 'You be careful!' I said. 'That boy won't stand for being smothered, least of all by a woman who neglected him when he was young—don't you be as possessive with him as you were with me!'

"It was a prophetic warning, wasn't it? Oh, I knew it would all end in disaster—I saw the disaster coming a mile off! When she wrote and told me in 1938 that she was going to live with you, I straight away invited her to return to Maltby to live with me; Ella had just died and I was on my own, but Adelaide wrote back, all pride, to say that nothing would induce her to live with me again, thanks very much, and she was all set to enjoy a golden old age with her darling boy.

"After you'd booted her out I called to see her at Emily's nasty little house in Balham. At first she wouldn't talk about what had happened, but she told me everything in the end. Adelaide always did tell me everything... *everything*... Poor Adelaide. Tragic... She never realised, you see, that you couldn't stop yourself behaving towards her as you'd behaved towards me... It was your way of paying us back, wasn't it, for all the misery you went through after Arthur's death? I understood. I'd worked that out years ago. Poor little lad, not even able to buy back his toys from the bailiffs... 'He can't help himself,' I said to Adelaide. 'He was a victim, just as we all were, of that bloody awful muddle.' But she only said: 'You don't understand. I've lived all these years under an illusion. There was no belated success with a child after all, no redemption, and I shall die a failure. I don't want to go on living any more,' she said weeping. 'What's the point of living if one's hated by the people one loves?'

"Well, I couldn't let her say a thing like that. I put my arms around her straight away and said: '*I* don't hate you! I still love you just as much as ever—which means that I'm now going to insist that you live with me in Maltby. No, don't argue!' I said, very masterful and confident. 'I'll not listen to any arguments this time! You're going to come back to Maltby and live happily ever after with me at last!'

"But she recoiled. *'You!'* she said in fury. 'You rejected me and forced me into exile in order to ensure you became Mayor of Maltby and rich as Croesus—you love no one but yourself! You and your prizes!' she said bitterly, hurling the words at me as if they were arrows dipped in poison. 'The only prize worth winning is love—and just you remember *that* when you're a lonely old man trying to comfort yourself with your bank balance and your fading memories!'

"And I've remembered. I've come here and I've remembered. Of course I tell myself how lucky I am. I've got my health and my wealth and I've even got an unmarried daughter to look after me. It would be wrong to be ungrateful. But Mercy irritates me. She's a silly woman, just like her mother—and so's Hope in Leeds. Faith was like me, but she was killed in the Blitz. No sons. One niece who sends Christmas cards but wouldn't care much if I died tomorrow. Two nephews who don't want to know me. My best friends all dead . . . But one mustn't complain, must one, and of course I'm a big man up in Yorkshire. I often remind myself of that when I'm feeling melancholy. I sit in my grand house and I look around at all the mementos of my past, all my prizes, and I think: What a success I was! How wonderfully well my life turned out and how wonderfully fortunate I still am . . . But after a while I begin to hear that silence, that long, long silence you hear when you're all alone in a large grand room, and then I think of your mother and I think of you and I know with a terrible certainty that the only prize worth chasing is the prize I've managed to lose."

He stopped talking. Gradually I became aware of the hum of the sea-wind beyond the tall windows, and the distant drone of other conversations on the far side of the room.

At last he said: "I'm sorry I didn't give you the money to buy back your toys, Nev."

And I answered: "It's all right, Uncle Will. The toys don't matter any more."

Then I poured the remainder of the champagne into our glasses and we sat for a while in silence in that long room which faced the sea.

6

BEFORE he could recover himself sufficiently to start talking about lunch I told him I had to return to the diocese. "I've taken time off from work to come here," I said, "and also my wife's expecting me to visit her in hospital."

"What's wrong with her?"

I failed to summon the strength to give him a precise answer. "Female troubles. But she's getting better."

"You look ripe for the hospital yourself. Did I give you the help you wanted? It looks more as if I've done you in."

"You gave me the help. I'm profoundly grateful to you, Uncle Will, more grateful than I can say."

"In that case," he said as we left the lounge, "perhaps we might drink champagne here again next year if you've nothing better to do."

"Oh, you'll see me long before then."

"I will? When?"

"August, when I take my holiday."

"You mean you'll come back to Yorkshire?"

"Well, I'm hardly likely to bump into you in Devon, am I?"

"If you think I'm going to die and let you off the hook—"

"You're going to live to be a hundred, remember? Start fattening the next calf."

He shook with mirth. Then he shoved out his gnarled old hand for me to shake and added with a masterly attempt at nonchalance: "It was a grand fattened calf, wasn't it, lad?"

"Champion!" I said, discarding my BBC accent. Then leaving him beaming in the hotel porch I stepped out into the stormy wind, which was sweeping east up the Channel, and struggled down the Esplanade beside the ragged roaring sea.

7

AS I entered the station the storm broke and rain began to stream from leaden skies. It was still raining when the train reached Starmouth. I ran as fast as I could to the car park but got soaked. Glancing into the driving-mirror I experienced the fleeting illusion that my face was streaked not with rain but with tears. I looked as white and drawn as someone who had bled to death.

I have little memory of my drive to Starbridge, but the motoring conditions were so unpleasant that the journey must have taken longer than usual. It was after five when I parked my car outside the Theological College. On my right the walls of the Cathedral rose in a vast wet cliff from the sodden sward and disappeared into the mist which hid the spire. Lights glowed in the windows of the ancient houses to combat the murk of the afternoon. The Close was at its most timeless. Only my car anchored me to the twentieth century.

Stumbling through the rain again I entered the modern world of the Theological College, all well-washed linoleum and white walls and bright electric light, and was informed by the secretary that although Darrow was chairing a meeting in the staff-room he had left instructions that I was to wait in his office. I spent ten minutes sitting at the table by the window and watching the Cathedral. It was in one of its inanimate moods, utterly silent, utterly still. No organ music played within and no sunlight flashed upon the glass. The Cathedral might have been waiting, just as I was, waiting for the infusion of life, waiting for the light to shine.

Good Friday had passed. It was Easter Saturday, and the Sunday of the Resurrection had still to dawn.

At twenty minutes past five Darrow walked in.

"Well?" he demanded as soon as he saw me, and without hesitation I said: "I want to confess."

XIX

"But what is wanted is a worthy object to which the individual can devote his whole energies, which shall grip and unify and inspire; only as he can see and occupy himself in relation to a single large purpose will he find peace and power."

CHARLES E. RAVEN
THE CREATOR SPIRIT

I

"I DID an evil thing," I said. "It was a very great sin. I destroyed someone."

Beyond the window, across the sward, someone switched on the lights in the Cathedral.

Without speaking Darrow sat down, and as I faced him once more across the table the bell began to toll for Evensong. "It wasn't my uncle," I said. "As I discovered today he's indestructible. And not only did he prove indestructible when I tried to destroy him all those years ago, but he even managed to understand my behaviour and forgive me. I never thought he would. That's why I had to distance myself from him—first physically, by never going back to Yorkshire, and then mentally, by calling him a villain. But deep down I knew he wasn't the villain of the piece at all. It was *I* who was the villain, and pushing the villainy onto him was the only way I could live with my guilt.

"I performed similar psychological contortions with my mother's memory. You remember that when we talked of Hedda Gabler I got upset by your suggestion that she could have been a victim and a monster as well as a *femme fatale?* You were right, of course, but I couldn't bear to think of my mother being a victim. Yet she was. She was *my* victim. And I couldn't bear to accept Willy's definition of her as a monster either, because that raised too many questions about the way I chose to remember her. How could I have got on so well with a monster? What could have driven me to do such a thing? I didn't want to answer those questions, so I had to say she wasn't a monster at all. I had to develop a portrait which was acceptable, a portrait I could bear to live with, so I played up the fact that she was a witty charming woman who adored me. But what I could never face—until today when it was rammed down my throat—was the fact that it was this adoration which enabled me to destroy her."

I stopped speaking, unsure which direction to take next. Then I said: "I hated my mother." I was unable to look at Darrow. I could only stare at the glowing windows of the Cathedral.

Darrow said casually: "Did you always hate her?" He might have been asking me if I had always taken sugar in my tea.

"No," I said, thinking hard of Emily's teapot and sugar-bowl, "in the beginning I was fascinated by my mother and so was Willy. She was so extraordinary, lying on her chaise-longue all day and reading books. No one else we knew had a mother who did that. Father said she was very special. That was why we had to be kept out of her way—she was so special that she had to have peace and quiet in order to think. 'Keep those stupid noisy boys out of my way so that I can think!' she said once to Tabitha. That was when I made up my mind to become very clever and quiet so that she would want to see more of me. That was when I realised . . . well, all that withheld love was such a prize, you see, *such a prize,* and I felt I could never rest in peace until it was won.

"Later, after my father died and Uncle Willoughby talked to us for the first time about winning the prizes, I felt I'd always known exactly what he meant. The prizes consisted of winning the attention of the people who mattered, and the ultimate prizes consisted of winning their love and approval. Father, Mother, Uncle Willoughby . . . they all offered prizes, but Mother's ultimate prize, her love and approval, was the most fascinating—the most enslaving prize of all. Those visits to the parlour for the daily kiss, those occasional pats on the head, those rare smiles . . . Whenever I won a smile I felt fit to burst with pride. Ah, what a chase it was for that prize, so addictive, so compulsive, so endlessly exciting . . .

"Then Father died and everything changed. No more kisses. No more pats on the head. No more smiles. No more Mother. We weren't even allowed to live with her in the school holidays. Of course now I know she was having a nervous breakdown—now I know she was a poor, pathetic, muddled, unhappy woman not responsible for her actions—but at the time I could only put her alongside Uncle Willoughby and think: I'll never forgive them, never, and one day I'll make them pay.

"Well, I got over that. Or at least I thought I did. After a while I realised that I couldn't go on living in a white-hot fever of misery; it was too debilitating, and I needed all my energy to Get On, Travel Far and stay out of the failure-pit; I didn't want to end up like my father who (so I wrongly thought) had deliberately abandoned me. So Uncle Willoughby had to become the hero, even though he was the villain, treating us so cruelly, and Mother had to become the heroine again, even though she was the villainess, rejecting us after Father's death. It was the way to survive, you see. I had to keep in with the people who mattered. My true feelings had to be buried, the curtain rung down on the past. I was acting for my life on a new stage, and I couldn't afford to let anything impair my performance.

"My mother became better in St. Leonards. I told myself it wasn't her fault that Willy and I could only see her occasionally. She had to be by the sea for her health and we had to be in London to Get On. It was no one's fault. It was just the way of the world, the luck of the draw.

"I was always making excuses for her—but then one always does make excuses for the great prizes, and my mother had become a prize again, I was back in pursuit of her love and attention, back in pursuit of my big addiction as if that hellish period of detoxification had never happened. What a quest it was, what a challenge! I wrote and I wrote and I wrote to her. I saved and I saved and I saved so that I could bring her a present on every visit—there were always second-hand books that I could pick up cheaply in London, and how gratified she always was, how enchanted! I'd be in a haze of pleasure afterwards for hours.

"Willy thought my behaviour was disgusting. 'It makes me sick,' he said, 'to see the way you fawn on that awful woman.' That was after his illness, after he'd stopped chasing the prizes and no longer cared about winning her love and approval. He just wrote her neglect off as unforgivable and went his own misogynist's way.

"But I remained addicted, and—as I can now see so clearly—the chase for the prize became in a bizarre way more exciting than the prize itself. The real truth was I was happiest when my mother and I were at a distance from each other; it was easier to sustain the fantasy of devotion. All those delectable letters to write, all those delectable expeditions to find the right present, all those delectable day-dreams when I would imagine our next witty dialogue down to the last comma—yes, *then* I was in ecstasy. But the actual visits themselves were hard going. Her rooms at St. Leonards were unsuitable for visitors. She remained awkward with children. I was shy with her. There was a perpetual atmosphere of constraint, but matters improved when I was old enough to engage in sparkling intellectual discussions. The meetings were exhausting but at least I felt I was making progress. Of course I can see now why they were so exhausting; it wasn't just because they required intellectual stamina. It was because although we were dazzling each other with this glittering mother-son relationship, none of the emotions were real. She was just trying to assuage her guilt by playing the devoted mother, while I . . . well, I still hated her. That was the truth of it. I'd never forgiven her for all that neglect and rejection when I was a child.

"I used to feel very violent emotions towards women when I was growing up. The normal women I found tolerable; the devoted wives and mothers were good, they were the way women were supposed to be, but as for the rest . . . Up at Oxford when I lost my virginity I started to beat the woman up afterwards. That shocked me. I told myself it would never have happened if I hadn't been drinking, but I knew the drink had only underlined feelings which were already present. I thought: *There's* a demon who has to be locked up. So for years I drank very sparingly and I became a clergyman, keeping my demon clamped down beneath a clerical collar, and I married a wife whom I could put on a pedestal and revere . . . She was safe there, you see, up on her pedestal, the perfect marital prize. I couldn't have harmed her there . . . Oh, how hard I worked to sew up my demon in a straitjacket so that I'd feel safe, and in the end I did feel safe, I thought I'd mastered him, I thought I had everything under control.

"But I didn't. He was just waiting for the right opportunity to burst free and take possession of me again, and in 1938, when my mother came to live with me, his moment finally came.

"I'm not sure when my mother genuinely began to love me. Sometimes it's hard to know when fantasy ends and reality begins, but I first knew beyond doubt that the love was real soon after Emily had announced her engagement. I said to my mother: 'Of course you'll come to live with me—how wonderful that we can be together at last!' And when her eyes filled with tears of happiness I knew I could say to the child I had been long ago: 'There! You've done it! You've won your ultimate prize!'

"After that my demon didn't have to wait long for the chance to take control, but the apparent cause of that final quarrel with my mother was so trivial that it's a wonder I can still remember it. She made some casual criticism of Grace's choice of curtains for the nursery. Then without warning the demon burst free. I turned on my mother and said: 'What the devil do you know about nurseries? You spent all my childhood keeping out of mine!'

"Then the violence began. That was the moment when all the acting had to stop. That was the moment when reality broke into the theatre and swept our long-running drama right off the stage.

"The verbal violence came first. It always does. That's the warm-up.

Words streamed out of me, words I never thought I'd ever utter, words expressing all the emotions I'd buried so deep for so long. I told her she was rubbish, a caricature of a woman, a contemptible monstrosity which any normal man could only despise and ridicule, and then when she tried to defend herself, I—

"Then the demon wiped me out. No, I can't say that. That sounds as if I'm disclaiming responsibility for what happened. I must say: I let the demon wipe me out. But no, I can't say that either, that makes me sound passive. And I wasn't passive at all.

"I was actively expressing what I can only describe as an ecstasy, the vilest and blackest of ecstasies, a perverted rush of power. At that moment I *was* the demon; he wasn't a separate entity any more. It was a moment of very great evil and I committed a very great sin. I must say that. I have to say it out loud. I was inflicting physical, mental and emotional pain on an old woman who loved me. I hit her and hit her and . . . oh, God only knows what would have happened if Grace hadn't heard my mother's screams and rushed into the room, but as soon as Grace appeared . . . Darrow, it was the most extraordinary thing. I know you think I'm absurdly infatuated with science, but this really was like the illustration of some immutable scientific principle; it was as if two substances had been placed in a test-tube and one had somehow instantly dissolved the other—"

"No demon can withstand the power of Christ."

"That's it. I suppose a Modernist would say it was the Christian principle in action, and talk about the power of moral force on a dissociated mind. But in the end descriptions aren't important; all that matters now is that my demon couldn't stay in the same room as Grace. He had to scuttle away and bury himself in the woodwork of my mind again. She was so good, you see. She'd never liked my mother, but without hesitation she took her in her arms and tried to comfort her—she couldn't have been more gentle and kind. My mother hated her for that, of course. She didn't want Grace to know what had happened—she didn't want anyone to know, and neither did I. Later, as I discovered today, she broke down and told Uncle Willoughby, but at that moment all we wanted to do was crawl back into our fantasy world as soon as possible because the world of reality was far too terrible to endure. In the end we rang down the curtain by agreeing to treat the incident as if it had never happened.

"So my mother went to live with Emily and we began writing our witty letters again as if nothing was wrong. Meanwhile I'd made it clear to Grace that I never wanted to speak of the quarrel, so naturally, perfect as always, she never referred to it. But perhaps she was too frightened to refer to it. I don't know, but time passed and nothing was said and in the end I was able to tell myself: I'm fine now, I'm safe, I'm surviving . . .

"But I wasn't. That was just a delusion. I wasn't surviving at all.

"I can't describe to you how terrible I felt when my mother died in 1941. I kept thinking: I won't feel guilty, I won't. But then the curtain would go up—all the curtains would go up—and I'd remember my mother loving me, my uncle loving me, my father loving me—and I knew I'd rejected them all. I told myself I was justified, I made myself believe that everything I'd done could be justified, but it was becoming harder and harder to keep this fiction nailed in place because once my mother was dead my private myth inexorably began to disintegrate. Then a very curious thing happened. I became aware that a black hole had opened up in my life, a gnawing emptiness which was stealthily expanding. At first I thought it was just a bizarre form of bereavement—and I suppose it was, in a way. But it wasn't a true bereavement. It was the addict's deprivation.

"All my life, in one way or another, I'd been bound up with my great prize, and now she was gone I found I didn't know what to do without her. I forgot the nightmare scene in 1938, blotted it right out. All I could remember was the thrill of the chase, the thrill which made me feel so powerfully alive—and then it occurred to me that if only I could embark on another delirious chase I could keep the horror perpetually at bay.

"I became restless. I became irritable. And my wonderful Grace, up there on her pedestal, began to seem so dull, so dreary, so incapable of providing me with the excitement I knew I just had to have . . . and which I finally found, in the May of 1942, when I met Dido for the first time.

"Oh, how happy I was! The demented addict had at last found a new supply of dope—and what a supply it was, what quality, what a perfect antidote to my malaise! Here was a brand-new eccentric female, sharp as a needle, deliciously amusing, withholding her love and absolutely unobtainable. What more could I possibly want? Only the freedom to chase her—which, as you'll remember, I soon received.

"I chased and I chased and I chased—oh, how I enjoyed myself! And every time she rejected me and humiliated me I thought: I'll pay her back in the end. The curious part was that I made exactly the same mistake as I made with my mother, and fooled myself into believing that the ultimate prize I was chasing was her love. But perhaps the mistake was inevitable; I'd buried the truth about my mother deep in my subconscious by that time, and looking back I can see clearly that during my long pursuit of Dido I never succeeded in analysing my behaviour truthfully.

By that time I was incapable of it. I was even incapable of linking Dido consciously with my mother—although all those *déjà vu* experiences were certainly hints of the truth I didn't dare acknowledge. It was only when the baby was born dead and I read Dido's letter, in which she finally told me she loved me, that I realised I'd been re-enacting the whole appalling ritual with my mother. Part of me was saying to myself: That's it, there's no prize left to win, what on earth do I do now? And the other part, the part I had to shovel out of sight behind the curtain, was whispering: Now you claim the *real* prize. You tear up her love and fling it back in her face and beat her till she screams for mercy.

"I couldn't look the truth squarely in the face, but I knew it was there. That was when I realised I'd wound up in a black pit with my demon. He'd finally triumphed; I was in the coffin and he was nailing down the lid. He'd put me through one revolting ritual and now he'd put me through the same disgusting charade all over again—"

"I'm afraid the hallmark of an unexorcised demon is a mania for repetition."

"But it's no use talking of exorcism now, is it? He's destroyed me, I've lost my battle with him—"

"No," said Darrow. "The battle's finished, but you haven't lost. Your days as a loser are over, Aysgarth. This is where you start to win."

2

"YOU'VE grasped the truth," said Darrow. "You're demonstrating with every syllable you utter that you repent. Can't you see your demon's vanquished, cowering with terror in his pit?"

"You're saying this is another example of the Christian principle in action, but it can't be."

"Why not? If you've repented, then Christ is on your side, and if no demon can withstand the power of Christ—"

"Christ couldn't possibly be on my side."

"Why not?"

"I may have repented, but I can't expect to receive his compassion and forgiveness. I'm too contaminated by what I've done."

"My dear Aysgarth, you know as well as I do that provided a genuine repentance is present, not even the most contaminated man on earth is unforgivable!"

"I know that intellectually, yes. It's what we're taught to believe. But—"

"You feel the forgiveness has no reality for you. I understand. But do you seriously believe that Our Lord's response to this agony of yours would be: 'Go your way and never darken my door again'?"

"No, of course in theory he'd say: 'Go your way and sin no more.' I know that intellectually too. But I still can't believe that if I were actually to meet him face to face now in 1946, he'd ever be able to bring himself to say such a thing to me."

Darrow said suddenly: "What did your uncle say to you today when you actually met him face to face? Did he say: 'Bugger off, you bastard, and never come near me again'?"

I was transfixed.

"He didn't say that, did he?" said Darrow. "Yet he knew what you'd done not only to him but to your mother. So if even an old Yorkshire rogue still loved you enough to forgive you in such very unpromising circumstances, how much more likely it is that Our Lord—"

But I was no longer listening to him. I could only whisper: "The old boy killed the fatted calf," and then the demon began to die at last as the black pit filled with light.

3

IT was at least five minutes before I could speak again. I remember being vaguely interested in the fact that Darrow kept quiet as a mouse and never bothered me. That was good. All speech would have been an intrusion and any physical contact an impertinence. But no doubt his telepathic intuition would have told him that. I didn't believe in telepathy, of course, but I could see how useful it was in pastoral work.

After I had finished revolting myself by snuffling despicably in this disgusting fashion, I managed to say: "I've been so busy going off my head that I haven't yet thanked you for flogging me along to see Uncle Will. It was the most important thing you could possibly have done."

"Can you tell me about the meeting now, do you think? I'd like to hear how he illuminated the past."

I talked for some time before concluding: "So in fact there were no heroes and villains, as in my melodrama. There were just three ordinary people who got in a mess and wound up in a tragedy. I can understand them all now."

"And having understood them—"

"Yes, I can forgive them. My poor pathetic parents—and that funny old villain talking today about his loveless marriage and his lonely life . . . Poor old sod. I promised I'd go up to Maltby in August to see him."

"And if your mother were alive, would you go and see her?"

"But she's not alive." It took me a great effort of will to add in a level voice: "I'll never be able to tell her I'm sorry. I'll never be able to say to her: 'Forgive me for being so stupid and ignorant, not understanding anything, forgive me for never realising how unhappy you were, forgive me for causing you so much pain.' I'll never be able to make amends for what I did."

"That's the negative side of your new enlightenment. But now look at the positive side. Having repented, your anger towards her's dead. You don't really want to go around hitting women any more, do you?"

I could only shudder in revulsion.

"Well, isn't that a step forward? Of course we mustn't make the mistake of thinking you're miraculously cured of your weakness for violence; you've got a tough aggressive streak which thrives on combat, and that's not going to change. But what *can* be changed is your susceptibility to demonic infiltration. We've got to make sure this aggressive streak isn't kidnapped by the next passing demon who thinks he spots an attractively violent home."

"How do we do that?"

"We find you a resourceful older clergyman whom you can consult whenever you're tempted to sweep violent feelings under the rug and ring down the curtain. With any luck he'll be able to ring up the curtain, whisk away the rug and disarm those dangerous emotions before they can fester and cause trouble."

I considered this solution carefully and said at last: "You could do that."

Darrow smiled. "I hope I've been useful to you in this emergency," he said in his best modest voice, the one he used on those rare occasions when he genuinely wanted to be humble and friendly, "but I'm sure Aidan would be the first to agree I couldn't help you in more normal circumstances. I rub you up the wrong way, with the result that I stimulate just the kind of aggressive feelings you can do without—and besides, our professional lives are too interconnected. Once we start wrangling about the College extension—"

"Yes, it would be disastrous. You're right." I heaved a sigh before adding: "It's a pity, because I can see how gifted you are at this kind of work. That remarkable intuition of yours must make up for your lack of personal experience."

Darrow looked startled. "Lack of personal experience?"

"Well, I'm sure you never had any trouble with your parents, did you? I remember your wife saying once to Grace that you were an only child brought up in a quiet happy home."

Darrow at once commented dryly: "I concede I never had an uncle to complicate family life!" Then he added: "Don't worry for the moment about your new counsellor. He'll probably turn up in exactly the right place once your future becomes clear."

"The future! Good heavens, I'd forgotten about it. What on earth's going to happen next?"

"Aysgarth, I know you think I'm a fortune-teller manqué, the sort of charlatan who ekes out a living in a booth on a seaside pier, but I assure you that I have no esoteric knowledge of your future. However I'll tell you this: I think the future will become clear very soon. You've faced up to your past; the present has been transformed by your new understanding and the stage is now all set for the next act."

"Please don't think I'm being sarcastic," I said, valiantly beating back the sarcasm, "but do you really think there'll be a magic moment when I'll clap my hands, shout 'Eureka!' and know beyond all doubt whether I'm to work for Bell in Europe or in London among the aristocracy?"

"Oh, those are just side-issues," said Darrow with the authority which I had once found so infuriating but which now commanded my respect. "The crucial question, which you seem to have forgotten, is: How do you survive your marriage in order to have any career in the Church at all?"

I felt close to despair once more. "Well?" I demanded. "What's the answer?"

"There you go again, treating me as if I can produce a detailed synopsis of your future just by flicking a switch in my brain! Aysgarth, there's no board outside this office which says: 'Fortune-Telling by Appointment.' All I can tell you as a priest is that you've sinned, you've repented and now by the grace of God you'll be redeemed—although the manner of the redemption is still to be revealed." He glanced up at the clock. "And talking of your wife, I see it's time you were on your way to visit her. Can you give me a lift to the station?"

"Yes, but I don't think I can visit Dido tonight—I feel too exhausted. I'll phone the hospital and say—"

"No," said Darrow so firmly that I jumped.

"But I just don't have the strength at present to play the devoted husband! And I certainly don't have the strength to listen to her rattling on and on and on about herself in her usual tiresome fashion!"

Darrow suddenly became very tough. I was reminded of Aidan taking one of his daring risks.

"Aysgarth, has it never occurred to you to wonder why your wife rattles on and on and on about herself?"

"Well, I always assumed it was simply part of her egocentric personality—"

"That's not much of an assumption, is it? It explains nothing. Have you never asked yourself if she's perhaps trying desperately to attract your attention? Is it not possible, do you suppose, that this unattractive egocentricity might even be a cry for help? What in fact is the hidden message here which your wife is so frantically trying to convey to you amidst the torrents of self-centred monologue?"

I could only stare at him.

"Why does she indulge in her famous eccentric behaviour?" pursued Darrow ruthlessly. "Is it because she's discovered in the past that it guarantees people notice her? If so, why is she so afraid of being passed over and ignored? How far can it be attributed to the fact that she was the youngest of a large ebullient family? Was she neglected when she was young? What was her childhood relationship with her mother, the mysterious woman who, so I hear, is kept out of sight in Scotland and only allowed to visit London for her daughters' weddings? What was your wife's childhood relationship with her father, who was probably too busy making his millions to bother much about the last daughter in his family? Does your wife's intense devotion to the sister closest to her in age indicate that she had failed to find a worthy object for her devotion elsewhere in the family? Does it hint at some kind of emotional deprivation analogous to your own at that time when you came to depend so heavily on your brother's companionship? In other words, to cut a long list of unanswered questions short, what's really going on in your wife's psyche? How well, in fact, do you know her? Have you ever made any profound attempt to understand why she's the way she is? Aysgarth, now is not the moment, believe me, to play the wilting flower and claim you're too exhausted to see her. Exert your very considerable will-power, give the appropriate instructions to your ox-like constitution and get over to that hospital to minister to this stranger who so desperately wants to communicate with you."

No argument was possible. Mute with shame, I levered myself to my feet and trudged outside with him to my car.

4

WHEN we reached the station Darrow said troubled: "I don't like leaving you, but I promised my wife I'd be home at a reasonable hour."

"I'm better now."

"Telephone me later this evening."

"Very well—if I'm still conscious."

"Any whisky in the house?"

"None. Run along, Nanny, or you'll miss your train."

Reluctantly he unfolded his tall frame, hauled himself out of the passenger seat and trailed away across the cobbled forecourt into the station.

I drove on to the hospital.

5

AS soon as I walked into Dido's flower-filled room I experienced yet again that eerie phenomenon of *déjà vu* and saw so clearly that this was no inexplicable delusion. I felt as if the scene had taken place before because it had indeed taken place before, over and over again in the past which had so tormented me. I looked at the pathetic, tragic invalid who loved me and saw not my wife but the mother I had so hideously mistreated. And then I saw the road to redemption.

The exhausted despair with which I had contemplated Dido such a short time earlier was now instantly erased; it was as if a blackboard had been wiped clean with the single sweep of a hand. Strength poured into me; it was as if a man dying from loss of blood had received a single mighty transfusion. I knew then—it required no reasoning, for the knowledge arrived fully formed in my mind—that I could embrace my role of husband until it became so familiar that no acting was necessary. I was reminded of how I had acquired my BBC accent. At first it had taken a conscious effort to maintain, but now I automatically spoke in that manner. All that had been required was the will to keep practising, and already, as I experienced the infusion of strength, I knew I had the will not only to accept my role but to perfect it. I had been granted the power to survive.

"My dearest Dido!" I exclaimed, and although in one sense I was acting, in another sense—the only sense that mattered as I thought of my mother—I was painfully sincere. "What must you be thinking of me? I'm sure you're feeling utterly deserted!"

She burst into tears but now I could deal with them without turning a hair. I took her in my arms and kissed her and pulled the visitor's chair close to the bed so that I could hold her hand while we talked.

"Oh Stephen, I've been feeling such a dreadful failure—"

"A failure?" I said to my mother as the past caught fire from the present and the pain was consumed by the flames. "You? Never describe yourself to me in that way again!"

"But Stephen—"

"You're a masterpiece!"

"Oh darling, how terribly sweet of you to say so, but I don't quite see how I can be when I'm so horribly abnormal—"

"I don't want anyone normal. I'd be bored to death. I want a magnificent aberration from the norm . . ." The fire was raging in the past now. I could see the bones of all the suffering bleached white as they were purified, and still the cleansing flames burnt on and on.

"How can I be magnificent when I produced that wretched travesty of a baby?"

"Where on earth did you get the idea that he was a wretched travesty? Why, I was so proud and pleased that I even called him Arthur after my father . . ." The flames were dying at last but a great light shone backwards from the present into my memory, and when I saw my mother reading quietly on her chaise-longue I knew we were both at peace. It was a memory I could live with, a small serene cameo which I could recall without flinching.

". . . and you see, I thought that as you never mentioned him he was too horrible to speak of—and I thought that had made you angry and disappointed—"

"I didn't mention him because I thought it would upset you. Obviously we've been crucifying ourselves over an absurd misunderstanding."

"But if he wasn't a wretched travesty after all . . . oh my God, how dreadful that I didn't see him! How can I ever forgive myself for—"

"No, there's no need for you to feel guilty. You were much too ill to cope with such a bereavement, so it was my job to attend to him—and my job to remember him in detail so that I could share him with you later." And as I thought of my mother toiling through her years of childbearing I embarked on a description not of poor little Arthur in his plain, waxen lifelessness but of Christian, perfect shining Christian with his pink-and-white skin and his long dark eyelashes and his soft brown down on the top of his small elegant head. ". . . and you mustn't feel he's been erased as if he never existed," I heard myself say. "He has his own special grave and his own special name. You can think of him and feel proud, just as I do."

As the tears streamed down her face again she whispered: "So it was all a sort of success after all."

"Oh, no doubt about it! And what a brave thing it was for you to embark on a pregnancy after what happened to Laura! I see now I never fully appreciated your great courage—or indeed the great love you offered me in your last letter. I've really been very obtuse and stupid."

"I was beginning to think that now you'd won my love you didn't want it any more—"

"My dear," I said as my mother turned over a page in her book, "when one wins someone's love—that ultimate prize—one doesn't tear it up and chuck it away in the nearest wastepaper basket. One looks after it and cherishes it and thinks how lucky one is to have won it. I know we've had a terrible first year of married life, but if we can now put that behind us—"

"That's what I want." Dido's tears had stopped. Suddenly she said: "My God, I do believe you mean every word you say—I believe the nightmare's finally coming to an end. Oh Stephen, if you only knew how frightened I've been! You see, I thought I was going to wind up like my mother—"

"Ah yes," I said, "your mother. I've never asked you much about her, have I, and I can see now that was yet another big mistake of mine, but—"

"No, I thought you were being quite wonderfully tactful. It's not a subject I can usually bear to talk about—or if I do talk about it I turn it into a joke and talk of Mother's beautiful retiring nature and Father's exceptional good taste in never having a mistress in the same city as his wife—"

"I should have realised the reality was very much more painful than the sophisticated fantasy you presented."

"Painful? It was unspeakable. Oh Stephen, when I grew up and saw how awful marriage could be, I didn't want to have anything to do with it! I never wanted to give any man the opportunity to treat me as my father treated my mother. All that neglect, all that contempt, all that humiliation . . . Mother gave up in the end, couldn't cope, walled herself up in Edinburgh, made up her mind to live a twilight existence as a complete failure, too stupid and feeble to keep up with her husband, too dull and common to be treated by her children as anything but a social encumbrance . . . Poor Mother! But on the other hand, why the hell should I feel sorry for her? She never took any notice of me. I'm sure I was a very unwelcome pregnancy. She never really cared."

"But your father cared, surely? He always seems to treat you with affection—"

"Oh yes—the sort of affection a farmer will feel for a prize cow who wins him a lot of prestige in the cattle-show! The only way I ever got him to take notice of me was to become a stunning social success in that great cattle-show the London Season, but as soon as I started to get a bit long in the tooth he became vile. 'There's nothing more pathetic than an aging spinster with a glittering future behind her!' he snarled at me once. 'Oh yes, there is!' I shot back. 'A married woman whose husband treats her like dirt!' He nearly burst with fury when I said that. 'You get yourself to the altar pretty damn quick,' he shouted, 'or your mother won't be the only woman I treat like dirt!' Oh, I could have killed him! I'd tried so hard to be the sort of daughter he wanted yet I'd never managed to be more than a lump of meat on parade. I thought: I'll show him! I'll show the bastard I'm a very different woman from my mother! I'll marry my Archdeacon and be a huge success as a married woman—but then I found that what I wanted to do and what I was capable of doing were two entirely different things and I became so confused, so frightened, so—"

"I blame myself very much. If only I'd—"

"No, there was nothing you could have done. I couldn't have confided in you before—I didn't trust you not to stop loving me once you found out how imperfect I really was. I thought that once you'd found out that I could never be a second Grace you wouldn't want me any more, and that was why, when you hardly ever came here to visit me, I felt I had no choice but to assume you were disillusioned and fed up."

"I don't want a second Grace. In fact I can say with absolute truth that I've never wanted a second Grace. I wanted to marry someone exactly like you."

"Yes, but *why,* Archdeacon dear? I could never quite work that out, but never mind, God moves in mysterious ways and I'm quite sure that although I'm so peculiar I'm going to be of absolutely *vital* importance to you in your career. And that reminds me—" She paused to dry her eyes and blow her nose. "Who do you think came to see me today?"

"About half Starbridge, I should think, judging by your battalions of flowers."

"Oh, most of them just arrived via the florist. But you see that really sumptuous lot over there? They were delivered in person by none other than that devoted gardener—"

"Lady Flaxton," I said, and found I could only watch with an appalled resignation as the future began to unfold before my eyes.

6

"MY dear!" said Dido, recovering fast now and even becoming animated. "How guilty I feel that I implied to you she was just a garden-obsessed old hag! She was so kind to me and promised she'd invite us both down to Flaxton Pauncefoot as soon as I was better. Apparently Lord F. is running around saying you've got the brains to be Dean of St. Paul's."

"Unfortunately for Lord Flaxton, Dean Matthews isn't considering retirement."

"Maybe you could be Dean of Westminster instead!"

"My dear, I think a modest canonry would be the most I could hope for at present at either Westminster Abbey or—"

"But wouldn't becoming a canon be a step down from being an archdeacon? No," said Dido, rushing excitedly on without giving me time to reply, "not at Westminster or St. Paul's—a canonry there is inevitably the prelude to Great Things!"

"Well, that's not *necessarily* true—"

"Oh darling, do stop quibbling! Of course it's not necessarily true if the man's old or boring or only moderately clever, but if the man's young and dynamic and brilliant—"

"Do I take this spirited defence of a London canonry to mean that you're hankering for the great metropolis?"

"Well . . . oh hell, let's be honest! Darling, you know as well as I do that London's where things happen because London's where one meets the people who matter. I mean, of course I'm mad about Starbridge—so beautiful, so romantic, so historic, so spiritual, so divine, so utterly wonderful in every possible way—but honestly, Stephen, when all's said and done . . . isn't it just the teensiest bit boring?"

"If we could somehow stifle our yawns for another two or three years, I'd almost certainly receive preferment anyway. I don't have to move to London in order to keep travelling up the ecclesiastical ladder."

"Yes, but if you stay here, not meeting the people who matter, you might be posted to some ghastly place in the back of beyond simply because you didn't go to Eton or Harrow, whereas if you're in London and people can see for themselves how triumphantly you've overcome your social disabilities—"

"How would you like to live in Geneva?"

"Geneva?"

"It's a city in Switzerland."

"Oh Stephen, don't be so idiotic, I know Blackboard was the most hopeless governess that ever lived, but even *I* know Geneva's in Switzerland! I only repeated the name because I thought I must have misheard you. What on earth could an English clergyman do in Geneva?"

"That's where the secretariat of the World Council of Churches is based, and now that the war's over everyone there's preparing for the Council's first meeting. Bishop Bell, as the most influential churchman in Europe, is bound to be heavily involved and that means there'll be plenty of liaison work with the German churches—and since I speak fluent German and have the experience of working with German POWs—"

"Yes, I'm sure that was all very interesting for you, darling, but the German POWs belong to the past, don't they—or they will do when the horrid camp closes—and you can't possibly chuck up your career here in order to romp around Europe with Bishop Bell."

"Can't I?"

"No, of course not—oh Stephen, *do* come down to earth and stop wafting along on your clouds of romantic idealism! I always did look askance at your secret passion for that dangerous saint Dr. Bell—he's your Pied Piper, all set to lead you hopelessly astray. World Council of Churches indeed! It'll be worse than the League of Nations, nothing but bickering and futility and grand idealistic statements that mean absolutely nothing. And Switzerland! All those cuckoo-clocks and shop-windows full of watches and men in leather shorts yodelling among the banks! It's so terribly unstimulating, isn't it, and just think of all the dreary exhausting problems attached to setting up house in a foreign country with all the endless difficulties about the children's education. It would cost a fortune to shunt them back and forth for the school holidays, and where's the money going to come from?"

"I suppose one could say that God would provide—"

"No, one jolly well couldn't! Honestly, you idealists are the limit sometimes, you really are—I bet Mrs. Bell has a hard slog keeping her George on the rails! Now, darling, do try to be *realistic.* Apart from all the financial problems which will arise if you go skipping off to Geneva in pursuit of your Pied Piper, what's going to happen to your future? Everyone will soon forget about you once you're lost in Europe, and then there'll be no deaneries, no bishoprics, no seat in the House of Lords, no invitations to Buckingham Palace, no glamour, no excitement, no simply *pulsating* professional fulfillment—"

"Not for you, no."

"Nor for you either, darling—oh, come down out of those clouds of self-deception and *be honest!* If we went to Switzerland—"

"No, let's forget Switzerland. And let's forget Bishop Bell. I was only toying with a passing whim."

"Well, I didn't think you could possibly be serious, but knowing your divinely romantic but absolutely lethal idealistic streak—"

"You think you could be happy and fulfilled in London, do you?"

"Oh, of course—there'd be no end to the help I could give you! I could create such a smart home for us and cultivate all the right people and give dazzling little dinner-parties for sixteen every week—"

"Ah yes," I said smiling at her, "I can see it all."

"Oh God, Stephen, are you secretly horrified? Do you want to rush off to Switzerland after all?"

"All I want," I said, "is for you to feel cherished, successful and happy."

"Well, darling, that's simply too noble of you and I'm on the point of soaking at least another six handkerchiefs, but our marriage won't be worth tuppence if I wind up happy as a lark and you wind up miserable!"

"I couldn't be happy if I felt I was causing you to suffer in any way. I couldn't live with myself. So in the end it's all mercifully simple," I said to Aidan as if he were beside me instead of far away in Yorkshire, "as clear as it was long ago when Raven spoke in Christ Church Cathedral." And to Darrow I added in the famous words of Martin Luther: " 'Here I stand. I can do no other.' "

Dido said: "Darling, that's all simply too wonderful, but I confess I do feel *slightly* worried that you sound as if you've been condemned to death."

I laughed, genuinely amused, and as I relaxed at last I found it easy to produce the answer which might have been so very difficult to frame. "Raven once wrote: 'All roads honestly followed lead to God: of that I am very sure,' " I said. "I believe that if I now go steadily on, trying to serve God by doing what I believe to be right and not looking too far ahead, then my road will eventually lead me where God intends me to go."

But Dido in her excitement was already peering far into the future. "Of course Westminster Abbey is more central than St. Paul's but perhaps the houses for the clergy in Amen Court are better than the ones in Little Cloister—I must try and find out exactly what the extent of the bomb damage was . . . On the other hand, the Abbey's near St. James's Park—so nice for the children—and there's nothing around the Cathedral except bomb-sites . . . And then of course one mustn't forget that the taxi-ride to Harrods would be so much cheaper from Parliament Square than from Ludgate Hill—"

The nurse entered the room to terminate my visit. I kissed Dido, and then leaving her still radiant at the thought of our golden future, I slipped quietly out of the brightly lit hospital into the rain-sodden twilight beyond.

7

OPENING the door of my car I found that Darrow had once more folded himself into the passenger seat.

"I couldn't get on the train," he said as I gasped in surprise. "I couldn't have forgiven myself if you'd left the hospital and started hitting the bottle."

"Why should I now start hitting the bottle?"

"Because you'll have seen the exact nature of the hard lonely road which lies ahead."

I slumped behind the wheel, slammed the door shut and said: "Are you quite sure you don't tell fortunes by appointment?"

"My dear Aysgarth, it was moderately obvious to a detached observer that you'd feel bound to redeem your mother's tragedy in the God-given way now available. Why else do you think I dragooned you to the hospital? But there was no clairvoyance. I merely made a deduction based on reason and experience."

We sat there in our makeshift metal confessional and eventually I found the words to tell him what had happened.

Darrow said soberly afterwards: "You've been called to perform a very difficult task."

"It could be worse," I said, and as I spoke I heard myself as if I were a stranger and saw with detachment the cool, laconic Yorkshireman, dogged and determined, wedded irrevocably to the British understatement and the stiff upper lip, despising any masculine display of emotion or self-pity, trained in the hardest of schools which had ensured he was prepared to tackle the hardest of tasks. "All that matters," I said, "is that I've been shown the way to survive my marriage, a miracle which means I can continue to serve God in the Church. I should be grateful for such a reprieve. It's more than I deserve." I paused before adding: "I daresay we'll become good friends in the end. At least life won't be dull. When I left she was planning her first little dinner-party for sixteen at Amen Court."

"Amusing for her. But perhaps Lord Flaxton will fail to produce the magic preferment out of his coronet."

"Perhaps. But on the other hand—"

"Yes, I can imagine the other hand too. I've been thinking again about your prospects, and I can now see that this might just be one of those rare occasions when an amateur like Flaxton finds no serious professional opposition to the scheme which allows him to flex his power and his eccentricity in such satisfying harmony. The gentlemen in authority may well think that a London canonry would give you a useful finishing polish after your years as an unusually youthful archdeacon in the provinces."

"And to cap it all—as you may have seen in *The Times* last week—"

"There's a canonry falling vacant at Westminster. Yes, I saw Woodhouse's appointment as Dean of Radbury."

We fell silent again. It had stopped raining, and the raindrops, clinging to their pattern on the windscreen, were sparkling in the light of the street-lamp. At last I said: "I spent my youth in London. I'll soon settle down. What right have I, after all that's happened, to go whining to God that I'd rather work somewhere else?"

"Whining, I agree, would be unattractive, but never think God doesn't listen when you tell Him what you want." Darrow paused for a moment before adding idly: "Of course Bishop Bell's often in London, attending the House of Lords and dealing with his international concerns. Except for Chichester there's no city other than London where you're more likely to encounter him."

Suddenly I switched on the windscreen wipers to clear the glass. The city street which had been blurred and indistinct was now clear-cut in the light from the street-lamp. "Perhaps in my spare time I could work for one of Bell's causes," I said.

"Of course you could."

"So London needn't be the end of the world, need it?"

"No, Aysgarth. London needn't be the end of the world."

I took a deep breath, expelled it slowly and then reached out to start the engine. "I'll take you back to the station."

"I still have this feeling I oughtn't to leave you—"

"My dear Darrow, unless you get the next train home *you're* the one who'll wind up being left—by your long-suffering wife!"

Darrow said vaguely: "Oh, she'll understand," but he seemed to resign himself to leaving me. It was only when we reached the station that I realised he still had his doubts. As I halted the car he said: "You're quite sure there's no whisky in your house?"

"Positive. Darrow, do you really think, after you've so cleverly given me hope for the future, that there's any serious risk of me winding up tonight dead drunk on the Cathedral sward and singing 'Lili Marlene' at the top of my voice?"

"No, but I confess your drinking does worry me. I feel it's your Achilles' heel."

"I usually have it well in control."

" 'Usually' isn't good enough. It must be 'always.' "

"Very well—in future I'll always have my drinking under control!"

"Even when you're under intense marital strain? There's inevitably going to be marital strain in the years ahead, Aysgarth, and since your whole future in the Church depends on your ability to survive your marriage—"

"I'll survive. If you think I'm on the road to alcoholism, I assure you you're mistaken—I'm not the suicidal type."

"You don't have to be an alcoholic to blight your service to God, Aysgarth. All you need to be is a heavy drinker, and you've already proved that's well within your capabilities." Opening the car door he unfolded himself once more from the passenger seat and stepped out into the damp evening air. "Think it over," he said, turning to face me, "and I believe your conscience will tell you I'm talking sense when I advise you to give up alcohol altogether. Now look after yourself, please, and phone me at once if you need to talk. I'll pray for you."

He strode away into the station and vanished so abruptly that I blinked.

"Sinister old magician!" I muttered to myself as I put the car in gear. As I reflected on his advice I was obliged to concede it was justified, but nevertheless I felt irritable. "I rub you up the wrong way," Darrow had said, and it was true. With my Modernist leanings I could hardly fail to be irritated by even the most benign wizard who practised white magic; I had long since made up my mind that wizards and white magic could not exist, and yet there was Darrow, bouncing along on a tidal wave of telepathy, clairvoyance and heaven only knows what else—and even creating the illusion that he could vanish in a puff of smoke at a railway station. In the old days, of course, he would have been burnt at the stake . . .

But then, no doubt, I would have been sorry.

8

PRIMROSE rushed downstairs to meet me as I arrived home. She was wearing her nightdress and had obviously been keeping herself awake for my arrival. "Daddy, Daddy, Daddy, you're out so much that I've almost forgotten what you look like!"

Dear little Primrose. She would be the one who had time for me when Dido was rushing around organising smart little dinner-parties for sixteen, but I knew this truth was far from salubrious, implying that I would come to regard my daughter as a substitute for my wife. I made up my mind to believe that Dido would in time become capable of assuaging my loneliness.

"Are you all right, Daddy?"

"Yes, fine," I said, and at once realised with painful clarity how hard it was for me to relax my guard even when I was with those who were closest to me. The long years of acting a part with my mother had left their scar; my inclination was still to play parts, to build a protective wall around myself and keep even those who loved me at a distance which they could sense but never quite describe. In a moment of enlightenment I saw at last how I must appear to my children: kind, quiet, friendly—but never revealing myself in depth, buttoning up all my deepest feelings and unconsciously encouraging them all to participate in my emotionally maimed charade.

The rose-tinted spectacles through which I had viewed my children for so long finally disintegrated. In a moment of further revelation I saw them not as the cyphers who reflected my image in such a pleasing light, but as the troubled strangers I had been too complacent to know. I saw Christian, that astonishing glorified version of myself, torn apart by the tragedy of his mother's death and acting the crippling role of the perfect son to the father who was so fatally remote; I saw Norman stepping into Willy's shoes, the shoes of a boy who would never be as clever as his closest sibling, and grappling with jealousy and despair; I saw James, whose sunny-natured simplicity I had always so naively taken for granted, struggling to come to terms with his average intelligence but becoming haunted by feelings of inferiority which would cast a heavy shadow over his life; I saw Sandy, perhaps the cleverest of them all but the most emotionally deprived, grieving in later years for the mother he could not remember as he tried not to resent his stepmother's insensitive neglect. And I saw Primrose—"

"Daddy, what are you thinking about?"

"You. I was thinking that I must try to be a much better father to my children in future."

"You couldn't be better. You're perfect."

Dear little Primrose. I gave her a hug, hung up my hat and drifted from the hall to the drawing-room. The first thing I saw as I crossed the threshold was the bottle of whisky. It was sitting boldly on the mantel-shelf.

I stopped dead. "Where on earth did that whisky come from?"

"Aunt Merry bought it."

"Merry! Good heavens, I'd forgotten her. Where is she?"

"Gone to the hospital. Didn't you see her? She left some time ago."

"I was talking for a while afterwards with Mr. Darrow." Turning my back on the bottle I said to Primrose quickly: "Time you were in bed—I'll tuck you up," and we headed at once upstairs away from temptation.

9

WHEN Merry arrived back half an hour later I was still talking to Primrose upstairs. I knew it was too great a risk to be on my own within reach of that bottle of whisky.

"I'm sorry I've been so beastly to you lately, Stephen," Merry said as

I returned downstairs to meet her, "but I was just so worried about Dido. However I now discover you've put everything right. Congratulations." She unexpectedly handed me an envelope. "Here's another billet-doux—she scribbled it after you left. Excuse the pong but before I could stop her she'd succumbed to a burst of romantic fervour and drenched the envelope with cologne . . . Now where did I put that hooch?"

"In a scandalous position on the drawing-room mantelshelf."

"Oh God, so I did—sorry. I meant to put it away but I forgot. Will you join me in a quick swill? I'm sure you disapprove of women drinking whisky, but hospitals always make me want to hit the bottle."

"Thanks for the offer, but I do actually have some work to do, so if you'll excuse me—" I escaped.

In my study I sank down in the chair behind my desk and slit open the reeking envelope. Unfolding the sheet of paper within, I read:

Darling,

I can't tell you how much better I feel, I really think there might be life after birth after all, and I'm so terribly glad about dear little Arthur, although of course still dreadfully sad he had to die, but it wasn't all in vain, was it, if he's something we can share, and when I'm better I'll put flowers on his grave and thank God for sending him to us, although I really do think God might have let him live, but then one can't argue with God, can one, it's just a waste of time and energy, and now I want to devote all my time and energy to being a simply *matchless* wife to you and an *equally* matchless mother to my children, because of course I'll have more since I'm now sure that if I can survive this experience I can survive anything and I shan't be nearly so frightened next time.

Talking about my parents with you this evening made me think of *your* parents, and suddenly out of the blue I had what I can only describe as a REVELATION. Darling, I know you'll be thrilled when I tell you that I've decided to be just like your mother whom you always adored so much because if I become just like her then I can be sure you'll always adore me too—yes, I do now believe you still love me, but I want to make certain you stay keen and I do think a wife needs to make an effort instead of lolling around in a complacent fog until she finds her husband in bed with her best friend—although of course I'd never find *you* in bed with anybody, such a *relief* you're a clergyman, but all the same I must never take you for granted—so as I was saying, I'm going to secure your adoration by being just like your mother and having a baby every year for five years and then once we've got all that boring old parturition out of the way we can look forward to endless years of devoted companionship—because by that time you'll be pushing fifty and too old to want sex much—if at all—so that little difficulty will all be quite *effortlessly* resolved—and as I picture our heavenly companionship, I can see we'll have just the sort of idyllic marriage your parents must have had before that divinely handsome father of yours died at the wrong moment and transformed your fascinating mother into a sort of intellectual Queen Victoria. Now, isn't that the most *inspired* and *blissful* REVELATION you could ever wish me to have?

Darling Stephen, no words of mine could express how much I adore you—and I mean *really* adore you—and so all I can do is swear this letter comes to you with eternal love from your utterly devoted

DIDO.

Eventually I refolded the letter, dropped it on the blotter and decided to remove the reeking envelope before the scent could asphyxiate me. On my way back to the study from the wastepaper basket in the hall I glanced into the drawing-room. It was empty. Merry had evidently departed with her stiff drink to the kitchen in search of the cold chicken which, according to Primrose, the housekeeper had left prepared for us. The bottle of whisky had been removed from its scandalous position on the mantelshelf.

To make sure Merry had put the whisky away in the sideboard I went into the dining-room and discovered, just as I had feared, that the bottle was standing among the decanters. Grabbing it by the neck I wrenched open the door of the sideboard, and as I did so all the glasses on the top shelf glittered in the artificial light.

After a while—it seemed a long while but probably it lasted no more than a few seconds—I found I was thinking of scandal, the scandal of a whisky bottle on a clerical mantelshelf, the scandal of a clergyman who drank too much, the scandal of putting a career at risk by dicing with disaster. Then I told myself I really would give up drink, that scandalous risk, I really would. But not just yet.

After all, I reflected as I uncapped the bottle and reached for a glass, I was an old hand at taking scandalous risks. Had I not told Dido long ago when we had first met that I liked to live dangerously? Born survivors could always get away with taking a scandalous risk or two, and I was born to survive.

I mixed myself a mild whisky-and-soda, very respectable, nothing gross, and having put the bottle out of sight I withdrew once more to my study. For a long time I sat looking at my untouched drink to prove to myself how strong my will-power was. The glass was still untouched when I picked up Dido's letter again and it even remained untouched when having contemplated my marital future I exclaimed aloud in despair: "How do I endure it?" Yet I knew the answer to that question even as I framed it in my mind. I thought of my mother saying to Uncle Willoughby: "The only prize worth winning is love!" and I knew I was being offered the prize which Uncle Willoughby had let slip through his fingers. With love all things were possible, even sexual happiness between apparently ill-assorted partners, and I saw again so clearly that by never rejecting Dido as I had so cruelly rejected my mother, I would step into Aidan's land of paradox, that mysterious country where he who saves his life for his own sake shall lose it, but he who loses his life for the sake of Christ shall find not death but life eternal.

With a cool rational eye I surveyed the alternative to the road I had been called to travel. I could walk away from Dido, leave the Church and settle for a life devoted to attaining material success and self-gratification, but what would be left of me after I had torn the heart out of my true self in such a fashion? I would be no more than a corpse bleeding to death. I could not have borne such a profound spiritual failure; then indeed in my despair and self-hatred I would have wound up a drunkard and alone. But my life, any life, real life, wasn't about pursuing the prizes of materialism and practising the gospel of self-gratification. Life was about enduring adversity, about being true to oneself, about striving to do the will of one's Creator so that one could live in harmony with all that was finest in one's nature. The real prizes were not, as my uncle had thought, health, wealth and happiness, that facile trio which could be destroyed so easily by the first breath of misfortune, but faith, hope and, above all, love. Once these were won, the real happiness, the lasting happiness of a fully integrated personality responding to the will of God, could finally begin to unfold.

Picking up my pen to answer Dido's letter, I thought of St. Paul writing: "It is not I who live, but Christ who lives in me," and at once I was comforted by the image of the immanent God, loving and forgiving—that Liberal vision which for me the world's evil could never diminish. But then I thought of the stern transcendent God of neo-orthodoxy, standing over and against a world which was under judgement and offering those who repented the chance of salvation. After my recent experiences, how could I deny this vision wasn't equally true? God was immanent *and* transcendent. I was once more in the land of paradox, and as my father cried in my memory: "It's all a unity! It's all one!" I knew Christ had risen from the dead, just as he always did, again—and again—and again—to be at one with the disciples who were willing to sacrifice all they had in order to follow him to the end.

It was Easter Sunday at last, and I was rising from the grave of my past to embark on my new life in absolute faith. Taking a sip of whisky, I thought no more of failure and misery, but began to write my Christian message of hope in the most loving terms I could devise.

Author's Note

ULTIMATE PRIZES is the third in a series of novels about the Church of England in the twentieth century. The first, *Glittering Images*, was narrated by Charles Ashworth, and the second, *Glamorous Powers*, was narrated by Jon Darrow. The next book, *Scandalous Risks*, set in the 1960s, will look at the Church from the point of view of an outsider, Venetia Flaxton.

NEVILLE AYSGARTH'S religious thought (though not his private life) is based on the writings of Charles Earle Raven (1885–1964). The son of a barrister, Raven was born in London and began his long association with Cambridge University in 1904 when he won a scholarship to Caius College to read Classics. He achieved a first-class honours in the Classical Tripos and followed this a year later with a first in Theology. He also devoted time during this final year to the study of biology, long a special interest of his, and became convinced that the two disciplines of theology and science should be drawn together. After some months working in a secular job in Liverpool, where he gained experience of squalid social conditions, he was ordained in 1909 and became Dean of Emmanuel College, Cambridge, until 1914. Having spent a short time as a schoolmaster at Tonbridge, he served as an Army chaplain in France from 1917 to 1918 and experienced the horrors of war at first hand; later he was to become famous as a pacifist. After the war he resumed his duties at Emmanuel College but in 1920 he became Rector of Bletchingley, Surrey, and in 1924 he was appointed a canon of the new Liverpool Cathedral, where he won great fame as a preacher. He returned to Cambridge in 1932 as Regius Professor of Divinity, and from 1939 to 1950 he was Master of Christ's College.

Raven was married three times. By his first wife, whom he met during his days as a Cambridge undergraduate, he had four children. After her death, in 1944, he remained a widower for some time before marrying an elderly American friend whom he had known for many years; she died soon after the wedding. In 1956 he married a Belgian who during the war had taken an active role in the Resistance. Thinking highly of women and delighting in their company, he believed it was wrong that they should be confined to a limited form of service in the Church, and he spoke out in favour of their ordination.

He never became a bishop.

In his theology Raven believed that a divine purpose operated through and in the evolutionary process, and that there was an essential unity in all created things. He had no time for a God conceived as sitting up on high outside the world. For him God was in the world, immanent, and the pinnacle of God's creative evolutionary process was the human personality. Having placed this great emphasis on personality, Raven stressed the idea of a personal God and saw religion at its best in terms of personal communication with this divine figure. Nature, he thought, offered a design which could be attributed to God's personal purpose, and Jesus was the manifestation of God's personal presence in its highest form. All was a unity in this immanent, creating, loving God; all was one.

This fundamentally optimistic approach to the world meant that in Raven's writings there was little room for paradox and tragedy, alienation and ambiguity, and when the new neo-orthodox school of theology tried to grapple with these problems, he was bitterly opposed not only to the idea of a transcendent God who stood apart from mankind but to the idea that truth could be reached through disunity, by the clash of opposing principles. For him, committed as he was to the concept of unity, it was impossible to concede that there could be an equally valid model of God based on a duality. It seemed to him that to pursue such a paradox was to pursue a policy of despair. Throughout his career he saw his theology go increasingly out of fashion, but towards the end of his life the neo-orthodox school began to wane in England, until at last in the 1960s Liberal theology, in a new and far more radical form, started to move back to the centre of the stage.

GEORGE KENNEDY ALLEN BELL, two years Raven's senior, was Bishop of Chichester from 1929 to 1957. Though distressed by the harshness of the Treaty of Versailles and sympathetic to the German people in consequence, he spoke out firmly in the 1930s against Hitler's persecution of the Jews and the Christian Churches, and during the war he urged the British Government, though without success, to support the Germans who were plotting to overthrow Hitler. He was not a pacifist, but his speeches appealing for the preservation of Christian values in the conduct of the war soon brought him into conflict with the Government's policies, and he earned himself many enemies in high places; people often failed to understand that Bell remained passionately anti-Nazi. After the war he went to Berlin and preached the Christian message of reconciliation to the thousands who flocked to hear him. Deeply involved in the reconstruction of Christian Europe, he became a leading figure in the World Council of Churches. He was eventually awarded the Grand Cross of the Order of Merit, with sash and star, the highest honour the Federal Republic of Germany could bestow, but he died a few hours before the news of the award arrived. Mrs. Bell received the decoration from the German Ambassador in November 1958.

A NOTE ON THE TYPE

THE text of this book was set in Bembo, a facsimile of a typeface cut by one of the most celebrated goldsmiths of his time, Francesco Griffo, for Aldus Manutius, the Venetian printer, in 1495. The face was named for Pietro Bembo, the author of the small treatise entitled De Aetna *in which it first appeared. Through the research of Stanley Morison, it is now acknowledged that all old-face type designs up to the time of William Caslon can be traced to the Bembo cut.*

THE present-day version of Bembo was introduced by the Monotype Corporation, London, in 1929. Sturdy, well balanced, and finely proportioned, Bembo is a face of rare beauty and great legibility in all of its sizes.

Composed by ComCom, a division of
The Haddon Craftsmen, Inc.,
Allentown, Pennsylvania
Printed and bound by Fairfield Graphics,
Fairfield, Pennsylvania
Book and ornament designed by
Margaret Wagner